Detective Tales from the
A.B.C Tea-Rooms

Detective Tales from the A.B.C Tea-Rooms

Two Detective Story Collections

The Old Man in the Corner

and

Unravelled Knots

Baroness Orczy

LEONAUR

Detective Tales from the A.B.C Tea-Rooms
Two Detective Story Collections
The Old Man in the Corner
and
Unravelled Knots
by Baroness Orczy

FIRST EDITION

First published under the titles
The Old Man in the Corner
and
Unravelled Knots

Leonaur is an imprint of Oakpast Ltd

Copyright in this form © 2022 Oakpast Ltd

ISBN: 978-1-915234-24-7 (hardcover)
ISBN: 978-1-915234-25-4 (softcover)

http://www.leonaur.com

Publisher's Notes

The views expressed in this book are not necessarily those of the publisher.

Contents

The Old Man in the Corner

Contents

The Fenchurch Street Mystery

1

The man in the corner pushed aside his glass, and leant across the table.

"Mysteries!"he commented. "There is no such thing as a mystery in connection with any crime, provided intelligence is brought to bear upon its investigation."

Very much astonished Polly Burton looked over the top of her newspaper, and fixed a pair of very severe, coldly inquiring brown eyes upon him.

She had disapproved of the man from the instant when he shuffled across the shop and sat down opposite to her, at the same marble-topped table which already held her large coffee (3d.), her roll and butter (2d.), and plate of tongue (6d.).

Now this particular corner, this very same table, that special view of the magnificent marble hall—known as the Norfolk Street branch of the Aerated Bread Company's depots—were Polly's own corner, table, and view. Here she had partaken of eleven pennyworth of luncheon and one pennyworth of daily information ever since that glorious never-to-be-forgotten day when she was enrolled on the staff of the *Evening Observer* (we'll call it that, if you please), and became a member of that illustrious and world-famed organisation known as the British Press.

She was a personality, was Miss Burton of the *Evening Observer.* Her cards were printed thus:

MISS MARY J. BURTON.

Evening Observer.

She had interviewed Miss Ellen Terry and the Bishop of Madagascar, Mr. Seymour Hicks and the Chief Commissioner of Police. She had been present at the last Marlborough House garden party—in the cloakroom, that is to say, where she caught sight of Lady Thingummy's hat, Miss What-you-may-call's sunshade, and of various other things modistical or fashionable, all of which were duly described under the heading "Royalty and Dress" in the early afternoon edition of the *Evening Observer*.

(The article itself is signed M. J. B., and is to be found in the files of that leading halfpennyworth.)

For these reasons—and for various others, too—Polly felt irate with the man in the corner, and told him so with her eyes, as plainly as any pair of brown eyes can speak.

She had been reading an article in the *Daily Telegraph*. The article was palpitatingly interesting. Had Polly been commenting audibly upon it? Certain it is that the man over there had spoken in direct answer to her thoughts.

She looked at him and frowned; the next moment she smiled. Miss Burton (of the *Evening Observer*) had a keen sense of humour, which two years' association with the British Press had not succeeded in destroying, and the appearance of the man was sufficient to tickle the most ultra-morose fancy. Polly thought to herself that she had never seen anyone so pale, so thin, with such funny light-coloured hair, brushed very smoothly across the top of a very obviously bald crown. He looked so timid and nervous as he fidgeted incessantly with a piece of string; his long, lean, and trembling fingers tying and untying it into knots of wonderful and complicated proportions.

Having carefully studied every detail of the quaint personality Polly felt more amiable.

"And yet," she remarked kindly but authoritatively, "this article, in an otherwise well-informed journal, will tell you that, even within the last year, no fewer than six crimes have completely baffled the police, and the perpetrators of them are still at large."

"Pardon me," he said gently, "I never for a moment ventured to suggest that there were no mysteries to the *police*; I merely remarked that there were none where intelligence was brought to bear upon the investigation of crime."

"Not even in the Fenchurch Street *mystery*, I suppose," she asked sarcastically.

"Least of all in the so-called Fenchurch Street *mystery*," he replied quietly.

Now the Fenchurch Street mystery, as that extraordinary crime had popularly been called, had puzzled—as Polly well knew—the brains of every thinking man and woman for the last twelve months. It had puzzled her not inconsiderably; she had been interested, fascinated; she had studied the case, formed her own theories, thought about it all often and often, had even written one or two letters to the Press on the subject—suggesting, arguing, hinting at possibilities and probabilities, adducing proofs which other amateur detectives were equally ready to refute. The attitude of that timid man in the corner, therefore, was peculiarly exasperating, and she retorted with sarcasm destined to completely annihilate her self-complacent interlocutor.

"What a pity it is, in that case, that you do not offer your priceless services to our misguided though well-meaning police."

"Isn't it?" he replied with perfect good-humour. "Well, you know, for one thing I doubt if they would accept them; and in the second place my inclinations and my duty would—were I to become an active member of the detective force—nearly always be in direct conflict. As often as not my sympathies go to the criminal who is clever and astute enough to lead our entire police force by the nose.

"I don't know how much of the case you remember," he went on quietly. "It certainly, at first, began even to puzzle me. On the 12th of last December, a woman, poorly dressed, but with an unmistakable air of having seen better days, gave information at Scotland Yard of the disappearance of her husband, William Kershaw, of no occupation, and apparently of no fixed abode. She was accompanied by a friend—a fat, oily-looking German—and between them they told a tale which set the police immediately on the move.

"It appears that on the 10th of December, at about three o'clock in the afternoon, Karl Müller, the German, called on his friend, William Kershaw, for the purpose of collecting a small debt—some ten pounds or so—which the latter owed him. On arriving at the squalid lodging in Charlotte Street, Fitzroy Square, he found William Kershaw in a wild state of excitement, and his wife in tears. Müller attempted to state the object of his visit, but Kershaw, with wild gestures, waved him aside, and—in his own words—flabbergasted him by asking him point-blank for another loan of two pounds, which sum, he declared, would be the means of a speedy fortune for himself and the friend who would help him in his need.

"After a quarter of an hour spent in obscure hints, Kershaw, finding

13

the cautious German obdurate, decided to let him into the secret plan, which, he averred, would place thousands into their hands."

Instinctively Polly had put down her paper; the mild stranger, with his nervous air and timid, watery eyes, had a peculiar way of telling his tale, which somehow fascinated her.

"I don't know," he resumed, "if you remember the story which the German told to the police, and which was corroborated in every detail by the wife or widow. Briefly it was this: Some thirty years previously, Kershaw, then twenty years of age, and a medical student at one of the London hospitals, had a chum named Barker, with whom he roomed, together with another.

"The latter, so it appears, brought home one evening a very considerable sum of money, which he had won on the turf, and the following morning he was found murdered in his bed. Kershaw, fortunately for himself, was able to prove a conclusive *alibi*; he had spent the night on duty at the hospital; as for Barker, he had disappeared, that is to say, as far as the police were concerned, but not as far as the watchful eyes of his friend Kershaw were able to spy—at least, so the latter said. Barker very cleverly contrived to get away out of the country, and, after sundry vicissitudes, finally settled down at Vladivostok, in Eastern Siberia, where, under the assumed name of Smethurst, he built up an enormous fortune by trading in furs.

"Now, mind you, everyone knows Smethurst, the Siberian millionaire. Kershaw's story that he had once been called Barker, and had committed a murder thirty years ago, was never proved, was it? I am merely telling you what Kershaw said to his friend the German and to his wife on that memorable afternoon of December the 10th.

"According to him Smethurst had made one gigantic mistake in his clever career—he had on four occasions written to his late friend, William Kershaw. Two of these letters had no bearing on the case, since they were written more than twenty-five years ago, and Kershaw, moreover, had lost them—so he said—long ago. According to him, however, the first of these letters was written when Smethurst, alias Barker, had spent all the money he had obtained from the crime, and found himself destitute in New York.

"Kershaw, then in fairly prosperous circumstances, sent him a £10 note for the sake of old times. The second, when the tables had turned, and Kershaw had begun to go downhill, Smethurst, as he then already called himself, sent his whilom friend £50. After that, as Müller gathered, Kershaw had made sundry demands on Smethurst's ever-increasing purse, and had accompanied these demands by various threats, which, considering the distant country in which the millionaire lived, were worse than futile.

"But now the climax had come, and Kershaw, after a final moment of hesitation, handed over to his German friend the two last letters purporting to have been written by Smethurst, and which, if you remember, played such an important part in the mysterious story of this extraordinary crime. I have a copy of both these letters here," added the man in the corner, as he took out a piece of paper from a very worn-out pocket-book, and, unfolding it very deliberately, he began to read:—

Sir,—Your preposterous demands for money are wholly unwarrantable. I have already helped you quite as much as you deserve. However, for the sake of old times, and because you once helped me when I was in a terrible difficulty, I am willing to once more let you impose upon my good nature. A friend of mine here, a Russian merchant, to whom I have sold my business, starts in a few days for an extended tour to many European and Asiatic ports in his yacht, and has invited me to accompany him as far as England. Being tired of foreign parts, and desirous of seeing the old country once again after thirty years' absence, I have decided to accept his invitation. I don't know when we may actually be in Europe, but I promise you that as soon as we touch a suitable port, I will write to you again, making an appointment for you to see me in London. But remember that if your demands are too preposterous I will not for a moment listen to them, and that I am the last man in the world to submit to persistent and unwarrantable blackmail.

I am, sir,
Yours truly,
Francis Smethurst.

"The second letter was dated from Southampton," continued the old man in the corner calmly, "and, curiously enough, was the only letter which Kershaw professed to have received from Smethurst of which he had kept the envelope, and which was dated. It was quite brief," he added, referring once more to his piece of paper.

Dear Sir,—Referring to my letter of a few weeks ago, I wish to inform you that the *Tsarskoe Selo* will touch at Tilbury on Tuesday next, the 10th. I shall land there, and immediately go up to London by the first train I can get. If you like, you may meet me at Fenchurch Street Station, in the first-class waiting-room, in the late afternoon. Since I surmise that after thirty years' absence my face may not be familiar to you, I may as well tell you that you will recognise me by a heavy Astrakhan fur coat, which I shall wear, together with a cap of the same. You may then introduce yourself to me, and I will personally listen to what you may have to say.

Yours faithfully,

Francis Smethurst.

"It was this last letter which had caused William Kershaw's excitement and his wife's tears. In the German's own words, he was walking up and down the room like a wild beast, gesticulating wildly, and muttering sundry exclamations. Mrs. Kershaw, however, was full of apprehension. She mistrusted the man from foreign parts—who, according to her husband's story, had already one crime upon his conscience—who might, she feared, risk another, in order to be rid of a dangerous enemy. Woman-like, she thought the scheme a dishonourable one, for the law, she knew, is severe on the blackmailer.

"The assignation might be a cunning trap, in any case it was a curious one; why, she argued, did not Smethurst elect to see Kershaw at his hotel the following day? A thousand whys and wherefores made her anxious, but the fat German had been won over by Kershaw's visions of untold gold, held tantalisingly before his eyes. He had lent the necessary £2, with which his friend intended to tidy himself up a bit before he went to meet his friend the millionaire. Half an hour afterwards Kershaw had left his lodgings, and that was the last the unfortunate woman saw of her husband, or Müller, the German, of his friend.

"Anxiously his wife waited that night, but he did not return; the next day she seems to have spent in making purposeless and futile inquiries about the neighbourhood of Fenchurch Street; and on the 12th she went to Scotland Yard, gave what particulars she knew, and placed in the hands of the police the two letters written by Smethurst."

2

The man in the corner had finished his glass of milk. His watery blue eyes looked across at Miss Polly Burton's eager little face, from which all traces of severity had now been chased away by an obvious and intense excitement.

"It was only on the 31st," he resumed after a while, "that a body, decomposed past all recognition, was found by two lightermen in the bottom of a disused barge. She had been moored at one time at the foot of one of those dark flights of steps which lead down between tall warehouses to the river in the East End of London. I have a photograph of the place here," he added, selecting one out of his pocket, and placing it before Polly.

"The actual barge, you see, had already been removed when I took this snapshot, but you will realise what a perfect place this alley is for the purpose of one man cutting another's throat in comfort, and without fear of detection. The body, as I said, was decomposed beyond all recognition; it had probably been there eleven days, but sundry articles, such as a silver ring and a tie pin, were recognisable, and were identified by Mrs. Kershaw as belonging to her husband.

"She, of course, was loud in denouncing Smethurst, and the police had no doubt a very strong case against him, for two days after the discovery of the body in the barge, the Siberian millionaire, as he was already popularly called by enterprising interviewers, was arrested in his luxurious suite of rooms at the Hotel Cecil.

"To confess the truth, at this point I was not a little puzzled. Mrs. Kershaw's story and Smethurst's letters had both found their way into the papers, and following my usual method—mind you, I am only an amateur, I try to reason out a case for the love of the thing—I sought about for a motive for the crime, which the police declared Smethurst had committed. To effectually get rid of a dangerous blackmailer was the generally accepted theory. Well! did it ever strike you how paltry that motive really was?"

Miss Polly had to confess, however, that it had never struck her in that light.

"Surely a man who had succeeded in building up an immense fortune by his own individual efforts, was not the sort of fool to believe that he had anything to fear from a man like Kershaw. He must have *known* that Kershaw held no damning proofs against him—not enough to hang him, anyway. Have you ever seen Smethurst?" he added, as he once more fumbled in his pocket-book.

Polly replied that she had seen Smethurst's picture in the illustrated papers at the time. Then he added, placing a small photograph before her:

"What strikes you most about the face?"

"Well, I think its strange, astonished expression, due to the total absence of eyebrows, and the funny foreign cut of the hair."

"So close that it almost looks as if it had been shaved. Exactly. That is what struck me most when I elbowed my way into the court that morning and first caught sight of the millionaire in the dock. He was a tall, soldierly-looking man, upright in stature, his face very bronzed and tanned. He wore neither moustache nor beard, his hair was cropped quite close to his head, like a Frenchman's; but, of course, what was so very remarkable about him was that total absence of eyebrows and even eyelashes, which gave the face such a peculiar appearance—as you say, a perpetually astonished look.

"He seemed, however, wonderfully calm; he had been accommodated with a chair in the dock—being a millionaire—and chatted pleasantly with his lawyer, Sir Arthur Inglewood, in the intervals between the calling of the several witnesses for the prosecution; whilst during the examination of these witnesses he sat quite placidly, with his head shaded by his hand.

"Müller and Mrs. Kershaw repeated the story which they had already told to the police. I think you said that you were not able, owing to pressure of work, to go to the court that day, and hear the case, so perhaps you have no recollection of Mrs. Kershaw. No? Ah, well! Here is a snapshot I managed to get of her once. That is her. Exactly as she stood in the box—overdressed—in elaborate crape, with a bonnet which once had contained pink roses, and to which a remnant of pink petals still clung obtrusively amidst the deep black.

"She would not look at the prisoner, and turned her head resolutely towards the magistrate. I fancy she had been fond of that vagabond husband of hers: an enormous wedding-ring encircled her finger, and that, too, was swathed in black. She firmly believed that Kershaw's murderer sat there in the dock, and she literally flaunted her grief before him.

"I was indescribably sorry for her. As for Müller, he was just fat, oily, pompous, conscious of his own importance as a witness; his fat fingers, covered with brass rings, gripped the two incriminating letters, which he had identified. They were his passports, as it were, to a delightful land of importance and notoriety. Sir Arthur Inglewood, I think, disappointed him by stating that he had no questions to ask of him. Müller had been brimful of answers, ready with the most perfect indictment, the most elaborate accusations against the bloated millionaire who had decoyed his dear friend Kershaw, and murdered him in Heaven knows what an out-of-the-way corner of the East End.

"After this, however, the excitement grew apace. Müller had been dismissed, and had retired from the court altogether, leading away Mrs. Kershaw, who had completely broken down.

"Constable D 21 was giving evidence as to the arrest in the meanwhile. The prisoner, he said, had seemed completely taken by surprise, not understanding the cause or history of the accusation against him; however, when put in full possession of the facts, and realising, no doubt, the absolute futility of any resistance, he had quietly enough followed the constable into the cab. No one at the fashionable and crowded Hotel Cecil had even suspected that anything unusual had occurred.

"Then a gigantic sigh of expectancy came from every one of the spectators. The 'fun' was about to begin. James Buckland, a porter at Fenchurch Street railway station, had just sworn to tell all the truth, *etc.* After all, it did not amount to much. He said that at six o'clock in the afternoon of December the 10th, in the midst of one of the densest fogs he ever remembers, the 5.5 from Tilbury steamed into the station, being just about an hour late. He was on the arrival platform, and was hailed by a passenger in a first-class carriage. He could see very little of him beyond an enormous black fur coat and a travelling cap of fur also.

"The passenger had a quantity of luggage, all marked F. S., and he directed James Buckland to place it all upon a four-wheel cab, with the exception of a small hand-bag, which he carried himself. Having seen that all his luggage was safely bestowed, the stranger in the fur coat paid the porter, and, telling the cabman to wait until he returned, he walked away in the direction of the waiting-rooms, still carrying his small hand-bag.

"'I stayed for a bit,' added James Buckland, 'talking to the driver about the fog and that: then I went about my business, seein' that the local from Southend 'ad been signalled.'

"The prosecution insisted most strongly upon the hour when the stranger in the fur coat, having seen to his luggage, walked away towards the waiting-rooms. The porter was emphatic. 'It was not a minute later than 6.15,' he averred.

"Sir Arthur Inglewood still had no questions to ask, and the driver of the cab was called.

"He corroborated the evidence of James Buckland as to the hour when the gentleman in the fur coat had engaged him, and having filled his cab in and out with luggage, had told him to wait. And cabby did wait. He waited in the dense fog—until he was tired, until he seriously thought of depositing all the luggage in the lost property office, and of looking out for another fare—waited until at last, at a quarter before nine, whom should he see walking hurriedly towards his cab but the gentleman in the fur coat and cap, who got in quickly and told the driver to take him at once to the Hotel Cecil. This, cabby declared, had occurred at a quarter before nine. Still Sir Arthur Inglewood made no comment, and Mr. Francis Smethurst, in the crowded, stuffy court, had calmly dropped to sleep.

"The next witness, Constable Thomas Taylor, had noticed a shabbily dressed individual, with shaggy hair and beard, loafing about the station and waiting-rooms in the afternoon of December the 10th. He seemed to be watching the arrival platform of the Tilbury and Southend trains.

"Two separate and independent witnesses, cleverly unearthed by the police, had seen this same shabbily dressed individual stroll into the first-class waiting-room at about 6.15 on Wednesday, December the 10th, and go straight up to a gentleman in a heavy fur coat and cap, who had also just come into the room. The two talked together for a while; no one heard what they said, but presently they walked off together. No one seemed to know in which direction.

"Francis Smethurst was rousing himself from his apathy; he whispered to his lawyer, who nodded with a bland smile of encouragement. The *employés* of the Hotel Cecil gave evidence as to the arrival of Mr. Smethurst at about 9.30 p.m. on Wednesday, December the 10th, in a cab, with a quantity of luggage; and this closed the case for the prosecution.

"Everybody in that court already *saw* Smethurst mounting the gallows. It was uninterested curiosity which caused the elegant audience to wait and hear what Sir Arthur Inglewood had to say. He, of course, is the most fashionable man in the law at the present moment. His lolling attitudes, his drawling speech, are quite the rage, and imitated by the gilded youth of society.

"Even at this moment, when the Siberian millionaire's neck literally and metaphorically hung in the balance, an expectant titter went round the fair spectators as Sir Arthur stretched out his long loose limbs and lounged across the table. He waited to make his effect—Sir Arthur is a born actor—and there is no doubt that he made it, when in his slowest, most drawly tones he said quietly;

"'With regard to this alleged murder of one William Kershaw, on

Wednesday, December the 10th, between 6.15 and 8.45 p.m., Your Honour, I now propose to call two witnesses, who saw this same William Kershaw alive on Tuesday afternoon, December the 16th, that is to say, six days after the supposed murder.'

"It was as if a bombshell had exploded in the court. Even His Honour was aghast, and I am sure the lady next to me only recovered from the shock of the surprise in order to wonder whether she need put off her dinner party after all.

"As for me," added the man in the corner, with that strange mixture of nervousness and self-complacency which had set Miss Polly Burton wondering, "well, you see, *I* had made up my mind long ago where the hitch lay in this particular case, and I was not so surprised as some of the others.

"Perhaps you remember the wonderful development of the case, which so completely mystified the police—and in fact everybody except myself. Torriani and a waiter at his hotel in the Commercial Road both deposed that at about 3.30 p.m. on December the 10th a shabbily dressed individual lolled into the coffee-room and ordered some tea. He was pleasant enough and talkative, told the waiter that his name was William Kershaw, that very soon all London would be talking about him, as he was about, through an unexpected stroke of good fortune, to become a very rich man, and so on, and so on, nonsense without end.

"When he had finished his tea, he lolled out again, but no sooner had he disappeared down a turning of the road than the waiter discovered an old umbrella, left behind accidentally by the shabby, talkative individual. As is the custom in his highly respectable restaurant, Signor Torriani put the umbrella carefully away in his office, on the chance of his customer calling to claim it when he had discovered his loss. And sure enough, nearly a week later, on Tuesday, the 16th, at about 1 p.m., the same shabbily dressed individual called and asked for his umbrella. He had some lunch, and chatted once again to the waiter. Signor Torriani and the waiter gave a description of William Kershaw, which coincided exactly with that given by Mrs. Kershaw of her husband.

"Oddly enough he seemed to be a very absentminded sort of person, for on this second occasion, no sooner had he left than the waiter found a pocket-book in the coffee-room, underneath the table. It contained sundry letters and bills, all addressed to William Kershaw. This pocketbook was produced, and Karl Müller, who had returned to the court, easily identified it as having belonged to his dear and

21

lamented friend 'Villiam.'

"This was the first blow to the case against the accused. It was a pretty stiff one, you will admit. Already it had begun to collapse like a house of cards. Still, there was the assignation, and the undisputed meeting between Smethurst and Kershaw, and those two and a half hours of a foggy evening to satisfactorily account for."

The man in the corner made a long pause, keeping the girl on tenterhooks. He had fidgeted with his bit of string till there was not an inch of it free from the most complicated and elaborate knots.

"I assure you," he resumed at last, "that at that very moment the whole mystery was, to me, as clear as daylight. I only marvelled how His Honour could waste his time and mine by putting what he thought were searching questions to the accused relating to his past. Francis Smethurst, who had quite shaken off his somnolence, spoke with a curious nasal twang, and with an almost imperceptible *soupçon* of foreign accent. He calmly denied Kershaw's version of his past; declared that he had never been called Barker, and had certainly never been mixed up in any murder case thirty years ago.

"'But you knew this man Kershaw,' persisted His Honour, 'since you wrote to him?'

"'Pardon me, Your Honour,' said the accused quietly, 'I have never, to my knowledge, seen this man Kershaw, and I can swear that I never wrote to him.'

"'Never wrote to him?' retorted His Honour warningly. 'That is a strange assertion to make when I have two of your letters to him in my hands at the present moment.'

"'I never wrote those letters, Your Honour,' persisted the accused quietly, 'they are not in my handwriting.'

"'Which we can easily prove,' came in Sir Arthur Inglewood's drawly tones, as he handed up a packet to His Honour; 'here are a number of letters written by my client since he has landed in this country, and some of which were written under my very eyes.'

"As Sir Arthur Inglewood had said, this could be easily proved, and the prisoner, at His Honour's request, scribbled a few lines, together with his signature, several times upon a sheet of note-paper. It was easy to read upon the magistrate's astounded countenance, that there was not the slightest similarity in the two handwritings.

"A fresh mystery had cropped up. Who, then, had made the assignation with William Kershaw at Fenchurch Street railway station? The prisoner gave a fairly satisfactory account of the employment of his time since his landing in England.

"'I came over on the *Tsarskoe Selo*,' he said, 'a yacht belonging to a friend of mine. When we arrived at the mouth of the Thames there was such a dense fog that it was twenty-four hours before it was thought safe for me to land. My friend, who is a Russian, would not land at all; he was regularly frightened at this land of fogs. He was going on to Madeira immediately.

"'I actually landed on Tuesday, the 10th, and took a train at once for town. I did see to my luggage and a cab, as the porter and driver told Your Honour; then I tried to find my way to a refreshment-room, where I could get a glass of wine. I drifted into the waiting-room, and there I was accosted by a shabbily dressed individual, who began telling me a piteous tale. Who he was I do not know. He said he was an old soldier who had served his country faithfully, and then been left to starve. He begged of me to accompany him to his lodgings, where I could see his wife and starving children, and verify the truth and piteousness of his tale.

"'Well, Your Honour,' added the prisoner with noble frankness, 'it was my first day in the old country. I had come back after thirty years with my pockets full of gold, and this was the first sad tale I had heard; but I am a business man, and did not want to be exactly "done" in the eye. I followed my man through the fog, out into the streets. He walked silently by my side for a time. I had not a notion where I was.

"'Suddenly I turned to him with some question, and realised in a moment that my gentleman had given me the slip. Finding, probably, that I would not part with my money till I *had* seen the starving wife and children, he left me to my fate, and went in search of more willing bait.

"'The place where I found myself was dismal and deserted. I could see no trace of cab or omnibus. I retraced my steps and tried to find my way back to the station, only to find myself in worse and more deserted neighbourhoods. I became hopelessly lost and fogged. I don't wonder that two and a half hours elapsed while I thus wandered on in the dark and deserted streets; my sole astonishment is that I ever found the station at all that night, or rather close to it a policeman, who showed me the way.'

"'But how do you account for Kershaw knowing all your movements?' still persisted His Honour, 'and his knowing the exact date of your arrival in England? How do you account for these two letters, in fact?'

23

"'I cannot account for it or them, Your Honour,' replied the prisoner quietly. 'I have proved to you, have I not, that I never wrote those letters, and that the man—er—Kershaw is his name?—was not murdered by me?'

"'Can you tell me of anyone here or abroad who might have heard of your movements, and of the date of your arrival?'

"'My late *employés* at Vladivostok, of course, knew of my departure, but none of them could have written these letters, since none of them know a word of English.'

"'Then you can throw no light upon these mysterious letters? You cannot help the police in any way towards the clearing up of this strange affair?'

"'The affair is as mysterious to me as to Your Honour, and to the police of this country.'

"Francis Smethurst was discharged, of course; there was no semblance of evidence against him sufficient to commit him for trial. The two overwhelming points of his defence which had completely routed the prosecution were, firstly, the proof that he had never written the letters making the assignation, and secondly, the fact that the man supposed to have been murdered on the 10th was seen to be alive and well on the 16th. But then, who in the world was the mysterious individual who had apprised Kershaw of the movements of Smethurst, the millionaire?"

3

The man in the corner cocked his funny thin head on one side and looked at Polly; then he took up his beloved bit of string and deliberately untied every knot he had made in it. When it was quite smooth, he laid it out upon the table.

"I will take you, if you like, point by point along the line of reasoning which I followed myself, and which will inevitably lead you, as it led me, to the only possible solution of the mystery.

"First take this point," he said with nervous restlessness, once more taking up his bit of string, and forming with each point raised a series of knots which would have shamed a navigating instructor, "obviously it was *impossible* for Kershaw not to have been acquainted with Smethurst, since he was fully apprised of the latter's arrival in England by two letters. Now it was clear to me from the first that no one could have written those two letters except Smethurst. You will argue that those letters were proved not to have been written by the man in the dock. Exactly. Remember, Kershaw was a careless man—he had lost both envelopes. To him they were insignificant. Now it was never disproved that those letters were written by Smethurst."

"But—" suggested Polly.

"Wait a minute," he interrupted, while knot number two appeared upon the scene, "it was proved that six days after the murder, William Kershaw was alive, and visited the Torriani Hotel, where already he was known, and where he conveniently left a pocket-book behind, so that there should be no mistake as to his identity; but it was never questioned where Mr. Francis Smethurst, the millionaire, happened to spend that very same afternoon."

"Surely, you don't mean—?" gasped the girl.

"One moment, please," he added triumphantly. "How did it come about that the landlord of the Torriani Hotel was brought into court at all? How did Sir Arthur Inglewood, or rather his client, know that William Kershaw had on those two memorable occasions visited the hotel, and that its landlord could bring such convincing evidence forward that would for ever exonerate the millionaire from the imputation of murder?"

"Surely," I argued, "the usual means, the police—"

"The police had kept the whole affair very dark until the arrest at the Hotel Cecil. They did not put into the papers the usual: 'If anyone happens to know of the whereabouts, *etc. etc.*' Had the landlord of that hotel heard of the disappearance of Kershaw through the usual channels, he would have put himself in communication with the police. Sir Arthur Inglewood produced him. How did Sir Arthur Inglewood come on his track?"

"Surely, you don't mean—?"

"Point number four," he resumed imperturbably, "Mrs. Kershaw was never requested to produce a specimen of her husband's handwriting. Why? Because the police, clever as you say they are, never started on the right tack. They believed William Kershaw to have been murdered; they looked for William Kershaw.

"On December the 31st, what was presumed to be the body of William Kershaw was found by two lightermen: I have shown you a photograph of the place where it was found. Dark and deserted it is in all conscience, is it not? Just the place where a bully and a coward would decoy an unsuspecting stranger, murder him first, then rob him of his valuables, his papers, his very identity, and leave him there to rot. The body was found in a disused barge which had been moored some time against the wall, at the foot of these steps. It was in the last stages of decomposition, and, of course, could not be identified; but the police would have it that it was the body of William Kershaw.

"It never entered their heads that it was the body of *Francis Smethurst, and that William Kershaw was his murderer.*

"Ah! it was cleverly, artistically conceived! Kershaw is a genius. Think of it all! His disguise! Kershaw had a shaggy beard, hair, and moustache. He shaved up to his very eyebrows! No wonder that even his wife did not recognise him across the court; and remember she never saw much of his face while he stood in the dock. Kershaw was shabby, slouchy, he stooped. Smethurst, the millionaire, might have served in the Prussian Army.

"Then that lovely trait about going to revisit the Torriani Hotel. Just a few days' grace, in order to purchase moustache and beard and wig, exactly similar to what he had himself shaved off. Making up to look like himself! Splendid! Then leaving the pocket-book behind! He! he! he! Kershaw was not murdered! Of course not. He called at the Torriani Hotel six days after the murder, whilst Mr. Smethurst, the millionaire, hobnobbed in the park with duchesses! Hang such a man! Fie!"

He fumbled for his hat. With nervous, trembling fingers he held it deferentially in his hand whilst he rose from the table. Polly watched him as he strode up to the desk, and paid twopence for his glass of milk and his bun. Soon he disappeared through the shop, whilst she still found herself hopelessly bewildered, with a number of snap-shot photographs before her, still staring at a long piece of string, smothered from end to end in a series of knots, as bewildering, as irritating, as puzzling as the man who had lately sat in the corner.

The Robbery in Phillimore Terrace

Whether Miss Polly Burton really did expect to see the man in the corner that Saturday afternoon, 'twere difficult to say; certain it is that when she found her way to the table close by the window and realised that he was not there, she felt conscious of an overwhelming sense of disappointment. And yet during the whole of the week she had, with more pride than wisdom, avoided this particular A.B.C. shop.

"I thought you would not keep away very long," said a quiet voice close to her ear.

She nearly lost her balance—where in the world had he come from? She certainly had not heard the slightest sound, and yet there he sat, in the corner, like a veritable Jack-in-the-box, his mild blue eyes staring apologetically at her, his nervous fingers toying with the inevitable bit of string.

The waitress brought him his glass of milk and a cheese-cake. He ate it in silence, while his piece of string lay idly beside him on the table. When he had finished, he fumbled in his capacious pockets, and drew out the inevitable pocket-book.

Placing a small photograph before the girl, he said quietly:

"That is the back of the houses in Phillimore Terrace, which overlook Adam and Eve Mews."

She looked at the photograph, then at him, with a kindly look of indulgent expectancy.

"You will notice that the row of back gardens have each an exit into the mews. These mews are built in the shape of a capital F. The photograph is taken looking straight down the short horizontal line, which ends, as you see, in a *cul-de-sac*. The bottom of the vertical line turns into Phillimore Terrace, and the end of the upper long horizontal line into High Street, Kensington. Now, on that particular night, or rather early morning, of January 15th, Constable D 21, having turned

" It was some time before the constable succeeded
in rescuing the tramp."

into the mews from Phillimore Terrace, stood for a moment at the angle formed by the long vertical artery of the mews and the short horizontal one which, as I observed before, looks on to the back gardens of the Terrace houses, and ends in a *cul-de-sac*.

"How long D 21 stood at that particular corner he could not exactly say, but he thinks it must have been three or four minutes before he noticed a suspicious-looking individual shambling along under the shadow of the garden walls. He was working his way cautiously in the direction of the *cul-de-sac*, and D 21, also keeping well within the shadow, went noiselessly after him.

"He had almost overtaken him—was, in fact, not more than thirty yards from him—when from out of one of the two end houses—No. 22, Phillimore Terrace, in fact—a man, in nothing but his night-shirt, rushed out excitedly, and, before D 21 had time to intervene, literally threw himself upon the suspected individual, rolling over and over with him on the hard cobble-stones, and frantically shrieking, 'Thief! Thief! Police!'

"It was some time before the constable succeeded in rescuing the tramp from the excited grip of his assailant, and several minutes before he could make himself heard.

"'There! there! that'll do!' he managed to say at last, as he gave the man in the shirt a vigorous shove, which silenced him for the moment. 'Leave the man alone now, you mustn't make that noise this time o' night, wakin' up all the folks.' The unfortunate tramp, who in the meanwhile had managed to get on to his feet again, made no attempt to get away; probably he thought he would stand but a poor chance. But the man in the shirt had partly recovered his power of speech, and was now blurting out jerky, half intelligible sentences:

"'I have been robbed—-robbed—I—-that is—my master—Mr. Knopf. The desk is open—the diamonds gone—all in my charge—and—now they are stolen! That's the thief—I'll swear—I heard him—not three minutes ago—I rushed downstairs—the door into the garden was smashed—I ran across the garden—he was sneaking about here still—Thief! Thief! Police! Diamonds! Constable, don't let him go—I'll make you responsible if you let him go—'

"'Now then—that'll do!' admonished D 21 as soon as he could get a word in, 'stop that row, will you?'

"The man in the shirt was gradually recovering from his excitement.

"'Can I give this man in charge?' he asked.

29

"'What for?'

"'Burglary and housebreaking. I heard him, I tell you. He must have Mr. Knopf's diamonds about him at this moment.'

"'Where is Mr. Knopf?'

"'Out of town,' groaned the man in the shirt. 'He went to Brighton last night, and left me in charge, and now this thief has been and—'

"The tramp shrugged his shoulders and suddenly, without a word, he quietly began taking off his coat and waistcoat. These he handed across to the constable. Eagerly the man in the shirt fell on them, and turned the ragged pockets inside out. From one of the windows a hilarious voice made some facetious remark, as the tramp with equal solemnity began divesting himself of his nether garments.

"'Now then, stop that nonsense,' pronounced D 21 severely, 'what were you doing here this time o' night, anyway?'

"'The streets o' London is free to the public, ain't they?' queried the tramp.

"'This don't lead nowhere, my man.'

"'Then I've lost my way, that's all,' growled the man surlily, 'and p'raps you'll let me get along now.'

"By this time a couple of constables had appeared upon the scene. D 21 had no intention of losing sight of his friend the tramp, and the man in the shirt had again made a dash for the latter's collar at the bare idea that he should be allowed to 'get along.'

"I think D 21 was alive to the humour of the situation. He suggested that Robertson (the man in the night-shirt) should go in and get some clothes on, whilst he himself would wait for the inspector and the detective, whom D 15 would send round from the station immediately.

"Poor Robertson's teeth were chattering with cold. He had a violent fit of sneezing as D 21 hurried him into the house. The latter, with another constable, remained to watch the burglared premises both back and front, and D 15 took the wretched tramp to the station with a view to sending an inspector and a detective round immediately.

"When the two latter gentlemen arrived at No. 22, Phillimore Terrace, they found poor old Robertson in bed, shivering, and still quite blue. He had got himself a hot drink, but his eyes were streaming and his voice was terribly husky. D 21 had stationed himself in the dining-room, where Robertson had pointed the desk out to him, with its broken lock and scattered contents.

"Robertson, between his sneezes, gave what account he could of the events which happened immediately before the robbery.

"His master, Mr. Ferdinand Knopf, he said, was a diamond merchant, and a bachelor. He himself had been in Mr. Knopf's employ over fifteen years, and was his only indoor servant. A charwoman came every day to do the housework.

"Last night Mr. Knopf dined at the house of Mr. Shipman, at No. 26, lower down. Mr. Shipman is the great jeweller who has his place of business in South Audley Street. By the last post there came a letter with the Brighton postmark, and marked 'urgent,' for Mr. Knopf, and he (Robertson) was just wondering if he should run over to No. 26 with it, when his master returned. He gave one glance at the contents of the letter, asked for his A.B.C. Railway Guide, and ordered him (Robertson) to pack his bag at once and fetch him a cab.

"'I guessed what it was,' continued Robertson after another violent fit of sneezing. 'Mr. Knopf has a brother, Mr. Emile Knopf, to whom he is very much attached, and who is a great invalid. He generally goes about from one seaside place to another. He is now at Brighton, and has recently been very ill.

"'If you will take the trouble to go downstairs, I think you will still find the letter lying on the hall table.

"'I read it after Mr. Knopf left; it was not from his brother, but from a gentleman who signed himself J. Collins, M.D. I don't remember the exact words, but, of course, you'll be able to read the letter—Mr. J. Collins said he had been called in very suddenly to see Mr. Emile Knopf, who, he added, had not many hours to live, and had begged of the doctor to communicate at once with his brother in London.

"'Before leaving, Mr. Knopf warned me that there were some valuables in his desk—diamonds mostly, and told me to be particularly careful about locking up the house. He often has left me like this in charge of his premises, and usually there have been diamonds in his desk, for Mr. Knopf has no regular City office, as he is a commercial traveller.'

"This, briefly, was the gist of the matter which Robertson related to the inspector with many repetitions and persistent volubility.

"The detective and inspector, before returning to the station with their report, thought they would call at No. 26, on Mr. Shipman, the great jeweller.

"You remember, of course," added the man in the corner, dreamily contemplating his bit of string, "the exciting developments of this extraordinary case. Mr. Arthur Shipman is the head of the firm of Shipman and Co., the wealthy jewellers. He is a widower, and lives very quietly by himself in his own old-fashioned way in the small Kensington house, leaving it to his two married sons to keep up the style and swagger befitting the representatives of so wealthy a firm.

"'I have only known Mr. Knopf a very little while,' he explained to the detectives. 'He sold me two or three stones once or twice, I think; but we are both single men, and we have often dined together. Last night he dined with me. He had that afternoon received a very fine consignment of Brazilian diamonds, as he told me, and knowing how beset I am with callers at my business place, he had brought the stones with him, hoping, perhaps, to do a bit of trade over the nuts and wine.

"'I bought £25,000 worth of him,' added the jeweller, as if he were speaking of so many farthings, 'and gave him a cheque across the dinner table for that amount. I think we were both pleased with our bargain, and we had a final bottle of '48 port over it together. Mr. Knopf left me at about 9.30, for he knows I go very early to bed, and I took my new stock upstairs with me, and locked it up in the safe. I certainly heard nothing of the noise in the mews last night. I sleep on the second floor, in the front of the house, and this is the first I have heard of poor Mr. Knopf's loss'

"At this point of his narrative Mr. Shipman very suddenly paused, and his face became very pale. With a hasty word of excuse, he unceremoniously left the room, and the detective heard him running quickly upstairs.

"Less than two minutes later Mr. Shipman returned. There was no need for him to speak; both the detective and the inspector guessed the truth in a moment by the look upon his face.

"'The diamonds—!' he gasped. 'I have been robbed.'"

2

"Now I must tell you," continued the man in the corner, "that after I had read the account of the double robbery, which appeared in the early afternoon papers, I set to work and had a good think—yes!" he added with a smile, noting Polly's look at the bit of string, on which he was still at work, "yes! aided by this small adjunct to continued thought—I made notes as to how I should proceed to discover the clever thief, who had carried off a small fortune in a single night. Of course, my methods are not those of a London detective; he has his own way of going to work. The one who was conducting this case questioned the unfortunate jeweller very closely about his servants and his household generally.

"'I have three servants,' explained Mr. Shipman, 'two of whom have been with me for many years; one, the housemaid, is a fairly newcomer—she has been here about six months. She came recommended by a friend, and bore an excellent character. She and the parlourmaid room together. The cook, who knew me when I was a schoolboy, sleeps alone; all three servants sleep on the floor above. I locked the jewels up in the safe which stands in the dressing-room. My keys and watch I placed, as usual, beside my bed. As a rule, I am a fairly light sleeper.

"'I cannot understand how it could have happened—but—you had better come up and have a look at the safe. The key must have been abstracted from my bedside, the safe opened, and the keys replaced—all while I was fast asleep. Though I had no occasion to look into the safe until just now, I should have discovered my loss before going to business, for I intended to take the diamonds away with me—'

"The detective and the inspector went up to have a look at the safe. The lock had in no way been tampered with—it had been opened with its own key. The detective spoke of chloroform, but Mr. Shipman declared that when he woke in the morning at about half-past seven there was no smell of chloroform in the room. However, the proceedings of the daring thief certainly pointed to the use of an anaesthetic. An examination of the premises brought to light the fact that the burglar had, as in Mr. Knopf's house, used the glass-panelled door from the garden as a means of entrance, but in this instance, he had carefully cut out the pane of glass with a diamond, slipped the bolts, turned the key, and walked in.

"'Which among your servants knew that you had the diamonds in your house last night, Mr. Shipman?' asked the detective.

"'Not one, I should say,' replied the jeweller, 'though, perhaps, the parlourmaid, whilst waiting at table, may have heard me and Mr. Knopf discussing our bargain.'

"'Would you object to my searching all your servants' boxes?'

"'Certainly not. They would not object, either, I am sure. They are perfectly honest-.'

"The searching of servants' belongings is invariably a useless proceeding," added the man in the corner, with a shrug of the shoulders. "No one, not even a latter-day domestic, would be fool enough to keep stolen property in the house. However, the usual farce was gone through, with more or less protest on the part of Mr. Shipman's servants, and with the usual result.

"The jeweller could give no further information; the detective and inspector, to do them justice, did their work of investigation minutely and, what is more, intelligently. It seemed evident, from their deductions, that the burglar had commenced proceedings on No. 26, Phillimore Terrace, and had then gone on, probably climbing over the garden walls between the houses to No. 22, where he was almost caught in the act by Robertson. The facts were simple enough, but the mystery remained as to the individual who had managed to glean the information of the presence of the diamonds in both the houses, and the means which he had adopted to get that information. It was obvious that the thief or thieves knew more about Mr. Knopf's affairs than Mr. Shipman's, since they had known how to use Mr. Emile Knopf's name in order to get his brother out of the way.

"'It was now nearly ten o'clock, and the detectives, having taken leave of Mr. Shipman, went back to No. 22, in order to ascertain whether Mr. Knopf had come back; the door was opened by the old charwoman, who said that her master had returned, and was having some breakfast in the dining-room.

"'Mr. Ferdinand Knopf was a middle-aged man, with sallow complexion, black hair and beard, of obviously Hebrew extraction. He spoke with a marked foreign accent, but very courteously, to the two officials, who, he begged, would excuse him if he went on with his breakfast.

"'I was fully prepared to hear the bad news,' he explained, 'which my man Robertson told me when I arrived. The letter I got last night was a bogus one; there is no such person as J. Collins, M.D. My brother had never felt better in his life. You will, I am sure, very soon trace the cunning writer of that epistle—ah! but I was in a rage, I can tell you, when I got to the Metropole at Brighton, and found that Emile, my brother, had never heard of any Doctor Collins.

"'The last train to town had gone, although I raced back to the station as hard as I could. Poor old Robertson, he has a terrible cold. Ah yes! my loss! it is for me a very serious one; if I had not made that lucky bargain with Mr. Shipman last night I should, perhaps, at this moment be a ruined man.

"'The stones I had yesterday were, firstly, some magnificent Brazilians; these I sold to Mr. Shipman mostly. Then I had some very good Cape diamonds—all gone; and some quite special Parisians, of wonderful work and finish, entrusted to me for sale by a great French house. I tell you, sir, my loss will be nearly £10,000 altogether. I sell on commission, and, of course, have to make good the loss.'

"He was evidently trying to bear up manfully, and as a business man should, under his sad fate. He refused in any way to attach the slightest blame to his old and faithful servant Robertson, who had caught, perhaps, his death of cold in his zeal for his absent master. As for any hint of suspicion falling even remotely upon the man, the very idea appeared to Mr. Knopf absolutely preposterous.

"With regard to the old charwoman, Mr. Knopf certainly knew nothing about her, beyond the fact that she had been recommended to him by one of the tradespeople in the neighbourhood, and seemed perfectly honest, respectable, and sober.

"About the tramp Mr. Knopf knew still less, nor could he imagine how he, or in fact anybody else, could possibly know that he happened to have diamonds in his house that night.

"This certainly seemed the great hitch in the case.

"Mr. Ferdinand Knopf, at the instance of the police, later on went to the station and had a look at the suspected tramp. He declared that he had never set eyes on him before.

"Mr. Shipman, on his way home from business in the afternoon, had done likewise, and made a similar statement.

"Brought before the magistrate, the tramp gave but a poor account of himself. He gave a name and address, which latter, of course, proved to be false. After that he absolutely refused to speak. He seemed not to care whether he was kept in custody or not. Very soon even the police realised that, for the present, at any rate, nothing could be got out of the suspected tramp.

"Mr. Francis Howard, the detective, who had charge of the case, though he would not admit it even to himself, was at his wits' ends. You must remember that the burglary, through its very simplicity, was an exceedingly mysterious affair. The constable, D 21, who had stood in Adam and Eve Mews, presumably while Mr. Knopf's house was being robbed, had seen no one turn out from the *cul-de-sac* into the main passage of the mews.

"The stables, which immediately faced the back entrance of the Phillimore Terrace houses, were all private ones belonging to residents in the neighbourhood. The coachmen, their families, and all the grooms who slept in the stablings were rigidly watched and questioned. One and all had seen nothing, heard nothing, until Robertson's shrieks had roused them from their sleep.

"As for the letter from Brighton, it was absolutely commonplace, and written upon notepaper which the detective, with Machiavellian cunning, traced to a stationer's shop in West Street. But the trade at that particular shop was a very brisk one; scores of people had bought note-paper there, similar to that on which the supposed doctor had written his tricky letter. The handwriting was cramped, perhaps a disguised one; in any case, except under very exceptional circumstances, it could afford no clue to the identity of the thief. Needless to say, the tramp, when told to write his name, wrote a totally different and absolutely uneducated hand.

"Matters stood, however, in the same persistently mysterious state when a small discovery was made, which suggested to Mr. Francis Howard an idea, which, if properly carried out, would, he hoped, inevitably bring the cunning burglar safely within the grasp of the police.

"That was the discovery of a few of Mr. Knopf's diamonds," continued the man in the corner after a slight pause, "evidently trampled into the ground by the thief whilst making his hurried exit through the garden of No. 22, Phillimore Terrace.

"At the end of this garden there is a small studio which had been built by a former owner of the house, and behind it a small piece of waste ground about seven feet square which had once been a rockery, and is still filled with large loose stones, in the shadow of which earwigs and woodlice innumerable have made a happy hunting ground.

"It was Robertson who, two days after the robbery, having need of a large stone, for some household purpose or other, dislodged one from that piece of waste ground, and found a few shining pebbles beneath it. Mr. Knopf took them round to the police-station himself immediately, and identified the stones as some of his Parisian ones.

"Later on, the detective went to view the place where the find had been made, and there conceived the plan upon which he built his cherished hopes.

"Acting upon the advice of Mr. Francis Howard, the police decided to let the anonymous tramp out of his safe retreat within the station, and to allow him to wander whithersoever he chose. A good idea, perhaps—the presumption being that, sooner or later, if the man was in any way mixed up with the cunning thieves, he would either rejoin his comrades or even lead the police to where the remnant of his hoard lay hidden; needless to say, his footsteps were to be literally dogged.

"The wretched tramp, on his discharge, wandered out of the yard, wrapping his thin coat round his shoulders, for it was a bitterly cold afternoon. He began operations by turning into the Town Hall Tavern for a good feed and a copious drink. Mr. Francis Howard noted that he seemed to eye every passer-by with suspicion, but he seemed to enjoy his dinner, and sat some time over his bottle of wine.

"It was close upon four o'clock when he left the tavern, and then began for the indefatigable Mr. Howard one of the most wearisome and uninteresting chases, through the mazes of the London streets, he ever remembers to have made. Up Notting Hill, down the slums of Notting Dale, along the High Street, beyond Hammersmith, and through Shepherd's Bush did that anonymous tramp lead the unfortunate detective, never hurrying himself, stopping every now and then at a public-house to get a drink, whither Mr. Howard did not always care to follow him.

"In spite of his fatigue, Mr. Francis Howard's hopes rose with every half-hour of this weary tramp. The man was obviously striving to kill time; he seemed to feel no weariness, but walked on and on, perhaps suspecting that he was being followed.

"At last, with a beating heart, though half perished with cold, and with terribly sore feet, the detective began to realise that the tramp was gradually working his way back towards Kensington. It was then close upon eleven o'clock at night; once or twice the man had walked up and down the High Street, from St. Paul's School to Derry and Toms' shops and back again, he had looked down one or two of the side streets and—at last—he turned into Phillimore Terrace. He seemed in no hurry, he even stopped once in the middle of the road, trying to light a pipe, which, as there was a high east wind, took him some considerable time. Then he leisurely sauntered down the street, and turned into Adam and Eve Mews, with Mr. Francis Howard now close at his heels.

"Acting upon the detective's instructions, there were several men in plain clothes ready to his call in the immediate neighbourhood. Two stood within the shadow of the steps of the Congregational Church at the corner of the mews, others were stationed well within a soft call.

"Hardly, therefore, had the hare turned into the *cul-de-sac* at the back of Phillimore Terrace than, at a slight sound from Mr. Francis Howard, every egress was barred to him, and he was caught like a rat in a trap.

"As soon as the tramp had advanced some thirty yards or so (the whole length of this part of the mews is about one hundred yards) and was lost in the shadow, Mr. Francis Howard directed four or five of his men to proceed cautiously up the mews, whilst the same number were to form a line all along the front of Phillimore Terrace between the mews and the High Street.

"Remember, the back-garden walls threw long and dense shadows, but the silhouette of the man would be clearly outlined if he made any attempt at climbing over them. Mr. Howard felt quite sure that the thief was bent on recovering the stolen goods, which, no doubt, he had hidden in the rear of one of the houses. He would be caught *in flagrante delicto*, and, with a heavy sentence hovering over him, he would probably be induced to name his accomplice. Mr. Francis Howard was thoroughly enjoying himself.

"The minutes sped on; absolute silence, in spite of the presence of so many men, reigned in the dark and deserted mews.

"Of course, this night's adventure was never allowed to get into the papers," added the man in the corner with his mild smile. "Had the plan been successful, we should have heard all about it, with a long eulogistic article as to the astuteness of our police; but as it was—well, the tramp sauntered up the mews—and—there he remained for aught Mr. Francis Howard or the other constables could ever explain. The earth or the shadows swallowed him up. No one saw him climb one of the garden walls, no one heard him break open a door; he had retreated within the shadow of the garden walls, and was seen or heard of no more."

"One of the servants in the Phillimore Terrace houses must have belonged to the gang," said Polly with quick decision.

"Ah, yes! but which?" said the man in the corner, making a beautiful knot in his bit of string. "I can assure you that the police left not a stone unturned once more to catch sight of that tramp whom they had had in custody for two days, but not a trace of him could they find, nor of the diamonds, from that day to this."

3

"The tramp was missing," continued the man in the corner, "and Mr. Francis Howard tried to find the missing tramp. Going round to the front, and seeing the lights at No. 26 still in, he called upon Mr. Shipman. The jeweller had had a few friends to dinner, and was giving them whiskies-and-sodas before saying goodnight. The servants had just finished washing up, and were waiting to go to bed; neither they nor Mr. Shipman nor his guests had seen or heard anything of the suspicious individual.

"Mr. Francis Howard went on to see Mr. Ferdinand Knopf. This gentleman was having his warm bath, preparatory to going to bed. So, Robertson told the detective. However, Mr. Knopf insisted on talking to Mr. Howard through his bathroom door. Mr. Knopf thanked him for all the trouble he was taking, and felt sure that he and Mr. Shipman would soon recover possession of their diamonds, thanks to the persevering detective.

"He! he! he!" laughed the man in the corner. "Poor Mr. Howard. He persevered—but got no farther; no, nor anyone else, for that matter. Even I might not be able to convict the thieves if I told all I knew to the police.

"Now, follow my reasoning, point by point," he added eagerly.

"Who knew of the presence of the diamonds in the house of Mr. Shipman and Mr. Knopf? Firstly," he said, putting up an ugly claw-like finger, "Mr. Shipman, then Mr. Knopf, then, presumably, the man Robertson."

"And the tramp?" said Polly.

"Leave the tramp alone for the present since he has vanished, and take point number two. Mr. Shipman was drugged. That was pretty obvious; no man under ordinary circumstances would, without waking, have his keys abstracted and then replaced at his own bedside. Mr. Howard suggested that the thief was armed with some anaesthetic; but how did the thief get into Mr. Shipman's room without waking him from his natural sleep? Is it not simpler to suppose that the thief had taken the precaution to drug the jeweller *before* the latter went to bed?"

"But—"

"Wait a moment, and take point number three. Though there was every proof that Mr. Shipman had been in possession of £25,000 worth of goods since Mr. Knopf had a cheque from him for that amount, there was no proof that in Mr. Knopf's house there was even an odd stone worth a sovereign.

"And then again," went on the scarecrow, getting more and more excited, "did it ever strike you, or anybody else, that at no time, while the tramp was in custody, while all that searching examination was being gone on with, no one ever saw Mr. Knopf and his man Robertson together at the same time?

"Ah!" he continued, whilst suddenly the young girl seemed to see the whole thing as in a vision, "they did not forget a single detail—follow them with me, point by point. Two cunning scoundrels—geniuses they should be called—well provided with some ill-gotten funds—but determined on a grand *coup*. They play at respectability, for six months, say. One is the master, the other the servant; they take a house in the same street as their intended victim, make friends with him, accomplish one or two creditable but very small business transactions, always drawing on the reserve funds, which might even have amounted to a few hundreds—and a bit of credit.

"Then the Brazilian diamonds, and the Parisians—which, remember, were so perfect that they required chemical testing to be detected. The Parisian stones are sold—not in business, of course—in the evening, after dinner and a good deal of wine. Mr. Knopf's Brazilians were beautiful; perfect! Mr. Knopf was a well-known diamond merchant.

"Mr. Shipman bought—but with the morning would have come sober sense, the cheque stopped before it could have been presented, the swindler caught. No! those exquisite Parisians were never intended to rest in Mr. Shipman's safe until the morning. That last bottle of '48 port, with the aid of a powerful soporific, ensured that Mr. Shipman would sleep undisturbed during the night.

"Ah! remember all the details, they were so admirable! the letter posted in Brighton by the cunning rogue to himself, the smashed desk, the broken pane of glass in his own house. The man Robertson on the watch, while Knopf himself in ragged clothing found his way into No. 26. If Constable D 21 had not appeared upon the scene that exciting comedy in the early morning would not have been enacted. As it was, in the supposed fight, Mr. Shipman's diamonds passed from the hands of the tramp into those of his accomplice.

"Then, later on, Robertson, ill in bed, while his master was supposed to have returned—by the way, it never struck anybody that no one saw Mr. Knopf come home, though he surely would have driven up in a cab. Then the double part played by one man for the next two days. It certainly never struck either the police or the inspector. Remember they only saw Robertson when in bed with a streaming cold. But Knopf had to be got out of gaol as soon as possible; the dual role could not have been kept up for long. Hence the story of the diamonds found in the garden of No. 22. The cunning rogues guessed that the usual plan would be acted upon, and the suspected thief allowed to visit the scene where his hoard lay hidden.

"It had all been foreseen, and Robertson must have been constantly on the watch. The tramp stopped, mind you, in Phillimore Terrace for some moments, lighting a pipe. The accomplice, then, was fully on the alert; he slipped the bolts of the back garden gate. Five minutes later Knopf was in the house, in a hot bath, getting rid of the disguise of our friend the tramp. Remember that again here the detective did not actually see him.

"The next morning Mr. Knopf, black hair and beard and all, was himself again. The whole trick lay in one simple art, which those two cunning rascals knew to absolute perfection, the art of impersonating one another.

"They are brothers, presumably—-twin brothers, I should say,"

"But Mr. Knopf—" suggested Polly.

"Well, look in the Trades' Directory; you will see F. Knopf & Co. diamond merchants, of some City address. Ask about the firm among the trade; you will hear that it is firmly established on a sound financial basis. He! he! he! and it deserves to be," added the man in the corner, as, calling for the waitress, he received his ticket, and taking up his shabby hat, took himself and his bit of string rapidly out of the room.

The York Mystery

1

The man in the corner looked quite cheerful that morning; he had had two glasses of milk and had even gone to the extravagance of an extra cheese-cake. Polly knew that he was itching to talk police and murders, for he cast furtive glances at her from time to time, produced a bit of string, tied and untied it into scores of complicated knots, and finally, bringing out his pocket-book, he placed two or three photographs before her.

"Do you know who that is?" he asked, pointing to one of these.

The girl looked at the face on the picture. It was that of a woman, not exactly pretty, but very gentle and childlike, with a strange pathetic look in the large eyes which was wonderfully appealing.

"That was Lady Arthur Skelmerton," he said, and in a flash there flitted before Polly's mind the weird and tragic history which had broken this loving woman's heart. Lady Arthur Skelmerton! That name recalled one of the most bewildering, most mysterious passages in the annals of undiscovered crimes.

"Yes. It was sad, wasn't it?" he commented, in answer to Polly's thoughts. "Another case which but for idiotic blunders on the part of the police must have stood clear as daylight before the public and satisfied general anxiety. Would you object to my recapitulating its preliminary details?"

She said nothing, so he continued without waiting further for a reply.

"It all occurred during the York racing week, a time which brings to the quiet cathedral city its quota of shady characters, who congregate wherever money and wits happen to fly away from their owners. Lord Arthur Skelmerton, a very well-known figure in London society and in racing circles, had rented one of the fine houses which overlook the racecourse. He had entered Peppercorn, by St. Armand—

Notre Dame, for the Great Ebor Handicap. Peppercorn was the winner of the Newmarket, and his chances for the Ebor were considered a practical certainty.

"If you have ever been to York, you will have noticed the fine houses which have their drive and front entrances in the road called 'The Mount,' and the gardens of which extend as far as the racecourse, commanding a lovely view over the entire track. It was one of these houses, called 'The Elms,' which Lord Arthur Skelmerton had rented for the summer.

"Lady Arthur came down some little time before the racing week with her servants—she had no children; but she had many relatives and friends in York, since she was the daughter of old Sir John Etty, the cocoa manufacturer, a rigid Quaker, who, it was generally said, kept the tightest possible hold on his own purse-strings and looked with marked disfavour upon his aristocratic son-in-law's fondness for gaming tables and betting books.

"As a matter of fact, Maud Etty had married the handsome young lieutenant in the —th Hussars, quite against her father's wishes. But she was an only child, and after a good deal of demur and grumbling, Sir John, who idolised his daughter, gave way to her whim, and a reluctant consent to the marriage was wrung from him.

"But, as a Yorkshireman, he was far too shrewd a man of the world not to know that love played but a very small part in persuading a duke's son to marry the daughter of a cocoa manufacturer, and as long as he lived, he determined that since his daughter was being wed because of her wealth, that wealth should at least secure her own happiness. He refused to give Lady Arthur any capital, which, in spite of the most carefully worded settlements, would inevitably, sooner or later, have found its way into the pockets of Lord Arthur's racing friends. But he made his daughter a very handsome allowance, amounting to over £3,000 a year, which enabled her to keep up an establishment befitting her new rank.

"A great many of these facts, intimate enough as they are, leaked out, you see, during that period of intense excitement which followed the murder of Charles Lavender, and when the public eye was fixed searchingly upon Lord Arthur Skelmerton, probing all the inner details of his idle, useless life.

"It soon became a matter of common gossip that poor little Lady Arthur continued to worship her handsome husband in spite of his obvious neglect, and not having as yet presented him with an heir, she settled herself down into a life of humble apology for her plebeian existence, atoning for it by condoning all his faults and forgiving all his vices, even to the extent of cloaking them before the prying eyes of Sir John, who was persuaded to look upon his son-in-law as a paragon of all the domestic virtues and a perfect model of a husband.

"Among Lord Arthur Skelmerton's many expensive tastes there was certainly that for horseflesh and cards. After some successful betting at the beginning of his married life, he had started a racing-stable which it was generally believed—as he was very lucky—was a regular source of income to him.

"Peppercorn, however, after his brilliant performances at Newmarket did not continue to fulfil his master's expectations. His collapse at York was attributed to the hardness of the course and to various other causes, but its immediate effect was to put Lord Arthur Skelmerton in what is popularly called a tight place, for he had backed his horse for all he was worth, and must have stood to lose considerably over £5,000 on that one day.

"The collapse of the favourite and the grand victory of King Cole, a rank outsider, on the other hand, had proved a golden harvest for the bookmakers, and all the York hotels were busy with dinners and suppers given by the confraternity of the Turf to celebrate the happy occasion. The next day was Friday, one of few important racing events, after which the brilliant and the shady throng which had flocked into the venerable city for the week would fly to more congenial climes, and leave it, with its fine old Minster and its ancient walls, as sleepy, as quiet as before.

"Lord Arthur Skelmerton also intended to leave York on the Saturday, and on the Friday night he gave a farewell bachelor dinner party at 'The Elms,' at which Lady Arthur did not appear. After dinner the gentlemen settled down to bridge, with pretty stiff points, you may be sure. It had just struck eleven at the Minster Tower, when constables McNaught and Murphy, who were patrolling the racecourse, were startled by loud cries of 'murder' and 'police.'

"Quickly ascertaining whence these cries proceeded, they hurried on at a gallop, and came up—quite close to the boundary of Lord Arthur Skelmerton's grounds—upon a group of three men, two of whom seemed to be wrestling vigorously with one another, whilst the third was lying face downwards on the ground. As soon as the constables drew near, one of the wrestlers shouted more vigorously, and with a certain tone of authority:

"'Here, you fellows, hurry up, sharp; the brute is giving me the slip!'

"But the brute did not seem inclined to do anything of the sort; he certainly extricated himself with a violent jerk from his assailant's grasp, but made no attempt to run away. The constables had quickly dismounted, whilst he who had shouted for help originally added more quietly:

"'My name is Skelmerton. This is the boundary of my property. I was smoking a cigar at the pavilion over there with a friend when I heard loud voices, followed by a cry and a groan. I hurried down the steps, and saw this poor fellow lying on the ground, with a knife sticking between his shoulder-blades, and his murderer,' he added, pointing to the man who stood quietly by with Constable McNaught's firm grip upon his shoulder, 'still stooping over the body of his victim. I was too late, I fear, to save the latter, but just in time to grapple with the assassin—'

"'It's a lie!' here interrupted the man hoarsely. 'I didn't do it, constable; I swear I didn't do it. I saw him fall—I was coming along a couple of hundred yards away, and I tried to see if the poor fellow was dead. I swear I didn't do it.'

"'You'll have to explain that to the inspector presently, my man,' was Constable McNaught's quiet comment, and, still vigorously protesting his innocence, the accused allowed himself to be led away, and the body was conveyed to the station, pending fuller identification.

"The next morning the papers were full of the tragedy; a column and a half of the *York Herald* was devoted to an account of Lord Arthur Skelmerton's plucky capture of the assassin. The latter had continued to declare his innocence, but had remarked, it appears, with grim humour, that he quite saw he was in a tight place, out of which, however, he would find it easy to extricate himself. He had stated to the police that the deceased's name was Charles Lavender, a well-known bookmaker, which fact was soon verified, for many of the murdered man's 'pals' were still in the city.

"So far, the most pushing of newspaper reporters had been unable to glean further information from the police; no one doubted, however, but that the man in charge, who gave his name as George Higgins, had killed the bookmaker for purposes of robbery. The inquest had been fixed for the Tuesday after the murder.

"Lord Arthur had been obliged to stay in York a few days, as his evidence would be needed. That fact gave the case, perhaps, a certain amount of interest as far as York and London 'society' were concerned. Charles Lavender, moreover, was well known on the turf; but no bombshell exploding beneath the walls of the ancient cathedral city could more have astonished its inhabitants than the news which, at about five in the afternoon on the day of the inquest, spread like wildfire throughout the town.

"That news was that the inquest had concluded at three o'clock with a verdict of 'Wilful murder against some person or persons unknown,' and that two hours later the police had arrested Lord Arthur Skelmerton at his private residence, 'The Elms,' and charged him on a warrant with the murder of Charles Lavender, the bookmaker."

2

"The police, it appears, instinctively feeling that some mystery lurked round the death of the bookmaker and his supposed murderer's quiet protestations of innocence, had taken a very considerable amount of trouble in collecting all the evidence they could for the inquest which might throw some light upon Charles Lavender's life, previous to his tragic end. Thus, it was that a very large array of witnesses was brought before the coroner, chief among whom was, of course, Lord Arthur Skelmerton.

"The first witnesses called were the two constables, who deposed that, just as the church clocks in the neighbourhood were striking eleven, they had heard the cries for help, had ridden to the spot whence the sounds proceeded, and had found the prisoner in the tight grasp of Lord Arthur Skelmerton, who at once accused the man of murder, and gave him in charge. Both constables gave the same version of the incident, and both were positive as to the time when it occurred.

"Medical evidence went to prove that the deceased had been stabbed from behind between the shoulder-blades whilst he was walking, that the wound was inflicted by a large hunting knife, which was produced, and which had been left sticking in the wound.

"Lord Arthur Skelmerton was then called and substantially repeated what he had already told the constables. He stated, namely, that on the night in question he had some gentlemen friends to dinner, and afterwards bridge was played. He himself was not playing much, and at a few minutes before eleven he strolled out with a cigar as far as the pavilion at the end of his garden; he then heard the voices, the cry and the groan previously described by him, and managed to hold the murderer down until the arrival of the constables.

"At this point the police proposed to call a witness, James Terry by name and a bookmaker by profession, who had been chiefly instrumental in identifying the deceased, a 'pal' of his. It was his evidence which first introduced that element of sensation into the case which culminated in the wildly exciting arrest of a duke's son upon a capital charge.

"It appears that on the evening after the Ebor, Terry and Lavender were in the bar of the Black Swan Hotel having drinks.

"'I had done pretty well over Peppercorn's fiasco,' he explained, 'but poor old Lavender was very much down in the dumps; he had held only a few very small bets against the favourite, and the rest of the day had been a poor one with him. I asked him if he had any bets with the owner of Peppercorn, and he told me that he only held one for less than £500.

"'I laughed and said that if he held one for £5,000 it would make no difference, as from what I had heard from the other fellows, Lord Arthur Skelmerton must be about stumped. Lavender seemed terribly put out at this, and swore he would get that £500 out of Lord Arthur, if no one else got another penny from him.

"'It's the only money I've made today,' he says to me. 'I mean to get it.'

"'You won't,' I says.

"'I will,' he says.

"'You will have to look pretty sharp about it then,' I says, 'for everyone will be wanting to get something, and first come first served.'

"'Oh! He'll serve me right enough, never you mind!' says Lavender to me with a laugh. 'If he don't pay up willingly, I've got that in my pocket which will make him sit up and open my lady's eyes and Sir John Etty's too about their precious noble lord.'

"'Then he seemed to think he had gone too far, and wouldn't say anything more to me about that affair. I saw him on the course the next day. I asked him if he had got his £500. He said: "No, but I shall get it today."'

"Lord Arthur Skelmerton, after having given his own evidence, had left the court; it was therefore impossible to know how he would take this account, which threw so serious a light upon an association with the dead man, of which he himself had said nothing.

"Nothing could shake James Terry's account of the facts he had placed before the jury, and when the police informed the coroner that they proposed to place George Higgins himself in the witness-box, as his evidence would prove, as it were, a complement and corollary of that of Terry, the jury very eagerly assented.

"If James Terry, the bookmaker, loud, florid, vulgar, was an unprepossessing individual, certainly George Higgins, who was still under the accusation of murder, was ten thousand times more so.

"None too clean, slouchy, obsequious yet insolent, he was the very personification of the cad who haunts the racecourse and who lives not so much by his own wits as by the lack of them in others. He described himself as a turf commission agent, whatever that may be.

"He stated that at about six o'clock on the Friday afternoon, when the racecourse was still full of people, all hurrying after the day's excitements, he himself happened to be standing close to the hedge which marks the boundary of Lord Arthur Skelmerton's grounds. There is a pavilion there at the end of the garden, he explained, on slightly elevated ground, and he could hear and see a group of ladies and gentlemen having tea. Some steps lead down a little to the left of the garden on to the course, and presently he noticed at the bottom of these steps Lord Arthur Skelmerton and Charles Lavender standing talking together. He knew both gentlemen by sight, but he could not see them very well as they were both partly hidden by the hedge. He was quite sure that the gentlemen had not seen him, and he could not help overhearing some of their conversation.

"'That's my last word, Lavender,' Lord Arthur was saying very quietly. 'I haven't got the money and I can't pay you now. You'll have to wait.'

"'Wait? I can't wait,' said old Lavender in reply. 'I've got my engagements to meet, same as you. I'm not going to risk being posted up as a defaulter while you hold £500 of my money. You'd better give it me now or—'

"But Lord Arthur interrupted him very quietly, and said:

"'Yes, my good man . . . . or?'

"'Or I'll let Sir John have a good look at that little bill I had of yours a couple of years ago. If you'll remember, my lord, it has got at the bottom of it Sir John's signature in your handwriting. Perhaps Sir John, or perhaps my lady, would pay me something for that little bill. If not, the police can have a squint at it. I've held my tongue long enough, and—'

"'Look here, Lavender,' said Lord Arthur, 'do you know what this little game of yours is called in law?'

"'Yes, and I don't care,' says Lavender. 'If I don't have that £500, I am a ruined man. If you ruin me, I'll do for you, and we shall be quits. That's my last word.'

"He was talking very loudly, and I thought some of Lord Arthur's friends up in the pavilion must have heard. He thought so, too, I think, for he said quickly:

"'If you don't hold your confounded tongue, I'll give you in charge for blackmail this instant.'

"'You wouldn't dare,' says Lavender, and he began to laugh. But just then a lady from the top of the steps said: 'Your tea is getting cold,' and Lord Arthur turned to go; but just before he went Lavender says to him: 'I'll come back tonight. You'll have the money then.'

"George Higgins, it appears, after he had heard this interesting conversation, pondered as to whether he could not turn what he knew into some sort of profit. Being a gentleman who lives entirely by his wits, this type of knowledge forms his chief source of income. As a preliminary to future moves, he decided not to lose sight of Lavender for the rest of the day.

"'Lavender went and had dinner at The Black Swan,' explained Mr. George Higgins, 'and I, after I had had a bite myself, waited outside till I saw him come out. At about ten o'clock I was rewarded for my trouble. He told the hall porter to get him a fly and he jumped into it. I could not hear what direction he gave the driver, but the fly certainly drove off towards the racecourse.

"'Now, I was interested in this little affair,' continued the witness, 'and I couldn't afford a fly. I started to run. Of course, I couldn't keep up with it, but I thought I knew which way my gentleman had gone. I made straight for the racecourse, and for the hedge at the bottom of Lord Arthur Skelmerton's grounds.

"'It was rather a dark night and there was a slight drizzle. I couldn't see more than about a hundred yards before me. All at once it seemed to me as if I heard Lavender's voice talking loudly in the distance. I hurried forward, and suddenly saw a group of two figures—mere blurs in the darkness—for one instant, at a distance of about fifty yards from where I was.

"'The next moment one figure had fallen forward and the other had disappeared. I ran to the spot, only to find the body of the murdered man lying on the ground. I stooped to see if I could be of any use to him, and immediately I was collared from behind by Lord Arthur himself.'

"You may imagine," said the man in the corner, "how keen was the excitement of that moment in court. Coroner and jury alike literally hung breathless on every word that shabby, vulgar individual uttered. You see, by itself his evidence would have been worth very little, but coming on the top of that given by James Terry, its significance—more, its truth—had become glaringly apparent. Closely cross-examined, he adhered strictly to his statement; and having finished his evidence, George Higgins remained in charge of the constables, and the next witness of importance was called up.

"This was Mr. Chipps, the senior footman in the employment of Lord Arthur Skelmerton. He deposed that at about 10.30 on the Friday evening a 'party' drove up to 'The Elms' in a fly, and asked to see Lord Arthur. On being told that his lordship had company he seemed terribly put out.

"'I hasked the party to give me 'is card,' continued Mr. Chipps, 'as I didn't know, perhaps, that 'is lordship might wish to see 'im, but I kept 'im standing at the 'all door, as I didn't altogether like his looks. I took the card in. His lordship and the gentlemen was playin' cards in the smoking-room, and as soon as I could do so without disturbing 'is lordship, I give him the party's card.'

"'What name was there on the card?' here interrupted the coroner.

"'I couldn't say now, sir,' replied Mr. Chipps; 'I don't really remember. It was a name I had never seen before. But I see so many visiting cards one way and the other in 'is lordship's 'all that I can't remember all the names.'

"'Then, after a few minutes' waiting, you gave his lordship the card? What happened then?'

"''Is lordship didn't seem at all pleased,' said Mr. Chipps with much guarded dignity; 'but finally he said: "Show him into the library, Chipps, I'll see him," and he got up from the card table, saying to the gentlemen: "Go on without me; I'll be back in a minute or two."

"'I was about to open the door for 'is lordship when my lady came into the room, and then his lordship suddenly changed his mind like, and said to me: "Tell that man I'm busy and can't see him," and 'e sat down again at the card table. I went back to the 'all, and told the party 'is lordship wouldn't see 'im. 'E said: "Oh! it doesn't matter," and went away quite quiet like.'

"'Do you recollect at all at what time that was?' asked one of the jury.

"'Yes, sir, while I was waiting to speak to 'is lordship I looked at the clock, sir; it was twenty past ten, sir.'

"There was one more significant fact in connection with the case, which tended still more to excite the curiosity of the public at the time, and still further to bewilder the police later on, and that fact was mentioned by Chipps in his evidence. The knife, namely, with which Charles Lavender had been stabbed, and which, remember, had been left in the wound, was now produced in court. After a little hesitation Chipps identified it as the property of his master, Lord Arthur Skelmerton.

"Can you wonder, then, that the jury absolutely refused to bring in a verdict against George Higgins? There was really, beyond Lord Arthur Skelmerton's testimony, not one particle of evidence against him, whilst, as the day wore on and witness after witness was called up, suspicion ripened in the minds of all those present that the murderer could be no other than Lord Arthur Skelmerton himself.

"The knife was, of course, the strongest piece of circumstantial evidence, and no doubt the police hoped to collect a great deal more now that they held a clue in their hands. Directly after the verdict, therefore, which was guardedly directed against some person unknown, the police obtained a warrant and later on arrested Lord Arthur in his own house."

"The sensation, of course, was tremendous. Hours before he was brought up before the magistrate the approach to the court was thronged. His friends, mostly ladies, were all eager, you see, to watch the dashing society man in so terrible a position. There was universal sympathy for Lady Arthur, who was in a very precarious state of health. Her worship of her worthless husband was well known; small wonder that his final and awful misdeed had practically broken her heart. The latest bulletin issued just after his arrest stated that her ladyship was not expected to live. She was then in a comatose condition, and all hope had perforce to be abandoned.

"At last, the prisoner was brought in. He looked very pale, perhaps, but otherwise kept up the bearing of a high-bred gentleman. He was accompanied by his solicitor, Sir Marmaduke Ingersoll, who was evidently talking to him in quiet, reassuring tones.

"Mr. Buchanan prosecuted for the Treasury, and certainly his indictment was terrific. According to him but one decision could be arrived at, namely, that the accused in the dock had, in a moment of passion, and perhaps of fear, killed the blackmailer who threatened him with disclosures which might for ever have ruined him socially, and, having committed the deed and fearing its consequences, probably realising that the patrolling constables might catch sight of his retreating figure, he had availed himself of George Higgins's presence on the spot to loudly accuse him of the murder.

"Having concluded his able speech, Mr. Buchanan called his witnesses, and the evidence, which on second hearing seemed more damning than ever, was all gone through again.

"Sir Marmaduke had no question to ask of the witnesses for the prosecution; he stared at them placidly through his gold-rimmed spectacles. Then he was ready to call his own for the defence. Colonel McIntosh, R.A., was the first. He was present at the bachelors' party given by Lord Arthur the night of the murder. His evidence tended at first to corroborate that of Chipps the footman with regard to Lord Arthur's orders to show the visitor into the library, and his counter-order as soon as his wife came into the room.

"'Did you not think it strange, colonel?' asked Mr. Buchanan, 'that Lord Arthur should so suddenly have changed his mind about seeing his visitor?'

"'Well, not exactly strange,' said the colonel, a fine, manly, soldierly figure who looked curiously out of his element in the witness-box. 'I don't think that it is a very rare occurrence for racing men to have certain acquaintances whom they would not wish their wives to know anything about.'

"'Then it did not strike you that Lord Arthur Skelmerton had some reason for not wishing his wife to know of that particular visitor's presence in his house?'

"'I don't think that I gave the matter the slightest serious consideration,' was the colonel's guarded reply.

"Mr. Buchanan did not press the point, and allowed the witness to conclude his statements.

"'I had finished my turn at bridge,' he said, 'and went out into the garden to smoke a cigar. Lord Arthur Skelmerton joined me a few minutes later, and we were sitting in the pavilion when I heard a loud and, as I thought, threatening voice from the other side of the hedge.

"'I did not catch the words, but Lord Arthur said to me: "There seems to be a row down there. I'll go and have a look and see what it is." I tried to dissuade him, and certainly made no attempt to follow him, but not more than half a minute could have elapsed before I heard a cry and a groan, then Lord Arthur's footsteps hurrying down the wooden stairs which lead on to the racecourse.'

"You may imagine," said the man in the corner, "what severe cross-examination the gallant colonel had to undergo in order that his assertions might in some way be shaken by the prosecution, but with military precision and frigid calm he repeated his important statements amidst a general silence, through which you could have heard the proverbial pin.

"He had heard the threatening voice *while* sitting with Lord Arthur Skelmerton; then came the cry and groan, and, *after that*, Lord Arthur's steps down the stairs. He himself thought of following to see what had happened, but it was a very dark night and he did not know the grounds very well. While trying to find his way to the garden steps he heard Lord Arthur's cry for help, the tramp of the patrolling constables' horses, and subsequently the whole scene between Lord Arthur, the man Higgins, and the constables. When he finally found his way to the stairs, Lord Arthur was returning in order to send a groom for police assistance.

"The witness stuck to his points as he had to his guns at Beckfontein a year ago; nothing could shake him, and Sir Marmaduke looked triumphantly across at his opposing colleague.

"With the gallant colonel's statements the edifice of the prosecution certainly began to collapse. You see, there was not a particle of evidence to show that the accused had met and spoken to the deceased after the latter's visit at the front door of 'The Elms.' He told Chipps that he wouldn't see the visitor, and Chipps went into the hall directly and showed Lavender out the way he came. No assignation could have been made, no hint could have been given by the murdered man to Lord Arthur that he would go round to the back entrance and wished to see him there.

"Two other guests of Lord Arthur's swore positively that after Chipps had announced the visitor, their host stayed at the card-table until a quarter to eleven, when evidently he went out to join Colonel McIntosh in the garden. Sir Marmaduke's speech was clever in the extreme. Bit by bit he demolished that tower of strength, the case against the accused, basing his defence entirely upon the evidence of Lord Arthur Skelmerton's guests that night.

"Until 10.45 Lord Arthur was playing cards; a quarter of an hour later the police were on the scene, and the murder had been committed. In the meanwhile, Colonel McIntosh's evidence proved conclusively that the accused had been sitting with him, smoking a cigar. It was obvious, therefore, clear as daylight, concluded the great lawyer, that his client was entitled to a full discharge; nay, more, he thought that the police should have been more careful before they harrowed up public feeling by arresting a high-born gentleman on such insufficient evidence as they had brought forward.

"The question of the knife remained certainly, but Sir Marmaduke passed over it with guarded eloquence, placing that strange question in the category of those inexplicable coincidences which tend to puzzle the ablest detectives, and cause them to commit such unpardonable blunders as the present one had been. After all, the footman may have been mistaken. The pattern of that knife was not an exclusive one, and he, on behalf of his client, flatly denied that it had ever belonged to him.

"Well," continued the man in the corner, with the chuckle peculiar to him in moments of excitement, "the noble prisoner was discharged. Perhaps it would be invidious to say that he left the court without a stain on his character, for I daresay you know from experience that the crime known as the York Mystery has never been satisfactorily cleared up.

"Many people shook their heads dubiously when they remembered that, after all, Charles Lavender was killed with a knife which one witness had sworn belonged to Lord Arthur; others, again, reverted to the original theory that George Higgins was the murderer, that he and James Terry had concocted the story of Lavender's attempt at blackmail on Lord Arthur, and that the murder had been committed for the sole purpose of robbery.

"Be that as it may, the police have not so far been able to collect sufficient evidence against Higgins or Terry, and the crime has been classed by press and public alike in the category of so-called impenetrable mysteries,"

3

The man in the corner called for another glass of milk, and drank it down slowly before he resumed:

"Now Lord Arthur lives mostly abroad," he said. "His poor, suffering wife died the day after he was liberated by the magistrate. She never recovered consciousness even sufficiently to hear the joyful news that the man she loved so well was innocent after all.

"Mystery!" he added as if in answer to Polly's own thoughts. "The murder of that man was never a mystery to me. I cannot understand how the police could have been so blind when every one of the witnesses, both for the prosecution and defence, practically pointed all the time to the one guilty person. What do you think of it all yourself?"

"I think the whole case so bewildering," she replied, "that I do not see one single clear point in it."

"You don't?" he said excitedly, while the bony fingers fidgeted again with that inevitable bit of string. "You don't see that there is one point clear which to me was the key of the whole thing?

"Lavender was murdered, wasn't he? Lord Arthur did not kill him. He had, at least, in Colonel McIntosh an unimpeachable witness to prove that he could not have committed that murder—and yet," he added with slow, excited emphasis, marking each sentence with a knot, "and yet he deliberately tries to throw the guilt upon a man who obviously was also innocent. Now why?"

"He may have thought him guilty."

"Or wished to shield or cover the retreat of *one he knew to be guilty.*"

"I don't understand."

"Think of someone," he said excitedly, "someone whose desire would be as great as that of Lord Arthur to silence a scandal round that gentleman's name. Someone who, unknown perhaps to Lord Arthur, had overheard the same conversation which George Higgins related to the police and the magistrate, someone who, whilst Chipps was taking Lavender's card in to his master, had a few minutes' time wherein to make an assignation with Lavender, promising him money, no doubt, in exchange for the compromising bills."

"Surely you don't mean—" gasped Polly.

"Point number one," he interrupted quietly, "utterly missed by the police. George Higgins in his deposition stated that at the most animated stage of Lavender's conversation with Lord Arthur, and when the bookmaker's tone of voice became loud and threatening, a voice from the top of the steps interrupted that conversation, saying: 'Your tea is getting cold.'"

"Yes—but—" she argued.

"Wait a moment, for there is point number two. That voice was a lady's voice. Now, I did exactly what the police should have done, but did not do. I went to have a look from the racecourse side at those garden steps which to my mind are such important factors in the discovery of this crime. I found only about a dozen rather low steps; anyone standing on the top must have heard every word Charles Lavender uttered the moment he raised his voice."

"Even then—"

"Very well, you grant that," he said excitedly. "Then there was the

55

great, the all-important point which, oddly enough, the prosecution never for a moment took into consideration. When Chipps, the footman, first told Lavender that Lord Arthur could not see him the bookmaker was terribly put out; Chipps then goes to speak to his master; a few minutes elapse, and when the footman once again tells Lavender that his lordship won't see him, the latter says 'Very well,' and seems to treat the matter with complete indifference.

"Obviously, therefore, something must have happened in between to alter the bookmaker's frame of mind. Well! What had happened? Think over all the evidence, and you will see that one thing only had occurred in the interval, namely, Lady Arthur's advent into the room.

"In order to go into the smoking-room, she must have crossed the hall; she must have seen Lavender. In that brief interval she must have realised that the man was persistent, and therefore a living danger to her husband. Remember, women have done strange things; they are a far greater puzzle to the student of human nature than the sterner, less complex sex has ever been. As I argued before—as the police should have argued all along—why did Lord Arthur deliberately accuse an innocent man of murder if not to shield the guilty one?

"Remember, Lady Arthur may have been discovered; the man, George Higgins, may have caught sight of her before she had time to make good her retreat. His attention, as well as that of the constables, had to be diverted. Lord Arthur acted on the blind impulse of saving his wife at any cost."

"She may have been met by Colonel McIntosh," argued Polly.

"Perhaps she was," he said. "Who knows? The gallant colonel had to swear to his friend's innocence. He could do that in all conscience—after that his duty was accomplished. No innocent man was suffering for the guilty. The knife which had belonged to Lord Arthur would always save George Higgins. For a time, it had pointed to the husband; fortunately, never to the wife. Poor thing, she died probably of a broken heart, but women when they love, think only of one object on earth—the one who is beloved.

"To me the whole thing was clear from the very first. When I read the account of the murder the knife! stabbing!—bah! Don't I know enough of *English* crime not to be certain at once that no Englishman, be he ruffian from the gutter or be he duke's son, ever stabs his victim in the back. Italians. French, Spaniards do it, if you will, and women of most nations. An Englishman's instinct is to strike and not to stab. George Higgins or Lord Arthur Skelmerton would have knocked their victim down; the woman only would lie in wait till the enemy's back was turned. She knows her weakness, and she does not mean to miss.

"Think it over. There is not one flaw in my argument, but the police never thought the matter out——perhaps in this case it was as well."

He had gone and left Miss Polly Burton still staring at the photograph of a pretty, gentle-looking woman, with a decided, wilful curve round the mouth, and a strange, unaccountable look in the large pathetic eyes; and the little journalist felt quite thankful that in this case the murder of Charles Lavender the bookmaker—cowardly, wicked as it was—had remained a mystery to the police and the public.

The Mysterious Death on the Underground Railway

It was all very well for Mr. Richard Frobisher (of the *London Mail*) to cut up rough about it. Polly did not altogether blame him.

She liked him all the better for that frank outburst of manlike ill-temper which, after all said and done, was only a very flattering form of masculine jealousy.

Moreover, Polly distinctly felt guilty about the whole thing. She had promised to meet Dickie—that is Mr. Richard Frobisher—at two o'clock sharp outside the Palace Theatre, because she wanted to go to a Maud Allan *matinée*, and because he naturally wished to go with her.

But at two o'clock sharp she was still in Norfolk Street, Strand, inside an A.B.C. shop, sipping cold coffee opposite a grotesque old man who was fiddling with a bit of string.

How could she be expected to remember Maud Allan or the Palace Theatre, or Dickie himself for a matter of that? The man in the corner had begun to talk of that mysterious death on the underground railway, and Polly had lost count of time, of place, and circumstance.

She had gone to lunch quite early, for she was looking forward to the *matinée* at the Palace.

The old scarecrow was sitting in his accustomed place when she came into the A.B.C. shop, but he had made no remark all the time that the young girl was munching her scone and butter. She was just busy thinking how rude he was not even to have said "Good morning," when an abrupt remark from him caused her to look up.

"Will you be good enough," he said suddenly, "to give me a description of the man who sat next to you just now, while you were having your cup of coffee and scone."

Involuntarily Polly turned her head towards the distant door, through which a man in a light overcoat was even now quickly passing. That man had certainly sat at the next table to hers, when she first sat down to her coffee and scone: he had finished his luncheon—whatever it was—a moment ago, had paid at the desk and gone out. The incident did not appear to Polly as being of the slightest consequence.

Therefore, she did not reply to the rude old man, but shrugged her shoulders, and called to the waitress to bring her bill.

"Do you know if he was tall or short, dark or fair?" continued the man in the corner, seemingly not the least disconcerted by the young girl's indifference. "Can you tell me at all what he was like?"

"Of course, I can," rejoined Polly impatiently, "but I don't see that my description of one of the customers of an A.B.C. shop can have the slightest importance."

He was silent for a minute, while his nervous fingers fumbled about in his capacious pockets in search of the inevitable piece of string. When he had found this necessary "adjunct to thought," he viewed the young girl again through his half-closed lids, and added maliciously:

"But supposing it were of paramount importance that you should give an accurate description of a man who sat next to you for half an hour today, how would you proceed?"

"I should say that he was of medium height—"

"Five foot eight, nine, or ten?" he interrupted quietly.

"How can one tell to an inch or two?" rejoined Polly crossly. "He was between colours."

"What's that?" he inquired blandly.

"Neither fair nor dark—his nose—"

"Well, what was his nose like? Will you sketch it?"

"I am not an artist. His nose was fairly straight—his eyes———"

"Were neither dark nor light—his hair had the same striking peculiarity—he was neither short nor tall—his nose was neither aquiline nor snub—" he recapitulated sarcastically.

"No," she retorted; "he was just ordinary-looking."

"Would you know him again—say tomorrow, and among a number of other men who were 'neither tall nor short, dark nor fair, aquiline nor snub-nosed,' etc.?"

"I don't know—I might—he was certainly not striking enough to be specially remembered."

"Exactly," he said, while he leant forward excitedly, for all the world like a Jack-in-the-box let loose. "Precisely; and you are a journalist—call yourself one, at least—and it should be part of your business to notice and describe people. I don't mean only the wonderful personage with the clear Saxon features, the fine blue eyes, the noble brow and classic face, but the ordinary person—the person who represents ninety out of every hundred of his own kind—the average Englishman, say, of the middle classes, who is neither very tall nor very short, who wears a moustache which is neither fair nor dark, but which masks his mouth, and a top hat which hides the shape of his head and brow, a man, in fact, who dresses like hundreds of his fellow-creatures, moves like them, speaks like them, has no peculiarity.

"Try to describe *him*, to recognise him, say a week hence, among his other eighty-nine doubles; worse still, to swear his life away, if he happened to be implicated in some crime, wherein *your* recognition of him would place the halter round his neck.

"Try that, I say, and having utterly failed you will more readily understand how one of the greatest scoundrels unhung is still at large, and why the mystery on the Underground Railway was never cleared up.

"I think it was the only time in my life that I was seriously tempted to give the police the benefit of my own views upon the matter. You see, though I admire the brute for his cleverness, I did not see that his being unpunished could possibly benefit anyone.

"In these days of tubes and motor traction of all kinds, the old-fashioned 'best, cheapest, and quickest route to City and West End' is often deserted, and the good old Metropolitan Railway carriages cannot at any time be said to be overcrowded. Anyway, when that particular train steamed into Aldgate at about 4 p.m. on March 18th last, the first-class carriages were all but empty.

"The guard marched up and down the platform looking into all the carriages to see if anyone had left a halfpenny evening paper behind for him, and opening the door of one of the first-class compartments, he noticed a lady sitting in the further corner, with her head turned away towards the window, evidently oblivious of the fact that on this line Aldgate is the terminal station.

"'Where are you for, lady?' he said.

"The lady did not move, and the guard stepped into the carriage, thinking that perhaps the lady was asleep. He touched her arm lightly and looked into her face. In his own poetic language, he was 'struck all of a 'eap.' In the glassy eyes, the ashen colour of the cheeks, the rigidity

"He was struck all of a 'eap."

of the head, there was the unmistakable look of death.

"Hastily the guard, having carefully locked the carriage door, summoned a couple of porters, and sent one of them off to the police-station, and the other in search of the station-master.

"Fortunately, at this time of day the up platform is not very crowded, all the traffic tending westward in the afternoon. It was only when an inspector and two police constables, accompanied by a detective in plain clothes and a medical officer, appeared upon the scene, and stood round a first-class railway compartment, that a few idlers realised that something unusual had occurred, and crowded round, eager and curious.

"Thus, it was that the later editions of the evening papers, under the sensational heading, 'Mysterious Suicide on the Underground Railway,' had already an account of the extraordinary event. The medical officer had very soon come to the decision that the guard had not been mistaken, and that life was indeed extinct.

"The lady was young, and must have been very pretty before the look of fright and horror had so terribly distorted her features. She was very elegantly dressed, and the more frivolous papers were able to give their feminine readers a detailed account of the unfortunate woman's gown, her shoes, hat, and gloves.

"It appears that one of the latter, the one on the right hand, was partly off, leaving the thumb and wrist bare. That hand held a small satchel, which the police opened, with a view to the possible identification of the deceased, but which was found to contain only a little loose silver, some smelling-salts, and a small empty bottle, which was handed over to the medical officer for purposes of analysis.

"It was the presence of that small bottle which had caused the report to circulate freely that the mysterious case on the Underground Railway was one of suicide. Certain it was that neither about the lady's person, nor in the appearance of the railway carriage, was there the slightest sign of struggle or even of resistance. Only the look in the poor woman's eyes spoke of sudden terror, of the rapid vision of an unexpected and violent death, which probably only lasted an infinitesimal fraction of a second, but which had left its indelible mark upon the face, otherwise so placid and so still."

"The body of the deceased was conveyed to the mortuary. So far, of course, not a soul had been able to identify her, or to throw the slightest light upon the mystery which hung around her death.

"Against that, quite a crowd of idlers—genuinely interested or not—obtained admission to view the body, on the pretext of having lost or mislaid a relative or a friend. At about 8.30 p.m. a young man, very well dressed, drove up to the station in a hansom, and sent in his card to the superintendent. It was Mr. Hazeldene, shipping agent, of 11, Crown Lane, E.C., and No. 19, Addison Row, Kensington.

"The young man looked in a pitiable state of mental distress; his hand clutched nervously a copy of the *St. James's Gazette*, which contained the fatal news. He said very little to the superintendent except that a person who was very dear to him had not returned home that evening.

"He had not felt really anxious until half an hour ago, when suddenly he thought of looking at his paper. The description of the deceased lady, though vague, had terribly alarmed him. He had jumped into a hansom, and now begged permission to view the body, in order that his worst fears might be allayed.

"You know what followed, of course," continued the man in the corner, "the grief of the young man was truly pitiable. In the woman lying there in a public mortuary before him, Mr. Hazeldene had recognised his wife.

"I am waxing melodramatic," said the man in the corner, who looked up at Polly with a mild and gentle smile, while his nervous fingers vainly endeavoured to add another knot on the scrappy bit of string with which he was continually playing, "and I fear that the whole story savours of the penny novelette, but you must admit, and no doubt you remember, that it was an intensely pathetic and truly dramatic moment.

"The unfortunate young husband of the deceased lady was not much worried with questions that night. As a matter of fact, he was not in a fit condition to make any coherent statement. It was at the coroner's inquest on the following day that certain facts came to light, which for the time being seemed to clear up the mystery surrounding Mrs. Hazeldene's death, only to plunge that same mystery, later on, into denser gloom than before.

"The first witness at the inquest was, of course, Mr. Hazeldene himself. I think everyone's sympathy went out to the young man as he stood before the coroner and tried to throw what light he could upon the mystery. He was well dressed, as he had been the day before, but he looked terribly ill and worried, and no doubt the fact that he had not shaved gave his face a careworn and neglected air.

"It appears that he and the deceased had been married some six years or so, and that they had always been happy in their married life. They had no children. Mrs. Hazeldene seemed to enjoy the best of health till lately, when she had had a slight attack of influenza, in which Dr. Arthur Jones had attended her. The doctor was present at this moment, and would no doubt explain to the coroner and the jury whether he thought that Mrs. Hazeldene had the slightest tendency to heart disease, which might have had a sudden and fatal ending.

"The coroner was, of course, very considerate to the bereaved husband. He tried by circumlocution to get at the point he wanted, namely, Mrs. Hazeldene's mental condition lately. Mr. Hazeldene seemed loath to talk about this. No doubt he had been warned as to the existence of the small bottle found in his wife's satchel.

"'It certainly did seem to me at times,' he at last reluctantly admitted, 'that my wife did not seem quite herself. She used to be very gay and bright, and lately I often saw her in the evening sitting, as if brooding over some matters, which evidently she did not care to communicate to me.'

"Still the coroner insisted, and suggested the small bottle.

"'I know, I know,' replied the young man, with a short, heavy sigh. 'You mean—the question of suicide—I cannot understand it at all—it seems so sudden and so terrible—she certainly had seemed listless and troubled lately—but only at times—and yesterday morning, when I went to business, she appeared quite herself again, and I suggested that we should go to the opera in the evening. She was delighted, I know, and told me she would do some shopping, and pay a few calls in the afternoon.'

"'Do you know at all where she intended to go when she got into the Underground Railway?'

"'Well, not with certainty. You see, she may have meant to get out at Baker Street, and go down to Bond Street to do her shopping. Then, again, she sometimes goes to a shop in St. Paul's Churchyard, in which case she would take a ticket to Aldersgate Street; but I cannot say.'

"'Now, Mr. Hazeldene,' said the coroner at last very kindly, 'will you try to tell me if there was anything in Mrs. Hazeldene's life which you know of, and which might in some measure explain the cause of the distressed state of mind, which you yourself had noticed? Did there exist any financial difficulty which might have preyed upon Mrs. Hazeldene's mind; was there any friend—to whose intercourse with Mrs. Hazeldene—you—er—at any time took exception? In fact,' added the coroner, as if thankful that he had got over an unpleasant moment, 'can you give me the slightest indication which would tend to confirm the suspicion that the unfortunate lady, in a moment of mental anxiety or derangement, may have wished to take her own life?'

"There was silence in the court for a few moments. Mr. Hazeldene seemed to every one there present to be labouring under some terrible moral doubt. He looked very pale and wretched, and twice attempted to speak before he at last said in scarcely audible tones:

"'No; there were no financial difficulties of any sort. My wife had an independent fortune of her own—she had no extravagant tastes.'

"'Nor any friend you at any time objected to?' insisted the coroner.

"'Nor any friend, I—at any time objected to,' stammered the unfortunate young man, evidently speaking with an effort.

"I was present at the inquest," resumed the man in the corner, after he had drunk a glass of milk and ordered another, "and I can assure you that the most obtuse person there plainly realised that Mr. Hazeldene was telling a lie. It was pretty plain to the meanest intelligence that the unfortunate lady had not fallen into a state of morbid dejection for nothing, and that perhaps there existed a third person who could throw more light on her strange and sudden death than the unhappy, bereaved young widower.

"That the death was more mysterious even than it had at first appeared became very soon apparent. You read the case at the time, no doubt, and must remember the excitement in the public mind caused by the evidence of the two doctors. Dr. Arthur Jones, the lady's usual medical man, who had attended her in a last very slight illness, and who had seen her in a professional capacity fairly recently, declared most emphatically that Mrs. Hazeldene suffered from no organic complaint which could possibly have been the cause of sudden death. Moreover, he had assisted Mr. Andrew Thornton, the district medical officer, in making a post-mortem examination, and together they had come to the conclusion that death was due to the action of prussic acid, which had caused instantaneous failure of the heart, but how the drug had been administered neither he nor his colleague were at present able to state.

"'Do I understand, then, Dr. Jones, that the deceased died, poisoned with prussic acid?'

"'Such is my opinion,' replied the doctor.

"'Did the bottle found in her satchel contain prussic acid?'

"'It had contained some at one time, certainly.'

"'In your opinion, then, the lady caused her own death by taking a dose of that drug?'

"'Pardon me, I never suggested such a thing; the lady died poisoned by the drug, but how the drug was administered we cannot say. By injection of some sort, certainly. The drug certainly was not swallowed; there was not a vestige of it in the stomach.'

"'Yes,' added the doctor in reply to another question from the coroner, 'death had probably followed the injection in this case almost immediately; say within a couple of minutes, or perhaps three. It was quite possible that the body would not have more than one quick and sudden convulsion, perhaps not that; death in such cases is absolutely sudden and crushing.'

"I don't think that at the time anyone in the room realised how important the doctor's statement was, a statement which, by the way, was confirmed in all its details by the district medical officer, who had conducted the post-mortem. Mrs. Hazeldene had died suddenly from an injection of prussic acid, administered no one knew how or when. She had been travelling in a first-class railway carriage in a busy time of the day. That young and elegant woman must have had singular nerve and coolness to go through the process of a self-inflicted injection of a deadly poison in the presence of perhaps two or three other persons.

"Mind you, when I say that no one there realised the importance of the doctor's statement at that moment, I am wrong; there were three persons, who fully understood at once the gravity of the situation, and the astounding development which the case was beginning to assume.

"Of course, I should have put myself out of the question," added the weird old man, with that inimitable self-conceit peculiar to himself. "I guessed then and there in a moment where the police were going wrong, and where they would go on going wrong until the mysterious death on the Underground Railway had sunk into oblivion, together with the other cases which they mismanage from time to time.

"I said there were three persons who understood the gravity of the two doctors' statements—the other two were, firstly, the detective who had originally examined the railway carriage, a young man of energy and plenty of misguided intelligence, the other was Mr. Hazeldene.

"At this point the interesting element of the whole story was first introduced into the proceedings, and this was done through the humble channel of Emma Funnel, Mrs. Hazeldene's maid, who, as far as was known then, was the last person who had seen the unfortunate lady alive and had spoken to her.

"'Mrs. Hazeldene lunched at home,' explained Emma, who was shy, and spoke almost in a whisper; 'she seemed well and cheerful. She went out at about half-past three, and told me she was going to Spence's, in St. Paul's Churchyard, to try on her new tailor-made gown. Mrs. Hazeldene had meant to go there in the morning, but was prevented as Mr. Errington called.'

"'Mr. Errington?' asked the coroner casually. 'Who is Mr. Errington?'

"But this Emma found difficult to explain. Mr. Errington was—Mr. Errington, that's all.

"'Mr. Errington was a friend of the family. He lived in a flat in the Albert Mansions. He very often came to Addison Row, and generally stayed late.'

"Pressed still further with questions, Emma at last stated that latterly Mrs. Hazeldene had been to the theatre several times with Mr. Errington, and that on those nights the master looked very gloomy, and was very cross.

"Recalled, the young widower was strangely reticent. He gave forth his answers very grudgingly, and the coroner was evidently absolutely satisfied with himself at the marvellous way in which, after a quarter of an hour of firm yet very kind questionings, he had elicited from the witness what information he wanted.

"Mr. Errington was a friend of his wife. He was a gentleman of means, and seemed to have a great deal of time at his command. He himself did not particularly care about Mr. Errington, but he certainly had never made any observations to his wife on the subject.

"'But who is Mr. Errington?' repeated the coroner once more. 'What does he do? What is his business or profession?'

"'He has no business or profession.'

"'What is his occupation, then?'

"'He has no special occupation. He has ample private means. But he has a great and very absorbing hobby.'

"'What is that?'

"'He spends all his time in chemical experiments, and is, I believe, as an amateur, a very distinguished toxicologist.'"

2

"Did you ever see Mr. Errington, the gentleman so closely connected with the mysterious death on the Underground Railway?" asked the man in the corner as he placed one or two of his little snapshot photos before Miss Polly Burton.

"There he is, to the very life. Fairly good-looking, a pleasant face enough, but ordinary, absolutely ordinary.

"It was this absence of any peculiarity which very nearly, but not quite, placed the halter round Mr. Errington's neck.

"But I am going too fast, and you will lose the thread.

"The public, of course, never heard how it actually came about that Mr. Errington, the wealthy bachelor of Albert Mansions, of the Grosvenor, and other young dandies' clubs, one fine day found himself before the magistrates at Bow Street, charged with being concerned in the death of Mary Beatrice Hazeldene, late of No. 19, Addison Row.

"I can assure you both press and public were literally flabbergasted. You see, Mr. Errington was a well-known and very popular member of a certain smart section of London society. He was a constant visitor at the opera, the racecourse, the Park, and the Carlton, he had a great many friends, and there was consequently quite a large attendance at the police court that morning.

"What had transpired was this:

"After the very scrappy bits of evidence which came to light at the inquest, two gentlemen bethought themselves that perhaps they had some duty to perform towards the State and the public generally. Accordingly, they had come forward, offering to throw what light they could upon the mysterious affair on the Underground Railway.

"The police naturally felt that their information, such as it was, came rather late in the day, but as it proved of paramount importance, and the two gentlemen, moreover, were of undoubtedly good position in the world, they were thankful for what they could get, and acted accordingly; they accordingly brought Mr. Errington up before the magistrate on a charge of murder.

"The accused looked pale and worried when I first caught sight of him in the court that day, which was not to be wondered at, considering the terrible position in which he found himself.

"He had been arrested at Marseilles, where he was preparing to start for Colombo.

"I don't think he realised how terrible his position really was until later in the proceedings, when all the evidence relating to the arrest had been heard, and Emma Funnel had repeated her statement as to Mr. Errington's call at 19, Addison Row, in the morning, and Mrs. Hazeldene starting off for St. Paul's Churchyard at 3.30 in the afternoon.

"Mr. Hazeldene had nothing to add to the statements he had made at the coroner's inquest. He had last seen his wife alive on the morning of the fatal day. She had seemed very well and cheerful.

"I think everyone present understood that he was trying to say as little as possible that could in any way couple his deceased wife's name with that of the accused.

"And yet, from the servant's evidence, it undoubtedly leaked out that Mrs. Hazeldene, who was young, pretty, and evidently fond of admiration, had once or twice annoyed her husband by her somewhat open, yet perfectly innocent, flirtation with Mr. Errington.

"I think everyone was most agreeably impressed by the widower's moderate and dignified attitude. You will see his photo there, among this bundle. That is just how he appeared in court. In deep black, of course, but without any sign of ostentation in his mourning. He had allowed his beard to grow lately, and wore it closely cut in a point.

"After his evidence, the sensation of the day occurred. A tall, dark-haired man, with the word 'City' written metaphorically all over him, had kissed the book, and was waiting to tell the truth, and nothing but the truth.

"He gave his name as Andrew Campbell, head of the firm of Campbell & Co., brokers, of Throgmorton Street.

"In the afternoon of March 18th Mr. Campbell, travelling on the Underground Railway, had noticed a very pretty woman in the same carriage as himself. She had asked him if she was in the right train for Aldersgate. Mr. Campbell replied in the affirmative, and then buried himself in the Stock Exchange quotations of his evening paper.

"At Gower Street, a gentleman in a tweed suit and bowler hat got into the carriage, and took a seat opposite the lady.

"She seemed very much astonished at seeing him, but Mr. Andrew Campbell did not recollect the exact words she said.

"The two talked to one another a good deal, and certainly the lady appeared animated and cheerful. Witness took no notice of them; he was very much engrossed in some calculations, and finally got out at Farringdon Street. He noticed that the man in the tweed suit also got out close behind him, having shaken hands with the lady, and said in a pleasant way: '*Au revoir!* Don't be late tonight.' Mr. Campbell did not hear the lady's reply, and soon lost sight of the man in the crowd.

"Everyone was on tenterhooks, and eagerly waiting for the palpitating moment when witness would describe and identify the man who last had seen and spoken to the unfortunate woman, within five minutes probably of her strange and unaccountable death.

"Personally, I knew what was coming before the Scotch stockbroker spoke.

"I could have jotted down the graphic and lifelike description he would give of a probable murderer. It would have fitted equally well the man who sat and had luncheon at this table just now; it would certainly have described five out of every ten young Englishmen you know.

"The individual was of medium height, he wore a moustache which was not very fair nor yet very dark, his hair was between colours. He wore a bowler hat, and a tweed suit—and—and—that was all—Mr. Campbell might perhaps know him again, but then again, he might not—he was not paying much attention—the gentleman was sitting on the same side of the carriage as himself—and he had his hat on all the time. He himself was busy with his newspaper—yes—he might know him again—-but he really could not say.

"Mr. Andrew Campbell's evidence was not worth very much, you will say. No, it was not in itself, and would not have justified any arrest were it not for the additional statements made by Mr. James Verner, manager of Messrs. Rodney & Co., colour printers.

"Mr. Verner is a personal friend of Mr. Andrew Campbell, and it appears that at Farringdon Street, where he was waiting for his train, he saw Mr. Campbell get out of a first-class railway carriage. Mr. Verner spoke to him for a second, and then, just as the train was moving off, he stepped into the same compartment which had just been vacated by the stockbroker and the man in the tweed suit. He vaguely recollects a lady sitting in the opposite corner to his own, with her face turned away from him, apparently asleep, but he paid no special attention to her.

"He was like nearly all business men when they are travelling—engrossed in his paper. Presently a special quotation interested him; he wished to make a note of it, took out a pencil from his waistcoat pocket, and seeing a clean piece of paste-board on the floor, he picked it up, and scribbled on it the memorandum, which he wished to keep. He then slipped the card into his pocket-book.

"'It was only two or three days later,' added Mr. Verner in the midst of breathless silence, 'that I had occasion to refer to these same notes again.

"'In the meanwhile, the papers had been full of the mysterious death on the Underground Railway, and the names of those connected with it were pretty familiar to me. It was, therefore, with much astonishment that on looking at the paste-board which I had casually picked up in the railway carriage I saw the name on it, "Frank Errington."'

"There was no doubt that the sensation in court was almost unprecedented. Never since the days of the Fenchurch Street mystery, and the trial of Smethurst, had I seen so much excitement. Mind you, I was not excited—I knew by now every detail of that crime as if I had committed it myself. In fact, I could not have done it better, although I have been a student of crime for many years now. Many people there—his friends, mostly—believed that Errington was doomed. I think he thought so, too, for I could see that his face was terribly white, and he now and then passed his tongue over his lips, as if they were parched.

"You see he was in the awful dilemma—a perfectly natural one, by the way—of being absolutely incapable of *proving an alibi*. The crime—if crime there was—had been committed three weeks ago. A man about town like Mr. Frank Errington might remember that he spent certain hours of a special afternoon at his club, or in the Park, but it is very doubtful in nine cases out of ten if he can find a friend who could positively swear as to having seen him there. No! no! Mr. Errington was in a tight corner, and he knew it. You see, there were—besides the evidence—two or three circumstances which did not improve matters for him. His hobby in the direction of toxicology, to begin with. The police had found in his room every description of poisonous susbtances, including prussic acid.

"Then, again, that journey to Marseilles, the start for Colombo, was, though perfectly innocent, a very unfortunate one. Mr. Errington had gone on an aimless voyage, but the public thought that he had fled, terrified at his own crime. Sir Arthur Inglewood, however, here again displayed his marvellous skill on behalf of his client by the masterly way in which he literally turned all the witnesses for the Crown inside out.

"Having first got Mr. Andrew Campbell to state positively that in the accused he certainly did *not* recognise the man in the tweed suit, the eminent lawyer, after twenty minutes' cross-examination, had so completely upset the stockbroker's equanimity that it is very likely he would not have recognised his own office-boy.

"But through all his flurry and all his annoyance Mr. Andrew Campbell remained very sure of one thing; namely, that the lady was alive and cheerful, and talking pleasantly with the man in the tweed suit up to the moment when the latter, having shaken hands with her, left her with a pleasant '*Au revoir!* Don't be late tonight.' He had heard neither scream nor struggle, and in his opinion, if the individual in the tweed suit had administered a dose of poison to his companion, it must have been with her own knowledge and free will; and the lady in the train most emphatically neither looked nor spoke like a woman prepared for a sudden and violent death.

"Mr. James Verner, against that, swore equally positively that he had stood in full view of the carriage door from the moment that Mr. Campbell got out until he himself stepped into the compartment, that there was no one else in that carriage between Farringdon Street and Aldgate, and that the lady, to the best of his belief, had made no movement during the whole of that journey.

"No; Frank Errington was *not* committed for trial on the capital charge," said the man in the corner with one of his sardonic smiles, "thanks to the cleverness of Sir Arthur Inglewood, his lawyer. He absolutely denied his identity with the man in the tweed suit, and swore he had not seen Mrs. Hazeldene since eleven o'clock in the morning of that fatal day. There was no *proof* that he had; moreover, according to Mr. Campbell's opinion, the man in the tweed suit was in all probability not the murderer. Common sense would not admit that a woman could have a deadly poison injected into her without her knowledge, while chatting pleasantly to her murderer.

"Mr. Errington lives abroad now. He is about to marry. I don't think any of his real friends for a moment believed that he committed the dastardly crime. The police think they know better. They do know this much, that it could not have been a case of suicide, that if the man who undoubtedly travelled with Mrs. Hazeldene on that fatal afternoon had no crime upon his conscience he would long ago have come forward and thrown what light he could upon the mystery.

"As to who that man was, the police in their blindness have not the faintest doubt. Under the unshakable belief that Errington is guilty they have spent the last few months in unceasing labour to try and find further and stronger proofs of his guilt. But they won't find them, because there are none. There are no positive proofs against the actual murderer, for he was one of those clever blackguards who think of everything, foresee every eventuality, who know human nature well, and can foretell exactly what evidence will be brought against them, and act accordingly.

"This blackguard from the first kept the figure, the personality, of

Frank Errington before his mind. Frank Errington was the dust which the scoundrel threw metaphorically in the eyes of the police, and you must admit that he succeeded in blinding them—to the extent even of making them entirely forget the one simple little sentence, overheard by Mr. Andrew Campbell, and which was, of course, the clue to the whole thing—the only slip the cunning rogue made—'*Au revoir!* Don't be late tonight.' Mrs. Hazeldene was going that night to the opera with her husband

"You are astonished?" he added with a shrug of the shoulders, "you do not see the tragedy yet, as I have seen it before me all along. The frivolous young wife, the flirtation with the friend?—all a blind, all pretence. I took the trouble which the police should have taken immediately, of finding out something about the finances of the Hazeldene *ménage*. Money is in nine cases out of ten the keynote to a crime.

"I found that the will of Mary Beatrice Hazeldene had been proved by the husband, her sole executor, the estate being sworn at £15,000. I found out, moreover, that Mr. Edward Sholto Hazeldene was a poor shipper's clerk when he married the daughter of a wealthy builder in Kensington—and then I made note of the fact that the disconsolate widower had allowed his beard to grow since the death of his wife.

"There's no doubt that he was a clever rogue," added the strange creature, leaning excitedly over the table, and peering into Polly's face. "Do you know how that deadly poison was injected into the poor woman's system? By the simplest of all means, one known to every scoundrel in Southern Europe. A ring—yes! a ring, which has a tiny hollow needle capable of holding a sufficient quantity of prussic acid to have killed two persons instead of one. The man in the tweed suit shook hands with his fair companion—probably she hardly felt the prick, not sufficiently in any case to make her utter a scream.

"And, mind you, the scoundrel had every facility, through his friendship with Mr. Errington, of procuring what poison he required, not to mention his friend's visiting card. We cannot gauge how many months ago he began to try and copy Frank Errington in his style of dress, the cut of his moustache, his general appearance, making the change probably so gradual, that no one in his own *entourage* would notice it. He selected for his model a man his own height and build, with the same coloured hair."

"But there was the terrible risk of being identified by his fellow-traveller in the Underground," suggested Polly.

"Yes, there certainly was that risk; he chose to take it, and he was wise. He reckoned that several days would in any case elapse before that person, who, by the way, was a business man absorbed in his newspaper, would actually see him again. The great secret of successful crime is to study human nature," added the man in the corner, as he began looking for his hat and coat. "Edward Hazeldene knew it well."

"But the ring?"

"He may have bought that when he was on his honeymoon," he suggested with a grim chuckle; "the tragedy was not planned in a week, it may have taken years to mature. But you will own that there goes a frightful scoundrel unhung. I have left you his photograph as he was a year ago, and as he is now. You will see he has shaved his beard again, but also his moustache. I fancy he is a friend now of Mr. Andrew Campbell."

He left Miss Polly Burton wondering, not knowing what to believe.

And that is why she missed her appointment with Mr. Richard Frobisher (of the *London Mail*) to go and see Maud Allan dance at the Palace Theatre that afternoon.

The Liverpool Mystery

1

"A title—a foreign title, I mean—is always very useful for purposes of swindles and frauds," remarked the man in the corner to Polly one day. "The cleverest robberies of modern times were perpetrated lately in Vienna by a man who dubbed himself Lord Seymour; whilst over here the same class of thief calls himself Count Something ending in 'o,' or Prince the other, ending in 'off.'"

"Fortunately for our hotel and lodging-house keepers over here," she replied, "they are beginning to be more alive to the ways of foreign swindlers, and look upon all titled gentry who speak broken English as possible swindlers or thieves."

"The result sometimes being exceedingly unpleasant to the real *grands seigneurs* who honour this country at times with their visits," replied the man in the corner. "Now, take the case of Prince Semionicz, a man whose sixteen quarterings are duly recorded in Gotha, who carried enough luggage with him to pay for the use of every room in an hotel for at least a week, whose gold cigarette case with diamond and turquoise ornament was actually stolen without his taking the slightest trouble to try and recover it; that same man was undoubtedly looked upon with suspicion by the manager of the Liverpool North-Western Hotel from the moment that his secretary—a dapper, somewhat vulgar little Frenchman—bespoke on behalf of his employer, with himself and a valet, the best suite of rooms the hotel contained.

"Obviously those suspicions were unfounded, for the little secretary, as soon as Prince Semionicz had arrived, deposited with the manager a pile of bank notes, also papers and bonds, the value of which would exceed tenfold the most outrageous bill that could possibly be placed before the noble visitor. Moreover, M. Albert Lambert explained that the prince, who only meant to stay in Liverpool a few days, was on his way to Chicago, where he wished to visit Princess

Anna Semionicz, his sister, who was married to Mr. Girwan, the great copper king and multimillionaire.

"Yet, as I told you before, in spite of all these undoubted securities, suspicion of the wealthy Russian prince lurked in the minds of most Liverpudlians who came in business contact with him. He had been at the North-Western two days when he sent his secretary to Winslow and Vassall, the jewellers of Bold Street, with a request that they would kindly send a representative round to the hotel with some nice pieces of jewellery, diamonds and pearls chiefly, which he was desirous of taking as a present to his sister in Chicago.

"Mr. Winslow took the order from M. Albert with a pleasant bow. Then he went to his inner office and consulted with his partner, Mr. Vassall, as to the best course to adopt. Both the gentlemen were desirous of doing business, for business had been very slack lately: neither wished to refuse a possible customer, or to offend Mr. Pettitt, the manager of the North-Western, who had recommended them to the prince. But that foreign title and the vulgar little French secretary stuck in the throats of the two pompous and worthy Liverpool jewellers, and together they agreed, firstly, that no credit should be given; and, secondly, that if a cheque or even a banker's draft were tendered, the jewels were not to be given up until that cheque or draft was cashed.

"Then came the question as to who should take the jewels to the hotel. It was altogether against business etiquette for the senior partners to do such errands themselves; moreover, it was thought that it would be easier for a clerk to explain, without giving undue offence, that he could not take the responsibility of a cheque or draft, without having cashed it previously to giving up the jewels.

"Then there was the question of the probable necessity of conferring in a foreign tongue. The head assistant, Charles Needham, who had been in the employ of Winslow and Vassall for over twelve years, was, in true British fashion, ignorant of any language save his own; it was therefore decided to dispatch Mr. Schwarz, a young German clerk lately arrived, on the delicate errand.

"Mr. Schwarz was Mr. Winslow's nephew and godson, a sister of that gentleman having married the head of the great German firm of Schwarz & Co., silversmiths, of Hamburg and Berlin.

"The young man had soon become a great favourite with his uncle, whose heir he would presumably be, as Mr. Winslow had no children.

"At first Mr. Vassall made some demur about sending Mr. Schwarz with so many valuable jewels alone in a city which he had not yet had the time to study thoroughly; but finally, he allowed himself to be persuaded by his senior partner, and a fine selection of necklaces, pendants, bracelets, and rings, amounting in value to over £16,000, having been made, it was decided that Mr. Schwarz should go to the North-Western in a cab the next day at about three o'clock in the afternoon. This he accordingly did, the following day being a Thursday.

"Business went on in the shop as usual under the direction of the head assistant, until about seven o'clock, when Mr. Winslow returned from his club, where he usually spent an hour over the papers every afternoon, and at once asked for his nephew. To his astonishment Mr. Needham informed him that Mr. Schwarz had not yet returned. This seemed a little strange, and Mr. Winslow, with a slightly anxious look in his face, went into the inner office in order to consult his junior partner. Mr. Vassall offered to go round to the hotel and interview Mr. Pettitt.

"'I was beginning to get anxious myself,' he said, 'but did not quite like to say so. I have been in over half an hour, hoping every moment that you would come in, and that perhaps you could give me some reassuring news. I thought that perhaps you had met Mr. Schwarz, and were coming back together.'

"However, Mr. Vassall walked round to the hotel and interviewed the hall porter. The latter perfectly well remembered Mr. Schwarz sending in his card to Prince Semionicz.

"'At what time was that?' asked Mr. Vassall.

"'About ten minutes past three, sir, when he came; it was about an hour later when he left.'

"'When he left?' gasped, more than said, Mr. Vassall.

"'Yes, sir. Mr. Schwarz left here about a quarter before four, sir.'

"'Are you quite sure?'

"'Quite sure. Mr. Pettitt was in the hall when he left, and he asked him something about business. Mr. Schwarz laughed and said, "not bad." I hope there's nothing wrong, sir,' added the man.

"'Oh—er—nothing—thank you. Can I see Mr. Pettitt?'

"'Certainly, sir.'

"Mr. Pettitt, the manager of the hotel, shared Mr. Vassall's anxiety, immediately he heard that the young German had not yet returned home.

"'I spoke to him a little before four o'clock. We had just switched on the electric light, which we always do these winter months at that hour. But I shouldn't worry myself, Mr. Vassall; the young man may have seen to some business on his way home. You'll probably find him in when you go back.'

"Apparently somewhat reassured, Mr. Vassall thanked Mr. Pettitt and hurried back to the shop, only to find that Mr. Schwarz had not returned, though it was now close on eight o'clock.

"Mr. Winslow looked so haggard and upset that it would have been cruel to heap reproaches upon his other troubles or to utter so much as the faintest suspicion that young Schwarz's permanent disappearance with £16,000 in jewels and money was within the bounds of probability.

"There was one chance left, but under the circumstances a very slight one indeed. The Winslows' private house was up the Birkenhead end of the town. Young Schwarz had been living with them ever since his arrival in Liverpool, and he may have—either not feeling well or for some other reason—gone straight home without calling at the shop. It was unlikely, as valuable jewellery was never kept at the private house, but—it just might have happened.

"It would be useless," continued the man in the corner, "and decidedly uninteresting, were I to relate to you Messrs. Winslow's and Vassall's further anxieties with regard to the missing young man. Suffice it to say that on reaching his private house Mr. Winslow found that his godson had neither returned nor sent any telegraphic message of any kind.

"Not wishing to needlessly alarm his wife, Mr. Winslow made an attempt at eating his dinner, but directly after that he hurried back to the North-Western Hotel, and asked to see Prince Semionicz. The prince was at the theatre with his secretary, and probably would not be home until nearly midnight.

"Mr. Winslow, then, not knowing what to think, nor yet what to fear, and in spite of the horror he felt of giving publicity to his nephew's disappearance, thought it his duty to go round to the police-station and interview the inspector. It is wonderful how quickly news of that type travels in a large city like Liverpool. Already the morning papers of the following day were full of the latest sensation: 'Mysterious disappearance of a well-known tradesman.'

"Mr. Winslow found a copy of the paper containing the sensational announcement on his breakfast-table. It lay side by side with a letter addressed to him in his nephew's handwriting, which had been posted in Liverpool.

"Mr. Winslow placed that letter, written to him by his nephew, into the hands of the police. Its contents, therefore, quickly became public property. The astounding statements made therein by Mr. Schwarz created, in quiet, business-like Liverpool, a sensation which has seldom been equalled.

"It appears that the young fellow did call on Prince Semionicz at a quarter past three on Wednesday, December 10th, with a bag full of jewels, amounting in value to some £16,000. The prince duly admired, and finally selected from among the ornaments a necklace, pendant, and bracelet, the whole being priced by Mr. Schwarz, according to his instructions, at £10,600. Prince Semionicz was most prompt and business-like in his dealings.

"'You will require immediate payment for these, of course,' he said in perfect English, 'and I know you business men prefer solid cash to cheques, especially when dealing with foreigners. I always provide myself with plenty of Bank of England notes in consequence,' he added with a pleasant smile, 'as £10,500 in gold would perhaps be a little inconvenient to carry. If you will kindly make out the receipt, my secretary, M. Lambert, will settle all business matters with you.'

"He thereupon took the jewels he had selected and locked them up in his dressing-case, the beautiful silver fittings of which Mr. Schwarz just caught a short glimpse of. Then, having been accommodated with paper and ink, the young jeweller made out the account and receipt, whilst M. Lambert, the secretary, counted out before him 105 crisp Bank of England notes of £100 each. Then, with a final bow to his exceedingly urbane and eminently satisfactory customer, Mr. Schwarz took his leave. In the hall he saw and spoke to Mr. Pettitt, and then he went out into the street.

"He had just left the hotel and was about to cross towards St. George's Hall when a gentleman, in a magnificent fur coat, stepped quickly out of a cab which had been stationed near the kerb, and, touching him lightly upon the shoulder, said with an unmistakable air of authority, at the same time handing him a card:

"'That is my name. I must speak with you immediately.'

"Schwarz glanced at the card, and by the light of the arc lamps above his head read on it the name of '*Dimitri Slaviansky Burgreneff, de la IIIe Section de la Police Imperial de S. M. le Czar.*'

"Quickly the owner of the unpronounceable name and the significant title pointed to the cab from which he had just alighted, and Schwarz, whose every suspicion with regard to his princely customer

"I must speak with you immediately."

bristled up in one moment, clutched his bag and followed his imposing interlocutor; as soon as they were both comfortably seated in the cab the latter began, with courteous apology in broken but fluent English:

"'I must ask your pardon, sir, for thus trespassing upon your valuable time, and I certainly should not have done so but for the certainty that our interests in a certain matter which I have in hand are practically identical, in so far that we both should wish to outwit a clever rogue.'

"Instinctively, and his mind full of terrible apprehension, Mr. Schwarz's hand wandered to his pocket-book, filled to overflowing with the banknotes which he had so lately received from the prince.

"'Ah, I see,' interposed the courteous Russian with a smile, 'he has played the confidence trick on you, with the usual addition of so many so-called banknotes.'

"'So-called,' gasped the unfortunate young man.

"'I don't think I often err in my estimate of my own country-men,' continued M. Burgreneff; 'I have vast experience, you must remember. Therefore, I doubt if I am doing M.—er—what does he call himself?—Prince something—an injustice if I assert, even without handling those crisp bits of paper you have in your pocket-book, that no bank would exchange them for gold.'

"Remembering his uncle's suspicions and his own, Mr. Schwarz cursed himself for his blindness and folly in accepting notes so easily without for a moment imagining that they might be false. Now, with every one of those suspicions fully on the alert, he felt the bits of paper with nervous, anxious fingers, while the imperturbable Russian calmly struck a match.

"'See here,' he said, pointing to one of the notes, 'the shape of that "w" in the signature of the chief cashier. I am not an English police officer, but I could pick out that spurious "w" among a thousand genuine ones. You see, I have seen a good many.'

"Now, of course, poor young Schwarz had not seen very many Bank of England notes. He could not have told whether one 'w' in Mr. Bowen's signature is better than another, but, though he did not speak English nearly as fluently as his pompous interlocutor, he understood every word of the appalling statement the latter had just made,

"'Then that prince,' he said, 'at the hotel——'

"'Is no more prince than you and I, my dear sir,' concluded the gentleman of His Imperial Majesty's police calmly.

"'And the jewels? Mr. Winslow's jewels?'

"'With the jewels there may be a chance—oh! a mere chance.

These forged banknotes, which you accepted so trustingly, may prove the means of recovering your property.'

"'How?'

"'The penalty of forging and circulating spurious banknotes is very heavy. You know that. The fear of seven years' penal servitude will act as a wonderful sedative upon the—er—prince's joyful mood. He will give up the jewels to me all right enough, never you fear. He knows,' added the Russian officer grimly, 'that there are plenty of old scores to settle up, without the additional one of forged banknotes. Our interests, you see, are identical. May I rely on your co-operation?'

"'Oh, I will do as you wish,' said the delighted young German. 'Mr. Winslow and Mr. Vassall, they trusted me, and I have been such a fool. I hope it is not too late.'

"'I think not,' said M. Burgreneff, his hand already on the door of the cab. 'Though I have been talking to you I have kept an eye on the hotel, and our friend the prince has not yet gone out. We are accustomed, you know, to have eyes everywhere, we of the Russian secret police. I don't think that I will ask you to be present at the confrontation. Perhaps you will wait for me in the cab. There is a nasty fog outside, and you will be more private. Will you give me those beautiful bank-notes? Thank you! Don't be anxious. I won't be long.'

"He lifted his hat, and slipped the notes into the inner pocket of his magnificent fur coat. As he did so, Mr. Schwarz caught sight of a rich uniform and a wide sash, which no doubt was destined to carry additional moral weight with the clever rogue upstairs.

"Then His Imperial Majesty's police officer stepped quickly out of the cab, and Mr. Schwarz was left alone."

2

"Yes, left severely alone," continued the man in the corner with a sarcastic chuckle. "So severely alone, in fact, that one quarter of an hour after another passed by and still the magnificent police officer in the gorgeous uniform did not return. Then, when it was too late, Schwarz cursed himself once again for the double-dyed idiot that he was. He had been only too ready to believe that Prince Semionicz was a liar and a rogue, and under these unjust suspicions he had fallen an all too easy prey to one of the most cunning rascals he had ever come across.

"An inquiry from the hall porter at the North-Western elicited the fact that no such personage as Mr. Schwarz described had entered the hotel. The young man asked to see Prince Semionicz, hoping against hope that all was not yet lost. The prince received him most courteously; he was dictating some letters to his secretary, while the valet was in the next room preparing his master's evening clothes. Mr. Schwarz found it very difficult to explain what he actually did want.

"There stood the dressing-case in which the prince had locked up the jewels, and there the bag from which the secretary had taken the banknotes. After much hesitation on Schwarz's part and much impatience on that of the prince, the young man blurted out the whole story of the so-called Russian police officer whose card he still held in his hand.

"The prince, it appears, took the whole thing wonderfully good-naturedly; no doubt he thought the jeweller a hopeless fool. He showed him the jewels, the receipt he held, and also a large bundle of banknotes similar to those Schwarz had with such culpable folly given up to the clever rascal in the cab.

"'I pay all my bills with Bank of England notes, Mr. Schwarz. It would have been wiser, perhaps, if you had spoken to the manager of the hotel about me before you were so ready to believe any cock-and-bull story about my supposed rogueries.'

"Finally, he placed a small 16mo volume before the young jeweller, and said with a pleasant smile:

"'If people in this country who are in a large way of business, and are therefore likely to come in contact with people of foreign nationality, were to study these little volumes before doing business with any foreigner who claims a title, much disappointment and a great loss would often be saved. Now in this case had you looked up page 797 of this little volume of Gotha's Almanach you would have seen my name in it and known from the first that the so-called Russian detective was a liar.'

"There was nothing more to be said, and Mr. Schwarz left the hotel. No doubt, now that he had been hopelessly duped, he dared not go home, and half hoped by communicating with the police that they might succeed in arresting the thief before he had time to leave Liverpool. He interviewed Detective-Inspector Watson, and was at once confronted with the awful difficulty which would make the recovery of the bank-notes practically hopeless. He had never had the time or opportunity of jotting down the numbers of the notes.

"Mr. Winslow, though terribly wrathful against his nephew, did not wish to keep him out of his home. As soon as he had received

Schwarz's letter, he traced him, with Inspector Watson's help, to his lodgings in North Street, where the unfortunate young man meant to remain hidden until the terrible storm had blown over, or perhaps until the thief had been caught red-handed with the booty still in his hands.

"This happy event, needless to say, never did occur, though the police made every effort to trace the man who had decoyed Schwarz into the cab. His appearance was such an uncommon one; it seemed most unlikely that no one in Liverpool should have noticed him after he left that cab. The wonderful fur coat, the long beard, all must have been noticeable, even though it was past four o'clock on a somewhat foggy December afternoon.

"But every investigation proved futile; no one answering Schwarz's description of the man had been seen anywhere. The papers contin-ued to refer to the case as 'the Liverpool Mystery.' Scotland Yard sent Mr. Fairburn down—the celebrated detective—at the request of the Liverpool police, to help in the investigations, but nothing availed.

"Prince Semionicz, with his suite, left Liverpool, and he who had attempted to blacken his character, and had succeeded in robbing Messrs. Winslow and Vassall of £10,500, had completely disappeared."

The man in the corner readjusted his collar and necktie, which, during the narrative of this interesting mystery, had worked its way up his long, crane-like neck under his large flappy ears. His costume of checked tweed of a peculiarly loud pattern had tickled the fancy of some of the waitresses, who were standing gazing at him and giggling in one corner. This evidently made him nervous. He gazed up very meekly at Polly, looking for all the world like a bald-headed adjutant dressed for a holiday.

"Of course, all sorts of theories of the theft got about at first. One of the most popular, and at the same time most quickly exploded, be-ing that young Schwarz had told a cock-and-bull story, and was the actual thief himself.

"However, as I said before, that was very quickly exploded, as Mr. Schwarz senior, a very wealthy merchant, never allowed his son's care-lessness to be a serious loss to his kind employers. As soon as he thor-oughly grasped all the circumstances of the extraordinary case, he drew a cheque for £10,500 and remitted it to Messrs. Winslow and Vassall. It was just, but it was also high-minded.

"All Liverpool knew of the generous action, as Mr. Winslow took care that it should; and any evil suspicion regarding young Mr. Schwarz vanished as quickly as it had come.

"Then, of course, there was the theory about the prince and his suite, and to this day I fancy there are plenty of people in Liverpool, and also in London, who declare that the so-called Russian police officer was a confederate. No doubt that theory was very plausible, and Messrs. Winslow and Vassall spent a good deal of money in trying to prove a case against the Russian prince.

"Very soon, however, that theory was also bound to collapse. Mr. Fairburn, whose reputation as an investigator of crime waxes in direct inverted ratio to his capacities, did hit upon the obvious course of interviewing the managers of the larger London and Liverpool *agents de change*. He soon found that Prince Semionicz had converted a great deal of Russian and French money into English bank-notes since his arrival in this country. More than £30,000 in good solid, honest money was traced to the pockets of the gentleman with the sixteen quarterings. It seemed, therefore, more than improbable that a man who was obviously fairly wealthy would risk imprisonment and hard labour, if not worse, for the sake of increasing his fortune by £10,000.

"However, the theory of the prince's guilt has taken firm root in the dull minds of our police authorities. They have had every information with regard to Prince Semionicz's antecedents from Russia; his position, his wealth, have been placed above suspicion, and yet they suspect and go on suspecting him or his secretary. They have communicated with the police of every European capital; and while they still hope to obtain sufficient evidence against those they suspect, they calmly allow the guilty to enjoy the fruit of his clever roguery."

"The guilty?" said Polly. "Who do you think—"

"Who do I think knew at that moment that young Schwarz had money in his possession?" he said excitedly, wriggling in his chair like a Jack-in-the-box. "Obviously someone was guilty of that theft who knew that Schwarz had gone to interview a rich Russian, and would in all probability return with a large sum of money in his possession?"

"Who, indeed, but the prince and his secretary?" she argued. "But just now you said—"

"Just now I said that the police were determined to find the prince and his secretary guilty; they did not look further than their own stumpy noses. Messrs. Winslow and Vassall spent money with a free hand in those investigations. Mr. Winslow, as the senior partner, stood to lose over £9,000 by that robbery. Now, with Mr. Vassall it was different.

"When I saw how the police went on blundering in this case, I took the trouble to make certain inquiries, the whole thing interested me so much, and I learnt all that I wished to know. I found out, namely, that Mr. Vassall was very much a junior partner in the firm, that he only drew ten *per cent* of the profits, having been promoted lately to a partnership from having been senior assistant.

"Now, the police did not take the trouble to find that out."

"But you don't mean that—"

"I mean that in all cases where robbery affects more than one person the first thing to find out is whether it affects the second party equally with the first. I proved that to you, didn't I, over that robbery in Phillimore Terrace? There, as here, one of the two parties stood to lose very little in comparison with the other—"

"Even then—" she began.

"Wait a moment, for I found out something more. The moment I had ascertained that Mr. Vassall was not drawing more than about £500 a year from the business profits I tried to ascertain at what rate he lived and what were his chief vices. I found that he kept a fine house in Albert Terrace. Now, the rents of those houses are £250 a year. Therefore speculation, horseracing or some sort of gambling, must help to keep up that establishment.

"Speculation and most forms of gambling are synonymous with debt and ruin. It is only a question of time. Whether Mr. Vassall was in debt or not at the time, that I cannot say, but this I do know, that ever since that unfortunate loss to him of about £1,000 he has kept his house in nicer style than before, and he now has a good banking account at the Lancashire and Liverpool bank, which he opened a year after his 'heavy loss.'"

"But it must have been very difficult——" argued Polly.

"What?" he said. "To have planned out the whole thing? For carrying it out was mere child's play. He had twenty-four hours in which to put his plan into execution. Why, what was there to do? Firstly, to go to a local printer in some out-of-the-way part of the town and get him to print a few cards with the high-sounding name. That, of course, is done 'while you wait.' Beyond that there was the purchase of a good second-hand uniform, fur coat, and a beard and a wig from a *costumier's*.

"No, no, the execution was not difficult; it was the planning of it all, the daring that was so fine. Schwarz, of course, was a foreigner; he had only been in England a little over a fortnight. Vassall's broken English misled him; probably he did not know the junior partner very intimately. I have no doubt that but for his uncle's absurd British prejudice and suspicions against the Russian Prince, Schwarz would not have been so ready to believe in the latter's roguery. As I said, it would be a great boon if English tradesmen studied Gotha more; but it was clever, wasn't it? I couldn't have done it much better myself."

That last sentence was so characteristic. Before Polly could think of some plausible argument against his theory he was gone, and she was trying vainly to find another solution to the Liverpool mystery.

The Edinburgh Mystery

1

The man in the corner had not enjoyed his lunch. Miss Polly Burton could see that he had something on his mind, for, even before he began to talk that morning, he was fidgeting with his bit of string, and setting all her nerves on the jar.

"Have you ever felt real sympathy with a criminal or a thief?" he asked her after a while.

"Only once, I think," she replied, "and then I am not quite sure that the unfortunate woman who did enlist my sympathies was the criminal you make her out to be."

"You mean the heroine of the York mystery?" he replied blandly. "I know that you tried very hard that time to discredit the only possible version of that mysterious murder, the version which is my own. Now, I am equally sure that you have at the present moment no more notion as to who killed and robbed poor Lady Donaldson in Charlotte Square, Edinburgh, than the police have themselves, and yet you are fully prepared to pooh-pooh my arguments, and to disbelieve my version of the mystery. Such is the lady journalist's mind."

"If you have some cock-and-bull story to explain that extraordinary case," she retorted, "of course I shall disbelieve it. Certainly, if you are going to try and enlist my sympathies on behalf of Edith Crawford, I can assure you you won't succeed."

"Well, I don't know that that is altogether my intention. I see you are interested in the case, but I dare say you don't remember all the circumstances. You must forgive me if I repeat that which you know already. If you have ever been to Edinburgh at all, you will have heard of Graham's bank, and Mr. Andrew Graham, the present head of the firm, is undoubtedly one of the most prominent notabilities of 'modern Athens.'"

The man in the corner took two or three photos from his pocket-book and placed them before the young girl; then, pointing at them with his long bony finger—

"That," he said, "is Mr. Elphinstone Graham, the eldest son, a typical young Scotchman, as you see, and this is David Graham, the second son."

Polly looked more closely at this last photo, and saw before her a young face, upon which some lasting sorrow seemed already to have left its mark. The face was delicate and thin, the features pinched, and the eyes seemed almost unnaturally large and prominent.

"He was deformed," commented the man in the corner in answer to the girl's thoughts, "and, as such, an object of pity and even of repugnance to most of his friends. There was also a good deal of talk in Edinburgh society as to his mental condition, his mind, according to many intimate friends of the Grahams, being at times decidedly unhinged. Be that as it may, I fancy that his life must have been a very sad one; he had lost his mother when quite a baby, and his father seemed, strangely enough, to have an almost unconquerable dislike towards him.

"Everyone got to know presently of David Graham's sad position in his father's own house, and also of the great affection lavished upon him by his godmother, Lady Donaldson, who was a sister of Mr. Graham's.

"She was a lady of considerable wealth, being the widow of Sir George Donaldson, the great distiller; but she seems to have been decidedly eccentric. Latterly she had astonished all her family—who were rigid Presbyterians—by announcing her intention of embracing the Roman Catholic faith, and then retiring to the convent of St. Augustine's at Newton Abbot in Devonshire.

"She had sole and absolute control of the vast fortune which a doting husband had bequeathed to her. Clearly, therefore, she was at liberty to bestow it upon a Devonshire convent if she chose. But this evidently was not altogether her intention.

"I told you how fond she was of her deformed godson, did I not? Being a bundle of eccentricities, she had many hobbies, none more pronounced than the fixed determination to see—before retiring from the world altogether—David Graham happily married.

"Now, it appears that David Graham, ugly, deformed, half-demented as he was, had fallen desperately in love with Miss Edith Crawford, daughter of the late Dr. Crawford, of Prince's Gardens. The young lady, however—very naturally, perhaps—fought shy of David Graham, who, about this time, certainly seemed very queer and morose, but Lady Donaldson, with characteristic determination, seems to have made up her mind to melt Miss Crawford's heart towards her unfortunate nephew.

"On October the 2nd last, at a family party given by Mr. Graham in his fine mansion in Charlotte Square, Lady Donaldson openly announced her intention of making over, by deed of gift, to her nephew, David Graham, certain property, money, and shares, amounting in total value to the sum of £100,000, and also her magnificent diamonds, which were worth £50,000, for the use of the said David's wife. Keith Macfinlay, a lawyer of Prince's Street, received the next day instructions for drawing up the necessary deed of gift, which she pledged herself to sign the day of her godson's wedding.

"A week later *The Scotsman* contained the following paragraph:—

"'A marriage is arranged and will shortly take place between David, younger son of Andrew Graham, Esq., of Charlotte Square, Edinburgh, and Dochnakirk, Perthshire, and Edith Lillian, only surviving daughter of the late Dr. Kenneth Crawford, of Prince's Gardens.'

"In Edinburgh society comments were loud and various upon the forthcoming marriage, and, on the whole, these comments were far from complimentary to the families concerned. I do not think that the Scotch are a particularly sentimental race, but there was such obvious buying, selling, and bargaining about this marriage that Scottish chivalry rose in revolt at the thought.

"Against that the three people most concerned seemed perfectly satisfied. David Graham was positively transformed; his moroseness was gone from him, he lost his queer ways and wild manners, and became gentle and affectionate in the midst of this great and unexpected happiness. Miss Edith Crawford ordered her trousseau, and talked of the diamonds to her friends, and Lady Donaldson was only waiting for the consummation of this marriage—her heart's desire—before she finally retired from the world, at peace with it and with herself.

"The deed of gift was ready for signature on the wedding day, which was fixed for November 7th, and Lady Donaldson took up her abode temporarily in her brother's house in Charlotte Square.

"Mr. Graham gave a large ball on October 23rd. Special interest is attached to this ball, from the fact that for this occasion Lady Donaldson insisted that David's future wife should wear the magnificent diamonds which were soon to become hers.

"They were, it seems, superb, and became Miss Crawford's stately beauty to perfection. The ball was a brilliant success, the last guest leaving at four a.m. The next day it was the universal topic of conversation, and the day after that, when Edinburgh unfolded the late editions of its morning papers, it learned with horror and dismay that Lady Donaldson had been found murdered in her room, and that the celebrated diamonds had been stolen.

"Hardly had the beautiful little city, however, recovered from this awful shock, than its newspapers had another thrilling sensation ready for their readers.

"Already all Scotch and English papers had mysteriously hinted at 'startling information' obtained by the Procurator Fiscal, and at an 'impending sensational arrest.'

"Then the announcement came, and everyone in Edinburgh read, horror-struck and aghast, that the 'sensational arrest' was none other than that of Miss Edith Crawford, for murder and robbery, both so daring and horrible that reason refused to believe that a young lady, born and bred in the best social circle, could have conceived, much less executed, so heinous a crime. She had been arrested in London at the Midland Hotel, and brought to Edinburgh, where she was judicially examined, bail being refused."

2

"Little more than a fortnight after that, Edith Crawford was duly committed to stand her trial before the High Court of Justiciary. She had pleaded 'Not Guilty' at the pleading diet, and her defence was entrusted to Sir James Fenwick, one of the most eminent advocates at the Criminal Bar.

"Strange to say," continued the man in the corner after a while, "public opinion from the first went dead against the accused. The public is absolutely like a child, perfectly irresponsible and wholly illogical; it argued that since Miss Crawford had been ready to contract a marriage with a half-demented, deformed creature for the sake of his £100,000 she must have been equally ready to murder and rob an old lady for the sake of £50,000 worth of jewellery, without the encumbrance of so undesirable a husband.

"Perhaps the great sympathy aroused in the popular mind for David Graham had much to do with this ill-feeling against the accused. David Graham had, by this cruel and dastardly murder, lost the best—if not the only—friend he possessed. He had also lost at one fell swoop the large fortune which Lady Donaldson had been about to assign to him.

"The deed of gift had never been signed, and the old lady's vast wealth, instead of enriching her favourite nephew, was distributed— since she had made no will—amongst her heirs-at-law. And now to crown this long chapter of sorrow David Graham saw the girl he loved accused of the awful crime which had robbed him of friend and fortune.

"It was, therefore, with an unmistakable thrill of righteous satisfaction that Edinburgh society saw this 'mercenary girl' in so terrible a plight.

"I was immensely interested in the case, and journeyed down to Edinburgh in order to get a good view of the chief actors in the thrilling drama which was about to be unfolded there.

"I succeeded—I generally do—in securing one of the front seats among the audience, and was already comfortably installed in my place in court when through the trapdoor I saw the head of the prisoner emerge. She was very becomingly dressed in deep black, and, led by two policemen, she took her place in the dock. Sir James Fenwick shook hands with her very warmly, and I could almost hear him instilling words of comfort into her.

"The trial lasted six clear days, during which time more than forty persons were examined for the prosecution, and as many for the defence. But the most interesting witnesses were certainly the two doctors, the maid Tremlett, Campbell, the High Street jeweller, and David Graham.

"There was, of course, a great deal of medical evidence to go through. Poor Lady Donaldson had been found with a silk scarf tied tightly round her neck, her face showing even to the inexperienced eye every symptom of strangulation.

"Then Tremlett, Lady Donaldson's confidential maid, was called. Closely examined by Crown Counsel, she gave an account of the ball at Charlotte Square on the 23rd, and the wearing of the jewels by Miss Crawford on that occasion.

"'I helped Miss Crawford on with the tiara over her hair,' she said; 'and my lady put the two necklaces round Miss Crawford's neck herself. There were also some beautiful brooches, bracelets, and earrings. At four o'clock in the morning when the ball was over, Miss Crawford brought the jewels back to my lady's room. My lady had already gone to bed, and I had put out the electric light, as I was going, too. There was only one candle left in the room, close to the bed.

"'Miss Crawford took all the jewels off, and asked Lady Donaldson for the key of the safe, so that she might put them away. My lady gave her the key and said to me, "You can go to bed, Tremlett, you must be dead tired." I was glad to go, for I could hardly stand up—I was so tired. I said "Goodnight!" to my lady and also to Miss Crawford, who was busy putting the jewels away. As I was going out of the room, I heard Lady Donaldson saying: "Have you managed it, my dear?" Miss Crawford said: "I have put everything away very nicely."'

"In answer to Sir James Fenwick, Tremlett said that Lady Donaldson always carried the key of her jewel safe on a ribbon round her neck, and had done so the whole day preceding her death.

"'On the night of the 24th,' she continued, 'Lady Donaldson still seemed rather tired, and went up to her room directly after dinner, and while the family were still sitting in the dining-room. She made me dress her hair, then she slipped on her dressing-gown and sat in the armchair with a book. She told me that she then felt strangely uncomfortable and nervous, and could not account for it.

"'However, she did not want me to sit with her, so I thought that the best thing I could do was to tell Mr. David Graham that her ladyship did not seem very cheerful. Her ladyship was so fond of Mr. David; it always made her happy to have him with her. I then went to my room, and at half-past eight Mr. David called me. He said: "Your mistress does seem a little restless tonight. If I were you, I would just go and listen at her door in about an hour's time, and if she has not gone to bed I would go in and stay with her until she has." At about ten o'clock I did as Mr. David suggested, and listened at her ladyship's door. However, all was quiet in the room, and, thinking her ladyship had gone to sleep, I went back to bed.

"'The next morning at eight o'clock, when I took in my mistress's cup of tea, I saw her lying on the floor, her poor dear face all purple and distorted. I screamed, and the other servants came rushing along. Then Mr. Graham had the door locked and sent for the doctor and the police.'

"The poor woman seemed to find it very difficult not to break down. She was closely questioned by Sir James Fenwick, but had nothing further to say. She had last seen her mistress alive at eight o'clock on the evening of the 24th.

"'And when you listened at her door at ten o'clock,' asked Sir James, 'did you try to open it?'

"'I did, but it was locked,' she replied.

"'Did Lady Donaldson usually lock her bedroom at night?'

"'Nearly always.'

"'And in the morning when you took in the tea?'

"'The door was open. I walked straight in.'

"'You are quite sure?' insisted Sir James.

"'I swear it,' solemnly asserted the woman.

"After that we were informed by several members of Mr. Graham's establishment that Miss Crawford had been in to tea at Charlotte Square in the afternoon of the 24th, that she told everyone she was going to London by the night mail, as she had some special shopping she wished to do there. It appears that Mr. Graham and David both tried to persuade her to stay to dinner, and then to go by the 9.10 p.m. from the Caledonian Station. Miss Crawford however had refused, saying she always preferred to go from the Waverley Station. It was nearer to her own rooms, and she still had a good deal of writing to do.

"In spite of this, two witnesses saw the accused in Charlotte Square later on in the evening. She was carrying a bag which seemed heavy, and was walking towards the Caledonian Railway Station.

"But the most thrilling moment in that sensational trial was reached on the second day, when David Graham, looking wretchedly ill, unkempt, and haggard, stepped into the witness-box. A murmur of sympathy went round the audience at sight of him, who was the second, perhaps, most deeply stricken victim of the Charlotte Square tragedy.

"David Graham, in answer to Crown Counsel, gave an account of his last interview with Lady Donaldson.

"'Tremlett had told me that she seemed anxious and upset, and I went to have a chat with her; she soon cheered up and ...'

"There the unfortunate young man hesitated visibly, but after a while resumed with an obvious effort.

"'She spoke of my marriage, and of the gift she was about to bestow upon me. She said the diamonds would be for my wife, and after that for my daughter, if I had one. She also complained that Mr. Macfinlay had been so punctilious about preparing the deed of gift, and that it was a great pity the £100,000 could not just pass from her hands to mine without so much fuss.

"'I stayed talking with her for about half an hour; then I left her, as she seemed ready to go to bed; but I told her maid to listen at the door in about an hour's time.'

"There was deep silence in the court for a few moments, a silence which to me seemed almost electrical. It was as if, some time before it was uttered, the next question put by Crown Counsel to the witness had hovered in the air.

"'You were engaged to Miss Edith Crawford at one time, were you not?'

"One felt, rather than heard, the almost inaudible 'Yes' which escaped from David Graham's compressed lips.

"'Under what circumstances was that engagement broken off?'

"Sir James Fenwick had already risen in protest, but David Graham had been the first to speak.

"'I do not think that I need answer that question.'

"'I will put it in a different form, then,' said Crown Counsel urbanely—'one to which my learned friend cannot possibly take exception. Did you or did you not on October 27th receive a letter from the accused, in which she desired to be released from her promise of marriage to you?'

"Again, David Graham would have refused to answer, and he certainly gave no audible reply to the learned counsel's question; but everyone in the audience there present—aye, every member of the jury and of the bar—read upon David Graham's pale countenance and large, sorrowful eyes that ominous 'Yes!' which had failed to reach his trembling lips."

3

"There is no doubt," continued the man in the corner, "that what little sympathy the young girl's terrible position had aroused in the public mind had died out the moment that David Graham left the witness-box on the second day of the trial. Whether Edith Crawford was guilty of murder or not, the callous way in which she had accepted a deformed lover, and then thrown him over, had set every one's mind against her.

"It was Mr. Graham himself who had been the first to put the Procurator Fiscal in possession of the fact that the accused had written to David from London, breaking off her engagement. This information had, no doubt, directed the attention of the Fiscal to Miss Crawford, and the police soon brought forward the evidence which had led to her arrest.

"We had a final sensation on the third day, when Mr. Campbell, jeweller, of High Street, gave his evidence. He said that on October 25th a lady came to his shop and offered to sell him a pair of diamond earrings. Trade had been very bad, and he had refused the bargain, although the lady seemed ready to part with the earrings for an extraordinarily low sum, considering the beauty of the stones.

"In fact, it was because of this evident desire on the lady's part to sell at *any* cost that he had looked at her more keenly than he otherwise would have done. He was now ready to swear that the lady that offered him the diamond earrings was the prisoner in the dock.

"I can assure you that as we all listened to this apparently damnatory evidence, you might have heard a pin drop amongst the audience in that crowded court. The girl alone, there in the dock, remained calm and unmoved. Remember that for two days we had heard evidence to prove that old Dr. Crawford had died leaving his daughter penniless, that having no mother she had been brought up by a maiden aunt, who had trained her to be a governess, which occupation she had followed for years, and that certainly she had never been known by any of her friends to be in possession of solitaire diamond earrings.

"The prosecution had certainly secured an ace of trumps, but Sir James Fenwick, who during the whole of that day had seemed to take little interest in the proceedings, here rose from his seat, and I knew at once that he had got a titbit in the way of a 'point' up his sleeve. Gaunt, and unusually tall, and with his beak-like nose, he always looks strangely impressive when he seriously tackles a witness. He did it this time with a vengeance, I can tell you. He was all over the pompous little jeweller in a moment.

"'Had Mr. Campbell made a special entry in his book, as to the visit of the lady in question?'

"'No.'

"'Had he any special means of ascertaining when that visit did actually take place?'

"'No—but—'

"'What record had he of the visit?'

"Mr. Campbell had none. In fact, after about twenty minutes of cross-examination, he had to admit that he had given but little thought to the interview with the lady at the time, and certainly not in connection with the murder of Lady Donaldson, until he had read in the papers that a young lady had been arrested.

"Then he and his clerk talked the matter over, it appears, and together they had certainly recollected that a lady had brought some beautiful earrings for sale on a day which *must have been* the very morning after the murder. If Sir James Fenwick's object was to discredit this special witness, he certainly gained his point.

"All the pomposity went out of Mr. Campbell; he became flurried, then excited, then he lost his temper. After that he was allowed to leave the court, and Sir James Fenwick resumed his seat, and waited like a vulture for its prey.

"It presented itself in the person of Mr. Campbell's clerk, who, before the Procurator Fiscal, had corroborated his employer's evidence in every respect. In Scotland no witness in any one case is present in court during the examination of another, and Mr. Macfarlane, the clerk, was, therefore, quite unprepared for the pitfalls which Sir James Fenwick had prepared for him. He tumbled into them, head foremost, and the eminent advocate turned him inside out like a glove.

"Mr. Macfarlane did not lose his temper; he was of too humble a frame of mind to do that, but he got into a hopeless quagmire of mixed recollections, and he too left the witness-box quite unprepared to swear as to the day of the interview with the lady with the diamond earrings.

"I dare say, mind you," continued the man in the corner with a chuckle, "that to most people present, Sir James Fenwick's cross-questioning seemed completely irrelevant. Both Mr. Campbell and his clerk were quite ready to swear that they had had an interview concerning some diamond earrings with a lady, of whose identity with the accused they were perfectly convinced, and to the casual observer the question as to the time or even the day when that interview took place could make but little difference in the ultimate issue.

"Now I took in, in a moment, the entire drift of Sir James Fenwick's defence of Edith Crawford. When Mr. Macfarlane left the witness-box, the second victim of the eminent advocate's caustic tongue, I could read as in a book the whole history of that crime, its investigation, and the mistakes made by the police first and the Public Prosecutor afterwards.

"Sir James Fenwick knew them, too, of course, and he placed a finger upon each one, demolishing—like a child who blows upon a house of cards—the entire scaffolding erected by the prosecution.

"Mr. Campbell's and Mr. Macfarlane's identification of the accused with the lady who, on some date—admitted to be uncertain—had tried to sell a pair of diamond earrings, was the first point. Sir James had plenty of witnesses to prove that on the 25th, the day after the murder, the accused was in London, whilst, the day before, Mr. Campbell's shop had been closed long before the family circle had seen the last of Lady Donaldson. Clearly the jeweller and his clerk must have seen some other lady, whom their vivid imagination had pictured as being identical with the accused.

"Then came the great question of time. Mr. David Graham had been evidently the last to see Lady Donaldson alive. He had spoken to her as late as 8.30 p.m. Sir James Fenwick had called two porters at the Caledonian Railway Station who testified to Miss Crawford having taken her seat in a first-class carriage of the 9.10 train, some minutes before it started.

"'Was it conceivable, therefore,' argued Sir James, 'that in the space of half an hour the accused—a young girl—could have found her way surreptitiously into the house, at a time when the entire household was still astir, that she should have strangled Lady Donaldson, forced open the safe, and made away with the jewels? A man—an experienced burglar might have done it, but I contend that the accused is physically incapable of accomplishing such a feat.

"'With regard to the broken engagement,' continued the eminent counsel with a smile, 'it may have seemed a little heartless, certainly, but heartlessness is no crime in the eyes of the law. The accused has stated in her declaration that at the time she wrote to Mr. David Graham, breaking off her engagement, she had heard nothing of the Edinburgh tragedy.

"'The London papers had reported the crime very briefly. The accused was busy shopping; she knew nothing of Mr. David Graham's altered position. In no case was the breaking off of the engagement a proof that the accused had obtained possession of the jewels by so foul a deed.'

"It is, of course, impossible for me," continued the man in the corner apologetically, "to give you any idea of the eminent advocate's eloquence and masterful logic. It struck everyone, I think, just as it did me, that he chiefly directed his attention to the fact that there was absolutely no proof against the accused.

"Be that as it may, the result of that remarkable trial was a verdict of 'Non Proven.' The jury was absent forty minutes, and it appears that in the mind of every one of them there remained, in spite of Sir James' arguments, a firmly rooted conviction—call it instinct, if you like—that Edith Crawford had done away with Lady Donaldson in order to become possessed of those jewels, and that in spite of the pompous jeweller's many contradictions, she had offered him some of those diamonds for sale. But there was not enough proof to convict, and she was given the benefit of the doubt.

"I have heard English people argue that in England she would have been hanged. Personally, I doubt that. I think that an English jury, not having the judicial loophole of 'Non Proven,' would have been bound to acquit her. What do you think?"

4

There was a moment's silence, for Polly did not reply immediately, and he went on making impossible knots in his bit of string. Then she said quietly—

"I think that I agree with those English people who say that an English jury would have condemned her. . . . I have no doubt that she was guilty. She may not have committed that awful deed herself. Someone in the Charlotte Square house may have been her accomplice and killed and robbed Lady Donaldson while Edith Crawford waited outside for the jewels. David Graham left his godmother at 8.30 p.m. If the accomplice was one of the servants in the house, he or she would have had plenty of time for any amount of villainy, and Edith Crawford could have yet caught the 9.10 p.m. train from the Caledonian Station."

"Then who, in your opinion," he asked sarcastically, and cocking his funny birdlike head on one side, "tried to sell diamond earrings to Mr. Campbell, the jeweller?"

"Edith Crawford, of course," she retorted triumphantly; "he and his clerk both recognised her."

"When did she try to sell them the earrings?"

"Ah, that is what I cannot quite make out, and there to my mind lies the only mystery in this case. On the 25th she was certainly in London, and it is not very likely that she would go back to Edinburgh in order to dispose of the jewels there, where they could most easily be traced."

"Not very likely, certainly," he assented drily.

"And," added the young girl, "on the day before she left for London, Lady Donaldson was alive."

"And pray," he said suddenly, as with comic complacency he surveyed a beautiful knot he had just twisted up between his long fingers, "what has that fact got to do with it?"

"But it has everything to do with it!" she retorted.

"Ah, there you go," he sighed with comic emphasis. "My teachings don't seem to have improved your powers of reasoning. You are as bad as the police. Lady Donaldson has been robbed and murdered, and you immediately argue that she was robbed and murdered by the same person."

"But——" argued Polly.

"There is no but," he said, getting more and more excited. "See how simple it is. Edith Crawford wears the diamonds one night, then she brings them back to Lady Donaldson's room. Remember the maid's statement: 'My lady said: "Have you put them back, my dear?"—a simple statement, utterly ignored by the prosecution. But what did it mean? That Lady Donaldson could not see for herself whether Edith Crawford had put back the jewels or not, since she *asked the question*."

"Then you argue——"

"I never argue," he interrupted excitedly; "I state undeniable facts. Edith Crawford, who wanted to steal the jewels, took them then and there, when she had the opportunity. Why in the world should she have waited? Lady Donaldson was in bed, and Tremlett, the maid, had gone.

"The next day—namely, the 25th—she tries to dispose of a pair of earrings to Mr. Campbell; she fails, and decides to go to London, where she has a better chance. Sir James Fenwick did not think it desirable to bring forward witnesses to prove what I have since ascertained is a fact, namely, that on the 27th of October, three days before her arrest, Miss Crawford crossed over to Belgium, and came back to London the next day. In Belgium, no doubt, Lady Donaldson's diamonds, taken out of their settings, calmly repose at this moment, while the money derived from their sale is safely deposited in a Belgian bank."

"But then, who murdered Lady Donaldson, and why?" gasped Polly.

"Cannot you guess?" he queried blandly. "Have I not placed the case clearly enough before you? To me it seems so simple. It was a daring, brutal murder, remember. Think of one who, not being the thief himself, would, nevertheless, have the strongest of all motives to shield the thief from the consequences of her own misdeed: aye! and the power too—since it would be absolutely illogical, nay, impossible, that he should be an accomplice."

"Surely——"

"Think of a curious nature, warped morally, as well as physically—do you know how those natures feel? A thousand times more strongly than the even, straight natures in everyday life. Then think of such a nature brought face to face with this awful problem.

"Do you think that such a nature would hesitate a moment before committing a crime to save the loved one from the consequences of

100

that deed? Mind you, I don't assert for a moment that David Graham had any *intention* of murdering Lady Donaldson. Tremlett tells him that she seems strangely upset; he goes to her room and finds that she has discovered that she has been robbed. She naturally suspects Edith Crawford, recollects the incidents of the other night, and probably expresses her feelings to David Graham, and threatens immediate prosecution, scandal, what you will.

"I repeat it again, I dare say he had no wish to kill her. Probably he merely threatened to. A medical gentleman who spoke of sudden heart failure was no doubt right. Then imagine David Graham's remorse, his horror and his fears. The empty safe probably is the first object that suggested to him the grim tableau of robbery and murder, which he arranges in order to ensure his own safety.

"But remember one thing: no miscreant was seen to enter or leave the house surreptitiously; the murderer left no signs of entrance, and none of exit. An armed burglar would have left some trace—*someone* would have heard *something*. Then who locked and unlocked Lady Donaldson's door that night while she herself lay dead?

"Someone in the house, I tell you—someone who left no trace—someone against whom there could be no suspicion—someone who killed without apparently the slightest premeditation, and without the slightest motive. Think of it—I know I am right—and then tell me if I have at all enlisted your sympathies in the author of the Edinburgh Mystery."

He was gone. Polly looked again at the photo of David Graham. Did a crooked mind really dwell in that crooked body, and were there in the world such crimes that were great enough to be deemed sublime?

5

"That question of motive is a very difficult and complicated one at times," said the man in the corner, leisurely pulling off a huge pair of flaming dog-skin gloves from his meagre fingers. "I have known experienced criminal investigators declare, as an infallible axiom, that to find the person interested in the committal of the crime is to find the criminal.

"Well, that may be so in most cases, but my experience has proved to me that there is one factor in this world of ours which is the mainspring of human actions, and that factor is human passions. For good or evil passions rule this poor humanity of ours. Remember, there are the women! French detectives, who are acknowledged masters in their craft, never proceed till after they have discovered the feminine element in a crime; whether in theft, murder, or fraud, according to their theory, there is always a woman.

"Perhaps the reason why the Phillimore Terrace robbery was never brought home to its perpetrators is because there was no woman in any way connected with it, and I am quite sure, on the other hand, that the reason why the thief at the English Provident Bank is still unpunished is because a clever woman has escaped the eyes of our police force."

He had spoken at great length and very dictatorially. Miss Polly Burton did not venture to contradict him, knowing by now that whenever he was irritable, he was invariably rude, and she then had the worst of it.

"When I am old," he resumed, "and have nothing more to do, I think I shall take professionally to the police force; they have much to learn."

Could anything be more ludicrous than the self-satisfaction, the abnormal conceit of this remark, made by that shrivelled piece of mankind, in a nervous, hesitating tone of voice? Polly made no comment, but drew from her pocket a beautiful piece of string, and knowing his custom of knotting such an article while unravelling his mysteries, she handed it across the table to him. She positively thought that he blushed.

"As an adjunct to thought," she said, moved by a conciliatory spirit.

He looked at the invaluable toy which the young girl had tantalisingly placed close to his hand: then he forced himself to look all round the coffee-room: at Polly, at the waitresses, at the piles of pallid buns upon the counter. But involuntarily, his mild blue eyes wandered back lovingly to the long piece of string, on which his playful imagination no doubt already saw a series of knots which would be equally tantalising to tie and to untie.

"Tell me about the theft at the English Provident Bank," suggested Polly condescendingly.

He looked at her, as if she had proposed some mysterious complicity in an unheard-of crime. Finally, his lean fingers sought the end of the piece of string, and drew it towards him. His face brightened up in a moment.

"There was an element of tragedy in that particular robbery," he began, after a few moments of beatified knotting, "altogether different to that connected with most crimes; a tragedy which, as far as I am concerned, would seal my lips for ever, and forbid them to utter a word, which might lead the police on the right track."

"Your lips," suggested Polly sarcastically, "are, as far as I can see, usually sealed before our long-suffering, incompetent police and——"

"And you should be the last to grumble at this," he quietly interrupted, "for you have spent some very pleasant half-hours already, listening to what you have termed my 'cock-and-bull' stories. You know the English Provident Bank, of course, in Oxford Street; there were plenty of sketches of it at the time in the illustrated papers. Here is a photo of the outside. I took it myself some time ago, and only wish I had been cheeky or lucky enough to get a snap-shot of the interior. But you see that the office has a separate entrance from the rest of the house, which was, and still is, as is usual in such cases, inhabited by the manager and his family.

"Mr. Ireland was the manager then; it was less than six months ago. He lived over the bank, with his wife and family, consisting of a son, who was clerk in the business, and two or three younger children. The house is really smaller than it looks on this photo, for it has no depth, and only one set of rooms on each floor looking out into the street, the back of the house being nothing but the staircase. Mr. Ireland and his family, therefore, occupied the whole of it.

"As for the business premises, they were, and, in fact, are, of the usual pattern; an office with its rows of desks, clerks, and cashiers, and beyond, through a glass door, the manager's private room, with the ponderous safe, and desk, and so on.

"The private room has a door into the hall of the house, so that the manager is not obliged to go out into the street in order to go to business. There are no living-rooms on the ground floor, and the house has no basement.

"I am obliged to put all these architectural details before you, though they may sound rather dry and uninteresting, but they are really necessary in order to make my argument clear.

"At night, of course, the bank premises are barred and bolted against the street, and as an additional precaution there is always a night watchman in the office. As I mentioned before, there is only a glass door between the office and the manager's private room. This, of course, accounted for the fact that the night watchman heard all that he did hear, on that memorable night, and so helped further to entangle the thread of that impenetrable mystery.

"Mr. Ireland as a rule went into his office every morning a little before ten o'clock, but on that particular morning, for some reason which he never could or would explain, he went down before having his breakfast at about nine o'clock. Mrs. Ireland stated subsequently that, not hearing him return, she sent the servant down to tell the master that breakfast was getting cold. The girl's shrieks were the first intimation that something alarming had occurred.

"Mrs. Ireland hastened downstairs. On reaching the hall she found the door of her husband's room open, and it was from there that the girl's shrieks proceeded.

"'The master, mum—the poor master—he is dead, mum—I am sure he is dead!'—accompanied by vigorous thumps against the glass partition, and not very measured language on the part of the watchman from the outer office, such as—'Why don't you open the door instead of making that row?'

"Mrs. Ireland is not the sort of woman who, under any circumstances, would lose her presence of mind. I think she proved that throughout the many trying circumstances connected with the investigation of the case. She gave only one glance at the room and realised the situation. On the armchair, with head thrown back and eyes closed, lay Mr. Ireland, apparently in a dead faint; some terrible shock must have very suddenly shattered his nervous system, and rendered him prostrate for the moment. What that shock had been it was pretty easy to guess.

"The door of the safe was wide open, and Mr. Ireland had evidently tottered and fainted before some awful fact which the open safe had revealed to him; he had caught himself against a chair which lay on the floor, and then finally sunk, unconscious, into the armchair.

"All this, which takes some time to describe," continued the man in the corner, "took, remember, only a second to pass like a flash through Mrs. Ireland's mind; she quickly turned the key of the glass door, which was on the inside, and with the help of James Fairbairn, the watchman, she carried her husband upstairs to his room, and immediately sent both for the police and for a doctor.

"As Mrs. Ireland had anticipated, her husband had received a severe mental shock which had completely prostrated him. The doctor prescribed absolute quiet, and forbade all worrying questions for the present. The patient was not a young man; the shock had been very severe—it was a case, a very slight one, of cerebral congestion—and Mr. Ireland's reason, if not his life, might be gravely jeopardised by any attempt to recall before his enfeebled mind the circumstances which had preceded his collapse.

"The police therefore could proceed but slowly in their investigations. The detective who had charge of the case was necessarily handicapped, whilst one of the chief actors concerned in the drama was unable to help him in his work.

"To begin with, the robber or robbers had obviously not found their way into the manager's inner room through the bank premises. James Fairbairn had been on the watch all night, with the electric light full on, and obviously no one could have crossed the outer office or forced the heavily barred doors without his knowledge.

"There remained the other access to the room, that is, the one through the hall of the house. The hall door, it appears, was always barred and bolted by Mr. Ireland himself when he came home, whether from the theatre or his club. It was a duty he never allowed anyone to perform but himself. During his annual holiday, with his wife and family, his son, who usually had the sub-manager to stay with him on those occasions, did the bolting and barring—but with the distinct understanding that this should be done by ten o'clock at night.

"As I have already explained to you, there is only a glass partition between the general office and the manager's private room, and, according to James Fairbairn's account, this was naturally always left wide open so that he, during his night watch, would of necessity hear the faintest sound. As a rule, there was no light left in the manager's room, and the other door—that leading into the hall—was bolted from the inside by James Fairbairn the moment he had satisfied himself that the premises were safe, and he had begun his night-watch. An electric bell in both the offices communicated with Mr. Ireland's bedroom and that of his son, Mr. Robert Ireland, and there was a telephone installed to the nearest district messengers' office, with an understood signal which meant 'Police.'

"At nine o'clock in the morning it was the night watchman's duty, as soon as the first cashier had arrived, to dust and tidy the manager's room, and to undo the bolts; after that he was free to go home to his breakfast and rest.

"You will see, of course, that James Fairbairn's position in the English Provident Bank is one of great responsibility and trust; but then in every bank and business house there are men who hold similar positions. They are always men of well-known and tried characters, often old soldiers with good-conduct records behind them. James Fairbairn is a fine, powerful Scotchman; he had been night watchman to the English Provident Bank for fifteen years, and was then not more than forty-three or forty-four years old. He is an ex-guardsman, and stands six feet three inches in his socks.

"It was his evidence, of course, which was of such paramount importance, and which somehow or other managed, in spite of the utmost care exercised by the police, to become public property, and to cause the wildest excitement in banking and business circles.

"James Fairbairn stated that at eight o'clock in the evening of March 25th, having bolted and barred all the shutters and the door of the back premises, he was about to lock the manager's door as usual, when Mr. Ireland called to him from the floor above, telling him to leave that door open, as he might want to go into the office again for a minute when he came home at eleven o'clock. James Fairbairn asked if he should leave the light on, but Mr. Ireland said: 'No, turn it out. I can switch it on if I want it.'

"The night watchman at the English Provident Bank has permission to smoke, he also is allowed a nice fire, and a tray consisting of a plate of substantial sandwiches and one glass of ale, which he can take when he likes. James Fairbairn settled himself in front of the fire, lit his pipe, took out his newspaper, and began to read. He thought he had heard the street door open and shut at about a quarter to ten; he supposed that it was Mr. Ireland going out to his club, but at ten minutes to ten o'clock the watchman heard the door of the manager's room open, and someone enter, immediately closing the glass partition door and turning the key.

"He naturally concluded it was Mr. Ireland himself.

"From where he sat, he could not see into the room, but he noticed that the electric light had not been switched on, and that the manager seemingly had no light but an occasional match.

"'For the minute,' continued James Fairbairn, 'a thought did just cross my mind that something might perhaps be wrong, and I put my newspaper aside and went to the other end of the room towards the glass partition. The manager's room was still quite dark, and I could not clearly see into it, but the door into the hall was open, and there was, of course, a light through there. I had got quite close to the partition, when I saw Mrs. Ireland standing in the doorway, and heard her saying in a very astonished tone of voice: 'Why, Lewis, I thought you had gone to your club ages ago. What in the world are you doing here in the dark?'

"'Lewis is Mr. Ireland's Christian name,' was James Fairbairn's further statement. 'I did not hear the manager's reply, but quite satisfied now that nothing was wrong, I went back to my pipe and my newspaper. Almost directly afterwards I heard the manager leave his room, cross the hall and go out by the street door. It was only after he had gone that I recollected that he must have forgotten to unlock the glass partition and that I could not therefore bolt the door into the hall the same as usual, and I suppose that is how those confounded thieves got the better of me.'"

6

"By the time the public had been able to think over James Fairbairn's evidence, a certain disquietude and unrest had begun to make itself felt both in the bank itself and among those of our detective force who had charge of the case. The newspapers spoke of the matter with very obvious caution, and warned all their readers to await the further development of this sad case.

"While the manager of the English Provident Bank lay in such a precarious condition of health, it was impossible to arrive at any definite knowledge as to what the thief had actually made away with. The chief cashier, however, estimated the loss at about £5,000 in gold and notes of the bank money—that was, of course, on the assumption that Mr. Ireland had no private money or valuables of his own in the safe.

"Mind you, at this point public sympathy was much stirred in favour of the poor man who lay ill, perhaps dying, and yet whom, strangely enough, suspicion had already slightly touched with its poisoned wing.

"Suspicion is a strong word, perhaps, to use at this point in the story. No one suspected anybody at present. James Fairbairn had told his story, and had vowed that some thief with false keys must have sneaked through the house into the inner office.

"Public excitement, you will remember, lost nothing by waiting. Hardly had we all had time to wonder over the night watchman's singular evidence, and, pending further and fuller details, to check our growing sympathy for the man who was ill, than the sensational side of this mysterious case culminated in one extraordinary, absolutely unexpected fact. Mrs. Ireland, after a twenty-four hours' untiring watch beside her husband's sick bed, had at last been approached by the detective, and been asked to reply to a few simple questions, and thus help to throw some light on the mystery which had caused Mr.

Ireland's illness and her own consequent anxiety.

"She professed herself quite ready to reply to any questions put to her, and she literally astounded both inspector and detective when she firmly and emphatically declared that James Fairbairn must have been dreaming or asleep when he thought he saw her in the doorway at ten o'clock that night, and fancied he heard her voice.

"She may or may not have been down in the hall at that particular hour, for she usually ran down herself to see if the last post had brought any letters, but most certainly she had neither seen nor spoken to Mr. Ireland at that hour, for Mr. Ireland had gone out an hour before, she herself having seen him to the front door. Never for a moment did she swerve from this extraordinary statement. She spoke to James Fairbairn in the presence of the detective, and told him he must absolutely have been mistaken, that she had not seen Mr. Ireland, and that she had not spoken to him.

"One other person was questioned by the police, and that was Mr. Robert Ireland, the manager's eldest son. It was presumed that he would know something of his father's affairs; the idea having now taken firm hold of the detective's mind that perhaps grave financial difficulties had tempted the unfortunate manager to appropriate some of the firm's money.

"Mr. Robert Ireland, however, could not say very much. His father did not confide in him to the extent of telling him all his private affairs, but money never seemed scarce at home certainly, and Mr. Ireland had, to his son's knowledge, not a single extravagant habit. He himself had been dining out with a friend on that memorable evening, and had gone on with him to the Oxford Music Hall. He met his father on the doorstep of the bank at about 11.30 p.m. and they went in together. There certainly was nothing remarkable about Mr. Ireland then, his son averred; he appeared in no way excited, and bade his son good night quite cheerfully.

"There was the extraordinary, the remarkable hitch," continued the man in the corner, waxing more and more excited every moment. "The public—who is at times very dense—saw it clearly nevertheless: of course, everyone at once jumped to the natural conclusion that Mrs. Ireland was telling a lie—a noble lie, a self-sacrificing lie, a lie endowed with all the virtues if you like, but still a lie.

"She was trying to save her husband, and was going the wrong way to work. James Fairbairn, after all, could not have dreamt quite all that he declared he had seen and heard. No one suspected James Fairbairn;

108

there was no occasion to do that; to begin with he was a great heavy Scotchman with obviously no powers of invention, such as Mrs. Ireland's strange assertion credited him with; moreover, the theft of the banknotes could not have been of the slightest use to him.

"But, remember, there was the hitch; without it the public mind would already have condemned the sick man upstairs, without hope of rehabilitation. This fact struck everyone.

"Granting that Mr. Ireland had gone into his office at ten minutes to ten o'clock at night for the purpose of extracting £5,000 worth of notes and gold from the bank safe, whilst giving the theft the appearance of a night burglary; granting that he was disturbed in his nefarious project by his wife, who, failing to persuade him to make restitution, took his side boldly, and very clumsily attempted to rescue him out of his difficult position—why should he, at nine o'clock the following morning, fall in a dead faint and get cerebral congestion at sight of a defalcation he knew had occurred? One might simulate a fainting fit, but no one can assume a high temperature and a congestion, which the most ordinary practitioner who happened to be called in would soon see were non-existent.

"Mr. Ireland, according to James Fairbairn's evidence, must have gone out soon after the theft, come in again with his son an hour and a half later, talked to him, gone quietly to bed, and waited for nine hours before he fell ill at sight of his own crime. It was not logical, you will admit. Unfortunately, the poor man himself was unable to give any explanation of the night's tragic adventures.

"He was still very weak, and though under strong suspicion, he was left, by the doctor's orders, in absolute ignorance of the heavy charges which were gradually accumulating against him. He had made many anxious inquiries from all those who had access to his bedside as to the result of the investigation, and the probable speedy capture of the burglars, but everyone had strict orders to inform him merely that the police so far had no clue of any kind.

"You will admit, as everyone did, that there was something very pathetic about the unfortunate man's position, so helpless to defend himself, if defence there was, against so much overwhelming evidence. That is why I think public sympathy remained with him. Still, it was terrible to think of his wife presumably knowing him to be guilty, and anxiously waiting whilst dreading the moment when, restored to health, he would have to face the doubts, the suspicions, probably the open accusations, which were fast rising up around him."

7

"It was close on six weeks before the doctor at last allowed his patient to attend to the grave business which had prostrated him for so long.

"In the meantime, among the many people who directly or indirectly were made to suffer in this mysterious affair, no one, I think, was more pitied, and more genuinely sympathised with, than Robert Ireland, the manager's eldest son.

"You remember that he had been clerk in the bank? Well, naturally, the moment suspicion began to fasten on his father his position in the business became untenable. I think everyone was very kind to him. Mr. Sutherland French, who was made acting manager 'during Mr. Lewis Ireland's regrettable absence,' did everything in his power to show his goodwill and sympathy to the young man, but I don't think that he or anyone else was much astonished when, after Mrs. Ireland's extraordinary attitude in the case had become public property, he quietly intimated to the acting manager that he had determined to sever his connection with the bank.

"The best of recommendations was, of course, placed at his disposal, and it was finally understood that, as soon as his father was completely restored to health and would no longer require his presence in London, he would try to obtain employment somewhere abroad. He spoke of the new volunteer corps organised for the military policing of the new colonies, and, truth to tell, no one could blame him that he should wish to leave far behind him all London banking connections. The son's attitude certainly did not tend to ameliorate the father's position. It was pretty evident that his own family had ceased to hope in the poor manager's innocence.

"And yet he was absolutely innocent. You must remember how that fact was clearly demonstrated as soon as the poor man was able to say a word for himself. And he said it to some purpose, too.

"Mr. Ireland was, and is, very fond of music. On the evening in question, while sitting in his club, he saw in one of the daily papers the announcement of a peculiarly attractive programme at the Queen's Hall concert. He was not dressed, but nevertheless felt an irresistible desire to hear one or two of these attractive musical items, and he strolled down to the Hall. Now, this sort of alibi is usually very difficult to prove, but Dame Fortune, oddly enough, favoured Mr. Ireland on this occasion, probably to compensate him for the hard knocks she had been dealing him pretty freely of late.

"It appears that there was some difficulty about his seat, which was sold to him at the box office, and which he, nevertheless, found wrongfully occupied by a determined lady, who refused to move. The management had to be appealed to; the attendants also remembered not only the incident, but also the face and appearance of the gentleman who was the innocent cause of the altercation.

"As soon as Mr. Ireland could speak for himself he mentioned the incident and the persons who had been witness to it. He was identified by them, to the amazement, it must be confessed, of police and public alike, who had comfortably decided that no one *could* be guilty save the manager of the Provident Bank himself. Moreover, Mr. Ireland was a fairly wealthy man, with a good balance at the Union Bank, and plenty of private means, the result of years of provident living.

"He had but to prove that if he really had been in need of an immediate £5,000—which was all the amount extracted from the bank safe that night—he had plenty of securities on which he could, at an hour's notice, have raised twice that sum. His life insurances had been fully paid up; he had not a debt which a £5 note could not easily have covered.

"On the fatal night he certainly did remember asking the watchman not to bolt the door to his office, as he thought he might have one or two letters to write when he came home, but later on he had forgotten all about this. After the concert he met his son in Oxford Street, just outside the house, and thought no more about the office, the door of which was shut, and presented no unusual appearance.

"Mr. Ireland absolutely denied having been in his office at the hour when James Fairbairn positively asserted he heard Mrs. Ireland say in an astonished tone of voice:'Why, Lewis, what in the world are you doing here?' It became pretty clear therefore that James Fairbairn's view of the manager's wife had been a mere vision.

"Mr. Ireland gave up his position as manager of the English Provident: both he and his wife felt no doubt that on the whole, perhaps, there had been too much talk, too much scandal connected with their name, to be altogether advantageous to the bank. Moreover, Mr. Ireland's health was not so good as it had been. He has a pretty house now at Sittingbourne, and amuses himself during his leisure hours with amateur horticulture, and I, who alone in London besides the persons directly connected with this mysterious affair, know the true solution of the enigma, often wonder how much of it is known to the ex-manager of the English Provident Bank."

The man in the corner had been silent for some time. Miss Polly Burton, in her presumption, had made up her mind, at the commencement of his tale, to listen attentively to every point of the evidence in connection with the case which he recapitulated before her, and to follow the point, in order to try and arrive at a conclusion of her own, and overwhelm the antediluvian scarecrow with her sagacity.

She said nothing, for she had arrived at no conclusion; the case puzzled every one, and had amazed the public in its various stages, from the moment when opinion began to cast doubt on Mr. Ireland's honesty to that when his integrity was proved beyond a doubt. One or two people had suspected Mrs. Ireland to have been the actual thief, but that idea had soon to be abandoned.

Mrs. Ireland had all the money she wanted; the theft occurred six months ago, and not a single bank-note was ever traced to her pocket; moreover, she must have had an accomplice, since someone else was in the manager's room that night; and if that someone else was her accomplice, why did she risk betraying him by speaking loudly in the presence of James Fairbairn, when it would have been so much simpler to turn out the light and plunge the hall into darkness?

"You are altogether on the wrong track," sounded a sharp voice in direct answer to Polly's thoughts—"altogether wrong. If you want to acquire my method of induction, and improve your reasoning power, you must follow my system. First think of the one absolutely undisputed, positive fact. You must have a starting-point, and not go wandering about in the realms of suppositions."

"But there are no positive facts," she said irritably.

"You don't say so?" he said quietly. "Do you not call it a positive fact that the bank safe was robbed of £5,000 on the evening of March 25th before 11.30 p.m."

"Yes, that is all which is positive and—"

"Do you not call it a positive fact," he interrupted quietly, "that the lock of the safe not being picked, it must have been opened by its own key?"

"I know that," she rejoined crossly, "and that is why everyone agreed that James Fairbairn could not possibly—"

"And do you not call it a positive fact, then, that James Fairbairn could not possibly, *etc., etc.*, seeing that the glass partition door was locked from the inside; Mrs. Ireland herself let James Fairbairn into her husband's office when she saw him lying fainting before the open safe. Of course, that was a positive fact, and so was the one that proved to any thinking mind that if that safe was opened with a key, it could only have been done by a person having access to that key."

"But the man in the private office—"

"Exactly! the man in the private office. Enumerate his points, if you please," said the funny creature, marking each point with one of his favourite knots. "He was a man who might that night have had access to the key of the safe, unsuspected by the manager or even his wife, and a man for whom Mrs. Ireland was willing to tell a downright lie. Are there many men for whom a woman of the better middle class, and an Englishwoman, would be ready to perjure herself? Surely not! She might do it for her husband. The public thought she had. It never struck them that she might have done it for her son!"

"Her son!" exclaimed Polly.

"Ah! she was a clever woman," he ejaculated enthusiastically, "one with courage and presence of mind, which I don't think I have ever seen equalled. She runs downstairs before going to bed in order to see whether the last post has brought any letters. She sees the door of her husband's office ajar, she pushes it open, and there, by the sudden flash of a hastily struck match she realises in a moment that a thief stands before the open safe, and in that thief, she has already recognised her son. At that very moment she hears the watchman's step approaching the partition. There is no time to warn her son; she does not know the glass door is locked; James Fairbairn may switch on the electric light and see the young man in the very act of robbing his employers' safe.

"One thing alone can reassure the watchman. One person alone had the right to be there at that hour of the night, and without hesitation she pronounces her husband's name.

"Mind you, I firmly believe that at the time the poor woman only wished to gain time, that she had every hope that her son had not yet had the opportunity to lay so heavy a guilt upon his conscience.

"What passed between mother and son we shall never know, but this much we do know, that the young villain made off with his booty, and trusted that his mother would never betray him. Poor woman! what a night of it she must have spent; but she was clever and far-seeing. She knew that her husband's character could not suffer through her action. Accordingly, she took the only course open to her to save her son even from his father's wrath, and boldly denied James Fairbairn's statement.

"Of course, she was fully aware that her husband could easily clear himself, and the worst that could be said of her was that she had thought him guilty and had tried to save him. She trusted to the future to clear her of any charge of complicity in the theft.

"By now everyone has forgotten most of the circumstances; the police are still watching the career of James Fairbairn and Mrs. Ireland's expenditure. As you know, not a single note, so far, has been traced to her. Against that, one or two of the notes have found their way back to England. No one realises how easy it is to cash English banknotes at the smaller *agents de change* abroad. The *changeurs* are only too glad to get them; what do they care where they come from as long as they are genuine? And a week or two later *M. le Changeur* could not swear who tendered him any one particular note.

"You see, young Robert Ireland went abroad; he will come back some day having made a fortune. There's his photo. And this is his mother—a clever woman, wasn't she?"

And before Polly had time to reply he was gone. She really had never seen anyone move across a room so quickly. But he always left an interesting trail behind: a piece of string knotted from end to end and a few photos.

The Dublin Mystery

1

"I always thought that the history of that forged will was about as interesting as any I had read," said the man in the corner that day. He had been silent for some time, and was meditatively sorting and looking through a packet of small photographs in his pocket-book. Polly guessed that some of these would presently be placed before her for inspection—and she had not long to wait.

"That is old Brooks," he said, pointing to one of the photographs, "Millionaire Brooks, as he was called, and these are his two sons, Percival and Murray. It was a curious case, wasn't it? Personally, I don't wonder that the police were completely at sea. If a member of that highly estimable force happened to be as clever as the clever author of that forged will, we should have very few undetected crimes in this country."

"That is why I always try to persuade you to give our poor ignorant police the benefit of your great insight and wisdom," said Polly, with a smile.

"I know," he said blandly, "you have been most kind in that way, but I am only an amateur. Crime interests me only when it resembles a clever game of chess, with many intricate moves which all tend to one solution, the checkmating of the antagonist—the detective force of the country. Now, confess that, in the Dublin mystery, the clever police there were absolutely checkmated."

"Absolutely."

"Just as the public was. There were actually two crimes committed in one city which have completely baffled detection: the murder of Patrick Wethered the lawyer, and the forged will of Millionaire Brooks. There are not many millionaires in Ireland; no wonder old Brooks was a notability in his way, since his business—bacon curing, I believe it is—is said to be worth over £2,000,000 of solid money.

"His younger son Murray was a refined, highly educated man, and was, moreover, the apple of his father's eye, as he was the spoilt darling of Dublin society; good-looking, a splendid dancer, and a perfect rider, he was the acknowledged 'catch' of the matrimonial market of Ireland, and many a very aristocratic house was opened hospitably to the favourite son of the millionaire.

"Of course, Percival Brooks, the eldest son, would inherit the bulk of the old man's property and also probably the larger share in the business; he, too, was good-looking, more so than his brother; he, too, rode, danced, and talked well, but it was many years ago that mammas with marriageable daughters had given up all hopes of Percival Brooks as a probable son-in-law. That young man's infatuation for Maisie Fortescue, a lady of undoubted charm but very doubtful antecedents, who had astonished the London and Dublin music-halls with her extravagant dances, was too well known and too old-established to encourage any hopes in other quarters.

"Whether Percival Brooks would ever marry Maisie Fortescue was thought to be very doubtful. Old Brooks had the full disposal of all his wealth, and it would have fared ill with Percival if he introduced an undesirable wife into the magnificent Fitzwilliam Place establishment.

"That is how matters stood," continued the man in the corner, "when Dublin society one morning learnt, with deep regret and dismay, that old Brooks had died very suddenly at his residence after only a few hours' illness. At first it was generally understood that he had had an apoplectic stroke; anyway, he had been at business hale and hearty as ever the day before his death, which occurred late on the evening of February 1st.

"It was the morning papers of February 2nd which told the sad news to their readers, and it was those self-same papers which on that eventful morning contained another even more startling piece of news, that proved the prelude to a series of sensations such as tranquil, placid Dublin had not experienced for many years. This was, that on that very afternoon which saw the death of Dublin's greatest millionaire, Mr. Patrick Wethered, his solicitor, was murdered in Phoenix Park at five o'clock in the afternoon while actually walking to his own house from his visit to his client in Fitzwilliam Place.

"Patrick Wethered was as well-known as the proverbial town pump; his mysterious and tragic death filled all Dublin with dismay. The lawyer, who was a man sixty years of age, had been struck on the back of the head by a heavy stick, garrotted, and subsequently robbed, for neither money, watch, or pocket-book were found upon his person, whilst the police soon gathered from Patrick Wethered's household that he had left home at two o'clock that afternoon, carrying both watch and pocket-book, and undoubtedly money as well.

"An inquest was held, and a verdict of wilful murder was found against some person or persons unknown.

"But Dublin had not exhausted its stock of sensations yet. Millionaire Brooks had been buried with due pomp and magnificence, and his will had been proved (his business and personalty being estimated at £2,500,000) by Percival Gordon Brooks, his eldest son and sole executor. The younger son, Murray, who had devoted the best years of his life to being a friend and companion to his father, while Percival ran after ballet-dancers and music-hall stars—Murray, who had avowedly been the apple of his father's eye in consequence—was left with a miserly pittance of £300 a year, and no share whatever in the gigantic business of Brooks & Sons, bacon curers, of Dublin.

"Something had evidently happened within the precincts of the Brooks' town mansion, which the public and Dublin society tried in vain to fathom. Elderly mammas and blushing *débutantes* were already thinking of the best means whereby next season they might more easily show the cold shoulder to young Murray Brooks, who had so suddenly become a hopeless 'detrimental' in the marriage market, when all these sensations terminated in one gigantic, overwhelming bit of scandal, which for the next three months furnished food for gossip in every drawing-room in Dublin.

"Mr. Murray Brooks, namely, had entered a claim for probate of a will, made by his father in 1891, declaring that the later will made the very day of his father's death and proved by his brother as sole executor, was null and void, that will being a forgery."

2

"The facts that transpired in connection with this extraordinary case were sufficiently mysterious to puzzle everybody. As I told you before, all Mr. Brooks' friends never quite grasped the idea that the old man should so completely have cut off his favourite son with the proverbial shilling.

"You see, Percival had always been a thorn in the old man's flesh. Horse-racing, gambling, theatres, and music-halls were, in the old pork-butcher's eyes, so many deadly sins which his son committed every day of his life, and all the Fitzwilliam Place household could testify to the many and bitter quarrels which had arisen between father and son over the latter's gambling or racing debts. Many people asserted that Brooks would sooner have left his money to charitable institutions than seen it squandered upon the brightest stars that adorned the music-hall stage.

"The case came up for hearing early in the autumn. In the meanwhile, Percival Brooks had given up his racecourse associates, settled down in the Fitzwilliam Place mansion, and conducted his father's business, without a manager, but with all the energy and forethought which he had previously devoted to more unworthy causes.

"Murray had elected not to stay on in the old house; no doubt associations were of too painful and recent a nature; he was boarding with the family of a Mr. Wilson Hibbert, who was the late Patrick Wethered's, the murdered lawyer's, partner. They were quiet, homely people, who lived in a very pokey little house in Kilkenny Street, and poor Murray must, in spite of his grief, have felt very bitterly the change from his luxurious quarters in his father's mansion to his present tiny room and homely meals.

"Percival Brooks, who was now drawing an income of over a hundred thousand a year, was very severely criticised for adhering so strictly to the letter of his father's will, and only paying his brother that paltry £300 a year, which was very literally but the crumbs off his own magnificent dinner table.

"The issue of that contested will case was therefore awaited with eager interest. In the meanwhile, the police, who had at first seemed fairly loquacious on the subject of the murder of Mr. Patrick Wethered, suddenly became strangely reticent, and by their very reticence aroused a certain amount of uneasiness in the public mind, until one day the *Irish Times* published the following extraordinary, enigmatic paragraph:

> We hear on authority which cannot be questioned, that certain extraordinary developments are expected in connection with the brutal murder of our distinguished townsman Mr. Wethered; the police, in fact, are vainly trying to keep it secret that they hold a clue which is as important as it is sensational, and that they only await the impending issue of a well-known litigation in the probate court to effect an arrest.

"The Dublin public flocked to the court to hear the arguments in the great will case. I myself journeyed down to Dublin. As soon as I succeeded in fighting my way to the densely crowded court, I took stock of the various actors in the drama, which I as a spectator was prepared to enjoy. There were Percival Brooks and Murray his brother, the two litigants, both good-looking and well dressed, and both striving, by keeping up a running conversation with their lawyer, to appear unconcerned and confident of the issue. With Percival Brooks was Henry Oranmore, the eminent Irish K.C., whilst Walter Hibbert, a rising young barrister, the son of Wilson Hibbert, appeared for Murray.

"The will of which the latter claimed probate was one dated 1891, and had been made by Mr. Brooks during a severe illness which threatened to end his days. This will had been deposited in the hands of Messrs. Wethered and Hibbert, solicitors to the deceased, and by it Mr. Brooks left his personalty equally divided between his two sons, but had left his business entirely to his youngest son, with a charge of £2,000 a year upon it, payable to Percival. You see that Murray Brooks therefore had a very deep interest in that second will being found null and void.

"Old Mr. Hibbert had very ably instructed his son, and Walter Hibbert's opening speech was exceedingly clever. He would show, he said, on behalf of his client, that the will dated February 1st, 1908, could never have been made by the late Mr. Brooks, as it was absolutely contrary to his avowed intentions, and that if the late Mr. Brooks did on the day in question make any fresh will at all, it certainly was not the one proved by Mr. Percival Brooks, for that was absolutely a forgery from beginning to end. Mr. Walter Hibbert proposed to call several witnesses in support of both these points.

"On the other hand, Mr. Henry Oranmore, K.C., very ably and courteously replied that he too had several witnesses to prove that Mr. Brooks certainly did make a will on the day in question, and that, whatever his intentions may have been in the past, he must have modified them on the day of his death, for the will proved by Mr. Percival Brooks was found after his death under his pillow, duly signed and witnessed and in every way legal.

"Then the battle began in sober earnest. There were a great many witnesses to be called on both sides, their evidence being of more or less importance—chiefly less. But the interest centred round the prosaic figure of John O'Neill, the butler at Fitzwilliam Place, who had been in Mr. Brooks' family for thirty years.

"'I was clearing away my breakfast things,' said John, 'when I heard the master's voice in the study close by. Oh my, he was that angry! I could hear the words "disgrace," and "villain," and "liar," and "ballet-dancer," and one or two other ugly words as applied to some female lady, which I would not like to repeat. At first, I did not take much notice, as I was quite used to hearing my poor dear master having words with Mr. Percival. So, I went downstairs carrying my breakfast things; but I had just started cleaning my silver when the study bell goes ringing violently, and I hear Mr. Percival's voice shouting in the hall: "John! quick! Send for Dr. Mulligan at once. Your master is not well! Send one of the men, and you come up and help me to get Mr. Brooks to bed."

"'I sent one of the grooms for the doctor,' continued John, who seemed still affected at the recollection of his poor master, to whom he had evidently been very much attached, 'and I went up to see Mr. Brooks. I found him lying on the study floor, his head supported in Mr. Percival's arms. "My father has fallen in a faint," said the young master; "help me to get him up to his room before Dr. Mulligan comes."

"'Mr. Percival looked very white and upset, which was only natural; and when we had got my poor master to bed, I asked if I should not go and break the news to Mr. Murray, who had gone to business an hour ago.

"However, before Mr. Percival had time to give me an order the doctor came. I thought I had seen death plainly writ in my master's face, and when I showed the doctor out an hour later, and he told me that he would be back directly, I knew that the end was near.

"'Mr. Brooks rang for me a minute or two later. He told me to send at once for Mr. Wethered, or else for Mr. Hibbert, if Mr. Wethered could not come. "I haven't many hours to live, John," he says to me—"my heart is broke, the doctor says my heart is broke. A man shouldn't marry and have children, John, for they will sooner or later break his heart." I was so upset I couldn't speak; but I sent round at once for Mr. Wethered, who came himself just about three o'clock that afternoon.

"'After he had been with my master about an hour I was called in, and Mr. Wethered said to me that Mr. Brooks wished me and one other of us servants to witness that he had signed a paper which was on a table by his bedside.

"I called Pat Mooney, the head footman, and before us both Mr. Brooks put his name at the bottom of that paper. Then Mr. Wethered give me the pen and told me to write my name as a witness, and that

Pat Mooney was to do the same. After that we were both told that we could go.'

"The old butler went on to explain that he was present in his late master's room on the following day when the undertakers, who had come to lay the dead man out, found a paper underneath his pillow. John O'Neill, who recognised the paper as the one to which he had appended his signature the day before, took it to Mr. Percival, and gave it into his hands.

"In answer to Mr. Walter Hibbert, John asserted positively that he took the paper from the undertaker's hand and went straight with it to Mr. Percival's room.

"'He was alone,' said John; 'I gave him the paper. He just glanced at it, and I thought he looked rather astonished, but he said nothing, and I at once left the room.'

"'When you say that you recognised the paper as the one which you had seen your master sign the day before, how did you actually recognise that it was the same paper?' asked Mr. Hibbert amidst breathless interest on the part of the spectators. I narrowly observed the witness's face.

"'It looked exactly the same paper to me, sir,' replied John, somewhat vaguely.

"'Did you look at the contents, then?'

"'No, sir; certainly not.'

"'Had you done so the day before?'

"'No, sir, only at my master's signature.'

"'Then you only thought by the *outside* look of the paper that it was the same?'

"'It looked the same thing, sir,' persisted John obstinately.

"You see," continued the man in the corner, leaning eagerly forward across the narrow marble table, "the contention of Murray Brooks' adviser was that Mr. Brooks, having made a will and hidden it—for some reason or other under his pillow—that will had fallen, through the means related by John O'Neill, into the hands of Mr. Percival Brooks, who had destroyed it and substituted a forged one in its place, which adjudged the whole of Mr. Brooks' millions to himself. It was a terrible and very daring accusation directed against a gentleman who, in spite of his many wild oats sowed in early youth, was a prominent and important figure in Irish high life.

"All those present were aghast at what they heard, and the whispered comments I could hear around me showed me that public opinion, at least, did not uphold Mr. Murray Brooks' daring accusation against his brother.

"But John O'Neill had not finished his evidence, and Mr. Walter Hibbert had a bit of sensation still up his sleeve. He had, namely, produced a paper, the will proved by Mr. Percival Brooks, and had asked John O'Neill if once again he recognised the paper.

"'Certainly, sir,' said John unhesitatingly, 'that is the one the undertaker found under my poor dead master's pillow, and which I took to Mr. Percival's room immediately.'

"Then the paper was unfolded and placed before the witness.

"'Now, Mr. O'Neill, will you tell me if that is your signature?'

"John looked at it for a moment; then he said: 'Excuse me, sir,' and produced a pair of spectacles which he carefully adjusted before he again examined the paper. Then he thoughtfully shook his head.

"'It don't look much like my writing, sir,' he said at last. 'That is to say,' he added, by way of elucidating the matter, 'it does look like my writing, but then I don't think it is.'

"There was at that moment a look in Mr. Percival Brooks' face," continued the man in the corner quietly, "which then and there gave me the whole history of that quarrel, that illness of Mr. Brooks, of the will, aye! and of the murder of Patrick Wethered too.

"All I wondered at was how every one of those learned counsel on both sides did not get the clue just the same as I did, but went on arguing, speechifying, cross-examining for nearly a week, until they arrived at the one conclusion which was inevitable from the very first, namely, that the will *was* a forgery—a gross, clumsy, idiotic forgery, since both John O'Neill and Pat Mooney, the two witnesses, absolutely repudiated the signatures as their own. The only successful bit of calligraphy the forger had done was the signature of old Mr. Brooks.

"It was a very curious fact, and one which had undoubtedly aided the forger in accomplishing his work quickly, that Mr. Wethered the lawyer having, no doubt, realised that Mr. Brooks had not many moments in life to spare, had not drawn up the usual engrossed, magnificent document dear to the lawyer heart, but had used for his client's will one of those regular printed forms which can be purchased at any stationer's.

"Mr. Percival Brooks, of course, flatly denied the serious allegation brought against him. He admitted that the butler had brought him the document the morning after his father's death, and that he certainly, on glancing at it, had been very much astonished to see that

that document was his father's will. Against that he declared that its contents did not astonish him in the slightest degree, that he himself knew of the testator's intentions, but that he certainly thought his father had entrusted the will to the care of Mr. Wethered, who did all his business for him.

"'I only very cursorily glanced at the signature,' he concluded, speaking in a perfectly calm, clear voice; 'you must understand that the thought of forgery was very far from my mind, and that my father's signature is exceedingly well imitated, if, indeed, it is not his own, which I am not at all prepared to believe. As for the two witnesses' signatures, I don't think I had ever seen them before. I took the document to Messrs. Barkston and Maud, who had often done business for me before, and they assured me that the will was in perfect form and order.'

"Asked why he had not entrusted the will to his father's solicitors, he replied:

"'For the very simple reason that exactly half an hour before the will was placed in my hands, I had read that Mr. Patrick Wethered had been murdered the night before. Mr. Hibbert, the junior partner, was not personally known to me.'

"After that, for form's sake, a good deal of expert evidence was heard on the subject of the dead man's signature. But that was quite unanimous, and merely went to corroborate what had already been established beyond a doubt, namely, that the will dated February 1st, 1908, was a forgery, and probate of the will dated 1891 was therefore granted to Mr. Murray Brooks, the sole executor mentioned therein."

3

"Two days later the police applied for a warrant for the arrest of Mr. Percival Brooks on a charge of forgery.

"The Crown prosecuted, and Mr. Brooks had again the support of Mr. Oranmore, the eminent K.C. Perfectly calm, like a man conscious of his own innocence and unable to grasp the idea that justice does sometimes miscarry, Mr. Brooks, the son of the millionaire, himself still the possessor of a very large fortune under the former will, stood up in the dock on that memorable day in October, 1908, which still no doubt lives in the memory of his many friends.

"All the evidence with regard to Mr. Brooks' last moments and the forged will was gone through over again. That will, it was the contention of the Crown, had been forged so entirely in favour of the accused, cutting out everyone else, that obviously no one but the beneficiary under that false will would have had any motive in forging it.

"Very pale, and with a frown between his deep-set, handsome Irish eyes, Percival Brooks listened to this large volume of evidence piled up against him by the Crown.

"At times he held brief consultations with Mr. Oranmore, who seemed as cool as a cucumber. Have you ever seen Oranmore in court? He is a character worthy of Dickens. His pronounced brogue, his fat, podgy, clean-shaven face, his not always immaculately clean large hands, have often delighted the caricaturist. As it very soon transpired during that memorable magisterial inquiry, he relied for a verdict in favour of his client upon two main points, and he had concentrated all his skill upon making these two points as telling as he possibly could.

"The first point was the question of time. John O'Neill, cross-examined by Oranmore, stated without hesitation that he had given the will to Mr. Percival at eleven o'clock in the morning. And now the eminent K.C. brought forward and placed in the witness-box the very lawyers into whose hands the accused had then immediately placed the will. Now, Mr. Barkston, a very well-known solicitor of King Street, declared positively that Mr. Percival Brooks was in his office at a quarter before twelve; two of his clerks testified to the same time exactly, and it was *impossible*, contended Mr. Oranmore, that within three-quarters of an hour Mr. Brooks could have gone to a stationer's, bought a will form, copied Mr. Wethered's writing, his father's signature, and that of John O'Neill and Pat Mooney.

"Such a thing might have been planned, arranged, practised, and ultimately, after a great deal of trouble, successfully carried out, but human intelligence could not grasp the other as a possibility.

"Still the judge wavered. The eminent K.C. had shaken but not shattered his belief in the prisoner's guilt. But there was one point more, and this Oranmore, with the skill of a dramatist, had reserved for the fall of the curtain.

"He noted every sign in the judge's face, he guessed that his client was not yet absolutely safe, then only did he produce his last two witnesses.

"One of them was Mary Sullivan, one of the housemaids in the Fitzwilliam mansion. She had been sent up by the cook at a quarter past four o'clock on the afternoon of February 1st with some hot water, which the nurse had ordered, for the master's room. Just as she was about to knock at the door Mr. Wethered was coming out of the room. Mary stopped with the tray in her hand, and at the door Mr. Wethered turned and said quite loudly: 'Now, don't fret, don't be anxious; do try and be calm. Your will is safe in my pocket, nothing can change it or alter one word of it but yourself.'

"It was, of course, a very ticklish point in law whether the housemaid's evidence could be accepted. You see, she was quoting the words of a man since dead, spoken to another man also dead. There is no doubt that had there been very strong evidence on the other side against Percival Brooks, Mary Sullivan's would have counted for nothing; but, as I told you before, the judge's belief in the prisoner's guilt was already very seriously shaken, and now the final blow aimed at it by Mr. Oranmore shattered his last lingering doubts.

"Dr. Mulligan, namely, had been placed by Mr. Oranmore into the witness-box. He was a medical man of unimpeachable authority, in fact, absolutely at the head of his profession in Dublin. What he said practically corroborated Mary Sullivan's testimony. He had gone in to see Mr. Brooks at half-past four, and understood from him that his lawyer had just left him.

"Mr. Brooks certainly, though terribly weak, was calm and more composed. He was dying from a sudden heart attack, and Dr. Mulligan foresaw the almost immediate end. But he was still conscious and managed to murmur feebly: 'I feel much easier in my mind now, doctor—I have made my will—Wethered has been—he's got it in his pocket—it is safe there—safe from that—' But the words died on his lips, and after that he spoke but little. He saw his two sons before he died, but hardly knew them or even looked at them.

"You see," concluded the man in the corner, "you see that the prosecution was bound to collapse. Oranmore did not give it a leg to stand on. The will was forged, it is true, forged in the favour of Percival Brooks and of no one else, forged for him and for his benefit. Whether he knew and connived at the forgery was never proved or, as far as I know, even hinted, but it was impossible to go against all the evidence, which pointed that, as far as the act itself was concerned, he at least was innocent. You see, Dr. Mulligan's evidence was not to be shaken. Mary Sullivan's was equally strong.

"There were two witnesses swearing positively that old Brooks' will was in Mr. Wethered's keeping when that gentleman left the Fitzwilliam mansion at a quarter past four. At five o'clock in the afternoon the lawyer was found dead in Phoenix Park. Between a quarter past four and eight o'clock in the evening Percival Brooks never left the house—that was subsequently proved by Oranmore up to the hilt and beyond a doubt. Since the will found under old Brooks' pillow was a forged will, where then was the will he did make, and which Wethered carried away with him in his pocket?"

"Stolen, of course," said Polly, "by those who murdered and robbed him; it may have been of no value to them, but they naturally would destroy it, lest it might prove a clue against them."

"Then you think it was mere coincidence?" he asked excitedly.

"What?"

"That Wethered was murdered and robbed at the very moment that he carried the will in his pocket, whilst another was being forged in its place?"

"It certainly would be very curious, if it *were* a coincidence," she said musingly.

"Very," he repeated with biting sarcasm, whilst nervously his bony fingers played with the inevitable bit of string. "Very curious indeed. Just think of the whole thing. There was the old man with all his wealth, and two sons, one to whom he is devoted, and the other with whom he does nothing but quarrel. One day there is another of these quarrels, but more violent, more terrible than any that have previously occurred, with the result that the father, heartbroken by it all, has an attack of apoplexy and practically dies of a broken heart. After that he alters his will, and subsequently a will is proved which turns out to be a forgery.

"Now everybody—police, press, and public alike—at once jump to the conclusion that, as Percival Brooks benefits by that forged will, Percival Brooks must be the forger."

"Seek for him whom the crime benefits, is your own axiom," argued the girl.

"I beg your pardon?"

"Percival Brooks benefited to the tune of £ 2,000,000."

"I beg your pardon. He did nothing of the sort. He was left with less than half the share that his younger brother inherited."

"Now, yes; but that was a former will and—"

"And that forged will was so clumsily executed, the signature so carelessly imitated, that the forgery was bound to come to light. Did *that* never strike you?"

"Yes, but—"

"There is no but," he interrupted. "It was all as clear as daylight to me from the very first. The quarrel with the old man, which broke

126

his heart, was not with his eldest son, with whom he was used to quarrelling, but with the second son whom he idolised, in whom he believed. Don't you remember how John O'Neill heard the words 'liar' and 'deceit'? Percival Brooks had never deceived his father. His sins were all on the surface. Murray had led a quiet life, had pandered to his father, and fawned upon him, until, like most hypocrites, he at last got found out. Who knows what ugly gambling debt or debt of honour, suddenly revealed to old Brooks, was the cause of that last and deadly quarrel?

"You remember that it was Percival who remained beside his father and carried him up to his room. Where was Murray throughout that long and painful day, when his father lay dying—he, the idolised son, the apple of the old man's eye? You never hear his name mentioned as being present there all that day. But he knew that he had offended his father mortally, and that his father meant to cut him off with a shilling. He knew that Mr. Wethered had been sent for, that Wethered left the house soon after four o'clock.

"And here the cleverness of the man comes in. Having lain in wait for Wethered and knocked him on the back of the head with a stick, he could not very well make that will disappear altogether. There remained the faint chance of some other witnesses knowing that Mr. Brooks had made a fresh will, Mr. Wethered's partner, his clerk, or one of the confidential servants in the house. Therefore, *a* will must be discovered after the old man's death.

"Now, Murray Brooks was not an expert forger, it takes years of training to become that. A forged will executed by himself would be sure to be found out—yes, that's it, sure to be found out. The forgery will be palpable—let it be palpable, and then it will be found out, branded as such, and the original will of 1891, so favourable to the young blackguard's interests, would be held as valid. Was it devilry or merely additional caution which prompted Murray to pen that forged will so glaringly in Percival's favour? It is impossible to say.

"Anyhow, it was the cleverest touch in that marvellously devised crime. To plan that evil deed was great, to execute it was easy enough. He had several hours' leisure in which to do it. Then at night it was simplicity itself to slip the document under the dead man's pillow. Sacrilege causes no shudder to such natures as Murray Brooks. The rest of the drama you know already——"

"But Percival Brooks?"

"The jury returned a verdict of 'Not guilty.' There was no evidence against him."

"But the money? Surely the scoundrel does not have the enjoyment of it still?"

"No; he enjoyed it for a time, but he died about three months ago, and forgot to take the precaution of making a will, so his brother Percival has got the business after all. If you ever go to Dublin, I should order some of Brooks' bacon if I were you. It is very good."

An Unparalleled Outrage

(A.k.a. *The Brighton Mystery*)

1

"Do you care for the seaside?" asked the man in the corner when he had finished his lunch. "I don't mean the seaside at Ostend or Trouville, but honest English seaside with n——r minstrels, three-shilling excursionists, and dirty, expensive furnished apartments, where they charge you a shilling for lighting the hall gas on Sundays and sixpence on other evenings. Do you care for that?"

"I prefer the country."

"Ah! perhaps it is preferable. Personally, I only liked one of our English seaside resorts once, and that was for a week, when Edward Skinner was up before the magistrate, charged with what was known as the 'Brighton Outrage.' I don't know if you remember the memorable day in Brighton, memorable for that elegant town, which deals more in amusements than mysteries, when Mr. Francis Morton, one of its most noted residents, disappeared. Yes! disappeared as completely as any vanishing lady in a music-hall. He was wealthy, had a fine house, servants, a wife and children, and he disappeared. There was no getting away from that.

"Mr. Francis Morton lived with his wife in one of the large houses in Sussex Square at the Kemp Town end of Brighton. Mrs. Morton was well known for her Americanisms, her swagger dinner parties, and beautiful Paris gowns. She was the daughter of one of the many American millionaires (I think her father was a Chicago pork-butcher), who conveniently provide wealthy wives for English gentlemen; and she had married Mr. Francis Morton a few years ago and brought him her quarter of a million, for no other reason but that she fell in love with him. He was neither good-looking nor distinguished, in fact, he was one of those men who seem to have City stamped all over their person.

"He was a gentleman of very regular habits, going up to London every morning on business and returning every afternoon by the 'hus-

129

band's train.' So regular was he in these habits that all the servants at the Sussex Square house were betrayed into actual gossip over the fact that on Wednesday, March 17th, the master was not home for dinner. Hales, the butler, remarked that the mistress seemed a bit anxious and didn't eat much food. The evening wore on and Mr. Morton did not appear.

"At nine o'clock the young footman was dispatched to the station to make inquiries whether his master had been seen there in the afternoon, or whether—which Heaven forbid—there had been an accident on the line. The young man interviewed two or three porters, the bookstall boy, and ticket clerk; all were agreed that Mr. Morton did not go up to London during the day; no one had seen him within the precincts of the station. There certainly had been no accident reported either on the up or down line.

"But the morning of the 18th came, with its usual postman's knock, but neither Mr. Morton nor any sign or news from him. Mrs. Morton, who evidently had spent a sleepless night, for she looked sadly changed and haggard, sent a wire to the hall porter at the large building in Cannon Street, where her husband had his office. An hour later she had the reply: 'Not seen Mr. Morton all day yesterday, not here today.' By the afternoon everyone in Brighton knew that a fellow-resident had mysteriously disappeared from or in the city.

"A couple of days, then another, elapsed, and still no sign of Mr. Morton. The police were doing their best. The gentleman was so well known in Brighton—as he had been a resident two years—that it was not difficult to firmly establish the one fact that he had not left the city, since no one saw him in the station on the morning of the 17th, nor at any time since then. Mild excitement prevailed throughout the town. At first the newspapers took the matter somewhat jocosely. 'Where is Mr. Morton?' was the usual placard on the evening's contents bills, but after three days had gone by and the worthy Brighton resident was still missing, while Mrs. Morton was seen to look more haggard and careworn every day, mild excitement gave place to anxiety.

"There were vague hints now as to foul play. The news had leaked out that the missing gentleman was carrying a large sum of money on the day of his disappearance. There were also vague rumours of a scandal not unconnected with Mrs. Morton herself and her own past history, which in her anxiety for her husband she had been forced to reveal to the detective-inspector in charge of the case.

"Then on Saturday the news which the late evening papers contained was this:

"'Acting on certain information received, the police today forced an entrance into one of the rooms of Russell House, a high-class furnished apartment on the King's Parade, and there they discovered our missing distinguished townsman, Mr. Francis Morton, who had been robbed and subsequently locked up in that room since Wednesday, the 17th. When discovered he was in the last stages of inanition; he was tied into an armchair with ropes, a thick wool shawl had been wound round his mouth, and it is a positive marvel that, left thus without food and very little air, the unfortunate gentleman survived the horrors of these four days of incarceration.

"'He has been conveyed to his residence in Sussex Square, and we are pleased to say that Doctor Mellish, who is in attendance, has declared his patient to be out of serious danger, and that with care and rest he will be soon quite himself again.

"'At the same time our readers will learn with unmixed satisfaction that the police of our city, with their usual acuteness and activity, have already discovered the identity and whereabouts of the cowardly ruffian who committed this unparalleled outrage.'"

2

"I really don't know," continued the man in the corner blandly, "what it was that interested me in the case from the very first. Certainly, it had nothing very out of the way or mysterious about it, but I journeyed down to Brighton nevertheless, as I felt that something deeper and more subtle lay behind that extraordinary assault, following a robbery, no doubt.

"I must tell you that the police had allowed it to be freely circulated abroad that they held a clue. It had been easy enough to ascertain who the lodger was who had rented the furnished room in Russell House. His name was supposed to be Edward Skinner, and he had taken the room about a fortnight ago, but had gone away ostensibly for two or three days on the very day of Mr. Morton's mysterious disappearance. It was on the 20th that Mr. Morton was found, and thirty-six hours later the public were gratified to hear that Mr. Edward Skinner had been traced to London and arrested on the charge of assault upon the person of Mr. Francis Morton and of robbing him of the sum of £10,000.

"Then a further sensation was added to the already bewildering case by the startling announcement that Mr. Francis Morton refused to prosecute.

"Of course, the Treasury took up the case and subpoenaed Mr. Morton as a witness, so that gentleman—if he wished to hush the matter up, or had been in any way terrorised into a promise of doing so—gained nothing by his refusal, except an additional amount of curiosity in the public mind and further sensation around the mysterious case.

"It was all this, you see, which had interested me and brought me down to Brighton on March 23rd to see the prisoner Edward Skinner arraigned before the beak. I must say that he was a very ordinary-looking individual. Fair, of ruddy complexion, with snub nose and the beginning of a bald place on the top of his head, he, too, looked the embodiment of a prosperous, stodgy 'City gent.'

"I took a quick survey of the witnesses present, and guessed that the handsome, stylish woman sitting next to Mr. Reginald Pepys, the noted lawyer for the Crown, was Mrs. Morton.

"There was a large crowd in court, and I heard whispered comments among the feminine portion thereof as to the beauty of Mrs. Morton's gown, the value of her large picture hat, and the magnificence of her diamond rings.

"The police gave all the evidence required with regard to the finding of Mr. Morton in the room at Russell House and also to the arrest of Skinner at the Langham Hotel in London. It appears that the prisoner seemed completely taken aback at the charge preferred against him, and declared that though he knew Mr. Francis Morton slightly in business he knew nothing as to his private life.

"'Prisoner stated,' continued Inspector Buckle, 'that he was not even aware Mr. Morton lived in Brighton, but I have evidence here, which I will place before Your Honour, to prove that the prisoner was seen in the company of Mr. Morton at 9.30 o'clock on the morning of the assault.'

"Cross-examined by Mr. Matthew Quiller, the detective-inspector admitted that prisoner merely said that he did not know that Mr. Morton was a *resident* of Brighton—he never denied having met him there.

"The witness, or rather witnesses, referred to by the police were two Brighton tradesmen who knew Mr. Morton by sight and had seen him on the morning of the 17th walking with the accused.

"In this instance Mr. Quiller had no question to ask of the witnesses, and it was generally understood that the prisoner did not wish to contradict their statement.

"Constable Hartrick told the story of the finding of the unfortunate Mr. Morton after his four days' incarceration. The constable had been sent round by the chief inspector, after certain information given by Mrs. Chapman, the landlady of Russell House. He had found the door locked and forced it open. Mr. Morton was in an armchair, with several yards of rope wound loosely round him; he was almost unconscious, and there was a thick wool shawl tied round his mouth which must have deadened any cry or groan the poor gentleman might have uttered. But, as a matter of fact, the constable was under the impression that Mr. Morton had been either drugged or stunned in some way at first, which had left him weak and faint and prevented him from making himself heard or extricating himself from his bonds, which were very clumsily, evidently very hastily, wound round his body.

"The medical officer who was called in, and also Dr. Mellish who attended Mr. Morton, both said that he seemed dazed by some stupefying drug, and also, of course, terribly weak and faint with the want of food.

"The first witness of real importance was Mrs. Chapman, the proprietress of Russell House, whose original information to the police led to the discovery of Mr. Morton. In answer to Mr. Pepys, she said that on March 1st the accused called at her house and gave his name as Mr. Edward Skinner.

"'He required, he said, a furnished room at a moderate rental for a permanency, with full attendance when he was in, but he added that he would often be away for two or three days, or even longer, at a time.

"'He told me that he was a traveller for a tea-house,' continued Mrs. Chapman, 'and I showed him the front room on the third floor, as he did not want to pay more than twelve shillings a week. I asked him for a reference, but he put three sovereigns in my hand, and said with a laugh that he supposed paying for his room a month in advance was sufficient reference; if I didn't like him after that, I could give him a week's notice to quit.'

"'You did not think of asking him the name of the firm for which he travelled?' asked Mr. Pepys.

"'No, I was quite satisfied as he paid me for the room. The next day he sent in his luggage and took possession of the room. He went out most mornings on business, but was always in Brighton for Saturday and Sunday. On the 16th he told me that he was going to Liverpool

" He had found the door locked, and forced it open."

for a couple of days; he slept in the house that night, and went off early on the 17th, taking his portmanteau with him.'

"'At what time did he leave?' asked Mr. Pepys.

"'I couldn't say exactly,' replied Mrs. Chapman with some hesitation. 'You see this is the off season here. None of my rooms are let, except the one to Mr. Skinner, and I only have one servant. I keep four during the summer, autumn, and winter season,' she added with conscious pride, fearing that her former statement might prejudice the reputation of Russell House. 'I thought I had heard Mr. Skinner go out about nine o'clock, but about an hour later the girl and I were both in the basement, and we heard the front door open and shut with a bang, and then a step in the hall.

"'"That's Mr. Skinner," said Mary. "So it is," I said, "why, I thought he had gone an hour ago." "He did go out then," said Mary, "for he left his bedroom door open and I went in to do his bed and tidy his room." "Just go and see if that's him, Mary," I said, and Mary ran up to the hall and up the stairs, and came back to tell me that that was Mr. Skinner all right enough; he had gone straight up to his room. Mary didn't see him, but he had another gentleman with him, as she could hear them talking in Mr. Skinner's room.'

"'Then you can't tell us at what time the prisoner left the house finally?'

"'No, that I can't. I went out shopping soon after that. When I came in it was twelve o'clock. I went up to the third floor and found that Mr. Skinner had locked his door and taken the key with him. As I knew Mary had already done the room, I did not trouble more about it, though I did think it strange for a gentleman to lock up his room and not leave the key with me.'

"'And, of course, you heard no noise of any kind in the room then?'

"'No. Not that day or the next, but on the third day Mary and I both thought we heard a funny sound. I said that Mr. Skinner had left his window open, and it was the blind flapping against the window-pane; but when we heard that funny noise again, I put my ear to the keyhole and I thought I could hear a groan. I was very frightened, and sent Mary for the police.'

"Mrs. Chapman had nothing more of interest to say. The prisoner certainly was her lodger. She had last seen him on the evening of the 16th going up to his room with his candle. Mary the servant had much the same story to relate as her mistress.

135

"'I think it was 'im, right enough,' said Mary guardedly. 'I didn't see 'im, but I went up to 'is landing and stopped a moment outside 'is door. I could 'ear loud voices in the room—gentlemen talking.'

"'I suppose you would not do such a thing as to listen, Mary?' queried Mr. Pepys with a smile.

"'No, sir,' said Mary with a bland smile, 'I didn't catch what the gentlemen said, but one of them spoke so loud I thought they must be quarrelling.'

"'Mr. Skinner was the only person in possession of a latch-key, I presume. No one else could have come in without ringing at the door?'

"'Oh no, sir.'

"That was all. So far, you see, the case was progressing splendidly for the Crown against the prisoner. The contention, of course, was that Skinner had met Mr. Morton, brought him home with him, assaulted, drugged, then gagged and bound him, and finally robbed him of whatever money he had in his possession, which, according to certain affidavits which presently would be placed before the magistrate, amounted to £10,000 in notes.

"But in all this there still remained the great element of mystery for which the public and the magistrate would demand an explanation: namely, what were the relationships between Mr. Morton and Skinner, which had induced the former to refuse the prosecution of the man who had not only robbed him, but had so nearly succeeded in leaving him to die a terrible and lingering death?

"Mr. Morton was too ill as yet to appear in person. Dr. Mellish had absolutely forbidden his patient to undergo the fatigue and excitement of giving evidence himself in court that day. But his depositions had been taken at his bedside, were sworn to by him, and were now placed before the magistrate by the prosecuting counsel, and the facts they revealed were certainly as remarkable as they were brief and enigmatical.

"As they were read by Mr. Pepys, an awed and expectant hush seemed to descend over the large crowd gathered there, and all necks were strained eagerly forward to catch a glimpse of a tall, elegant woman, faultlessly dressed and wearing exquisite jewellery, but whose handsome face wore, as the prosecuting counsel read her husband's deposition, a more and more ashen hue.

"'This, Your Honour, is the statement made upon oath by Mr. Francis Morton,' commenced Mr. Pepys in that loud, sonorous voice of his which sounds so impressive in a crowded and hushed court. "'I was obliged, for certain reasons which I refuse to disclose, to make a payment of a large sum of money to a man whom I did not know and have never seen. It was in a matter of which my wife was cognisant and which had entirely to do with her own affairs. I was merely the go-between, as I thought it was not fit that she should see to this matter herself. The individual in question had made certain demands, of which she kept me in ignorance as long as she could, not wishing to unnecessarily worry me. At last, she decided to place the whole matter before me, and I agreed with her that it would be best to satisfy the man's demands.

""'I then wrote to that individual whose name I do not wish to disclose, addressing the letter, as my wife directed me to do, to the Brighton post office, saying that I was ready to pay the £10,000 to him, at any place or time and in what manner he might appoint. I received a reply which bore the Brighton postmark, and which desired me to be outside Furnival's, the drapers, in West Street, at 9.30 on the morning of March 17th, and to bring the money (£10,000) in Bank of England notes.

""'On the 16th my wife gave me a cheque for the amount and I cashed it at her bank—Bird's in Fleet Street. At half-past nine the following morning I was at the appointed place. An individual wearing a grey overcoat, bowler hat, and red tie accosted me by name and requested me to walk as far as his lodgings in the King's Parade. I followed him. Neither of us spoke. He stopped at a house which bore the name 'Russell House,' and which I shall be able to swear to as soon as I am able to go out. He let himself in with a latch-key, and asked me to follow him up to his room on the third floor. I thought I noticed when we were in the room that he locked the door; however, I had nothing of any value about me except the £10,000, which I was ready to give him. We had not exchanged the slightest word.

""'I gave him the notes, and he folded them and put them in his pocket-book. Then I turned towards the door, and, without the slightest warning, I felt myself suddenly gripped by the shoulder, while a handkerchief was pressed to my nose and mouth. I struggled as best I could, but the handkerchief was saturated with chloroform, and I soon lost consciousness. I hazily remember the man saying to me in short, jerky sentences, spoken at intervals while I was still weakly struggling:

""'What a fool you must think me, my dear sir! Did you really think that I was going to let you quietly walk out of here, straight to the police-station, eh? Such dodges have been done before, I know, when a man's silence has to be bought for money. Find out who he is, see where he lives, give him the money, then inform against him. No, you don't! not this time. I am off to the Continong with this £10,000, and I can get to Newhaven in time for the midday boat, so you'll have to keep quiet until I am the other side of the Channel, my friend. You won't be much inconvenienced; my landlady will hear your groans presently and release you, so you'll be all right. There, now, drink this—that's better.' He forced something bitter down my throat, then I remember nothing more.

"""When I regained consciousness, I was sitting in an armchair with some rope tied round me and a wool shawl round my mouth. I hadn't the strength to make the slightest effort to disentangle myself or to utter a scream. I felt terribly sick and faint.""

"Mr. Reginald Pepys had finished reading, and no one in that crowded court had thought of uttering a sound; the magistrate's eyes were fixed upon the handsome lady in the magnificent gown, who was mopping her eyes with a dainty lace handkerchief.

"The extraordinary narrative of the victim of so daring an outrage had kept everyone in suspense; one thing was still expected to make the measure of sensation as full as it had ever been over any criminal case, and that was Mrs. Morton's evidence. She was called by the prosecuting counsel, and slowly, gracefully, she entered the witness-box. There was no doubt that she had felt keenly the tortures which her husband had undergone, and also the humiliation of seeing her name dragged forcibly into this ugly, blackmailing scandal.

"Closely questioned by Mr. Reginald Pepys, she was forced to admit that the man who blackmailed her was connected with her early life in a way which would have brought terrible disgrace upon her and upon her children. The story she told, amidst many tears and sobs, and much use of her beautiful lace handkerchief and beringed hands, was exceedingly pathetic.

"It appears that when she was barely seventeen, she was inveigled into a secret marriage with one of those foreign adventurers who swarm in every country, and who styled himself Comte Armand de la Tremouille. He seems to have been a blackguard of unusually low pattern, for, after he had extracted from her some £200 of her pin money and a few diamond brooches, he left her one fine day with a laconic word to say that he was sailing for Europe by the *Argentina*, and would not be back for some time. She was in love with the brute, poor young soul, for when, a week later, she read that the *Argentina* was wrecked, and presumably every soul on board had perished, she wept very many bitter tears over her early widowhood.

"Fortunately, her father, a very wealthy pork-butcher of Chicago, had known nothing of his daughter's culpable foolishness. Four years later he took her to London, where she met Mr. Francis Morton and married him. She led six or seven years of very happy married life when one day, like a thunderbolt from a clear, blue sky, she received a typewritten letter, signed 'Armand de la Tremouille,' full of protestations of undying love, telling a long and pathetic tale of years of suffering in a foreign land, whither he had drifted after having been rescued almost miraculously from the wreck of the *Argentina*, and where he never had been able to scrape a sufficient amount of money to pay for his passage home. At last fate had favoured him. He had, after many vicissitudes, found the whereabouts of his dear wife, and was now ready to forgive all that was past and take her to his loving arms once again.

"What followed was the usual course of events when there is a blackguard and a fool of a woman. She was terrorised and did not dare to tell her husband for some time; she corresponded with the Comte de la Tremouille, begging him for her sake and in memory of the past not to attempt to see her. She found him amenable to reason in the shape of several hundred pounds which passed through the Brighton post office into his hands. At last, one day, by accident, Mr. Morton came across one of the Comte de la Tremouille's interesting letters. She confessed everything, throwing herself upon her husband's mercy.

"Now, Mr. Francis Morton was a business man, who viewed life practically and soberly. He liked his wife, who kept him in luxury, and wished to keep her, whereas the Comte de la Tremouille seemed willing enough to give her up for a consideration. Mrs. Morton, who had the sole and absolute control of her fortune, on the other hand, was willing enough to pay the price and hush up the scandal, which she believed—since she was a bit of a fool—would land her in prison for bigamy. Mr. Francis Morton wrote to the Comte de la Tremouille that his wife was ready to pay him the sum of £10,000 which he demanded in payment for her absolute liberty and his own complete disappearance out of her life now and for ever. The appointment was made, and Mr. Morton left his house at 9 a.m. on March 17th with the £10,000 in his pocket.

"The public and the magistrate had hung breathless upon her words. There was nothing but sympathy felt for this handsome woman, who throughout had been more sinned against than sinning, and whose gravest fault seems to have been a total lack of intelligence in dealing with her own life. But I can assure you of one thing, that in no case within my recollection was there ever such a sensation in a court as when the magistrate, after a few minutes' silence, said gently to Mrs. Morton:

"'And now, Mrs. Morton, will you kindly look at the prisoner, and tell me if in him you recognise your former husband?'

"And she, without even turning to look at the accused, said quietly:

"'Oh no! Your Honour! of course that man is *not* the Comte de la Tremouille.'"

3

"I can assure you that the situation was quite dramatic," continued the man in the corner, whilst his funny, claw-like hands took up a bit of string with renewed feverishness.

"In answer to further questions from the magistrate, she declared that she had never seen the accused; he might have been the go-between, however, that she could not say. The letters she received were all typewritten, but signed 'Armand de la Tremouille,' and certainly the signature was identical with that on the letters she used to receive from him years ago, all of which she had kept.

"'And did it *never* strike you,' asked the magistrate with a smile, 'that the letters you received might be forgeries?'

"'How could they be?' she replied decisively; 'no one knew of my marriage to the Comte de la Tremouille, no one in England certainly. And, besides, if someone did know the *comte* intimately enough to forge his handwriting and to blackmail me, why should that someone have waited all these years? I have been married seven years, Your Honour.'

"That was true enough, and there the matter rested as far as she was concerned. But the identity of Mr. Francis Morton's assailant had to be finally established, of course, before the prisoner was committed for trial. Dr. Mellish promised that Mr. Morton would be allowed to come to court for half an hour and identify the accused on the following day, and the case was adjourned until then. The accused was led away between two constables, bail being refused, and Brighton had perforce to moderate its impatience until the Wednesday.

"On that day the court was crowded to overflowing; actors, play-wrights, literary men of all sorts had fought for admission to study for themselves the various phases and faces in connection with the case. Mrs. Morton was not present when the prisoner, quiet and self-possessed, was brought in and placed in the dock. His solicitor was with him, and a sensational defence was expected.

"Presently there was a stir in the court, and that certain sound, half rustle, half sigh, which preludes an expected palpitating event. Mr. Morton, pale, thin, wearing yet in his hollow eyes the stamp of those five days of suffering, walked into court leaning on the arm of his doctor—Mrs. Morton was not with him.

"He was at once accommodated with a chair in the witness-box, and the magistrate, after a few words of kindly sympathy, asked him if he had anything to add to his written statement. On Mr. Morton replying in the negative, the magistrate added:

"'And now, Mr. Morton, will you kindly look at the accused in the dock and tell me whether you recognise the person who took you to the room in Russell House and then assaulted you?'

"Slowly the sick man turned towards the prisoner and looked at him; then he shook his head and replied quietly:

"'No, sir, that certainly was not the man.'

"'You are quite sure?' asked the magistrate in amazement, while the crowd literally gasped with wonder.

"'I swear it,' asserted Mr. Morton.

"'Can you describe the man who assaulted you?'

"'Certainly. He was dark, of swarthy complexion, tall, thin, with bushy eyebrows and thick black hair and short beard. He spoke English with just the faintest suspicion of a foreign accent.'

"The prisoner, as I told you before, was English in every feature. English in his ruddy complexion, and absolutely English in his speech.

"After that the case for the prosecution began to collapse. Everyone had expected a sensational defence, and Mr. Matthew Quiller, counsel for Skinner, fully justified all these expectations. He had no fewer than four witnesses present who swore positively that at 9.45 a.m. on the morning of Wednesday, March 17th, the prisoner was in the express train leaving Brighton for Victoria.

"Not being endowed with the gift of being in two places at once, and Mr. Morton having added the whole weight of his own evidence in Mr. Edward Skinner's favour, that gentleman was once more remanded by the magistrate, pending further investigation by the police, bail being allowed this time in two sureties of £50 each."

4

"Tell me what you think of it," said the man in the corner, seeing that Polly remained silent and puzzled.

"Well," she replied dubiously,"I suppose that the so-called Armand de la Tremouille's story was true in substance. That he did not perish on the *Argentina*, but drifted home, and blackmailed his former wife."

"Doesn't it strike you that there are at least two very strong points against that theory?" he asked, making two gigantic knots in his piece of string.

"Two?"

"Yes. In the first place, if the blackmailer was the 'Comte de la Tremouille' returned to life, why should he have been content to take £10,000 from a lady who was his lawful wife, and who could keep him in luxury for the rest of his natural life upon her large fortune, which was close upon a quarter of a million? The real Comte de la Tremouille, remember, had never found it difficult to get money out of his wife during their brief married life, whatever Mr. Morton's subsequent experience in the same direction might have been. And, secondly, why should he have typewritten his letters to his wife?"

"Because—"

"That was a point which, to my mind, the police never made the most of. Now, my experience in criminal cases has invariably been that when a typewritten letter figures in one, that letter is a forgery. It is not very difficult to imitate a signature, but it is a jolly sight more difficult to imitate a handwriting throughout an entire letter."

"Then, do you think—"

"I think, if you will allow me," he interrupted excitedly, "that we will go through the points—the sensible, tangible points of the case. Firstly: Mr. Morton disappears with £10,000 in his pocket for four entire days; at the end of that time, he is discovered loosely tied to an armchair, and a wool shawl round his mouth. Secondly: A man named Skinner is accused of the outrage. Mr. Morton, although he himself is able, mind you, to furnish the best defence possible for Skinner, by denying his identity with the man who assaulted him, refuses to prosecute. Why?"

"He did not wish to drag his wife's name into the case."

"He must have known that the Crown would take up the case. Then, again, how is it no one saw him in the company of the swarthy foreigner he described?"

"Two witnesses did see Mr. Morton in company with Skinner,"

argued Polly.

"Yes, at 9.20 in West Street; that would give Edward Skinner time to catch the 9.45 at the station, and to entrust Mr. Morton with the latch-key of Russell House," remarked the man in the corner dryly.

"What nonsense!" Polly ejaculated,

"Nonsense, is it?" he said, tugging wildly at his bit of string; "is it nonsense to affirm that if a man wants to make sure that his victim shall not escape, he does not usually wind rope 'loosely 'round his figure, nor does he throw a wool shawl lightly round his mouth. The police were idiotic beyond words; they themselves discovered that Morton was so 'loosely' fastened to his chair that very little movement would have disentangled him, and yet it never struck them that nothing was easier for that particular type of scoundrel to sit down in an armchair and wind a few yards of rope round himself, then, having wrapped a wool shawl round his throat, to slip his two arms inside the ropes."

"But what object would a man in Mr. Morton's position have for playing such extraordinary pranks?"

"Ah, the motive! There you are! What do I always tell you? Seek the motive! Now, what was Mr. Morton's position? He was the husband of a lady who owned a quarter of a million of money, not one penny of which he could touch without her consent, as it was settled on herself, and who, after the terrible way in which she had been plundered and then abandoned in her early youth, no doubt kept a very tight hold upon the purse-strings. Mr. Morton's subsequent life has proved that he had certain expensive, not altogether avowable, tastes. One day he discovers the old love letters of the 'Comte Armand de la Tremouille.'

"Then he lays his plans. He typewrites a letter, forges the signature of the erstwhile count, and awaits events. The fish does rise to the bait. He gets sundry bits of money, and his success makes him daring. He looks round him for an accomplice—clever, unscrupulous, greedy— and selects Mr. Edward Skinner, probably some former pal of his wild oats days.

"The plan was very neat, you must confess. Mr. Skinner takes the room in Russell House, and studies all the manners and customs of his landlady and her servant. He then draws the full attention of the police upon himself. He meets Morton in West Street, then disappears ostensibly after the 'assault.' In the meanwhile, Morton goes to Russell House. He walks upstairs, talks loudly in the room, then makes elaborate preparations for his comedy."

"Why! he nearly died of starvation!"

"That, I dare say, was not a part of his reckoning. He thought, no doubt, that Mrs. Chapman or the servant would discover and rescue him pretty soon. He meant to appear just a little faint, and endured quietly the first twenty-four hours of inanition. But the excitement and want of food told on him more than he expected. After twenty-four hours he turned very giddy and sick, and, falling from one fainting fit into another, was unable to give the alarm.

"However, he is all right again now, and concludes his part of a downright blackguard to perfection. Under the plea that his conscience does not allow him to live with a lady whose first husband is still alive, he has taken a bachelor flat in London, and only pays afternoon calls on his wife in Brighton. But presently he will tire of his bachelor life, and will return to his wife. And I'll guarantee that the Comte de la Tremouille will never be heard of again."

And that afternoon the man in the corner left Miss Polly Burton alone with a couple of photos of two uninteresting, stodgy, quiet-looking men—Morton and Skinner—who, if the old scarecrow was right in his theories, were a pair of the finest blackguards unhung.

The Regent's Park Murder

1

By this time Miss Polly Burton had become quite accustomed to her extraordinary *vis-à-vis* in the corner.

He was always there, when she arrived, in the self-same corner, dressed in one of his remarkable check tweed suits; he seldom said good morning, and invariably when she appeared he began to fidget with increased nervousness, with some tattered and knotty piece of string.

"Were you ever interested in the Regent's Park murder?" he asked her one day.

Polly replied that she had forgotten most of the particulars connected with that curious murder, but that she fully remembered the stir and flutter it had caused in a certain section of London Society.

"The racing and gambling set, particularly, you mean," he said, "All the persons implicated in the murder, directly or indirectly, were of the type commonly called 'Society men,' or 'men about town,' whilst the Harewood Club in Hanover Square, round which centred all the scandal in connection with the murder, was one of the smartest clubs in London.

"Probably the doings of the Harewood Club, which was essentially a gambling club, would for ever have remained 'officially' absent from the knowledge of the police authorities but for the murder in the Regent's Park and the revelations which came to light in connection with it.

"I dare say you know the quiet square which lies between Portland Place and the Regent's Park and is called Park Crescent at its south end, and subsequently Park Square East and West. The Marylebone Road, with all its heavy traffic, cuts straight across the large square and its pretty gardens, but the latter are connected together by a tunnel under the road; and of course, you must remember that the new tube station in the south portion of the Square had not yet been planned.

"February 6th, 1907, was a very foggy night, nevertheless Mr. Aaron Cohen, of 30, Park Square West, at two o'clock in the morning, having finally pocketed the heavy winnings which he had just swept off the green table of the Harewood Club, started to walk home alone. An hour later most of the inhabitants of Park Square West were aroused from their peaceful slumbers by the sounds of a violent altercation in the road. A man's angry voice was heard shouting violently for a minute or two, and was followed immediately by frantic screams of 'Police' and 'Murder.' Then there was the double sharp report of firearms, and nothing more.

"The fog was very dense, and, as you no doubt have experienced yourself, it is very difficult to locate sound in a fog. Nevertheless, not more than a minute or two had elapsed before Constable F 18, the point policeman at the corner of Marylebone Road, arrived on the scene, and, having first of all whistled for any of his comrades on the beat, began to grope his way about in the fog, more confused than effectually assisted by contradictory directions from the inhabitants of the houses close by, who were nearly falling out of the upper windows as they shouted out to the constable.

"'By the railings, policeman.'

"'Higher up the road.'

"'No, lower down.'

"'It was on this side of the pavement, I am sure.'

"'No, the other.'

"'At last, it was another policeman, F 22, who, turning into Park Square West from the north side, almost stumbled upon the body of a man lying on the pavement with his head against the railings of the Square. By this time quite a little crowd of people from the different houses in the road had come down, curious to know what had actually happened.

"The policeman turned the strong light of his bull's-eye lantern on the unfortunate man's face.

"'It looks as if he had been strangled, don't it?' he murmured to his comrade.

"And he pointed to the swollen tongue, the eyes half out of their sockets, bloodshot and congested, the purple, almost black, hue of the face.

"At this point one of the spectators, more callous to horrors, peered curiously into the dead man's face. He uttered an exclamation

"It looks as if he had been strangled."

of astonishment.

"'Why, surely, it's Mr. Cohen from No. 30!'

"The mention of a name familiar down the length of the street had caused two or three other men to come forward and to look more closely into the horribly distorted mask of the murdered man.

"'Our next-door neighbour, undoubtedly,' asserted Mr. Ellison, a young barrister, residing at No. 31.

"'What in the world was he doing this foggy night all alone, and on foot?' asked somebody else.

"'He usually came home very late. I fancy he belonged to some gambling club in town. I dare say he couldn't get a cab to bring him out here. Mind you, I don't know much about him. We only knew him to nod to.'

"'Poor beggar! it looks almost like an old-fashioned case of garrotting.'

"'Anyway, the blackguardly murderer, whoever he was, wanted to make sure he had killed his man!' added Constable P 18, as he picked up an object from the pavement. 'Here's the revolver, with two cartridges missing. You gentlemen heard the report just now?'

"'He don't seem to have hit him though. The poor bloke was strangled, no doubt.'

"'And tried to shoot at his assailant, obviously,' asserted the young barrister with authority.

"'If he succeeded in hitting the brute, there might be a chance of tracing the way he went.'

"'But not in the fog.'

"Soon, however, the appearance of the inspector, detective, and medical officer, who had quickly been informed of the tragedy, put an end to further discussion.

"The bell at No. 30 was rung, and the servants—all four of them women—were asked to look at the body.

"Amidst tears of horror and screams of fright, they all recognised in the murdered man their master, Mr. Aaron Cohen. He was therefore conveyed to his own room pending the coroner's inquest.

"The police had a pretty difficult task, you will admit; there were so very few indications to go by, and at first literally no clue.

"The inquest revealed practically nothing. Very little was known in the neighbourhood about Mr. Aaron Cohen and his affairs. His female servants did not even know the name or whereabouts of the various clubs he frequented.

"He had an office in Throgmorton Street and went to business every day. He dined at home, and sometimes had friends to dinner. When he was alone, he invariably went to the club, where he stayed until the small hours of the morning.

"The night of the murder he had gone out at about nine o'clock. That was the last his servants had seen of him. With regard to the revolver, all four servants swore positively that they had never seen it before, and that, unless Mr. Cohen had bought it that very day, it did not belong to their master.

"Beyond that, no trace whatever of the murderer had been found, but on the morning after the crime a couple of keys linked together by a short metal chain were found close to a gate at the opposite end of the Square, that which immediately faced Portland Place. These were proved to be, firstly, Mr. Cohen's latchkey, and, secondly, his gate-key of the Square.

"It was therefore presumed that the murderer, having accomplished his fell design and ransacked his victim's pockets, had found the keys and made good his escape by slipping into the Square, cutting under the tunnel, and out again by the further gate. He then took the precaution not to carry the keys with him any further, but threw them away and disappeared in the fog.

"The jury returned a verdict of wilful murder against some person or persons unknown, and the police were put on their mettle to discover the unknown and daring murderer. The result of their investigations, conducted with marvellous skill by Mr. William Fisher, led, about a week after the crime, to the sensational arrest of one of London's smartest young bucks.

"The case Mr. Fisher had got up against the accused briefly amounted to this:

"On the night of February 6th, soon after midnight, play began to run very high at the Harewood Club, in Hanover Square. Mr. Aaron Cohen held the bank at roulette against some twenty or thirty of his friends, mostly young fellows with no wits and plenty of money. 'The Bank' was winning heavily, and it appears that this was the third consecutive night on which Mr. Aaron Cohen had gone home richer by several hundreds than he had been at the start of play.

"Young John Ashley, who is the son of a very worthy county gentleman who is M.F.H. somewhere in the Midlands, was losing heavily, and in his case also it appears that it was the third consecutive night that Fortune had turned her face against him.

"Remember," continued the man in the corner, "that when I tell you all these details and facts, I am giving you the combined evidence of several witnesses, which it took many days to collect and to classify.

"It appears that young Mr. Ashley, though very popular in society, was generally believed to be in what is vulgarly termed 'low water'; up to his eyes in debt, and mortally afraid of his dad, whose younger son he was, and who had on one occasion threatened to ship him off to Australia with a £5 note in his pocket if he made any further extravagant calls upon his paternal indulgence.

"It was also evident to all John Ashley's many companions that the worthy M.F.H. held the purse-strings in a very tight grip. The young man, bitten with the desire to cut a smart figure in the circles in which he moved, had often recourse to the varying fortunes which now and again smiled upon him across the green tables in the Harewood Club.

"Be that as it may, the general consensus of opinion at the Club was that young Ashley had changed his last 'pony' before he sat down to a turn of roulette with Aaron Cohen on that particular night of February 6th.

"It appears that all his friends, conspicuous among whom was Mr. Walter Hatherell, tried their very best to dissuade him from pitting his luck against that of Cohen, who had been having a most unprecedented run of good fortune. But young Ashley, heated with wine, exasperated at his own bad luck, would listen to no one; he tossed one £5 note after another on the board, he borrowed from those who would lend, then played on parole for a while. Finally, at half-past one in the morning, after a run of nineteen on the red, the young man found himself without a penny in his pockets, and owing a debt—a gambling debt—a debt of honour of £1,500 to Mr. Aaron Cohen.

"Now we must render this much maligned gentleman that justice which was persistently denied to him by press and public alike; it was positively asserted by all those present that Mr. Cohen himself repeatedly tried to induce young Mr. Ashley to give up playing. He himself was in a delicate position in the matter, as he was the winner, and once or twice the taunt had risen to the young man's lips, accusing the holder of the bank of the wish to retire on a competence before the break in his luck.

"Mr. Aaron Cohen, smoking the best of Havanas, had finally shrugged his shoulders and said: 'As you please!'

"But at half-past one he had had enough of the player, who always lost and never paid—never could pay, so Mr. Cohen probably believed. He therefore at that hour refused to accept Mr. John Ashley's 'promissory' stakes any longer. A very few heated words ensued, quickly checked by the management, who are ever on the alert to avoid the least suspicion of scandal.

"In the meanwhile, Mr. Hatherell, with great good sense, persuaded young Ashley to leave the Club and all its temptations and go home; if possible, to bed.

"The friendship of the two young men, which was very well known in society, consisted chiefly, it appears, in Walter Hatherell being the willing companion and helpmeet of John Ashley in his mad and extravagant pranks. But tonight the latter, apparently tardily sobered by his terrible and heavy losses, allowed himself to be led away by his friend from the scene of his disasters. It was then about twenty minutes to two.

"Here the situation becomes interesting," continued the man in the corner in his nervous way. "No wonder that the police interrogated at least a dozen witnesses before they were quite satisfied that every statement was conclusively proved.

"Walter Hatherell, after about ten minutes' absence, that is to say at ten minutes to two, returned to the club room. In reply to several inquiries, he said that he had parted with his friend at the corner of New Bond Street, since he seemed anxious to be alone, and that Ashley said he would take a turn down Piccadilly before going home—he thought a walk would do him good.

"At two o'clock or thereabouts Mr. Aaron Cohen, satisfied with his evening's work, gave up his position at the bank and, pocketing his heavy winnings, started on his homeward walk, while Mr. Walter Hatherell left the club half an hour later.

"At three o'clock precisely the cries of 'Murder' and the report of firearms were heard in Park Square West, and Mr. Aaron Cohen was found strangled outside the garden railings."

2

"Now at first sight the murder in the Regent's Park appeared both to police and public as one of those silly, clumsy crimes, obviously the work of a novice, and absolutely purposeless, seeing that it could but inevitably lead its perpetrators, without any difficulty, to the gallows.

"You see, a motive had been established. 'Seek him whom the crime benefits,' say our French *confrères*. But there was something more than that.

"Constable James Funnell, on his beat, turned from Portland Place into Park Crescent a few minutes after he had heard the clock at Holy Trinity Church, Marylebone, strike half-past two. The fog at that moment was perhaps not quite so dense as it was later on in the morning, and the policeman saw two gentlemen in overcoats and top-hats leaning arm in arm against the railings of the Square, close to the gate. He could not, of course, distinguish their faces because of the fog, but he heard one of them saying to the other:

"'It is but a question of time, Mr. Cohen, I know my father will pay the money for me, and you will lose nothing by waiting.'

"To this the other apparently made no reply, and the constable passed on; when he returned to the same spot, after having walked over his beat, the two gentlemen had gone, but later on it was near this very gate that the two keys referred to at the inquest had been found.

"Another interesting fact," added the man in the corner, with one of those sarcastic smiles of his which Polly could not quite explain, "was the finding of the revolver upon the scene of the crime. That revolver, shown to Mr. Ashley's valet, was sworn to by him as being the property of his master.

"All these facts made, of course, a very remarkable, so far quite unbroken, chain of circumstantial evidence against Mr. John Ashley. No wonder, therefore, that the police, thoroughly satisfied with Mr. Fisher's work and their own, applied for a warrant against the young man, and arrested him in his rooms in Clarges Street exactly a week after the committal of the crime.

"As a matter of fact, you know, experience has invariably taught me that when a murderer seems particularly foolish and clumsy, and proofs against him seem particularly damning, that is the time when the police should be most guarded against pitfalls.

"Now in this case, if John Ashley had indeed committed the murder in Regent's Park in the manner suggested by the police, he would have been a criminal in more senses than one, for idiocy of that kind is to my mind worse than many crimes.

"The prosecution brought its witnesses up in triumphal array one after another. There were the members of the Harewood Club—who had seen the prisoner's excited condition after his heavy gambling losses to Mr. Aaron Cohen; there was Mr. Hatherell, who, in spite of his friendship for Ashley, was bound to admit that he had parted from him at the corner of Bond Street at twenty minutes to two, and had not seen him again till his return home at five a.m.

"Then came the evidence of Arthur Chipps, John Ashley's valet. It proved of a very sensational character.

"He deposed that on the night in question his master came home at about ten minutes to two. Chipps had then not yet gone to bed. Five minutes later Mr. Ashley went out again, telling the valet not to sit up for him. Chipps could not say at what time either of the young gentlemen had come home.

"That short visit home—presumably to fetch the revolver—was thought to be very important, and Mr. John Ashley's friends felt that his case was practically hopeless.

"The valet's evidence and that of James Funnell, the constable, who had overheard the conversation near the park railings, were certainly the two most damning proofs against the accused. I assure you I was having a rare old time that day. There were two faces in court to watch which was the greatest treat I had had for many a day. One of these was Mr. John Ashley's.

"Here's his photo—short, dark, dapper, a little 'racy' in style, but otherwise he looks a son of a well-to-do farmer. He was very quiet and placid in court, and addressed a few words now and again to his solicitor. He listened gravely, and with an occasional shrug of the shoulders, to the recital of the crime, such as the police had reconstructed it, before an excited and horrified audience.

"Mr. John Ashley, driven to madness and frenzy by terrible financial difficulties, had first of all gone home in search of a weapon, then waylaid Mr. Aaron Cohen somewhere on that gentleman's way home. The young man had begged for delay. Mr. Cohen perhaps was obdurate; but Ashley followed him with his importunities almost to his door.

"There, seeing his creditor determined at last to cut short the painful interview, he had seized the unfortunate man at an unguarded moment from behind, and strangled him; then, fearing that his dastardly work was not fully accomplished, he had shot twice at the already dead body, missing it both times from sheer nervous excitement. The murderer then must have emptied his victim's pockets, and, finding the key of the garden, thought that it would be a safe way of evading capture by cutting across the squares, under the tunnel, and so through the more distant gate which faced Portland Place.

"The loss of the revolver was one of those unforeseen accidents which a retributive Providence places in the path of the miscreant, delivering him by his own act of folly into the hands of human justice.

"Mr. John Ashley, however, did not appear the least bit impressed by the recital of his crime. He had not engaged the services of one of the most eminent lawyers, expert at extracting contradictions from witnesses by skilful cross-examinations—oh, dear me, no! he had been contented with those of a dull, prosy, very second-rate limb of the law, who, as he called his witnesses, was completely innocent of any desire to create a sensation.

"He rose quietly from his seat, and, amidst breathless silence, called the first of three witnesses on behalf of his client. He called three—but he could have produced twelve—gentlemen, members of the Ashton Club in Great Portland Street, all of whom swore that at three o'clock on the morning of February 6th, that is to say, at the very moment when the cries of 'Murder' roused the inhabitants of Park Square West, and the crime was being committed, Mr. John Ashley was sitting quietly in the clubrooms of the Ashton playing bridge with the three witnesses. He had come in a few minutes before three—as the hall porter of the Club testified—and stayed for about an hour and a half.

"I need not tell you that this undoubted, this fully proved, *alibi* was a positive bomb-shell in the stronghold of the prosecution. The most accomplished criminal could not possibly be in two places at once, and though the Ashton Club transgresses in many ways against the gambling laws of our very moral country, yet its members belong to the best, most unimpeachable classes of society. Mr. Ashley had been seen and spoken to at the very moment of the crime by at least a dozen gentlemen whose testimony was absolutely above suspicion.

"Mr. John Ashley's conduct throughout this astonishing phase of the inquiry remained perfectly calm and correct. It was no doubt the consciousness of being able to prove his innocence with such absolute conclusion that had steadied his nerves throughout the proceedings.

"His answers to the magistrate were clear and simple, even on the ticklish subject of the revolver.

"'I left the club, sir,' he explained, 'fully determined to speak with Mr. Cohen alone in order to ask him for a delay in the settlement of my debt to him. You will understand that I should not care to do this in the presence of other gentlemen.

"I went home for a minute or two—not in order to fetch a revolver, as the police assert, for I always carry a revolver about with me in foggy weather—but in order to see if a very important business letter had come for me in my absence.

"'Then I went out again, and met Mr. Aaron Cohen not far from

154

the Harewood Club. I walked the greater part of the way with him, and our conversation was of the most amicable character. We parted at the top of Portland Place, near the gate of the Square, where the policeman saw us. Mr. Cohen then had the intention of cutting across the Square, as being a shorter way to his own house. I thought the Square looked dark and dangerous in the fog, especially as Mr. Cohen was carrying a large sum of money.

"'We had a short discussion on the subject, and finally I persuaded him to take my revolver, as I was going home only through very frequented streets, and moreover carried nothing that was worth stealing. After a little demur Mr. Cohen accepted the loan of my revolver, and that is how it came to be found on the actual scene of the crime; finally, I parted from Mr. Cohen a very few minutes after I had heard the church clock striking a quarter before three. I was at the Oxford Street end of Great Portland Street at five minutes to three, and it takes at least ten minutes to walk from where I was to the Ashton Club.'

"This explanation was all the more credible, mind you, because the question of the revolver had never been very satisfactorily explained by the prosecution. A man who has effectually strangled his victim would not discharge two shots of his revolver for, apparently, no other purpose than that of rousing the attention of the nearest passer-by. It was far more likely that it was Mr. Cohen who shot—perhaps wildly into the air, when suddenly attacked from behind. Mr. Ashley's explanation therefore was not only plausible, it was the only possible one.

"You will understand therefore how it was that, after nearly half an hour's examination, the magistrate, the police, and the public were alike pleased to proclaim that the accused left the court without a stain upon his character."

3

"Yes," interrupted Polly eagerly, since, for once, her acumen had been at least as sharp as his, "but suspicion of that horrible crime only shifted its taint from one friend to another, and, of course, I know—"

"But that's just it," he quietly interrupted, "you don't know—Mr. Walter Hatherell, of course, you mean. So did everyone else at once. The friend, weak and willing, committing a crime on behalf of his cowardly, yet more assertive friend who had tempted him to evil. It was a good theory; and was held pretty generally, I fancy, even by the police.

"I say 'even' because they worked really hard in order to build up a case against young Hatherell, but the great difficulty was that of time. At the hour when the policeman had seen the two men outside Park Square together, Walter Hatherell was still sitting in the Harewood Club, which he never left until twenty minutes to two. Had he wished to waylay and rob Aaron Cohen he would not have waited surely till the time when presumably the latter would already have reached home.

"Moreover, twenty minutes was an incredibly short time in which to walk from Hanover Square to Regent's Park without the chance of cutting across the squares, to look for a man, whose whereabouts you could not determine to within twenty yards or so, to have an argument with him, murder him, and ransack his pockets. And then there was the total absence of motive."

"But—" said Polly meditatively, for she remembered now that the Regent's Park murder, as it had been popularly called, was one of those which had remained as impenetrable a mystery as any other crime had ever been in the annals of the police.

The man in the corner cocked his funny birdlike head well on one side and looked at her, highly amused evidently at her perplexity.

"You do not see how that murder was committed?" he asked with a grin.

Polly was bound to admit that she did not.

"If you had happened to have been in Mr. John Ashley's predicament," he persisted, "you do not see how you could conveniently have done away with Mr. Aaron Cohen, pocketed his winnings, and then led the police of your country entirely by the nose, by proving an indisputable *alibi?*"

"I could not arrange conveniently," she retorted, "to be in two different places half a mile apart at one and the same time."

"No! I quite admit that you could not do this unless you also had a friend—"

"A friend? But you say—"

"I say that I admired Mr. John Ashley, for his was the head which planned the whole thing, but he could not have accomplished the fascinating and terrible drama without the help of willing and able hands."

"Even then—" she protested.

"Point number one," he began excitedly, fidgeting with his inevitable piece of string. "John Ashley and his friend Walter Hatherell leave the club together, and together decide on the plan of campaign.

156

Hatherell returns to the club, and Ashley goes to fetch the revolver—the revolver which played such an important part in the drama, but not the part assigned to it by the police. Now try to follow Ashley closely, as he dogs Aaron Cohen's footsteps.

"Do you believe that he entered into conversation with him? That he walked by his side? That he asked for delay? No! He sneaked behind him and caught him by the throat, as the garrotters used to do in the fog. Cohen was apoplectic, and Ashley is young and powerful. Moreover, he meant to kill—"

"But the two men talked together outside the Square gates," protested Polly, "one of whom was Cohen, and the other Ashley."

"Pardon me," he said, jumping up in his seat like a monkey on a stick, "there were not two men talking outside the Square gates. According to the testimony of James Funnell, the constable, two men were leaning arm in arm against the railings and *one* man was talking."

"Then you think that—"

"At the hour when James Funnell heard Holy Trinity clock striking half-past two Aaron Cohen was already dead. Look how simple the whole thing is," he added eagerly, "and how easy after that—easy, but oh, dear me! how wonderfully, how stupendously clever. As soon as James Funnell has passed on, John Ashley, having opened the gate, lifts the body of Aaron Cohen in his arms and carries him across the Square. The Square is deserted, of course, but the way is easy enough, and we must presume that Ashley had been in it before. Anyway, there was no fear of meeting anyone.

"In the meantime, Hatherell has left the club: as fast as his athletic legs can carry him, he rushes along Oxford Street and Portland Place. It had been arranged between the two miscreants that the Square gate should be left on the latch.

"Close on Ashley's heels now, Hatherell too cuts across the Square, and reaches the further gate in good time to give his confederate a hand in disposing the body against the railings. Then, without another instant's delay, Ashley runs back across the gardens, straight to the Ashton Club, throwing away the keys of the dead man, on the very spot where he had made it a point of being seen and heard by a passer-by.

"Hatherell gives his friend six or seven minutes' start, then he begins the altercation which lasts two or three minutes, and finally rouses the neighbourhood with cries of 'Murder' and report of pistol in order to establish that the crime was committed at the hour when its perpetrator has already made out an indisputable *alibi*."

"I don't know what you think of it all, of course," added the funny creature as he fumbled for his coat and his gloves, "but I call the planning of that murder—on the part of novices, mind you—one of the cleverest pieces of strategy I have ever come across. It is one of those cases where there is no possibility whatever now of bringing the crime home to its perpetrator or his abettor. They have not left a single proof behind them; they foresaw everything, and each acted his part with a coolness and courage which, applied to a great and good cause, would have made fine statesmen of them both.

"As it is, I fear, they are just a pair of young blackguards, who have escaped human justice, and have only deserved the full and ungrudging admiration of yours very sincerely."

He had gone. Polly wanted to call him back, but his meagre person was no longer visible through the glass door. There were many things she would have wished to ask of him—what were his proofs, his facts? His were theories, after all, and yet, somehow, she felt that he had solved once again one of the darkest mysteries of great criminal London.

The De Genneville Peerage

(A.k.a. *The Birmingham Mystery*)

The man in the corner rubbed his chin thoughtfully, and looked out upon the busy street below.

"I suppose," he said, "there is some truth in the saying that Providence watches over bankrupts, kittens, and lawyers."

"I didn't know there was such a saying," replied Polly, with guarded dignity.

"Isn't there? Perhaps I am misquoting; anyway, there should be. Kittens, it seems, live and thrive through social and domestic upheavals which would annihilate a self-supporting tom-cat, and today I read in the morning papers the account of a noble lord's bankruptcy, and in the society ones that of his visit at the house of a Cabinet minister, where he is the most honoured guest. As for lawyers, when Providence had exhausted all other means of securing their welfare, it brought forth the peerage cases."

"I believe, as a matter of fact, that this special dispensation of Providence, as you call it, requires more technical knowledge than any other legal complication that comes before the law courts," she said.

"And also, a great deal more money in the client's pocket than any other complication. Now, take the Brockelsby peerage case. Have you any idea how much money was spent over that soap bubble, which only burst after many hundreds, if not thousands, of pounds went in lawyers' and counsels' fees?"

"I suppose a great deal of money was spent on both sides," she replied, "until that sudden, awful issue—"

"Which settled the dispute effectually," he interrupted with a dry chuckle. "Of course, it is very doubtful if any reputable solicitor would have taken up the case. Timothy Beddingfield, the Birmingham lawyer, is a gentleman who—well—has had some misfortunes, shall we say? He is still on the rolls, mind you, but I doubt if any case would have its chances improved by his conducting it. Against that there is just this to be said, that some of these old peerages have such peculiar histories, and own such wonderful archives, that a claim is always worth investigating—you never know what may be the rights of it.

"I believe that, at first, everyone laughed over the pretensions of the Hon. Robert Ingram de Genneville to the joint title and part revenues of the old barony of Genneville, but, obviously, he *might* have got his case. It certainly sounded almost like a fairy-tale, this claim based upon the supposed validity of an ancient document over 400 years old. It was *then* that a mediaeval Lord de Genneville, more endowed with muscle than common sense, became during his turbulent existence much embarrassed and hopelessly puzzled through the presentation made to him by his lady of twin-born sons.

"His embarrassment chiefly arose from the fact that my lady's attendants, while ministering to the comfort of the mother, had, in a moment of absent-mindedness, so placed the two infants in their cot that subsequently no one, not even—perhaps least of all—the mother, could tell which was the one who had been the first to make his appearance into this troublesome and puzzling world,

"After many years of cogitation, during which the Lord de Genneville approached nearer to the grave and his sons to man's estate, he gave up trying to solve the riddle as to which of the twins should succeed to his title and revenues; he appealed to his Liege Lord and King—Edward, fourth of that name—and with the latter's august sanction he drew up a certain document, wherein he enacted that both his sons should, after his death, share his titles and goodly revenues, and that the first son born in wedlock of *either* father should subsequently be the sole heir.

"In this document was also added that if in future times should any Lords de Genneville be similarly afflicted with twin sons, who had equal rights to be considered the eldest born, the same rule should apply as to the succession.

"Subsequently a Lord de Genneville was created Earl of Brockelsby by one of the Stuart kings, but for four hundred years after its enactment the extraordinary deed of succession remained a mere tradition, the Countesses of Brockelsby having, seemingly, no predilection for twins. But in 1878 the mistress of Brockelsby Castle presented her lord with twin-born sons.

"Fortunately, in modern times, science is more wide-awake, and attendants more careful. The twin brothers did not get mixed up, and

one of them was styled Viscount Tirlemont, and was heir to the earl-
dom, whilst the other, born two hours later, was that fascinating, dashing young Guardsman, well known at Hurlingham, Goodwood, London, and in his own county—the Hon. Robert Ingram de Genneville.

"It certainly was an evil day for this brilliant young scion of the
ancient race when he lent an ear to Timothy Beddingfield. This man,
and his family before him, had been solicitors to the Earls of Brockelsby for many generations, but Timothy, owing to certain 'irregularities,' had forfeited the confidence of his client, the late earl.

"He was still in practice in Birmingham, however, and, of course,
knew the ancient family tradition anent the twin succession. Whether
he was prompted by revenge or merely self-advertisement no one
knows.

"Certain it is that he did advise the Hon. Robert de Genneve-
ille—who apparently had more debts than he conveniently could pay,
and more extravagant tastes than he could gratify on a younger son's
portion—to lay a claim, on his father's death, to the joint title and a
moiety of the revenues of the ancient barony of Genneville, that claim
being based upon the validity of the fifteenth-century document.

"You may gather how extensive were the pretensions of the Hon.
Robert from the fact that the greater part of Edgbaston is now built
upon land belonging to the old barony. Anyway, it was the last straw
in an ocean of debt and difficulties, and I have no doubt that Beddingfield had not much trouble in persuading the Hon. Robert to
commence litigation at once.

"The young Earl of Brockelsby's attitude, however, remained one
of absolute quietude in his nine points of the law. He was in possession
both of the title and of the document. It was for the other side to force
him to produce the one or to share the other.

"It was at this stage of the proceedings that the Hon. Robert was
advised to marry, in order to secure, if possible, the first male heir of
the next generation, since the young earl himself was still a bachelor. A
suitable *fiancée* was found for him by his friends in the person of Miss
Mabel Brandon, the daughter of a rich Birmingham manufacturer,
and the marriage was fixed to take place at Birmingham on Thursday,
September 15th, 1907.

"On the 13th the Hon. Robert Ingram de Genneville arrived at
the Castle Hotel in New Street for his wedding, and on the 14th, at
eight o'clock in the morning, he was discovered lying on the floor of
his bedroom—murdered.

"The shrieks of the chambermaid attracted some
of the waiters."

"The sensation which the awful and unexpected sequel to the De Genneville peerage case caused in the minds of the friends of both litigants was quite unparalleled. I don't think any crime of modern times created quite so much stir in all classes of society. Birmingham was wild with excitement, and the *employés* of the Castle Hotel had real difficulty in keeping off the eager and inquisitive crowd who thronged daily to the hall, vainly hoping to gather details of news relating to the terrible tragedy.

"At present there was but little to tell. The shrieks of the chamber-maid, who had gone into the Hon. Robert's room with his shaving water at eight o'clock, had attracted some of the waiters. Soon the manager and his secretary came up, and immediately sent for the police.

"It seemed at first sight as if the young man had been the victim of a homicidal maniac, so brutal had been the way in which he had been assassinated. The head and body were battered and bruised by some heavy stick or poker, almost past human shape, as if the murderer had wished to wreak some awful vengeance upon the body of his victim. In fact, it would be impossible to recount the gruesome aspect of that room and of the murdered man's body such as the police and the medical officer took note of that day.

"It was supposed that the murder had been committed the evening before, as the victim was dressed in his evening clothes, and all the lights in the room had been left fully turned on. Robbery, also, must have had a large share in the miscreant's motives, for the drawers and cupboards, the portmanteau and dressing-bag had been ransacked as if in search of valuables. On the floor there lay a pocket-book torn in half and only containing a few letters addressed to the Hon. Robert de Genneville.

"The Earl of Brockelsby, next-of-kin to the deceased, was also telegraphed for. He drove over from Brockelsby Castle, which is about seven miles from Birmingham. He was terribly affected by the awful-ness of the tragedy, and offered a liberal reward to stimulate the activity of the police in search of the miscreant.

"The inquest was fixed for the 17th, three days later, and the public was left wondering where the solution lay of the terrible and grue-some murder at the Castle Hotel."

2

"The central figure in the coroner's court that day was undoubt-edly the Earl of Brockelsby in deep black, which contrasted strongly with his florid complexion and fair hair. Sir Marmaduke Ingersoll, his solicitor, was with him, and he had already performed the painful duty of identifying the deceased as his brother. This had been an exceedingly painful duty owing to the terribly mutilated state of the body and face; but the clothes and various trinkets he wore, including a signet ring, had fortunately not tempted the brutal assassin, and it was through them chiefly that Lord Brockelsby was able to swear to the identity of his brother.

"The various *employés* at the hotel gave evidence as to the discovery of the body, and the medical officer gave his opinion as to the immediate cause of death. Deceased had evidently been struck at the back of the head with a poker or heavy stick, the murderer then venting his blind fury upon the body by battering in the face and bruising it in a way that certainly suggested the work of a maniac.

"Then the Earl of Brockelsby was called, and was requested by the coroner to state when he had last seen his brother alive.

"'The morning before his death,' replied his lordship, 'he came up to Birmingham by an early train, and I drove up from Brockelsby to see him. I got to the hotel at eleven o'clock and stayed with him for about an hour.'

"'And that is the last you saw of the deceased?'

"'That is the last I saw of him,' replied Lord Brockelsby.

"He seemed to hesitate for a moment or two as if in thought whether he should speak or not, and then to suddenly make up his mind to speak, for he added: 'I stayed in town the whole of that day, and only drove back to Brockelsby late in the evening. I had some business to transact, and put up at the Grand, as I usually do, and dined with some friends.'

"'Would you tell us at what time you returned to Brockelsby Castle?'

"'I think it must have been about eleven o'clock. It is a seven-mile drive from here.'

"'I believe,' said the coroner after a slight pause, during which the attention of all the spectators was riveted upon the handsome figure of the young man as he stood in the witness-box, the very personification of a high-bred gentleman, 'I believe that I am right in stating that there was an unfortunate legal dispute between your lordship and your brother?'

"'That is so.'

"The coroner stroked his chin thoughtfully for a moment or two, then he added:

"'In the event of the deceased's claim to the joint title and revenues of De Genneville being held good in the courts of law, there would be a great importance, would there not, attached to his marriage, which was to have taken place on the 15th?'

"'In that event, there certainly would be.'

"'Is the jury to understand, then, that you and the deceased parted on amicable terms after your interview with him in the morning?'

"The Earl of Brockelsby hesitated again for a minute or two, while the crowd and the jury hung breathless on his lips.

"'There was no enmity between us,' he replied at last.

"'From which we may gather that there may have been—shall I say—a slight disagreement at that interview?'

"'My brother had unfortunately been misled by the misrepresentations or perhaps the too optimistic views of his lawyer. He had been dragged into litigation on the strength of an old family document which he had never seen, which, moreover, is antiquated, and, owing to certain wording in it, invalid. I thought that it would be kinder and more considerate if I were to let my brother judge of the document for himself. I knew that when he had seen it he would be convinced of the absolutely futile basis of his claim, and that it would be a terrible disappointment to him. That is the reason why I wished to see him myself about it, rather than to do it through the more formal—perhaps more correct—medium of our respective lawyers. I placed the facts before him with, on my part, a perfectly amicable spirit.'

"The young Earl of Brockelsby had made this somewhat lengthy, perfectly voluntary explanation of the state of affairs in a calm, quiet voice, with much dignity and perfect simplicity, but the coroner did not seem impressed by it, for he asked very drily:

"'Did you part good friends?'

"'On my side absolutely so.'

"'But not on his?' insisted the coroner.

"'I think he felt naturally annoyed that he had been so ill-advised by his solicitors.'

"'And you made no attempt later on in the day to adjust any ill-feeling that may have existed between you and him?' asked the coroner, marking with strange, earnest emphasis every word he uttered.

"'If you mean did I go and see my brother again that day—no, I did not.'

"'And your lordship can give us no further information which might throw some light upon the mystery which surrounds the Hon. Robert de Genneville's death?' still persisted the coroner.

"'I am sorry to say I cannot,' replied the Earl of Brockelsby with firm decision.

"The coroner still looked puzzled and thoughtful. It seemed at first as if he wished to press his point further; everyone felt that some deep import had lain behind his examination of the witness, and all were on tenterhooks as to what the next evidence might bring forth. The Earl of Brockelsby had waited a minute or two, then, at a sign from the coroner, had left the witness-box in order to have a talk with his solicitor.

"At first, he paid no attention to the depositions of the cashier and hall porter of the Castle Hotel, but gradually it seemed to strike him that curious statements were being made by these witnesses, and a frown of anxious wonder settled between his brows, whilst his young face lost some of its florid hue.

"Mr. Tremlett, the cashier at the hotel, had been holding the attention of the court. He stated that the Hon. Robert Ingram de Genneville had arrived at the hotel at eight o'clock on the morning of the 13th; he had the room which he usually occupied when he came to the 'Castle,' namely, No. 21, and he went up to it immediately on his arrival, ordering some breakfast to be brought up to him.

"At eleven o'clock the Earl of Brockelsby called to see his brother and remained with him until about twelve. In the afternoon the deceased went out, and returned for his dinner at seven o'clock in company with a gentleman whom the cashier knew well by sight, Mr. Timothy Beddingfield, the lawyer, of Paradise Street. The gentlemen had their dinner downstairs, and after that they went up to the Hon. Mr. de Genneville's room for coffee and cigars.

"'I could not say at what time Mr. Beddingfield left,' continued the cashier, 'but I rather fancy I saw him in the hall at about 9.15 p.m. He was wearing an Inverness cape over his dress clothes and a Glengarry cap. It was just at the hour when the visitors who had come down for the night from London were arriving thick and fast; the hall was very full, and there was a large party of Americans monopolising most of our personnel, so I could not swear positively whether I did see Mr. Beddingfield or not then, though I am quite sure that it was Mr. Timothy Beddingfield who dined and spent the evening with the Hon. Mr. de Genneville, as I know him quite well by sight. At ten o'clock I am off duty, and the night porter remains alone in the hall.'

166

"Mr. Tremlett's evidence was corroborated in most respects by a waiter and by the hall porter. They had both seen the deceased come in at seven o'clock in company with a gentleman, and their description of the latter coincided with that of the appearance of Mr. Timothy Beddingfield, whom, however, they did not actually know.

"At this point of the proceedings the foreman of the jury wished to know why Mr. Timothy Beddingfield's evidence had not been obtained, and was informed by the detective-inspector in charge of the case that that gentleman had seemingly left Birmingham, but was expected home shortly. The coroner suggested an adjournment pending Mr. Beddingfield's appearance, but at the earnest request of the detective he consented to hear the evidence of Peter Tyrrell, the night porter at the Castle Hotel, who, if you remember the case at all, succeeded in creating the biggest sensation of any which had been made through this extraordinary and weirdly gruesome case.

"'It was the first time I had been on duty at "The Castle,"' he said, 'for I used to be night porter at "Bright's," in Wolverhampton, but just after I had come on duty at ten o'clock a gentleman came and asked if he could see the Hon. Robert de Genneville. I said that I thought he was in, but would send up and see. The gentleman said: "It doesn't matter. Don't trouble; I know his room. Twenty-one, isn't it?" And up he went before I could say another word.'

"'Did he give you any name?' asked the coroner.

"'No, sir.'

"'What was he like?'

"'A young gentleman, sir, as far as I can remember, in an Inverness cape and Glengarry cap, but I could not see his face very well as he stood with his back to the light, and the cap shaded his eyes, and he only spoke to me for a minute.'

"'Look all round you,' said the coroner quietly. 'Is there anyone in this court at all like the gentleman you speak of?'

"An awed hush fell over the many spectators there present as Peter Tyrrell, the night porter of the Castle Hotel, turned his head towards the body of the court and slowly scanned the many faces there present; for a moment he seemed to hesitate—only for a moment though, then, as if vaguely conscious of the terrible importance his next words might have, he shook his head gravely and said:

"'I wouldn't like to swear.'

"The coroner tried to press him, but with true British stolidity he repeated: 'I wouldn't like to say.'

"'Well, then, what happened?' asked the coroner, who had perforce to abandon his point.

"'The gentleman went upstairs, sir, and about a quarter of an hour later he come down again, and I let him out. He was in a great hurry then, he threw me a half-crown and said: "Goodnight."'

"'And though you saw him again then, you cannot tell us if you would know him again?'

"Once more the hall porter's eyes wandered as if instinctively to a certain face in the court; once more he hesitated for many seconds which seemed like so many hours, during which a man's honour, a man's life, hung perhaps in the balance.

"Then Peter Tyrrell repeated slowly: 'I wouldn't swear.'

"But coroner and jury alike, aye, and every spectator in that crowded court, had seen that the man's eyes had rested during that one moment of hesitation upon the face of the Earl of Brockelsby."

3

The man in the corner blinked across at Polly with his funny mild blue eyes.

"No wonder you are puzzled," he continued, "so was everybody in the court that day, every one save myself. I alone could see in my mind's eye that gruesome murder such as it had been committed, with all its details, and, above all, its motive, and such as you will see it presently, when I place it all clearly before you.

"But before you see daylight in this strange case, I must plunge you into further darkness, in the same manner as the coroner and jury were plunged on the following day, the second day of that remarkable inquest. It had to be adjourned, since the appearance of Mr. Timothy Beddingfield had now become of vital importance. The public had come to regard his absence from Birmingham at this critical moment as decidedly remarkable, to say the least of it, and all those who did not know the lawyer by sight wished to see him in his Inverness cape and Glengarry cap such as he had appeared before the several witnesses on the night of the awful murder.

"When the coroner and jury were seated, the first piece of information which the police placed before them was the astounding statement that Mr. Timothy Beddingfield's whereabouts had not been ascertained, though it was confidently expected that he had not gone far and could easily be traced. There was a witness present who, the police thought, might throw some light as to the lawyer's probable destination, for obviously he had left Birmingham directly after his interview with the deceased.

"This witness was Mrs. Higgins, who was Mr. Beddingfield's housekeeper. She stated that her master was in the constant habit—especially latterly—of going up to London on business. He usually left by a late evening train on those occasions, and mostly was only absent thirty-six hours. He kept a portmanteau always ready packed for the purpose, for he often left at a few moments' notice. Mrs. Higgins added that her master stayed at the Great Western Hotel in London, for it was there that she was instructed to wire if anything urgent required his presence back in Birmingham.

"'On the night of the 14th,' she continued, 'at nine o'clock or thereabouts, a messenger came to the door with the master's card, and said that he was instructed to fetch Mr. Beddingfield's portmanteau, and then to meet him at the station in time to catch the 9.35 p.m. up train. I gave him the portmanteau, of course, as he had brought the card, and I had no idea there could be anything wrong; but since then I have heard nothing of my master, and I don't know when he will return.'

"Questioned by the coroner, she added that Mr. Beddingfield had never stayed away quite so long without having his letters forwarded to him. There was a large pile waiting for him now; she had written to the Great Western Hotel, London, asking what she should do about the letters, but had received no reply. She did not know the messenger by sight who had called for the portmanteau. Once or twice before Mr. Beddingfield had sent for his things in that manner when he had been dining out.

"Mr. Beddingfield certainly wore his Inverness cape over his dress clothes when he went out at about six o'clock in the afternoon. He also wore a Glengarry cap.

"The messenger had so far not yet been found, and from this point—namely, the sending for the portmanteau—all traces of Mr. Timothy Beddingfield seem to have been lost. Whether he went up to London by that 9.35 train or not could not be definitely ascertained. The police had questioned at least a dozen porters at the railway, as well as ticket collectors; but no one had any special recollection of a gentleman in an Inverness cape and Glengarry cap, a costume worn by more than one first-class passenger on a cold night in September.

"There was the hitch, you see; it all lay in this. Mr. Timothy Beddingfield, the lawyer, had undoubtedly made himself scarce. He was last seen in company with the deceased, and wearing an Inverness cape and Glengarry cap; two or three witnesses saw him leaving the hotel at about 9.15. Then the messenger calls at the lawyer's house for the portmanteau, after which Mr. Timothy Beddingfield seems to vanish into thin air; but—and that is a great 'but'—the night porter at the 'Castle' seems to have seen someone wearing the momentous Inverness and Glengarry half an hour or so later on, and going up to deceased's room, where he stayed about a quarter of an hour.

"Undoubtedly you will say, as everyone said to themselves that day after the night porter and Mrs. Higgins had been heard, that there was a very ugly and very black finger which pointed unpleasantly at Mr. Timothy Beddingfield, especially as that gentleman, for some reason which still required an explanation, was not there to put matters right for himself. But there was just one little thing—a mere trifle, perhaps—which neither the coroner nor the jury dared to overlook, though, strictly speaking, it was not evidence.

"You will remember that when the night porter was asked if he could, among the persons present in court, recognise the Hon. Robert de Genneville's belated visitor, everyone had noticed his hesitation, and marked that the man's eyes had rested doubtingly upon the face and figure of the young Earl of Brockelsby.

"Now, if that belated visitor had been Mr. Timothy Beddingfield—tall, lean, dry as dust, with a bird-like beak and clean-shaven chin—no one could for a moment have mistaken his face—even if they only saw it very casually and recollected it but very dimly—with that of young Lord Brockelsby, who was florid and rather short—the only point in common between them was their Saxon hair.

"You see that it was a curious point, don't you?" added the man in the corner, who now had become so excited that his fingers worked like long thin tentacles round and round his bit of string. "It weighed very heavily in favour of Timothy Beddingfield. Added to which you must also remember that, as far as he was concerned, the Hon. Robert de Genneville was to him the goose with the golden eggs.

"The 'De Geneville peerage case' had brought Beddingfield's name in great prominency. With the death of the claimant all hopes of prolonging the litigation came to an end. There was a total lack of motive as far as Beddingfield was concerned."

"Not so with the Earl of Brockelsby," said Polly, "and I've often maintained—"

"What?" he interrupted. "That the Earl of Brockelsby changed clothes with Beddingfield in order more conveniently to murder his own brother? Where and when could the exchange of costume have been effected, considering that the Inverness cape and Glengarry cap were in the hall of the Castle Hotel at 9.15, and at that hour and until ten o'clock Lord Brockelsby was at the Grand Hotel finishing dinner with some friends? That was subsequently proved, remember, and also that he was back at Brockelsby Castle, which is seven miles from Birmingham, at eleven o'clock sharp. Now, the visit of the individual in the Glengarry occurred sometime after 10 p.m."

"Then there was the disappearance of Beddingfield," said the girl musingly. "That certainly points very strongly to him. He was a man in good practice, I believe, and fairly well known."

"And has never been heard of from that day to this," concluded the old scarecrow with a chuckle. "No wonder you are puzzled. The police were quite baffled, and still are, for a matter of that. And yet see how simple it is! Only the police would not look further than these two men—Lord Brockelsby with a strong motive and the night porter's hesitation against him, and Beddingfield without a motive, but with strong circumstantial evidence and his own disappearance as condemnatory signs.

"If only they would look at the case as I did, and think a little about the dead as well as about the living. If they had remembered that peerage ease, the Hon. Robert's debts, his last straw which proved a futile claim.

"Only that very day the Earl of Brockelsby had, by quietly showing the original ancient document to his brother, persuaded him how futile were all his hopes. Who knows how many were the debts contracted, the promises made, the money borrowed and obtained on the strength of that claim which was mere romance? Ahead nothing but ruin, enmity with his brother, his marriage probably broken off, a wasted life, in fact.

"Is it small wonder that, though ill-feeling against the Earl of Brockelsby may have been deep, there was hatred, bitter, deadly hatred against the man who with false promises had led him into so hopeless a quagmire? Probably the Hon. Robert owed a great deal of money to Beddingfield, which the latter hoped to recoup at usurious interest, with threats of scandal and what not.

"Think of all that," he added, "and then tell me if you believe that a stronger motive for the murder of such an enemy could well be found."

"But what you suggest is impossible," said Polly, aghast.

"Allow me," he said, "it is more than possible—it is very easy and simple. The two men were alone together in the Hon. Robert de Genneville's room after dinner. You, as representing the public, and the police say that Beddingfield went away and returned half an hour later in order to kill his client. I say that it was the lawyer who was murdered at nine o'clock that evening, and that Robert de Genneville, the ruined man, the hopeless bankrupt, was the assassin."

"Then—"

"Yes, of course, now you remember, for I have put you on the track. The face and the body were so battered and bruised that they were past recognition. Both men were of equal height. The hair, which alone could not be disfigured or obliterated, was in both men similar in colour.

"Then the murderer proceeds to dress his victim in his own clothes. With the utmost care he places his own rings on the fingers of the dead man, his own watch in the pocket; a gruesome task, but an important one, and it is thoroughly well done. Then he himself puts on the clothes of his victim, with finally the Inverness cape and Glengarry, and when the hall is full of visitors, he slips out unperceived. He sends the messenger for Beddingfield's portmanteau and starts off by the night express."

"But then his visit at the Castle Hotel at ten o'clock—" she urged. "How dangerous!"

"Dangerous? Yes! but oh, how clever. You see, he was the Earl of Brockelsby's twin brother, and twin brothers are always somewhat alike. He wished to appear dead, murdered by someone, he cared not whom, but what he did care about was to throw clouds of dust in the eyes of the police, and he succeeded with a vengeance. Perhaps—who knows?—he wished to assure himself that he had forgotten nothing in the *mise en scène*, that the body, battered and bruised past all semblance of any human shape save for its clothes, really would appear to every one as that of the Hon. Robert de Genneville, while the latter disappeared for ever from the old world and started life again in the new.

"Then you must always reckon with the practically invariable rule that a murderer always revisits, if only once, the scene of his crime.

"Two years have elapsed since the crime; no trace of Timothy Beddingfield, the lawyer, has ever been found, and I can assure you that it will never be, for his plebeian body lies buried in the aristocratic family vault of the Earls of Brockelsby."

He was gone before Polly could say another word. The faces of

Timothy Beddingfield, of the Earl of Brockelsby, of the Hon. Robert de Genneville seemed to dance before her eyes and to mock her for the hopeless bewilderment in which she found herself plunged because of them; then all the faces vanished, or, rather, were merged in one long, thin, bird-like one, with bone-rimmed spectacles on the top of its beak, and a wide, rude grin beneath it, and, still puzzled, still doubtful, the young girl too paid for her scanty luncheon and went her way.

The Mysterious Death in Percy Street

1

Miss Polly Burton had had many an argument with Mr. Richard Frobisher about that old man in the corner, who seemed far more interesting and deucedly more mysterious than any of the crimes over which he philosophised. Dick thought, moreover, that Miss Polly spent more of her leisure time now in that A.B.C. shop than she had done in his own company before, and told her so, with that delightful air of sheepish sulkiness which the male creature invariably wears when he feels jealous and won't admit it.

Polly liked Dick to be jealous, but she liked that old scarecrow in the A.B.C. shop very much too, and though she made sundry vague promises from time to time to Mr. Richard Frobisher, she nevertheless drifted back instinctively day after day to the tea-shop in Norfolk Street, Strand, and stayed there, sipping coffee for as long as the man in the corner chose to talk. On this particular afternoon she went to the A.B.C. shop with a fixed purpose, that of making him give her his views of Mrs. Owen's mysterious death in Percy Street.

The facts had interested and puzzled her. She had had countless arguments with Mr. Richard Frobisher as to the three great possible solutions of the puzzle—"Accident, Suicide, Murder?"

"Undoubtedly neither accident nor suicide," he said dryly.

Polly was not aware that she had spoken. What an uncanny habit that creature had of reading her thoughts!

"You incline to the idea, then, that Mrs. Owen was murdered. Do you know by whom?"

He laughed, and drew forth the piece of string he always fidgeted with when unravelling some mystery.

"You would like to know who murdered that old woman?" he asked at last.

174

"I would like to hear your views on the subject," Polly replied.

"I have no views," he said dryly. "No one can know who murdered the woman, since no one ever saw the person who did it. No one can give the faintest description of the mysterious man who alone could have committed that clever deed, and the police are playing a game of blind man's buff."

"But you must have formed some theory of your own," she persisted.

It annoyed her that the funny creature was obstinate about this point, and she tried to nettle his vanity.

"I suppose that as a matter of fact your original remark that 'there are no such things as mysteries' does not apply universally. There is a mystery—that of the death in Percy Street, and you, like the police, are unable to fathom it."

He pulled up his eyebrows and looked at her for a minute or two.

"Confess that that murder was one of the cleverest bits of work accomplished outside Russian diplomacy," he said with a nervous laugh. "I must say that were I the judge, called upon to pronounce sentence of death on the man who conceived that murder, I could not bring myself to do it. I would politely request the gentleman to enter our Foreign Office—we have need of such men. The whole *mise en scène* was truly artistic, worthy of its *milieu*—the Rubens Studios in Percy Street, Tottenham Court Road.

"Have you ever noticed them? They are only studios by name, and are merely a set of rooms in a corner house, with the windows slightly enlarged, and the rents charged accordingly in consideration of that additional five inches of smoky daylight, filtering through dusty windows. On the ground floor there is the order office of some stained glass works, with a workshop in the rear, and on the first floor landing a small room allotted to the caretaker, with gas, coal, and fifteen shillings a week, for which princely income she is deputed to keep tidy and clean the general aspect of the house.

"Mrs. Owen, who was the caretaker there, was a quiet, respectable woman, who eked out her scanty wages by sundry—mostly very meagre—tips doled out to her by impecunious artists in exchange for promiscuous domestic services in and about the respective studios.

"But if Mrs. Owen's earnings were not large, they were very regular, and she had no fastidious tastes. She and her cockatoo lived on her wages; and all the tips added up, and never spent, year after year, went to swell a very comfortable little account at interest in the Birkbeck

"On the floor lay the body of Mrs. Owen."

Bank. This little account had mounted up to a very tidy sum, and the thrifty widow—or old maid—no one ever knew which she was—was generally referred to by the young artists of the Rubens Studios as a 'lady of means.' But this is a digression.

"No one slept on the premises except Mrs. Owen and her cockatoo. The rule was that one by one as the tenants left their rooms in the evening, they took their respective keys to the caretaker's room. She would then, in the early morning, tidy and dust the studios and the office downstairs, lay the fire and carry up coals.

"The foreman of the glass works was the first to arrive in the morning. He had a latchkey, and let himself in, after which it was the custom of the house that he should leave the street door open for the benefit of the other tenants and their visitors.

"Usually, when he came at about nine o'clock, he found Mrs. Owen busy about the house doing her work, and he had often a brief chat with her about the weather, but on this particular morning of February 2nd he neither saw nor heard her. However, as the shop had been tidied and the fire laid, he surmised that Mrs. Owen had finished her work earlier than usual, and thought no more about it. One by one the tenants of the studios turned up, and the day sped on without any one's attention being drawn noticeably to the fact that the caretaker had not appeared upon the scene.

"It had been a bitterly cold night, and the day was even worse; a cutting north-easterly gale was blowing, there had been a great deal of snow during the night which lay quite thick on the ground, and at five o'clock in the afternoon, when the last glimmer of the pale winter daylight had disappeared, the confraternity of the brush put palette and easel aside and prepared to go home. The first to leave was Mr. Charles Pitt; he locked up his studio and, as usual, took his key into the caretaker's room. He had just opened the door when an icy blast literally struck him in the face; both the windows were wide open, and the snow and sleet were beating thickly into the room, forming already a white carpet upon the floor.

"The room was in semi-obscurity, and at first Mr. Pitt saw nothing, but instinctively realising that something was wrong, he lit a match, and saw before him the spectacle of that awful and mysterious tragedy which has ever since puzzled both police and public. On the floor, already half covered by the drifting snow, lay the body of Mrs. Owen face downwards, in a nightgown, with feet and ankles bare, and these and her hands were of a deep purple colour; whilst in a corner of the room, huddled up with the cold, the body of the cockatoo lay stark and stiff."

2

"At first there was only talk of a terrible accident, the result of some inexplicable carelessness which perhaps the evidence at the inquest would help to elucidate.

"Medical assistance came too late; the unfortunate woman was indeed dead, frozen to death, inside her own room. Further examination showed that she had received a severe blow at the back of the head, which must have stunned her and caused her to fall, helpless, beside the open window. Temperature at five degrees below zero had done the rest. Detective Inspector Howell discovered close to the window a wrought-iron gas bracket, the height of which corresponded exactly with the bruise at the back of Mrs. Owen's head.

"Hardly however had a couple of days elapsed when public curiosity was whetted by a few startling headlines, such as the halfpenny evening papers alone know how to concoct.

'The mysterious death in Percy Street.' 'Is it Suicide or Murder?' 'Thrilling details—Strange developments.' 'Sensational Arrest.'

"What had happened was simply this:

"At the inquest a few certainly very curious facts connected with Mrs. Owen's life had come to light, and this had led to the apprehension of a young man of very respectable parentage on a charge of being concerned in the tragic death of the unfortunate caretaker.

"To begin with, it happened that her life, which in an ordinary way should have been very monotonous and regular, seemed, at any rate latterly, to have been more than usually chequered and excited. Every witness who had known her in the past concurred in the statement that since October last a great change had come over the worthy and honest woman.

"I happen to have a photo of Mrs. Owen as she was before this great change occurred in her quiet and uneventful life, and which led, as far as the poor soul was concerned, to such disastrous results.

"Here she is to the life," added the funny creature, placing the photo before Polly—"as respectable, as stodgy, as uninteresting as it is well possible for a member of your charming sex to be; not a face, you will admit, to lead any youngster to temptation or to induce him to commit a crime.

"Nevertheless, one day all the tenants of the Rubens Studios were surprised and shocked to see Mrs. Owen, quiet, respectable Mrs. Owen, sallying forth at six o'clock in the afternoon, attired in an extravagant bonnet and a cloak trimmed with imitation astrakhan which—slightly open in front—displayed a gold locket and chain of astonishing proportions.

"Many were the comments, the hints, the bits of sarcasm levelled at the worthy woman by the frivolous confraternity of the brush.

"The plot thickened when from that day forth a complete change came over the worthy caretaker of the Rubens Studios. While she appeared day after day before the astonished gaze of the tenants and the scandalised looks of the neighbours, attired in new and extravagant dresses, her work was hopelessly neglected, and she was always 'out' when wanted.

"There was, of course, much talk and comment in various parts of the Rubens Studios on the subject of Mrs. Owen's 'dissipations.' The tenants began to put two and two together, and after a very little while the general consensus of opinion became firmly established that the honest caretaker's demoralisation coincided week for week, almost day for day, with young Greenhill's establishment in No. 8 Studio.

"Everyone had remarked that he stayed much later in the evening than anyone else, and yet no one presumed that he stayed for purposes of work. Suspicions soon rose to certainty when Mrs. Owen and Arthur Greenhill were seen by one of the glass workmen dining together at Gambia's Restaurant in Tottenham Court Road.

"The workman, who was having a cup of tea at the counter, noticed particularly that when the bill was paid the money came out of Mrs. Owen's purse. The dinner had been sumptuous—veal cutlets, a cut from the joint, dessert, coffee and liqueurs. Finally, the pair left the restaurant apparently very gay, young Greenhill smoking a choice cigar.

"Irregularities such as these were bound sooner or later to come to the ears and eyes of Mr. Allman, the landlord of the Rubens Studios; and a month after the New Year, without further warning, he gave her a week's notice to quit his house.

"'Mrs. Owen did not seem the least bit upset when I gave her notice,' Mr. Allman declared in his evidence at the inquest; 'on the contrary, she told me that she had ample means, and had only worked latterly for the sake of something to do. She added that she had plenty of friends who would look after her, for she had a nice little pile to leave to anyone who would know how "to get the right side of her."'

"Nevertheless, in spite of this cheerful interview, Miss Bedford, the tenant of No. 6 Studio, had stated that when she took her key to the caretaker's room at 6.30 that afternoon, she found Mrs. Owen in tears. The caretaker refused to be comforted, nor would she speak of her trouble to Miss Bedford.

"Twenty-four hours later she was found dead.

"The coroner's jury returned an open verdict, and Detective-Inspector Jones was charged by the police to make some inquiries about young Mr. Greenhill, whose intimacy with the unfortunate woman had been universally commented upon.

"The detective, however, pushed his investigations as far as the Birkbeck Bank. There he discovered that after her interview with Mr. Allman, Mrs. Owen had withdrawn what money she had on deposit, some £800, the result of twenty-five years' saving and thrift.

"But the immediate result of Detective-Inspector Jones's labours was that Mr. Arthur Greenhill, lithographer, was brought before the magistrate at Bow Street on the charge of being concerned in the death of Mrs. Owen, caretaker of the Rubens Studios, Percy Street.

"Now that magisterial inquiry is one of the few interesting ones which I had the misfortune to miss," continued the man in the corner, with a nervous shake of the shoulders. "But you know as well as I do how the attitude of the young prisoner impressed the magistrate and police so unfavourably that, with every new witness brought forward, his position became more and more unfortunate.

"Yet he was a good-looking, rather coarsely built young fellow, with one of those awful Cockney accents which literally make one jump. But he looked painfully nervous, stammered at every word spoken, and repeatedly gave answers entirely at random.

"His father acted as lawyer for him, a rough-looking elderly man, who had the appearance of a common country attorney rather than of a London solicitor.

"The police had built up a fairly strong case against the lithographer. Medical evidence revealed nothing new: Mrs. Owen had died from exposure, the blow at the back of the head not being sufficiently serious to cause anything but temporary disablement. When the medical officer had been called in, death had intervened for some time; it was quite impossible to say how long, whether one hour or five or twelve.

"The appearance and state of the room, when the unfortunate

woman was found by Mr. Charles Pitt, were again gone over in minute detail. Mrs. Owen's clothes, which she had worn during the day, were folded neatly on a chair. The key of her cupboard was in the pocket of her dress. The door had been slightly ajar, but both the windows were wide open; one of them, which had the sash-line broken, had been fastened up most scientifically with a piece of rope.

"Mrs. Owen had obviously undressed preparatory to going to bed, and the magistrate very naturally soon made the remark how untenable the theory of an accident must be. No one in their five senses would undress with a temperature at below zero, and the windows wide open.

"After these preliminary statements the cashier of the Birkbeck was called and he related the caretaker's visit at the bank.

"'It was then about one o'clock,' he stated. 'Mrs. Owen called and presented a cheque to self for £827, the amount of her balance. She seemed exceedingly happy and cheerful, and talked about needing plenty of cash, as she was going abroad to join her nephew, for whom she would in future keep house. I warned her about being sufficiently careful with so large a sum, and parting from it injudiciously, as women of her class are very apt to do. She laughingly declared that not only was she careful of it in the present, but meant to be so for the far-off future, for she intended to go that very day to a lawyer's office and to make a will.'

"The cashier's evidence was certainly startling in the extreme, since in the widow's room no trace of any kind was found of any money; against that, two of the notes handed over by the bank to Mrs. Owen on that day were cashed by young Greenhill on the very morning of her mysterious death. One was handed in by him to the West End Clothiers Company, in payment for a suit of clothes, and the other he changed at the Post Office in Oxford Street.

"After that all the evidence had of necessity to be gone through again on the subject of young Greenhill's intimacy with Mrs. Owen. He listened to it all with an air of the most painful nervousness, his cheeks were positively green, his lips seemed dry and parched, for he repeatedly passed his tongue over them, and when Constable E 18 deposed that at 2 a.m. on the morning of February 2nd he had seen the accused and spoken to him at the corner of Percy Street and Tottenham Court Road, young Greenhill all but fainted.

"The contention of the police was that the caretaker had been murdered and robbed during that night before she went to bed, that young Greenhill had done the murder, seeing that he was the only person known to have been intimate with the woman, and that it was, moreover, proved unquestionably that he was in the immediate neighbourhood of the Rubens Studios at an extraordinarily late hour of the night.

"His own account of himself, and of that same night, could certainly not be called very satisfactory. Mrs. Owen was a relative of his late mother's, he declared. He himself was a lithographer by trade, with a good deal of time and leisure on his hands. He certainly had employed some of that time in taking the old woman to various places of amusement. He had on more than one occasion suggested that she should give up menial work, and come and live with him, but, unfortunately, she was a great deal imposed upon by her nephew, a man of the name of Owen, who exploited the good-natured woman in every possible way, and who had on more than one occasion made severe attacks upon her savings at the Birkbeck Bank.

"Severely cross-examined by the prosecuting counsel about this supposed relative of Mrs. Owen, Greenhill admitted that he did not know him—had, in fact, never seen him. He knew that his name was Owen and that was all. His chief occupation consisted in sponging on the kind-hearted old woman, but he only went to see her in the evenings, when he presumably knew that she would be alone, and invariably after all the tenants of the Rubens Studios had left for the day.

"I don't know whether at this point it strikes you at all, as it did both magistrate and counsel, that there was a direct contradiction in this statement and the one made by the cashier of the Birkbeck on the subject of his last conversation with Mrs. Owen. 'I am going abroad to join my nephew, for whom I am going to keep house,' was what the unfortunate woman had said.

"Now Greenhill, in spite of his nervousness and at times contradictory answers, strictly adhered to his point, that there was a nephew in London, who came frequently to see his aunt.

"Anyway, the sayings of the murdered woman could not be taken as evidence in law. Mr. Greenhill senior put the objection, adding:

'There may have been two nephews,' which the magistrate and the prosecution were bound to admit.

"With regard to the night immediately preceding Mrs. Owen's death, Greenhill stated that he had been with her to the theatre, had seen her home, and had had some supper with her in her room. Before he left her, at 2 a.m., she had of her own accord made him a present of £10, saying: 'I am a sort of aunt to you, Arthur, and if you don't have it, Bill is sure to get it.'

"She had seemed rather worried in the early part of the evening, but later on she cheered up.

"'Did she speak at all about this nephew of hers or about her money affairs?' asked the magistrate.

"Again, the young man hesitated, but said, 'No! she did not mention either Owen or her money affairs.'

"If I remember rightly," added the man in the corner, "for recollect I was not present, the case was here adjourned. But the magistrate would not grant bail. Greenhill was removed looking more dead than alive—though everyone remarked that Mr. Greenhill senior looked determined and not the least worried. In the course of his examination on behalf of his son, of the medical officer and one or two other witnesses, he had very ably tried to confuse them on the subject of the hour at which Mrs. Owen was last known to be alive.

"He made a very great point of the fact that the usual morning's work was done throughout the house when the inmates arrived. Was it conceivable, he argued, that a woman would do that kind of work overnight, especially as she was going to the theatre, and therefore would wish to dress in her smarter clothes? It certainly was a very nice point levelled against the prosecution, who promptly retorted: Just as conceivable as that a woman in those circumstances of life should, having done her work, undress beside an open window at nine o'clock in the morning with the snow beating into the room.

"Now it seems that Mr. Greenhill senior could produce any amount of witnesses who could help to prove a conclusive *alibi* on behalf of his son, if only some time subsequent to that fatal 2 a.m. the murdered woman had been seen alive by some chance passer-by.

"However, he was an able man and an earnest one, and I fancy the magistrate felt some sympathy for his strenuous endeavours on his son's behalf. He granted a week's adjournment, which seemed to satisfy Mr. Greenhill completely.

"In the meanwhile, the papers had talked of and almost exhausted the subject of the mystery in Percy Street. There had been, as you no doubt know from personal experience, innumerable arguments on the puzzling alternatives:—

"Accident?

"Suicide?

"Murder?

"A week went by, and then the case against young Greenhill was resumed. Of course, the court was crowded It needed no great penetration to remark at once that the prisoner looked more hopeful, and his father quite elated.

"Again, a great deal of minor evidence was taken, and then came the turn of the defence. Mr. Greenhill called Mrs. Hall, confectioner, of Percy Street, opposite the Rubens Studios. She deposed that at 8 o'clock in the morning of February 2nd, while she was tidying her shop window, she saw the caretaker of the Studios opposite, as usual, on her knees, her head and body wrapped in a shawl, cleaning her front steps. Her husband also saw Mrs. Owen, and Mrs. Hall remarked to her husband how thankful she was that her own shop had tiled steps, which did not need scrubbing on so cold a morning.

"Mr. Hall, confectioner, of the same address, corroborated this statement, and Mr. Greenhill, with absolute triumph, produced a third witness, Mrs. Martin, of Percy Street, who from her window on the second floor had, at 7.30 a.m., seen the caretaker shaking mats outside her front door. The description this witness gave of Mrs. Owen's get-up, with the shawl round her head, coincided point by point with that given by Mr. and Mrs. Hall.

"After that Mr. Greenhill's task became an easy one; his son was at home having his breakfast at 8 o'clock that morning—not only himself, but his servants would testify to that.

"The weather had been so bitter that the whole of that day Arthur had not stirred from his own fireside. Mrs. Owen was murdered after 8 a.m. on that day, since she was seen alive by three people at that hour, therefore his son could not have murdered Mrs. Owen. The police must find the criminal elsewhere, or else bow to the opinion originally expressed by the public that Mrs. Owen had met with a terrible untoward accident, or that perhaps she may have wilfully sought her own death in that extraordinary and tragic fashion.

"Before young Greenhill was finally discharged one or two witnesses were again examined, chief among these being the foreman of the glassworks. He had turned up at the Rubens Studios at 9 o'clock, and been in business all day. He averred positively that he did not specially notice any suspicious-looking individual crossing the hall that day. 'But,' he remarked with a smile, 'I don't sit and watch every one who goes up and down stairs. I am too busy for that. The street door is always left open; any one can walk in, up or down, who knows the way.'

"That there was a mystery in connection with Mrs. Owen's death—of that the police have remained perfectly convinced; whether young Greenhill held the key of that mystery or not they have never found out to this day.

"I could enlighten them as to the cause of the young lithographer's anxiety at the magisterial inquiry, but I assure you, I do not care to do the work of the police for them. Why should I? Greenhill will never suffer from unjust suspicions. He and his father alone—besides myself—know in what a terribly tight corner he all but found himself.

"The young man did not reach home till nearly *five* o'clock that morning. His last train had gone; he had to walk, lost his way, and wandered about Hampstead for hours. Think what his position would have been if the worthy confectioners of Percy Street had not seen Mrs. Owen 'wrapped up in a shawl, on her knees, doing the front steps.'

"Moreover, Mr. Greenhill senior is a solicitor, who has a small office in John Street, Bedford Row. The afternoon before her death Mrs. Owen had been to that office and had there made a will by which she left all her savings to young Arthur Greenhill, lithographer. Had that will been in other than paternal hands, it would have been proved, in the natural course of such things, and one other link would have been added to the chain which nearly dragged Arthur Greenhill to the gallows—'the link of a very strong motive.'

"Can you wonder that the young man turned livid, until such time as it was proved beyond a doubt that the murdered woman was alive hours after he had reached the safe shelter of his home?

"I saw you smile when I used the word 'murdered,'" continued the man in the corner, growing quite excited now that he was approaching the *dénouement* of his story. "I know that the public, after the magistrate had discharged Arthur Greenhill, were quite satisfied to think that the mystery in Percy Street was a case of accident—or suicide."

"No," replied Polly, "there could be no question of suicide, for two very distinct reasons."

He looked at her with some degree of astonishment. She supposed that he was amazed at her venturing to form an opinion of her own.

"And may I ask what, in your opinion, these reasons are?" he asked very sarcastically.

"To begin with, the question of money," she said—"has any more of it been traced so far?"

"Not another £5 note," he said with a chuckle; "they were all

185

cashed in Paris during the Exhibition, and you have no conception how easy a thing that is to do, at any of the hotels or smaller *agents de change*."

"That nephew was a clever blackguard," she commented.

"You believe, then, in the existence of that nephew?"

"Why should I doubt it? Someone must have existed who was sufficiently familiar with the house to go about in it in the middle of the day without attracting anyone's attention."

"In the middle of the day?" he said with a chuckle.

"Any time after 8.30 in the morning."

"So, you, too, believe in the 'caretaker, wrapped up in a shawl,' cleaning her front steps?" he queried.

"But—"

"It never struck you, in spite of the training your intercourse with me must have given you, that the person who carefully did all the work in the Rubens Studios, laid the fires and carried up the coals, merely did it in order to gain time; in order that the bitter frost might really and effectually do its work, and Mrs. Owen be not missed until she was truly dead."

"But—" suggested Polly again.

"It never struck you that one of the greatest secrets of successful crime is to lead the police astray with regard to the time when the crime was committed. That was, if you remember, the great point in the Regent's Park murder.

"In this case the 'nephew,' since we admit his existence, would—even if he were ever found, which is doubtful—be able to prove as good an alibi as young Greenhill."

"But I don't understand—"

"How the murder was committed?" he said eagerly. "Surely you can see it all for yourself, since you admit the 'nephew'—a scamp, perhaps—who sponges on the good-natured woman. He terrorises and threatens her, so much so that she fancies her money is no longer safe even in the Birkbeck Bank. Women of that class are apt at times to mistrust the Bank of England. Anyway, she withdraws her money. Who knows what she meant to do with it in the immediate future?

"In any case, she wishes to secure it after her death to a young man whom she likes, and who has known how to win her good graces. That afternoon the nephew begs, entreats for more money; they have a row; the poor woman is in tears, and is only temporarily consoled by a pleasant visit at the theatre.

186

"At 2 o'clock in the morning young Greenhill parts from her. Two minutes later the nephew knocks at the door. He comes with a plausible tale of having missed his last train, and asks for a 'shake down' somewhere in the house. The good-natured woman suggests a sofa in one of the studios, and then quietly prepares to go to bed. The rest is very simple and elementary. The nephew sneaks into his aunt's room, finds her standing in her nightgown; he demands money with threats of violence; terrified, she staggers, knocks her head against the gas bracket, and falls on the floor stunned, while the nephew seeks for her keys and takes possession of the £800. You will admit that the subsequent raise *en scène*—is worthy of a genius.

"No struggle, not the usual hideous accessories round a crime. Only the open windows, the bitter north-easterly gale, and the heavily falling snow—two silent accomplices, as silent as the dead.

"After that the murderer, with perfect presence of mind, busies himself in the house, doing the work which will ensure that Mrs. Owen shall not be missed, at any rate, for some time. He dusts and tidies; some few hours later he even slips on his aunt's skirt and bodice, wraps his head in a shawl, and boldly allows those neighbours who are astir to see what they believe to be Mrs. Owen. Then he goes back to her room, resumes his normal appearance, and quietly leaves the house."

"He may have been seen."

"He undoubtedly *was* seen by two or three people, but no one thought anything of seeing a man leave the house at that hour. It was very cold, the snow was falling thickly, and as he wore a muffler round the lower part of his face, those who saw him would not undertake to know him again."

"That man was never seen nor heard of again?" Polly asked.

"He has disappeared off the face of the earth. The police are searching for him, and perhaps someday they will find him—then society will be rid of one of the most ingenious men of the age,"

3

He had paused, absorbed in meditation. The young girl also was silent. Some memory too vague as yet to take a definite form was persistently haunting her—one thought was hammering away in her brain, and playing havoc with her nerves. That thought was the inexplicable feeling within her that there was something in connection with that hideous crime which she ought to recollect, something which—if she could only remember what it was—would give her the clue to the tragic mystery, and for once ensure her triumph over this self-conceited and sarcastic scarecrow in the corner.

He was watching her through his great bone-rimmed spectacles, and she could see the knuckles of his bony hands, just above the top of the table, fidgeting, fidgeting, fidgeting, till she wondered if there existed another set of fingers in the world which could undo the knots his lean ones made in that tiresome piece of string.

Then suddenly—à *propos* of nothing, Polly *remembered*—the whole thing stood before her, short and clear like a vivid flash of lightning:— Mrs. Owen lying dead in the snow beside her open window; one of them with a broken sash-line, tied up most scientifically with a piece of string. She remembered the talk there had been at the time about this improvised sash-line.

That was after young Greenhill had been discharged, and the question of suicide had been voted an impossibility.

Polly remembered that in the illustrated papers photographs appeared of this wonderfully knotted piece of string, so contrived that the weight of the frame could but tighten the knots, and thus keep the window open. She remembered that people deduced many things from that improvised sash-line, chief among these deductions being that the murderer was a sailor—so wonderful, so complicated, so numerous were the knots which secured that window-frame.

But Polly knew better. In her mind's eye she saw those fingers, rendered doubly nervous by the fearful cerebral excitement, grasping at first mechanically, even thoughtlessly, a bit of twine with which to secure the window; then the ruling habit strongest through all, the girl could see it; the lean and ingenious fingers fidgeting, fidgeting with that piece of string, tying knot after knot, more wonderful, more complicated, than any she had yet witnessed.

"If I were you," she said, without daring to look into that corner where he sat, "I would break myself of the habit of perpetually making knots in a piece of string."

He did not reply, and at last Polly ventured to look up—the corner was empty, and through the glass door beyond the desk, where he had just deposited his few coppers, she saw the tails of his tweed coat, his extraordinary hat, his meagre, shrivelled-up personality, fast disappearing down the street.

Miss Polly Burton (of the *Evening Observer*) was married the other day to Mr. Richard Frobisher (of the *London Mail*). She has never set eyes on the man in the corner from that day to this.

Unravelled Knots

"The old man in the corner."

Contents

The Mystery of the Khaki Tunic

I cannot pretend to say how it all happened: I can but relate what occurred, leaving those of my friends who are versed in psychic matters to find a plausible explanation for the fact that on that horrible foggy afternoon I chanced to walk into that blameless tea-shop at that particular hour. Now I had not been inside a tea-shop for years and I had practically ceased to think of the Man in the Corner—the weird, spook-like creature with the baggy trousers, the huge horn-rimmed spectacles, and the thin claw-like hands that went on fidgeting, fidgeting, fidgeting, with a piece of string, tying it with nervy deliberation into innumerable and complicated knots.

And yet when I walked into that tea-shop and saw him sitting in the corner by the fire, I was hardly conscious of surprise; but I did not think that he would recognise me. So, I sat down at the next table to him, and when I thought that he was most intent on fidgeting with his piece of string, I stole surreptitious glances at him. The last twenty years seemed to have passed him by; he was just the same; his hair was of the same colourless, lank texture and still lay plastered across his bald, pointed cranium, his pale eyes were no paler, his face no more wrinkled, his fingers were just as agile and restless as they had been when I last saw him twenty years ago.

Then all at once he spoke, just as he used to do, in the same cracked voice, with the dry, ironic chuckle.

"One of the most interesting cases it has ever been my good fortune to investigate," he said.

I had not realised that he had seen me, and I gave such a startled jump that I spilt half a cup of tea on my frock. With a long, bony finger he was pointing to a copy of the *Express Post* which lay beside his plate, and, almost against my will, my eyes wandered to the flaming headline: "The Mystery of the Khaki Tunic." Then I looked up enquiringly at my pixy-like interlocutor. His watery blue eyes contemplated me through his horn-rimmed spectacles and his thin, colourless lips smiled on me with placid benevolence. It never occurred to me to make a conventional little speech about the lapse of time since last we met; for the moment

I had the feeling as if I had seen him the day before yesterday. "You are still interested in criminology then?" I asked.

"More than ever," he replied with a bland smile, "and this case has given me some of the most delightful moments I have ever experienced in connection with my studies. I have watched the police committing one blunder after another, and today when they are completely baffled, and the public has started to write letters to the papers about another undetected crime and another criminal at large. I am having the time of my life."

"Of course, you have made up your mind," I retorted with what I felt was withering sarcasm.

"I have arrived at the only possible solution of the mystery," he replied unperturbed, "and you will do the same when I have put the facts clearly and logically before you. As for the police, let 'em flounder," he went on complacently. "For me it has been an exciting drama, to watch from beginning to end. Every one of the characters in it stands out before me like a clear-cut cameo. There was Miss Mary Clarke, a quiet middle-aged woman who rented 'Hardacres,' from Lord Foremeere. She had taken the place soon after the Armistice and ran a poultry farm there on a small scale with the occasional assistance of her brother Arthur, an ex-officer in the East Glebeshires, a young man who had an excellent war record, but who seemed, like so many other young men of his kind, to have fallen into somewhat shiftless and lazy ways since the glorious peace.

"No doubt you know the geography of the place. The halfpenny papers have been full of maps and plans of 'Hardacres.' It is rather a lonely house on the road between Langford and Barchester, about three quarters of a mile from Meere village. Meere Court is another half-mile or so further on, the house hidden by clumps of stately trees, above which can be perceived the towers of Barchester Cathedral.

"Very little seems to have been known about Miss Clarke in the neighbourhood; she seemed to be fairly well-to-do and undoubtedly a cut above the village folk; but, equally obviously, she did not belong to the county set. Nor did she encourage visitors, not even the vicar; she seldom went to church, and neither went to parties nor ever asked anyone to tea; she did most of her shopping herself, in Meere, and sold her poultry and eggs to Mr. Brook, the local dealer, who served all the best houses for miles around. Every morning at seven o'clock a girl from the village named Emily Baker came in to do the housework at 'Hardacres,' and left again after the midday dinner. Once a week regularly Miss Clarke called at Meere Court. Always on a Friday. She walked over in the afternoon, whatever the weather, brought a large basket of eggs with her, and was shown without ever being kept waiting, straight into Lady Foremeere's sitting-room. The interview lasted about ten minutes, sometimes more, and then she would be shown out again.

"Mind you," the funny creature went on glibly, and raising a, long, pointed finger to emphasise his words, "no one seems to have thought that there was anything mysterious about Miss Clarke. The fact that 'she kept 'erself to 'erself' was not in itself a sign of anything odd about her. People, especially women, in outlying country districts, often lead very self-centred lonely lives; they arouse a certain amount of curiosity when they first arrive in the neighbourhood, but after a while gossip dies out, if it is not fed, and the hermit's estrangements from village life is tacitly accepted.

"On the other hand, Miss Clarke's brother Arthur was exceedingly gregarious. He was a crack tennis player and an excellent dancer, and these two accomplishments procured him the entree into the best houses in the county—houses which, before the war, when people were more fastidious in the choice of their guests, would no doubt have not been quite so freely opened to him.

"It was common gossip that Arthur was deeply in love with April St. Jude, Lord Foremeere's beautiful daughter by a previous marriage, but public opinion was unanimous in the assertion that there never could be any question of marriage between an extemporary gentleman without money or property of any kind and the society beauty who had been courted by some of the smartest and richest men in London.

"Nor did Arthur Clarke enjoy the best of reputations in the neighbourhood: he was over fond of betting and loafing about the public-houses of Barchester. People said that he might help his sister in the farm more than he did, seeing that he did not appear to have a six-pence of his own, and that she gave him bed and board; but as he was very good looking and could make himself very agreeable if he chose, the women at any rate smiled at his misdeeds and were content to call

Arthur 'rather wild, but not really a bad boy.'

"Then came the tragedy.

"On the twenty-eighth of December last, when Emily Baker came to work as usual, she was rather surprised not to see or hear Miss Clarke moving about the place. As a rule, she was out in the yard by the time Emily arrived; the chickens would have had their hot mash and the empty pans would have been left for Emily to wash up. But this morning nothing. In the girl's own words, there was a creepy kind of lonely feeling about the house.

"She knew that Mr. Clarke was not at home. The day before the servants at Meere Court had their annual Christmas party, and Mr. Clarke had been asked to help with the tree and to entertain the children. He had announced his intention of putting up afterwards at the Deanery Hotel for the night, a thing he was rather fond of doing whenever he was asked out to parties, and did not know what time he might be able to get away.

"Emily when she arrived had found the front door on the latch as usual, therefore—she reflected—Miss Clarke must have been downstairs and drawn the bolts; but where could she be now? Never, never would she have gone out before feeding her chickens, on such a cold morning too!

"At this point Emily gave up reflecting and proceeded to action. She went up to her mistress's room. It was empty and the bed had not been slept in. Genuinely alarmed now, she ran down again, her next objective being the parlour. The door was, as usual, locked on the outside, but, contrary to precedent, the key was not in the lock; thinking it had dropped out, the girl searched for it, but in vain, and at one moment when she moved the small mat which stood before the door of the locked room, she at once became aware of an overpowering smell of gas.

"This proved the death-blow to Emily's fortitude; she took to her heels and ran out of the house and down the road toward the village, nor did she halt until she came to the local police station, where she gave as coherent an account as she could of the terrible state of things at 'Hardacres.'

"You will remember that when the police broke open the door of the parlour the first thing they saw was the body of Miss Clarke lying full length on the floor. The poor woman was quite dead, suffocated by the poisonous fumes of gas which was fully turned on in the old-fashioned chandelier above her head. The one window had

196

been carefully latched, and the thick curtains closely drawn together; the chimney had been stuffed up with newspaper and paper had been thrust into every aperture so as to exclude the slightest possible breath of air. There was a wad of it in the keyhole, and the mat on the landing outside had been carefully arranged against the door with the same sinister object.

"It was clearly a deliberate case of murder; the news spread like wildfire and soon the entire neighbourhood was gloating over a sensation the like of which had not come its way for generations past."

2

"The London evening papers got hold of the story for their noonday edition," the Man in the Corner went on after a slight pause, "and I, with my passion for the enigmatical and the perplexing, made up my mind then and there to probe the mystery on my own account, because I knew well enough that this was just the sort of case which would send the county police blundering all over the wrong track.

"I arrived at Barchester on the Tuesday in time for the inquest, but nothing of much importance transpired that day. Medical evidence went to prove that the deceased had first been struck on the back of the head by some heavy instrument, a weighted stick or something of the sort, which had no doubt stunned her; but she actually died of poisoning by gas which she had inhaled in large quantities while she was half-conscious. The medical officer went on to say that Miss Clarke must have been dead twelve hours or more when he was called in by the police at about eight o'clock in the morning.

"After this a couple of neighbours testified to having seen Miss Clarke at her front door at about half-past five the previous evening. It was a very dark night, if you remember, and a thick Scotch mist was falling. When the neighbours went by, Miss Clarke had apparently just introduced a visitor into her house, the gas was alight in the small hall and they had vaguely perceived the outline of a man or woman, they could not swear which, in a huge coat, standing for a moment immediately behind Miss Clarke; the neighbours also heard Miss Clarke's voice speaking to her visitor, but what she said they could not distinguish. The weather was so atrocious that everyone who was abroad that night hurried along without taking much notice of what went on around.

"Evidence of a more or less formal character followed and the inquest was then adjourned until the Friday, everyone going away with the feeling that sensational developments were already in the air.

"And the developments came tumbling in thick and fast. To begin with, it appears that Arthur Clarke, when first questioned by the police, had made a somewhat lame statement.

"'I was asked,' he said, 'to help with the servants' Christmas party at Meere Court. I walked over to Barchester at about three o'clock in the afternoon, with my suitcase, as I was going to spend the night at the Deanery Hotel. I went on to Meere Court soon after half-past three, and stayed until past seven, after which I walked back to the Deanery, had some dinner and went early to bed. I never knew that anything had happened to my sister until the police telephoned to me soon after eight o'clock the next morning. And,' he added, 'that's all about it.'

"But it certainly was not 'all about it', because several of the servants at Meere Court who were asked at what time Mr. Clarke went away that night, said that he must have gone very soon after five o'clock. They all finished their tea about that time, and then the gramophone was set going for dancing; they were quite sure that they had not seen Mr. Clarke after that. On the other hand, Miss St. Jude said that the servants were mistaken: they were far too deeply engrossed in their own amusements to be at all reliable in their statements. As a matter of fact, Mr. Clarke went away, as he said, at about seven o'clock; she herself had danced with him most of the time, and said goodnight to him in the hall at a few minutes after seven.

"Here was a neat little complication, do you see? A direct conflict of evidence at the very outset of this mysterious case. Can you wonder that amateur detectives already shrugged their shoulders and raised their eyebrows, declaring that the Honourable April St. Jude was obviously in love with Arthur Clarke and was trying to shield him, well knowing that he had something to hide?

"Of course, the police themselves were very reticent, but even they could not stop people from gossiping. And gossip, I can assure you, had enough and to spare to feed on. At first, of course, the crime had seemed entirely motiveless. The deceased had not an enemy or, as far as that goes, many acquaintances in the world. In the drawer of the desk, in the parlour, the sum of twenty pounds odd in notes and cash was found, and in a little box by the side of the money poor Mary Clarke's little bits of jewellery. But twenty-four hours later no one could remain in doubt as to the assassin's purpose. You will remember that on the day following the adjourned inquest there had arrived from the depths of Yorkshire an old sister of the deceased, a respectable spinster, to whom Arthur himself, it seems, had communicated the terrible news. She had come to Barchester for the funeral. This elder Miss Clarke, Euphemia by name, though she could not say much that was informative, did at any rate throw light upon one dark passage in her sister's history.

"'For the past four years,' she told the police, 'my sister had an allowance of £4 a week from a member of the aristocracy. I did not know much about her affairs, but I do know that she had a packet of letters on which she set great store. What these letters were I have not the slightest idea, nor do I know what Mary ultimately did with them. On one occasion, before she was actually settled at "Hardacres," she met me in London and asked me to take care of this packet for her, and she told me then that they were very valuable. I also know that she and my brother Arthur had most heated arguments together on the subject of these letters. Arthur was always wanting her to give them up to him and she always refused. On one occasion she told me that she could, if she wanted, sell that packet of letters for five thousand pounds. "Why on earth don't you?" I asked her. But she replied: "Oh, Arthur would only get the money out of me. It's better as it is."'

"This story, as you may well imagine, gave food enough for gossip; at once a romance was woven of blackmail and drama of love and passion, whilst the name of a certain great lady in the neighbourhood, to whom Miss Clarke had been in the habit of paying mysterious weekly visits, was already on everybody's lips.

"And then the climax came. By evening it had transpired that in Arthur Clarke's room at 'Hardacres' the police had found an old khaki tunic stuffed away at the bottom of a drawer, and in the pocket of the tunic the key of the locked parlour door. It was an officer's tunic, which had at some time had its buttons and badges taken off; its right sleeve was so torn that it was nearly out of its arm hole; the cuff was all crumpled as if it had been crushed in a damp, hot hand, and there was a small piece of the cloth torn clean out of it. And—I will leave you to guess the importance of this fact—in the tightly-clenched hand of the murdered woman was found the small piece of khaki cloth which corresponded to a hair's breadth with the missing bit in the sleeve of the tunic.

"After that the man in the street shook his head and declared that Arthur Clarke was as good as hung already."

The Man in the Corner had drawn out of his capacious pocket a fresh piece of string. And now his claw-like fingers started to work on it with feverish intentness. I watched him, fascinated, well knowing that his keen mind was just as busy with the problem of the "Hardacres" mystery as were his hands in the fashioning of some intricate and complicated knot.

"I am not," he said after a while, "going to give you an elaborate description of the inquest and of the crowds that collected both inside and out of the court room, hoping to get a glimpse of the principal actors in the exciting drama. By now, of course, all those who had talked of the crime being without apparent motive had effectually been silenced. To every amateur detective, as well as to the professional, the murderer and his nefarious object appeared absolutely revealed to the light of day. Every indication, every scrap of evidence collected up to this hour, both direct and circumstantial, pointed to Arthur Clarke as the murderer of his sister.

"There were the letters, which were alleged to be worth five thousand pounds to the mysterious member of the aristocracy who was paying Miss Clarke a weekly pittance, obviously in order to silence her; there was the strong love motive—the young man in love with the girl far above him in station and wanting to get hold of a large sum of money in order, no doubt, to embark on some profitable business which might help him in his wooing; and there, above all, was the damning bit of khaki cloth in the murdered woman's hand, and the tunic with the key of the locked door in its pocket found in a drawer in Clarke's own room. No, indeed, the inquest was not likely to be a dull affair, more especially as no one doubted what the verdict would be, whilst a good many people anticipated that Clarke would at once be arrested on the coroner's warrant and committed for trial at the next assizes on the capital charge.

"But though we all knew that the inquest would not be dull, yet we were not prepared for the surprises which were in store for us, and which will render that inquest a memorable one in the annals of criminal investigation. To begin with we already knew that Arthur Clarke had now the assistance of Mr. Markham, one of the leading solicitors of Barchester, in his difficult position. Acting on that gentleman's advice Clarke had amplified the statement which he had originally made as to his movements on the fatal afternoon. This amplified statement he now reiterated on oath, and though frankly no one believed him, we were bound to admit that if he could substantiate it, an extraordinary complication would arise, which though it might not eventually clear him altogether, in the minds of thinking people, would at any rate give him the benefit of the doubt. What he now stated was in substance this:

"'The servants at Meere Court,' he said, 'are quite right when they say that I left the party soon after five o'clock. I was rather tired, and after a last dance with Miss St. Jude I went upstairs to pay my respects to Lady Foremeere. Her ladyship, however, kept me talking for some considerable time on one subject and then another, until, to my astonishment, I saw that it was close on seven o'clock, when I hastily took my leave. While I was looking for my coat in the hall, I remember that Lord Foremeere came out of the smoking-room and asked me if I knew whether the party downstairs had broken up. "These things are such a bore," he said, "but I will see if I can get one of them to come up and show you out." I told his lordship not to trouble; however, he rang the bell, and presently the butler, Spinks, came through from the servants' quarters, and his lordship then went upstairs, I think. A minute or two later Miss St. Jude came, also from the servants' quarters; she sent Spinks away telling him that she would look after me; we then talked together for a few moments and then I said goodnight and went straight back to the hotel.'

"Now we had already learned from both the hall-porter and the headwaiter at the Deanery that Mr. Clarke was back at the hotel soon after seven o'clock, that he had his dinner in the restaurant at half-past, and that after spending an hour or so in the lounge after dinner he went up to his room and did not go out again until the following morning. Therefore, all that was needed now was a confirmatory statement from Lady Foremeere to prove Arthur Clarke's innocence, because in that case every hour of his time would be accounted for, from half-past three onwards, whilst Miss Clarke was actually seen alive by two neighbours when she introduced a visitor into her house at half-past five.

"The question would then resolve itself into, who was that visitor? leaving the more important one of the khaki tunic a baffling mystery, rather than a damning evidence.

"The entire court room was on the tiptoe of expectation when Lady Foremeere was formally called. I can assure you that the ubiquitous pin could have been heard to drop during the brief moment's silence when the elegant society woman stood up and disposed her exquisite sable cape about her shoulders and then swore to tell the whole truth and nothing but the truth.

"She answered the coroner's questions in a dear, audible voice, and never wavered in her assertions. She said that her stepdaughter had come up to her *boudoir* and asked her if she would see Mr. Arthur Clarke for a few moments; he had something very important to say to her.

"'I was rather surprised at the strange request,' Lady Foremeere continued with utmost composure, 'and suggested that Mr. Clarke should make his important communication to Lord Foremeere, but my step-daughter insisted and to please her I agreed. I thought that I would get my husband to be present at this mysterious interview, but his lordship was having a short rest in the smoking-room, so on second consideration I decided not to disturb him. A minute or two later Mr.—er—Clarke presented himself and at once I realised that he had had too much to drink.

"'He talked wildly about his desire to marry Miss St. Jude and very excitedly about some compromising letters which he alleged were in his possession and which he threatened to show to Lord Foremeere, if I did not at once give him so many thousand pounds. Naturally I ordered him out of the place, but he wouldn't go for a long time; he got more and more incoherent and excited and it was not until I threatened to fetch Lord Foremeere immediately that he sobered down and finally I went away. He had been in my room about half an hour.'

"'About half an hour?'" was the coroner's earnest comment on this amazing piece of evidence, 'but Mr. Clarke said that when he left your ladyship it was close on seven.'

"'Mr.—er—Clarke is in error,' her ladyship asserted firmly. 'The clock had just struck half-past five when I succeeded in ridding myself of him.'

"You can easily imagine how great was the excitement at this moment and how intensified it became when Lord Foremeere gave evidence in his turn and further confused the issues. He began by corroborating Arthur Clarke's statement about his having spoken to him in the hall at seven o'clock. It was almost unbelievable! Everybody gasped and the coroner almost gave a jump:

"'But her ladyship has just told us,' he said, 'that Clarke left her at half-past five!'

"'That, no doubt, is accurate,' Lord Foremeere rejoined in his stiff, prim manner, 'since her ladyship said so. All I know is that I was asleep in front of the fire in the smoking-room when I heard a loud bang issuing from the hall. I went to see what it was and there I certainly saw Clarke. He was just coming through the glass door which divides the outside vestibule from the hall, and he appeared to me to have come straight out of the wet and to have left his hat and coat in the outer vestibule.'

"'But,' the coroner insisted, 'what made your lordship think that he had come from outside?'

"'Well, for one thing his face and hands were quite wet and he was wiping them with his handkerchief when I first caught sight of him. His boots too were wet and so were the edges of his trousers, and then, as I said, he was coming into the hall from the outer vestibule, and it was the banging of the front door which had roused me.'

"'And the hour then was?'

"'The clock had not long since struck seven. But my butler will be able to confirm this.'

"And Spinks the butler did confirm this portion of his lordship's statement, though he could say nothing about Mr. Clarke's boots being wet; nor did he help Mr. Clarke on with his coat and hat, or open the door for him. Miss St. Jude had practically followed Spinks into the hall, and had at once dismissed him, saying she would look after Mr. Clarke. His lordship in the meanwhile had gone upstairs and Spinks went back into the servants' hall.

"Of course, Miss St. Jude was called. You remember that she had previously stated that Clarke had only left the party at about seven o'clock, that she herself had danced with him most of the time until then, and finally said goodbye to him in the hall. But as this statement was not even corroborated by Clarke's own assertions and entirely contradicted by both Lord and Lady Foremeere's evidence, she was fortunately advised not to repeat it on oath. But she hotly denied the suggestion that Clarke had come in from outside when she said goodbye to him in the hall. She saw him put on his hat and coat and they were quite dry. But nobody felt that her evidence was of any value because she would naturally do her utmost to help her sweetheart.

"Finally, one of the most interesting moments in that memorable enquiry was reached when Lady Foremeere was recalled and asked to state what she knew of Miss Clarke's antecedents.

"'Very little,' she replied. 'I only knew her in France when she worked under me in a hospital. I was very ill at one time and she nursed me devotedly; ever since that I helped her financially as much as I could.'

"'You made her a weekly allowance?' her ladyship was asked.

"'Not exactly,' she replied. 'I just bought her eggs and poultry at a higher figure than she would get from anyone else.'

"'Do you know anything about some letters that she thought were so valuable?'

"'Oh, yes!' the lady replied with a kindly smile. 'Mary had a collection of autograph letters which she had collected whilst she was nursing in France. Among them were some by august, and others by very distinguished personages. She had the idea that these were extraordinarily valuable.'

"'Do you know what became of those letters?'

"'No,' her ladyship replied,' I do not know.'

"'But there were other letters, were there not?' the coroner insisted, 'in which you yourself were interested? The ones Mr. Clarke spoke to you about?'

"'They existed only in Mr. Clarke's imagination, I fancy,' Lady Foremeere replied; 'but he was in such a highly excited state that afternoon that I really could not quite make out what it was that he desired to sell to me.'

"Lady Foremeere spoke very quietly and very simply, without a single note of spite or acerbity in her soft, musical voice. One felt that she was stating quite simple facts that rather bored her, but to which she did not attach any importance. And later on, when Miss Euphemia Clarke retold the story of the packet of letters and of the quarrels which the deceased and her brother had about them, and when the damning evidence of the khaki tunic stood out like an avenging Nemesis pointing at the unfortunate young man, those in court who had imagination saw—positively saw—the hangman's rope tightening around his neck.

4

"And yet the verdict was one of wilful murder against some person or persons unknown," I said, after a slight pause, waiting for the funny creature to take up his narrative again.

"Yes," he replied, "Arthur Clarke has been cleared of every suspicion. He left the court a free man. His innocence was proved beyond question through what everyone thought was the most damnatory piece of evidence against him—the evidence of the khaki tunic. The khaki tunic exonerated Arthur Clarke as completely as the most skilful defender could do. Because if did not fit him. Arthur Clarke was a rather heavy, full grown, broad-shouldered man, the khaki tunic would only fit a slim lad of eighteen. Clarke had admitted the tunic was his, but he had never thought of examining it, and certainly not of trying it on. It was Miss St. Jude who thought of that. Trust a woman in love for getting an inspiration.

"When she was called at the end of the day to affirm the statements which she had previously made to the police and realised that these statements of hers were actually in contradiction with Clarke's own assertions, she worked herself up into at state bordering on hysteria, in the midst of which she caught sight of the khaki tunic on the coroner's table. Of course, she, like everyone else in the neighbourhood, knew all about the tunic, but when April St. Jude actually saw it with her own eyes and realised what its existence meant to her sweetheart, she gave a wild shriek.

"'I'll not believe it,' she cried, 'I'll not believe it. It can't be. It is not Arthur's tunic at all.' Then her eyes dilated, her voice sank to a hoarse whisper, and with a trembling hand she pointed at the tunic: 'Why,' she murmured, 'it is so small, so small! Arthur! Where is Arthur! Why does he not show them all that he never could have worn that tunic?'

"Proverbially there is but a narrow dividing line between tragedy and farce: while some people shuddered and gasped and men literally held their breath, marvelling what would happen next, quite a number of women fell into hysterical giggling. Of course, you remember what happened. The papers have told you all about it. Arthur Clarke was made to try on the khaki tunic and he could not even get his arms into the sleeves. Under no circumstances could he ever have worn that particular tunic. It was several sizes too small for him. Then he examined it closely and recognised it as one he wore in his school O.T.C when he was a lad.

"When he was originally confronted with it, he explained he was so upset, so genuinely terrified at the consequences of certain follies which he undoubtedly had committed, that he could hardly see out of his eyes. The tunic was shown to him and he had admitted that it was his, for he had quite a collection of old tunics which he had always kept. But for the moment he had quite forgotten about the one which he had worn more than eight years ago at school.

"And so the khaki tunic, instead of condemning Clarke had entirely cleared him, for it now became quite evident that the miscreant who had committed the dastardly murder had added this hideous act to his greater crime, and deliberately set to work to fasten the guilt on an innocent man. He had gone up to Clarke's room, opened the wardrobe, picked up a likely garment, no doubt tearing a piece of cloth out of it whilst so doing, and thus getting the fiendish idea of inserting that piece of khaki between the fingers of the murdered woman. Finally, after locking the parlour door, he put the key in the pocket of the tunic and stuffed the latter in the bottom of a drawer.

"It was a clever and cruel trick which well-nigh succeeded in hanging an innocent man. As it is, it has enveloped the affair in an almost impenetrable mystery. I say 'almost' because I know who killed Miss Clarke, even though the public has thrown out an erroneous conjecture. 'It was Lady Foremeere,' they say, 'who killed Miss Clarke.' But at once comes the question:

'How could she?' And the query: 'When?' Arthur Clarke says he was with her until seven, and after that hour there were several members of her household who waited upon her, notably her maid who it seems came up to dress her at about that time, and she and Lord Foremeere sat down to dinner as usual at eight o'clock.

"That there had been one or two dark passages in Lady Foremeere's life, prior to her marriage four years ago, and that Miss Clarke was murdered for the sake of letters which were in some way connected with her ladyship were the only actual undisputable facts in that mysterious case. That it was not Arthur Clarke who killed his sister has been indubitably proved; that a great deal of the evidence was contradictory everyone has admitted. And if the police does not act on certain suggestions which I have made to them, the 'Hardacres' murder will remain a mystery to the public to the end of time.

"'And what are these suggestions?' I asked, without the slightest vestige of irony, for, much against my will, the man's personality exercised a curious fascination over me.

"To keep an eye on Lord Foremeere," the funny creature replied with his dry chuckle, "and see when and how he finally disposes of a wet coat, a dripping hat and soaked boots which he has succeeded in keeping concealed somewhere in the smoking-room, away from the prying eyes even of his own valet."

"'You mean—?' I asked, with an involuntary gasp.

"Yes," he replied. "I mean that it was Lord Foremeere who murdered Miss Clarke for the sake of those letters which apparently contained matter that was highly compromising to his wife. Everything to my mind points to him as the murderer. Whether he knew all along of the existence of the compromising letters, or whether he first knew of this through the conversation between her ladyship and Clarke the day of the servants' party, it is impossible to say; certain it is that he did overhear that conversation and that he made up his mind to end the impossible situation then and there, and to put a stop once and for all to any further attempt at blackmail. It was easy enough for him on that day to pass in and out of the house unperceived.

"No doubt his primary object in going to 'Hardacres' was to purchase the letters from Miss Clarke, money down; perhaps she proved obstinate, perhaps he merely thought that dead men tell no tales. This we shall never know. After the hideous deed, which must have revolted his otherwise fastidious senses, he must have become conscious of an overwhelming hatred for the man who had, as it were, pushed him into crime, and my belief is that the elaborate *mise en scene* of the khaki tunic, and the circumstantial lie that when he came out of the smoking-room Arthur Clarke had obviously just come in from outside was invented not so much with the object of averting any suspicion from himself as with the passionate desire to be revenged on Clarke.

"Think it over," the Man in the Corner concluded, as he stuffed his beloved bit of string into his capacious pocket; "time, opportunity, motive, all are in favour of my theory, so do not be surprised if the early editions of tomorrow's evening papers contain the final sensation in this interesting case."

He was gone before I could say another word, and all that I saw of him was his spook-like figure disappearing through the swing door. There was no one now in the place, so a moment or two later I too paid my bill and went away.

5

The Man in the Corner proved to be right in the end. At eleven o'clock the next morning the street corners were full of newspaper placards with the flaring headlines: "Sudden death of Lord Foremeere." It was reported that on the previous evening his lordship was examining a new automatic which he had just bought and explaining the mechanism to his valet. At one moment he actually made the remark: "It is all right, it isn't loaded," but apparently there was one cartridge left in one of the chambers. His lordship, it seems, was looking straight down the barrel and his finger must accidentally have touched the trigger; anyway, according to the valet's story, there was a sudden explosion, and Lord Foremeere fell, shot right between the eyes.

The verdict at the inquest was of course one of accidental death, the coroner and jury expressing the greatest possible sympathy with Lady Foremeere and Miss St. Jude. It was only subsequently that one or two facts came to light which appeared obscure and unimportant to the man in the street, but which for me, in the light of my conversation with the Man in the Corner, bore earnest significance.

It seems that an hour or two before the accident, the chief superintendent of police had called with two constables at Meere Court and was closeted for a considerable time with Lord Foremeere in the smoking-room. And Spinks, the butler, who subsequently let the three men out, noticed that one of the constables was carrying a coat and a hat, which Spinks knew were old ones belonging to his lordship.

Then I knew that the funny creature in the loud check tweeds and baggy trousers had found the true solution of the 'Hardacres' mystery.

Oh, and you wish to know what was the sequel to the pretty love story between April St. Jude and Arthur Clarke. Well, you know, she married Amos Rottenberg, the New York banker last year, and Clarke runs a successful garage now somewhere in the North. A kind friend must have lent him the capital wherewith to make a start. I can make a shrewd guess who that kind friend was.

The Mystery of the Ingres Masterpiece

1

I did not see the Man in the Corner for several weeks after that strange meeting in the blameless tea-shop. The exigencies of my work kept me busy, and somehow the sensational suicide of Lord Foremeere which had appeared like the logical sequence of the spook-like creature's deductions, had left a painful impression on my mind. Entirely illogically, I admit, I felt that the Man in the Corner had had something to do with the tragedy.

But when in March of that year we were all thrilled by the mystery of the valuable Ingres picture, and wherever one went one heard conjectures and explanations of that extraordinary case, my thoughts very naturally reverted to the funny creature and his bit of string, and I found myself often wondering what his explanation of what seemed a truly impenetrable mystery could possibly be.

The facts certainly were very puzzling in themselves. When first I was deputed by the *Express Post* to put them clearly and succinctly before its readers, I found the task strangely difficult; this, for the simple reason that I myself could not see daylight through it all, and often did I stand in front of the admirable reproduction which I possess of the Ingres "*La Fiancée*" wondering if those smiling lips would not presently speak and tell me how an original and exquisite picture could possibly have been in two different places at one and the same time.

For that, in truth, was the depth of the puzzle. We will, if you please, call the original owners of the picture the Duke and Duchess Paul de Rochechouart. That, of course, is not their name, but, as you all know what they really are, it matters not what I call them for the purpose of recording their singular adventure.

His Grace had early in life married a Swedish lady of great talent and singular beauty. She was an artist of no mean order, having exhibited pictures of merit both at the Paris *salon* and at the Royal Academy in London; she was also an accomplished musician, and had published one or two very charming volumes of poetry.

The duke and his wife were devoted to one another; they lived for the greater part of the year at their beautiful *château* on the Oise, not far from Chantilly, and here they entertained a great deal, more after the homely and hospitable manner of English country houses than in the more formal foreign fashion. Here, too, they had collected some rare furniture, tapestries, and objects of art and *vertu*, amongst which certain highly-prized pictures of the French School of the Nineteenth Century.

The war, we may imagine, left the Duc de Rochechouart and his charming wife a good deal poorer, as it left most other people in France, and soon it became known amongst the art dealers of London, Paris and New York that they had decided to sell one or two of their most valuable pictures; foremost amongst these was the celebrated "*La Fiancée*" by Ingres.

Immediately there was what is technically known as a ramp after the picture. Dealers travelled backwards and forwards from all the great Continental cities to the *château* on the Oise to view the picture. Offers were made for it by cable, telegram and telephone, and the whole art world was kept in a flutter over what certainly promised to be a sensational deal.

Alas! as with most of the beautiful possessions of this impoverished old world, the coveted prize was destined to go to the country that had the longest purse. A certain Mr. Aaron Jacobson, the Chicago multi-millionaire, presently cabled an offer of half a million dollars for the picture, an offer which, rumour had it, the Duc de Rochechouart had since accepted. Mr. Jacobs was said to be a charming, highly-cultured man, a great art connoisseur and a great art lover, and presently one heard that he had already set sail for Europe with the intention of fetching away his newly-acquired treasure himself.

On the very day following Mr. Jacob's arrival as the guest of the Duc and Duchesse de Rochechouart at the latter's *château*, the world-famous picture was stolen in broad daylight by a thief or thieves who contrived to make away with their booty without leaving the slightest clue, so it was said, that might put the police on their track. The picture was cut clean out of the frame, an operation which must have taken at least two or three minutes. It always used to hang above the tall chimneypiece in the *duchesse's* studio, but that self-same morning it had been lifted down and placed on an easel in the dining hall, no doubt for closer inspection by the purchaser. This easel stood in a corner of the hall, close to one of the great windows that overlooked the gardens of the *château*.

The amazing point in this daring theft was that a garden *fête* and tennis tournament were in progress at the time. A crowd of guests was spread all over the lawns and grounds in full view of the windows of the hall, and, as far as the preliminary investigations were able to establish, there were not more than twenty or twenty-five minutes at most during which some servant or other inmate of the *château* had not either actually been through the hall or had occasion to observe the windows.

The dining hall itself has monumental doors which open on the great central vestibule, and immediately facing it similar doors give on the library. The marble vestibule runs right through the centre of the main building, it has both a front and a garden entrance, and all the reception rooms open out of it, right and left. Close to the front door entrance is one of the main ways into the kitchens and offices.

Now right away until half-past four on that fateful afternoon the servants were up and down the vestibule, busy with arrangements for tea which they were serving outside on the lawns. The tennis tournament was then drawing to a close, the *duchesse* was on the lawn with her guests, dispensing tea, and at half-past four precisely the Duc de Rochechouart came into the *château* by way of the garden entrance, went across the vestibule and into the library to fetch the prizes which were to be distributed to the victors in the tournament, and which were locked up in his desk. The doors of the dining hall were wide open and the *duc* walking past them peeped into the room.

The picture was in its place then, and he gave a glance at it as he passed, conscious of a pang of regret at thought that he must needs part with this precious treasure. It took the *duc* some little time to sort the prizes, and as in the meanwhile the afternoon post had come in and a few letters had been laid on his desk, he could not resist the desire to glance through his correspondence. On the whole he thought that he might have been in the library about a quarter of an hour or perhaps more. He had closed the door when he entered the room, and when he came out again he certainly noticed that the doors of the dining-hall were shut. But there was nothing in this to arouse his suspicions, and with the neatly tied parcels containing the prizes under his arm, he recrossed the vestibule and went out once more into the garden.

At five o'clock M. Amede, the chief butler, had occasion to go into the dining hall to fetch a particular silver tray which he required. He owned to being astonished at finding the doors closed, because he had been past them a quarter of an hour before that and they were wide open then. However, he entered the room without any serious misgivings, but the next moment he nearly fainted with horror at sight of the empty frame upon the easel. The very first glance had indeed revealed the nefarious deed. The picture had not been moved out of its frame, it was the canvas that had been cut. M. Amede, however, knowing what was due to his own dignity did not disturb the entire household then and there; he made his way quietly back into the garden where the distribution of prizes after the tournament was taking place and, seizing a favourable opportunity, he caught *M le Duc's* eye and imparted to him the awful news.

Even so nothing was said until after the guests had departed. By the *duc's* orders the doors leading into the dining hall were locked, and to various enquiries after the masterpiece made by inquisitive ladies, the evasive answer was given that the picture was in the hands of the packers.

There remained the house party, which, of course, included Mr. Aaron Jacobs. There were also several ladies and gentlemen staying at the *château*, and before they all went up to their rooms to dress for dinner, they were told what had happened. In the meanwhile, the police had already been sent for, and *M le Commissaire* was conducting his preliminary investigations. The rooms and belongings of all the servants were searched, and, with the consent of the guests themselves, this search was extended to their rooms. A work of art worth half a million dollars could not thus be allowed to disappear and the thief to remain undetected for the sake of social conventions, and as the law stands in France any man may be guilty of a crime until he be proved innocent.

2

The theft of the Ingres masterpiece was one of those cases which interest the public in every civilised country, and here in England where most people are bitten with the craze for criminal investigation it created quite a sensation in its way.

I remember that when we all realised for the first time that the picture had in very truth disappeared, and that the French police, despite its much vaunted acumen, had entirely failed to find the slightest trace of the thief, we at once began to look about for a romantic solution of the mystery. M le Duc de Rochechouart and his pretty *duchesse* had above all our deepest sympathies, for it had very soon transpired that neither the Ingres masterpiece, nor indeed any of the *duc's* valuable collection of art works, was insured. This fact seems almost incredible to English minds, with whom every kind of insurance is part and parcel of the ordinary household routine. But abroad the system is not nearly so far-reaching or so extended, and there are numberless households in every degree of the social scale who never dream of spending money on insurances save, perhaps, against fire.

Be that as it may, the fact remained that "*La Fiancée*" was not insured against theft, and that through the action of an unknown miscreant the Duc and Duchesse de Rochechouart would, unless the police did ultimately succeed in tracing the stolen masterpiece, find themselves the poorer by half a million dollars. With their usual lack of logic, readers of the half-penny Press promptly turned their attention to Mr. Aaron Jacobs, the intending purchaser. Being a Chicago multi-millionaire does not, it appears, render a man immune from the temptation of acquiring by dishonest means the things which he covets.

Anyway, the public decided that Mr. Jacobs was not so rich as he was reputed to be, but that, on the other hand, being as greedy for the possession of European works of art as any ogre for human flesh, he had stolen the picture which he could not afford to buy; and ten, or mayhap fifteen years hence, when the story of the mysterious theft will have been consigned to oblivion, Mr. Jacobs would display the masterpiece in his gallery. How this was to be accomplished without the subsequent intervention of the police those wiseacres did not attempt to explain.

The mystery remained impenetrable for close on two years. Many other sensations, criminal or otherwise, had, during that time, driven the affair of the Ingres masterpiece out of the public mind. Then suddenly the whole story was revived and in a manner which proved far more exciting than anyone had surmised. It was linked—though the European public did not know this—with the death in July, 1919, of Charles B. Tupper, the head of one of the greatest cinematograph organisations in the States—a man who for the past few years had controlled over two thousand theatres, and had made millions in his day.

Sometime during the war, he had married the well-known cinema star, Anita Hodgkins, a beautiful entirely uneducated girl who hailed from Upper Tooting. The will of Mr. Charles B. Tupper was proved for a fabulous sum, and, as soon as his affairs were settled, Mrs. Tupper, who presumably had remained Cockney at heart as well as in speech, set sail for England with the intention of settling down once more in the country of her birth. She bought Holt Manor, a magnificent house in Buckinghamshire, sent for all her splendid furniture and belongings from America, and, early in 1920, when her palatial residence was ready for occupation, she married Lord Polchester, a decadent young nincompoop, who was said to have fallen in love with her when he first saw her face on the screen.

Presumably Mrs. Anita Tupper nee Hodgkins hugged herself with the belief that once she was styled my lady, she would automatically become a social star as she had been a cinema one in the past. But in this harmless ambition she was at first disappointed. Though she had furnished her new house lavishly, though paragraphs appeared in all the halfpenny and weekly Press giving details of the sumptuous establishment of which the new Lady Polchester was queen, though she appeared during the London season of 1920 at several official functions and went to an evening Court that year, wearing pearls that might have been envied by an empress, she found that in Buckinghamshire the best people were shy of calling on her, and the bits of pasteboard that were from time to time left at her door came chiefly from the neighbouring doctors, parsons, or retired London tradespeople, or from mothers with marriageable daughters who looked forward to parties at the big house and consequent possible matrimonial prizes.

This went on for a time and then Lady Polchester, wishing no doubt to test the intentions of the county towards her, launched out invitations for a garden party! The invitations included the London friends she had recently made, and a special train from Paddington was to bring those friends to the party. Among these was Mr. Aaron Jacobs. He had known the late Charles B. Tupper over in the States, and had met Lady Polchester more recently at one of the great functions at the United States Embassy in London. She had interested him with a glowing account of her splendid collection of works of art, of pictures and antique furniture which she had inherited from her first husband and which now adorned her house in Buckinghamshire, and when she asked him down to her party he readily accepted, more I imagine out of curiosity to see the objects in which he was as keenly interested as ever, than from a desire to establish closer acquaintanceship with the lady.

The garden party at Holt Manor, as the place was called, does not appear to have been a great social success. For one thing it rained the whole afternoon, and the military band engaged for the occasion proved too noisy for indoor entertainment. But some of the guests were greatly interested in the really magnificent collection of furniture, tapestries, pictures and works of art which adorned the mansion, and after tea Lady Polchester graciously conducted them all over the house, pointing out herself the most notable pieces in the collection and never failing to mention the price at which the late Mr. Charles B. Tupper purchased the work of art in question.

And that is when the sensation occurred. Following their hostess, the guests had already seen and duly admired two really magnificent Van Dycks that hung in the hall, when she turned to them and said, with a flourish of her plentifully be-gemmed hands;

"You must come into the library and see the picture for which Mr. Tupper gave over half a million dollars. I never knew I had it, as he never had it taken out of its case, and I never saw it until this year when it came over with all my other things from our house in New York. Lord Polchester had it unpacked and hung in the library. I don't care much about it myself, and the late Mr. Tupper hadn't the time to enjoy his purchase, because he died two days after the picture arrived in New York, and, as I say, he never had it unpacked. He bought it for use in a commercial undertaking which he had in mind at one time, then the scheme fell through, and I am sure I never thought any more about the old picture."

With that she led the way into the library, a nobly-proportioned room lined with books in choice bindings, and with a beautiful Adams chimneypiece, above which hung a picture.

Of course, there were some people present who had never heard of the stolen Ingres, but there must have been a few who, as they entered the room, must literally have gasped with astonishment, for there it certainly was. "*La Fiancée*" with her marvellously painted Eastern draperies, her exquisitely drawn limbs and enigmatic smile, was smiling down from the canvas, just as if she had every right to be in the house of the ex-cinema star, and as if there had not been a gigantic fuss about her throughout the whole art world of Europe.

We may take it that the person by far the most astonished at that moment was Mr. Aaron Jacobs. But he was too thoroughly a gentleman and too much a man of the world to betray his feelings then, and I suppose that those who, like himself, had thought they recognised the stolen masterpiece, did not like to say anything either until they

215

were more sure: English people in all grades of society being proverbi-ally averse to being what they would call "mixed up" in any kind of a fuss. Certain it is that nothing was said at the moment to disturb Lady Polchester's complacent equanimity, and after a while the party broke up and the guests departed.

Of course, people thought that Mr. Aaron Jacobs should have in-formed Lord Polchester of his intentions before he went to the police. But Lord Polchester was such a nonentity in his own household, such a frivolous fool, and, moreover, addicted to drink and violent fits of temper, that those who knew him easily realised how a sensible busi-ness man like Mr. Aaron Jacobs would avoid any personal explanations with him.

Mr. Jacobs went straight to the police that self-same evening, and the next day Lady Polchester had a visit from Detective Purley, one of the ablest as he was one of the most tactful men on the staff. But indeed, he had need of all his tact in face of the infuriated cinema star when that lady realised the object of his visit.

"How dared they come and ask her such impertinent questions?" she stormed. "Did they imagine she had stolen the beastly picture which she would as soon throw on the dust heap as look at again? She, who could buy up all the pictures in any gallery and not feel the pinch" and so on; and so on. The unfortunate Purley had a very unpleasant quarter of an hour, but after a while he succeeded in paci-fying the irate lady and got her to listen calmly to what he had to say.

He managed to make her understand that without casting the slightest aspersion upon her honourability or that of the late Charles B. Tupper, there was no getting away from the fact that the picture now hanging in the library of Holt Manor was the property of the Duc de Rochechouart from whose house in France it was stolen over two years before—to be quite accurate it was stolen on July 25th, 1919.

"Then," retorted the lady, by no means convinced or mollified, "I can prove you all to be liars, for the late Mr. Charles B. Tupper bought the old thing long before that. He had been on the Continent in the spring of 1919 and landed in New York again on May 18th. He told me then that he had made some interesting purchases in Europe, amongst them there was a picture for which he had paid half a mil-lion dollars. I scolded him about it, us I thought he was throwing his money away on such stuff, but he said that he wanted to make use of the picture for some wonderful advertising scheme he had in his mind, so I said no more about it. But that is the picture you say was stolen from some duke or other in July, when I tell you that it had been shipped for New York a month at least before that."

Perhaps at this point Detective Purley failed to conceal altogether a slight look of incredulity, for Lady Polchester turned on him once more like a fury.

"So, you still think I stole the dirty old picture, do you?" she cried, using further language that is quite unprintable, "and you think that I am such a ninny and that I will give it up simply because you are trying to bully me. But I won't, so there! I can prove the truth of every word I say, and I don't care if I have to spend another million dollars to put your old duke in prison for talking such rot about me."

Once again Purley's tact had to come into play, and after a while he succeeded in soothing the lady's outraged feelings. With infinite patience he gradually got her to view the matter more calmly and above all not to look upon him as an enemy, but as a friend whose one desire was to throw light upon what certainly seemed an extraordinary mystery.

"Very well, then," she said, after a while, "I'll tell you all I can. I don't know when the picture was shipped from Europe but I do know that a case addressed to Mr. Charles B. Tupper and marked 'valuable picture with great care' was delivered at our house in New York on July 18th. I can't mistake the date because Mr. Tupper was already very ill when the case arrived and he died two days later, that is on July 20th, 1919. That you can ascertain easily enough, can't you?" Lady Polchester added tartly. Then as Purley offered no comment she went on more quietly:

"That's all right, then. Now let me tell you that the case containing this picture was in my house two days before Mr. Tupper died, and that I never had it undone until a couple of months ago, here in this house. I had it shipped from New York, not along with all my things, but by itself; and there is the lawyer over there, Mr. George F. Topham, who can tell you all about the case.

"I was too upset what with Mr. Tupper's illness and then his death, and the will and the whole bag of tricks to trouble much about it myself, but I told the lawyer that it contained a picture for which Mr. Tupper had paid half a million dollars, and it was put down for probate for that amount; the lawyer took charge of the old thing, and he can swear, and lots of people over in the States can swear that the case was never undone. And the shipping company can swear that it never was touched whilst it was in their charge. They delivered it here and their men opened the case for us and helped us to hang the picture.

"And now," concluded Lady Polchester, not because she had nothing more to say but presumably because she was out of breath, "now perhaps you'll tell me how a picture which was over in New York on the 18th of July can have been stolen from France on the 25th; and if you can't tell me that, then I'll trouble you to clear out of my house, for I've no use for Nosey Parkers about the place."

The unfortunate Purley had certainly, by all accounts, rather a rough time of it with the lady. Nor could he arrive at any satisfactory arrangement with her. Needless to say, that she absolutely refused to give up the picture unless she were forced to do so by law, and even then, she dared say, she could make it very unpleasant for some people.

3

The next event of any importance in this extraordinary case was the action brought by the Duc and Duchesse de Rochechouart here in England against Lady Polchester for illegal detention of their property.

It very soon transpired that several witnesses had come over from the States in order to corroborate the lady's assertions with regard to her rightful ownership of the picture, and the public was once more on the tiptoe of expectation.

The case came on for hearing in March and only lasted two days. The picture was in court and was identified first by the Duc and the Duchesse de Rochechouart and then by two or three experts as the genuine work of Ingres: "*La Fiancée*" known throughout the entire art world as having been purchased by the *duc's* grandfather from the artist himself in 1850, and having been in the possession of the family uninterruptedly ever since. The *duc* himself had last seen it in his own *château* at half past four on the afternoon of July 25, 1919.

A well-known peculiarity about the masterpiece was that it had originally been painted on a somewhat larger canvas, and that the artist himself, at the request of the original purchaser, had it cut smaller and re-strained on a smaller stretcher; this alteration was, of course, distinctly visible on the picture. The frame was new; it was admittedly purchased by Lady Polchester recently. When the picture came into her possession it was unframed.

On that lady's behalf on the other hand there was a formidable array of witnesses, foremost amongst these being Mr. Anthony Kleeberger, who was the late Charles B. Tupper's secretary and manager. He was the first to throw some light on the original transaction whereby "*La Fiancée*" first came into his employer's possession.

"Mr. Tupper," he explained, "was the inventor of a new process of colour photography which he desired to test and then to advertise all over the world by means of reproduction from some world-famous masterpiece, and when during the spring of 1919 I accompanied him to Europe, one of the objects which he had in mind was the purchase of a picture suitable for his purpose. It pretty soon was known all over the art world of the Continent what we were after and that Mr. Tupper was prepared to pay a big price for his choice. You would be surprised if I were to tell you of some of the offers we had in Vienna, in London, even in Rome.

"At last, when we were staying in Paris, Mr. Tupper came to me one day and told me he had at last found the very picture he wanted. He had gone to the studio of a picture restorer who had written to him and offered him a genuine Ingres. He had seen the picture and liked it, and had agreed to give the owner half a million dollars for it. I thought this a terrific price and frankly I was a little doubtful whether my employer had a sufficient knowledge of art to enter into a transaction of this sort. I feared that he might be badly had, and buying some spurious imitation rather than a masterpiece.

"But Mr. Tupper was always a queer man in business. Once he had made up his mind there was no arguing with him. 'I like the picture,' was all that he ever said to me in response to some timid suggestion on my part that he should seek expert advice, 'and I have agreed to buy it for half a million dollars, simply because the fellow would not part with it for less. I believe it to be genuine. But if it is not, I don't care. It will answer my purpose and there it is.'

"He then gave me instructions to see about the packing and forwarding of the picture and this I did. I must say that I had terrible misgivings about the whole affair. I certainly thought the picture magnificent, but of course I am no judge. It had a worthless frame round it which I discarded in order to facilitate the packing. The picture restorer's studio was up a back street in the Montmartre quarter. He and his wife saw to the packing themselves; I never saw anybody else in the place. I arranged for the forwarding of the case, for the insurance and so on, and I myself handed over to the vendor, whose name was given to me as Matthieu Vignard, five hundred thousand dollar bills in the name and on account of my employer, Mr. Charles B. Tupper.

"Of course, I presumed that the snuffy old man and his blousey wife were acting for some personage who desired to remain unknown, and as time went on and there was no talk in the art world or in the newspapers then about any great masterpiece being stolen, I soon forgot my misgivings, and a couple of months later I set out on Mr. Tupper's business for Central America where I remained for close on two years.

"Half the time during those years I was up country in Costa Rica, Venezuela and so on where newspapers are scarce, and when the hue and cry was after a picture stolen from the house of the Duc de Rochechouart, I knew nothing about it. But this picture now in court is certainly the one which Mr. Tupper bought in Paris at the end of June 1919, and which I myself saw packed and nailed down in its case and forwarded to New York where it arrived two days before Mr. Tupper's death."

That was the substance of Mr. Kleeberger's evidence, by far the most important heard on the first day of the action. After that the testimony of other witnesses went to confirm the whole story. There was the well-known New York solicitor, Mr. George F. Topham, who took charge of the picture after the death of his client, Mr. Tupper, and the managing director of the Nebraska Safe Deposit Company where it was stored until Lady Polchester sent for it. There were the managers of the shipping companies who forwarded the picture from Paris to New York in June—July 1919, and from New York to Holt Manor in the following year, and there were the removal men and servants who saw the picture unpacked and hung in the library at the Manor.

It took two days to go through all that evidence, but it was never either conflicting or doubtful. Yet the one supreme, mysterious contradiction remained, namely, that the picture now in court, the wonderful Ingres masterpiece, was bought by Mr. Tupper in Paris in June 1919, and then and there shipped over by him to New York, and that, nevertheless, it was stated never to have left the Duc de Rochechouart's possession from the day when his grandfather bought it more than seventy years ago until that memorable twenty-fifth of July, 1919, when it was stolen on the very day it was about to pass into the possession of Mr. Aaron Jacobs. One felt one's head reeling when one thought out this amazing puzzle, and the decision of the learned judge was awaited with palpitating curiosity.

But after the second day of the action, just before it was adjourned, counsel on both sides were able to announce that their respective clients had come to an exceedingly satisfactory arrangement. All aspersions as to the honourability of the late Charles B. Tupper or of Lady Polchester would be publicly withdrawn and a notice to that effect would appear in all the leading newspapers of London, Paris and New York; and Lady Polchester would now remain in undisputed possession of the Ingres masterpiece, having paid its rightful owner the Duc de Rochechouart the sum of one hundred and twenty thousand pounds for it.

So, both parties we may take it were completely satisfied; at one time it had looked as if the unfortunate duke would be done both out of his picture and out of the money, and another as if Lady Polchester would be so defrauded. But now all was well and the learned judge declared himself pleased with the agreement. Not so the public who were left to face a mystery which everyone felt would never now be cleared up.

I for one felt completely at sea, so much so indeed that my thoughts instinctively flew to the curious creature in the blameless tea-shop who I felt sure would have a theory of his own which would account for what was puzzling us all.

And a day or two later I saw him, weaving a fantastic design of knots in a piece of string: He knew that I wished to hear his explanation of the mystery of the Ingres masterpiece, but he kept me on tenterhooks for some time, wearing out my patience with his sharp, sarcastic comments.

"Do you admit," he asked me at one time, with his exasperating chuckle, "that the Ingres masterpiece could have been in two places at one and the same time?"

"No, of course," I replied, "I do not admit such nonsense."

"Very well then," he resumed, "what is the logical conclusion?"

"That there were two pictures," I said coldly.

"Of course, there were two pictures. And as the great Mr. Ingres did not presumably paint his masterpiece in duplicate, we must take it that one picture was the original and the other the copy."

Now it was my turn to grow sarcastic and I retorted drily:

"Having done that, we are no nearer a solution of the mystery than we were before."

"Are we not?" he rejoined with a cackle like an old hen. "Now it seems to me that when we have admitted that one of the pictures was a copy of the other, and when we know that the picture which Mr. Charles B. Tupper bought was the original, because that was the one that was produced in court, we must come to the conclusion that the one which was stolen from the *château* in France could only have been the copy."

"Why yes," I admitted, "but then again we have been told that the grandfather of the present Duc de Rochechouart bought the picture from the artist himself, and that it has been in the uninterrupted possession of his family ever since."

"And I am willing to admit that the picture was in the uninterrupted possession of the Duc de Rochechouart until the present holder of the title or someone who had access to it in the same way as himself sold it to Mr. Charles B. Tupper in June 1919."

"But you don't mean—"

"Surely," the funny creature went on with his dry cackle, "it was not such a very difficult little bit of dishonesty to perpetrate, seeing that Mme la Duchesse was such an accomplished artist. Can you not imagine the lady being like many of us, very short of money, and then hearing of Mr. Charles B. Tupper, the American business man who was searching Europe through for a world-famous masterpiece; can you not see her during one of her husband's pleasure trips to Paris or elsewhere setting to work to make an exact replica of "*La Fiancée.*" We know that it always hung in her studio until the day when it was moved to the dining hall. Think how easy it was for her to substitute her own copy for the original. The only difficulty would be the conveying of the picture to Paris, but an artist knows how to take a canvas off its stretcher, to roll it up and re-strain it.

"Here I think that she must have had a confederate, probably some down-at-heel friend of her past artistic days, a man whom she paid lavishly both for his help and his silence. Who that man was I suppose we shall never know. The so-called Matthew Vignard and his 'blousey wife,' as Mr. Kleeberger picturesquely described her, have completely disappeared; no trace of them was ever found. They hired a studio at Montmartre for one month, paid the *concierge* the rent in advance, and at the end of that time they decamped and have never been heard of since, but unless I am much mistaken, they must at the present moment be carrying on a very lucrative little blackmailing business, because it must have been Vignard who conveyed the picture to Paris in the same way as we know it was he who first approached Charles B. Tupper and ultimately sold him the picture."

"But surely," I objected, for the funny creature had paused a moment, and I could not deny that his arguments were sound, "surely it would have been more practical to have sold the copy—which we suppose must have been perfect—to Mr. Tupper who was a layman and an outsider, and to have kept the original in the *château*, as the *duc* was even then negotiating for its sale, and most of the art dealers were coming to have a look at it."

He did not reply immediately but remained for a while deeply absorbed in the contemplation of his beloved bit of string.

"That," he admitted with complacent condescension, "would be a sound argument if we admit at once that the *duchesse* knew for a certainty that her husband intended to sell 'La Fiancée.' But my contention is that at the time that she sold the picture to Mr. Tupper she had no idea that the *duc* had any such intentions. No doubt when she knew this for a fact, she must have been beside herself with horror; no doubt also that she had a hard fight with her own terror before she made a clean breast of her misdeed to her husband. Apparently, she did not do this until the very last moment, until the day when the picture was actually taken out of her studio and placed upon an easel in the dining-hall for closer inspection. Then discovery was imminent and we must suppose that she made full confession.

"The *duc*, like a gallant gentleman, at once set his wits thinking how best to save his wife's reputation without endangering his own. To have admitted to Mr Aaron Jacobs and to the other experts and art dealers who had come to see the masterpiece that a Duc de Rochechouart was trying to sell a spurious imitation whilst having already disposed of the original was, of course, unthinkable; and thus, the idea presented itself to Their Graces that the copy must be made to disappear effectually. A favourable circumstance for the success of this scheme was the garden *fête* which was to take place that afternoon, when the house would be full of guests, of strangers and of servants, when surveillance would be slack and the comings and goings of the master of the house would easily pass unperceived.

"The *duc*, in my opinion, chose that one quarter of an hour when he was alone in the house to cut the picture out of its frame. He then hid the canvas sufficiently skilfully that it was never found. Probably he thought at the time that there the matter would end, but equally probably he never gave the future another thought. His own position was unassailable seeing he was not insured against loss, and it was the present alone that mattered: the fact that a Duc de Rochechouart was trying to sell a spurious picture for half a million dollars. To many French men and women ever since the war, America is a far country, and no doubt the *duc* and *duchesse* both hoped that the whole transaction, including the Ingres masterpiece, would soon lie buried somewhere at the bottom of the sea.

"Fate and Lady Polchester proved too strong for them; they ordained that '*La Fiancée*' should be brought back to Europe, and that the whole of its exciting history be revived. But fate proved kind in the end, and I think that you will agree with me that two such daring and resourceful adventurers as Their Graces deserve the extra half million dollars which, thanks to Lady Polchester's generosity or ostentation, they got unexpectedly.

"Soon afterwards you will remember that the Duc and Duchesse de Rochechouart sold their *château* on the Oise together with the bulk of their collection of pictures and furniture.

"They now live in Sweden, I understand, where the *duchesse* has many friends and relations and where the law of libel will not trouble you much if you publish my deductions in your valuable magazine.

"Think it all out," the Man in the Corner concluded glibly "and from every point of view, and you will see that there is not a single flaw in my argument. I have given you the only possible solution of the mystery of the Ingres masterpiece."

"You may be right—" I murmured thoughtfully.

"I know I am," he answered drily.

The Mystery of the Pearl Necklace

1

The Man in the Corner had a very curious theory about that mysterious affair of the pearl necklace, and though it all occurred a few years ago, I am tempted to put his deductions down on record, because, as far as I know, neither the police of this or any other country, nor the public, have ever found a satisfactory solution for what was undoubtedly a strange and mystifying adventure.

I remembered the case quite well when first he spoke to me about it one afternoon in what had become my favourite tea-haunt in Fleet Street; the only thing I was not quite certain of was the identity of the august personage to whom the pearl necklace was to be presented. I do know, of course, that she belonged to one of the reigning families of Europe, and that she had been an active and somewhat hot-headed and bitter opponent of the communist movement in her own country, in consequence of which both she and her exalted husband had been the object of more than one murderous attack by the other side. It was on the occasion of the august lady's almost miraculous escape from a peculiarly well-planned and brutal assault that a number of ladies in England subscribed the sum of £15,000 for the purchase of an exquisite pearl necklace to be presented to her as a congratulatory gift.

Rightly or wrongly, the donors of this princely gift feared that a certain well-known political organisation on the Continent would strive by every means in its power, fair or foul, to prevent this token of English goodwill from reaching the recipient, and also, as it chanced to happen, there had been during the past few months a large number of thefts of valuables on Continental railways, and it became a question who should be entrusted by the committee of subscribers with the perilous task of taking the necklace over for presentation; the trouble being further enhanced by the fact that in those days the insurance companies barred one or two European countries from their comprehensive policies against theft and petty larceny, and that it was to one of those countries thus barred that the bearer of the £15,000 necklace would have to journey.

Imagine the excitement, the anxiety, which reigned in the hearts of the thousands of middle-class English women who had subscribed their *mite* towards the gift! Their committee sat behind closed doors discussing the claims of various volunteers who were ready to undertake the journey: these worthy folk were quite convinced that certain well-known leaders of anarchical organisations would be on the lookout for the booty and would have special facilities for the theft of it at the frontier during the course of those endless customs and passport formalities for which that particular country was ever famous.

Finally, the committee's choice fell upon a certain Captain Arthur Saunders, nephew of Sir Montague Bowden, who was chairman of the ladies' committee. Captain Saunders had, it seems, travelled abroad a great deal, and his wife was foreign—Swedish, so it was understood; it was thought that if he went abroad now in the company of his wife, the object of their journey might be thought to be a visit to Mrs. Saunders's relations, and the conveying of the pearl necklace to its destination might thus remain more or less a secret.

The choice was approved of by all the subscribers, and it was decided that Captain and Mrs. Saunders should start by the 10 a.m. train for Paris on the 16th of March. Captain Saunders was to call the previous afternoon at a certain bank in Charing Cross where the necklace was deposited, and there receive it as an almost sacred trust from the hands of the manager. Further, it was arranged that Mrs. Saunders should, immediately on arrival in Paris, send a wire to Mrs. Berners, a great friend of hers who was the secretary of the committee, and in fact that she should keep the committee informed of Captain Saunders's wellbeing at all the more important points of their journey.

And thus, they started.

But no news came from Paris on the 16th. At first no anxiety was felt on that score, everyone being ready to surmise that the Calais-Paris train had been late in, and that the Saunders's had perhaps only barely time to clear their luggage at the Customs and catch the train *deluxe* which would take them on, *via* Cologne, without a chance of sending the promised telegram. But soon after midday of the 17th, Sir Montague Bowden had a wire from Mrs. Saunders from Paris saying:

Arthur disappeared since last night. Desperately anxious. Please

226

come at once. Save booked room for you here. Mary. Hotel Majestic.

The news was terrifying; however, Sir Montague Bowden, with commendable zeal, at once wired to Mary announcing his immediate departure for Paris, and as it was then too late for him to catch the afternoon Continental train, he started by the evening one, travelling all night and arriving at the Hotel Majestic in the early morning. He had thought it more prudent to say nothing about the matter before he left England. The news, he thought, would travel fast enough when it became necessary for the members of the committee to know what had occurred, and for the present, at any rate. Sir Montague was still hoping that as soon as he arrived in Paris, he would find that the whole thing was only an ugly nightmare.

As soon as he had had a bath and some breakfast he went in search of information. He found that the French police had already the "*affaire*" in hand, but that they had not so far, the slightest clue to the mysterious disappearance of the Capitaine Saunders. He found the management of the Majestic in a state of offended dignity, and Mrs. Saunders in one that verged on hysteria, but fortunately he also found at the hotel a Mr. Haasberg, brother of Mrs. Saunders, a Swedish business man of remarkable coolness and clearness of judgment, who promptly put him *au fait* of what had occurred.

It seems that Mr. Haasberg was settled in business in Paris, and that he had hoped to catch a glimpse of his sister and brother-in-law on the evening of the 16th at the Gare du Nord, on their way through to the East, but that on that very morning he had received a telegram from Mary asking him to book a couple of rooms—a bedroom and a sitting-room—for one night for them at the Hotel Majestic. This Mr. Haasberg did, glad enough that he would see something more of his sister than he had been led to hope.

On the afternoon of the 16th, he was kept late at business and was unable to meet the Saunders's at the station, but towards nine o'clock he walked to the Majestic hoping to find them in. Their room was on the third floor. Mr. Haasberg went up in the lift, and as soon as he reached No. 301, he became aware of a buzz of conversation coming from within, which, however, ceased as soon as he had pushed open the door. On entering the room, he saw that Captain Saunders had a visitor, a tall, thick-set man who wore an old-fashioned heavy moustache, and large, gold-rimmed spectacles. At sight of Mr. Haasberg the man clapped his hat—a bowler—on his head, pulled his coat collar over his ears, and with a hasty: "Well—s'long, old man. I'll wait till tomorrow!" spoken with a strong foreign accent, he walked rapidly out of the room and down the corridor. Haasberg stood for a moment in the doorway to watch the disappearing personage but he did this without any ulterior motive or thought of suspicion; then he turned back into the room and greeted his brother-in-law.

Saunders seemed to Haasberg to be nervous and ill-at-ease; in response to the latter's inquiry after Mary, he explained that she had remained in her room as he had a man to see on business. Haasberg made some casual remark about this visitor, and then Mary Saunders came in—she too appeared troubled and agitated and as soon as she had greeted her brother, she turned to her husband and asked very eagerly:

"Well, has he gone?"

Saunders, giving a significant glance in Haasberg's direction, replied with an obvious effort at indifference: "Yes, yes, he's gone. But he said he would be back tomorrow."

At which Mary seemed to give a sigh of relief.

Scenting some uncomfortable mystery Haasberg questioned her and also Saunders about their visitor, but could not elicit any satisfactory explanation.

"Oh, there is nothing mysterious about old Pasquier," was all that either of them would say.

"He is an old pal of Arthur's," Mary added lightly, "but he is such an awful bore that I got Arthur to say that I was out, so that he might get rid of him more quickly."

But somehow Haasberg felt that these explanations were very lame. He could not get it out of his head that there was something mysterious about the visitor, and knowing the purpose of the Saunders's journey, he thought it as well to give them a very serious word of warning about Continental hotels generally and to suggest that they should, after this stay in Paris, go straight through in the train *deluxe* and never halt again until the £15,000 necklace was safely in the hands of the august lady for whom it was intended. But both Arthur and Mary laughed at these words of warning.

"My dear fellow," Arthur said, seemingly rather in a huff, "we are not such mugs as you think us. Mary and I have travelled on the Continent at least as much as you have, and are fully alive to the dangers attendant upon our mission. As a matter of fact, the moment we arrived,

I gave the necklace in its own padlocked tin box, just as I brought it over from England in charge of the hotel management, who immediately locked it up in their strong room, so even if good old Pasquier had designs on it—which I can assure you he has not—he would stand no chance of getting hold of it. And now do sit down, there's a good chap, and talk of something else."

Only half reassured, Haasberg sat down and had a chat. But he did not stay long. Mary was obviously tired and soon said goodnight. Arthur offered to accompany his brother-in-law to the latter's lodgings in the Rue de Moncigny.

"I would like a walk," he said, "before going to bed."

So, the two men walked out together and Haasberg finally said goodnight to Arthur just outside his own lodgings. It was then close upon ten o'clock. The little party had agreed to spend the next day together, as the train *deluxe* did not go until the evening and Haasberg had promised to take a holiday from business. Before going to bed he attended to some urgent correspondence, and had just finished a letter when his telephone bell rang. To his horror he heard his sister's voice speaking in the greatest possible distress and anxiety;

"Don't keep Arthur up so late, Herman," she said. "I am dog tired and can't go to sleep until he returns."

"Arthur?" he replied, "but Arthur left me at my door two hours ago."

"He has not returned," she insisted, "and I am getting anxious."

"Of course, you are, but he can't be long now. He must have turned into a *café* and forgot the time. Do ring me up as soon as he comes in."

Unable to rest, however, and once more vaguely anxious, Haasberg went hastily back to the Majestic. He found Mary nearly distracted with anxiety, and as he himself felt anything but reassured, he did not know how to comfort her. At one time he went down into the hall to ascertain whether anything was known in the hotel about Saunders's movements earlier in the evening, but at this hour of the night there was only the night porter and the watchmen about, and they knew nothing of what had occurred before they came on duty.

There was nothing for it but to await the morning as calmly as possible. This was difficult enough as Mary Saunders was evidently in a terrible state of agitation. She was quite certain that something tragic had happened to her husband, but Haasberg tried in vain to get her to speak of the mysterious visitor who had from the first aroused his own suspicions. Mary persisted in asserting that the visitor was just an old pal of Arthur's and that no possible suspicion of any kind could possibly rest upon him.

In the early morning Haasberg went off to the nearest commissariat of police. They took the matter in hand without delay and within the hour had obtained some valuable information from the personnel of the hotel. To begin with it was established that at about ten minutes past ten the previous evening, that is to say a quarter of an hour or so after Haasberg had parted from Arthur Saunders outside his own lodgings, the latter had returned to the Majestic and at once asked for the tin box which he had deposited in the bureau. There was some difficulty in acceding to his request, because the clerk who was in charge of the keys of the strong room could not at once be found. However, *M le Capitaine* was so insistent that search was made for the clerk who presently appeared with the keys, and after the usual formalities handed over the tin box to Saunders who signed a receipt for it in the book. Haasberg had since then identified the signature which was quite clear and incontestable.

Saunders then went upstairs, refusing to take the lift, and five minutes later he had come down again, nodded to the hall porter and went out of the hotel. No one had seen him since, but during the course of the morning the valet on the fourth floor had found an empty tin box in the gentlemen's cloak-room. This box was produced, and to her unutterable horror Mary Saunders recognised it as the one which had held the pearl necklace.

The whole of this evidence as it gradually came to light was a staggering blow both to Mary and to Haasberg himself, because until this moment neither of them had thought that the necklace was in jeopardy: they both believed that it was safely locked up in the strong room of the hotel.

Haasberg now feared the worst. He blamed himself terribly for not having made more certain of the mysterious visitor's identity. He had not yet come to the point of accusing his brother-in-law, in his mind, of a conspiracy to steal the necklace, but frankly, at this stage, he did not know what to think. Saunders's conduct had—to say the least—been throughout extremely puzzling. Why had he elected to spend the night in Paris, when all arrangements had been made for him and his wife to travel straight through? Who was the mysterious visitor with the walrus moustache, vaguely referred to by both Arthur and Mary as "old Pasquier"? And above all why had Arthur withdrawn the necklace from the hotel strong room where it was quite safe and, with it in his pocket, walked about the streets of Paris at that hour of the night?

Haasberg was quite convinced that "old Pasquier" knew something about the whole affair, but, strangely enough, Mary persisted in asserting that he was quite harmless, and an old friend of Arthur's who was beyond suspicion. When further pressed with questions she declared that she had no idea where the man lodged, and that, in fact, she believed that he had left Paris the self-same evening *en route* for Brussels where he was settled in business.

Enquiry amongst the personnel of the hotel revealed the fact that Captain Saunders's visitor had been seen by the hall porter when he came soon after half-past eight, and asked whether *le Capitaine* Saunders had finished dinner; his question being answered in the affirmative, he went upstairs, refusing to take the lift.

Half an hour or so later he was seen by one of the waiters in the lounge hurriedly crossing the hall, and finally by the two boys in attendance at the swing doors when he went out of the hotel. All agreed that the man was very tall and thick-set, that he wore a heavy moustache and a pair of gold-rimmed spectacles. He had on a bowler hat and an overcoat with the collar pulled right up to his ears. The hall porter who himself spoke English fairly well, was under the impression that the man was not English, although he made his enquiries in that language.

In addition to all these investigations, the *commissaire de police,* on his second visit to the hotel, was able to assure Haasberg that all the commissariats in and around Paris had been communicated with by telephone so as to ascertain whether any man answering Saunders's description had been injured during the night in a street accident and taken in somewhere for shelter; also, that a description of the necklace had already been sent round to all the *Monts de Pieds* throughout the country. The police were also sharply on the lookout for the man with the walrus moustache, but so far without success.

Whether he had left for Brussels by the last train on the previous night could not be definitely established, nor when or by what route he had arrived in Paris. There are always such crowds at the Gare du Nord for the arrival and departure of important trains that any man can easily—if he wishes—pass unperceived.

And Mary Saunders obstinately persisted in her denial of any knowledge about him. "Arthur," she said "sometimes saw old Pasquier in London"; but she did not know anything about him, neither what his nationality was, nor where he lodged. She did not know when he had left London, nor where he could be found in Paris. All that she knew, so she said, was that his name was Pasquier, and that he was in business in Brussels; she therefore concluded that he was Belgian. Even to her own brother she would not say more, although he succeeded in making her understand how strange her attitude must appear both to the police and to her friends, and what harm she was doing to her husband, but at this she burst into floods of tears, and swore that she knew nothing about Pasquier's whereabouts, and that she believed him to be innocent of any attempt to steal the necklace or to injure Arthur.

There was nothing more to be said for the present and Haasberg sent the telegram in his sister's name to Sir Montague Bowden because he felt that someone less busy than himself should look after the affair and be a comfort to Mary, whose mental condition appeared pitiable in the extreme. In this first interview he was able to assure Sir Montague that everything had been done to trace the whereabouts of Arthur Saunders, and also of the necklace of which the unfortunate man had been the custodian; and it was actually while the two men were talking the whole case over that Haasberg received an intimation from the police that they believed the missing man had been found: at any rate would *Monsieur* give himself the trouble to come round to the commissariat at once.

This, of course, Haasberg did, accompanied by Sir Montague, and at the commissariat, to their horror they found the unfortunate Saunders in a terrible condition. Briefly the *commissaire* explained to them that about a quarter past ten last night an *agent de police,* making his rounds, saw a man crouching in the angle of a narrow blind alley that leads out of the Rue de Moncigny. On being shaken up by the agent the man struggled to his feet, but he appeared quite dazed and unable to reply to any questions that were put to him. He was then conveyed to the nearest commissariat where he spent the night.

He was obviously suffering from loss of memory; and could give no account of himself, nor were any papers of identification found upon him, not even a visiting card, but close beside him, on the pavement where he was crouching, the agent had picked up a handkerchief which was saturated with chloroform. The handkerchief bore the initials A. S. The man, of course, was Arthur Saunders. What had happened to him it was impossible to ascertain. He certainly did not appear to be physically hurt, although from time to time when Mr. Haasberg or Sir Montague tried to question him he passed his hand across the back of his head, and an expression of pathetic puzzlement came into his eyes.

His two friends, after the usual formalities of identification, were allowed to take him back to the Hotel Majestic where he was restored to the arms of his anxious wife; the English doctor, hastily summoned, could not find any trace of injury about the body, only the head appeared rather tender when touched. The doctor's theory was that Saunders had probably been sandbagged first and then rendered more completely insensible by means of the chloroformed handkerchief, and that excitement, anxiety and the blow on the head had caused temporary loss of memory which quietude and good nursing would soon put right. In the meanwhile, of the £15,000 necklace there was not the slightest trace.

2

Unfortunately, the disappearance of so valuable a piece of jewellery was one of those cases that could not be kept out of public knowledge. The matter was of course in the hands of the French police, and they had put themselves in communication with their English confreres, and the consternation—not to say the indignation—amongst the good ladies who had subscribed the money for the gift to the august lady was unbounded. Everybody was blaming everybody else; the choice of Captain Saunders as the accredited messenger was now severely criticised; pointed questions were asked as to his antecedents, as to his wife's foreign relations, and it was soon found that very little was known about either.

Of course, everybody knew that he was Sir Montague Bowden's nephew, and that, thanks to his uncle's influence, he had obtained a remunerative and rather important post in the office of one of the big Insurance Companies. But what his career had been before that no one knew. Some people said that he had fought in South Africa and later on had been correspondent for one of the great dailies during the Russo-Japanese War; altogether there seemed no doubt that he had been something of a rolling stone.

Rather tardily the committee was taken severely to task for having entrusted so important a mission to a man who was either a coward or a thief, or both, for at first no one doubted that Saunders had met a confederate in Paris and had handed over the necklace to him, whilst he himself enacted a farce of being waylaid, chloroformed and robbed, and subsequently of losing his memory.

But presently another version of the mystery was started by some amateur detective, and it found credence with quite a good many people. This was that Sir Montague Bowden had connived at the theft with Mrs. Saunders's relations; that the man with the walrus moustache either did not exist at all or was in very truth a harmless old friend of Captain Saunders, and that it was Haasberg who had induced his brother-in-law to withdraw the necklace from the hotel strong room and to bring it to the Rue de Moncigny; that in fact it was that same perfidious Swede who had waylaid the credulous Englishman, chloroformed and robbed him of the precious necklace.

In the meanwhile, the police in England had, of course, been communicated with by their French *confrères*, but before they could move in the matter or enjoin discretion on all concerned, an enterprising young man on the staff of the Express Post had interviewed Miss Elizabeth Spicer who was the parlourmaid at the Saunders's flat in Sloane Street.

That young lady it seems had something to say about a gentleman named Pasquier who was not an infrequent visitor at the flat. She described him as a fine, tall gentleman who wore large gold-rimmed spectacles and a full military moustache. It seems that the last time Miss Elizabeth saw him was two days before her master and mistress's departure for abroad. Mr. Pasquier called late that evening and stayed till past ten o'clock. When Elizabeth was rung for in order to show him out, he was saying goodbye to the captain in the hall, and she heard him say "in his funny foreign way," as she put it:

"Well, I shall be in Paris as soon as you. Tink it over, my friend."

And on the top of that came the story told by Henry Tidy, Sir Montague Bowden's butler. According to him Captain Saunders called at Sir Montague Bowden's house in Lowndes Street on the afternoon of the 15th. The two gentlemen remained closeted together in the library for nearly an hour when Tidy was summoned to show the visitor out. Sir Montague, it seems, went to the front door with his nephew, and as the latter finally wished him goodbye Sir Montague said to him:

"My dear boy, you can take it from me that there's nothing to worry about, and in any case, I am afraid that it is too late to make any fresh arrangements."

"It's because of Mary," the captain rejoined; "she has made herself quite ill over it."

"The journey will do her good," Sir Montague went on pleasantly, "but if I were you, I would have a good talk with your brother-in-law. He must know his Paris well. Take my advice and spend the night at the Majestic; you can always get rooms there."

This conversation Tidy heard quite distinctly, and he related the whole incident both to the journalist and to the police. After that the amateur investigators of crime were divided into two camps: there were those who persisted in thinking that Pasquier and Saunders, and probably Mrs. Saunders also, had conspired together to steal the necklace, and that Saunders had acted the farce of being waylaid and robbed and losing his memory; they based their deductions on Elizabeth Spicer's evidence and on Mary Saunders's extraordinary persistence in trying to shield the mysterious Pasquier. But other people, getting hold of Henry Tidy's story, deduced from it that it was indeed Sir Montague Bowden who had planned the whole thing in conjunction with Haasberg, since it was he who had persuaded Saunders to spend the night in Paris, thus giving his accomplice the opportunity of assaulting Saunders and stealing the necklace.

To these wiseacres "old Pasquier" was indeed a harmless old pal of Arthur's, whose presence that evening at the Majestic was either a fable invented by Haasberg, or one quite innocent in purpose. In vain did Sir Montague try to explain away Tidy's evidence. Arthur, he said, had certainly called on him that last afternoon, but what he seemed worried about was his wife's health; he feared that she would not be strong enough to undertake the long journey without a break, so Sir Montague advised him to spend the night in Paris and in any case to talk the matter over with Mary's brother.

The conversation overheard by Tidy could certainly admit of this explanation, but it did not satisfy the many amateur detectives who preferred to see a criminal in the chairman of the committee rather than a harmless old gentleman, as eager as themselves to find a solution of the mystery. And while people argued and wrangled there was no news of the necklace, and none of the man with the walrus moustache. No doubt that worthy had by now shaved off his hirsute adornment and grown a beard. He had certainly succeeded in evading the police; whether he had gone to Brussels or succeeded in crossing the German frontier no one could say, but his disappearance certainly bore out the theory of his being the guilty party with the connivance of Saunders, as against the Bowden-Haasberg theory.

As for the necklace it had probably been already taken to pieces and the pearls would presently be disposed of one by one to unscrupulous Continental dealers, when the first hue and cry after them had died away.

Captain Saunders was said to be slowly recovering from his loss of memory and subsequent breakdown. Everyone at home was waiting to hear what explanation he would give of his amazing conduct in taking the necklace out of the hotel strong room late that night and sallying forth with it into the streets of Paris at that hour. The explanation came after about a fortnight of suspense in a letter from Mary to her friend Mrs. Berners.

Arthur, she said, had told her that on the fateful evening, after he parted from Mr. Haasberg in the Rue de Moncigny, he had felt restless and anxious about what the latter had told him on the subject of foreign hotels, and he was suddenly seized with the idea that the necklace was not safe in the care of the management of the Majestic, because there would come a moment when he would have to claim the tin box and this would probably be handed over to him when the hall of the hotel was crowded, and the eyes of expert thieves would then follow his every movement.

Therefore, he went back to the hotel, claimed the tin box, and as the latter was large and cumbersome, he got rid of it in one of the cloak-rooms of the hotel, slipped the necklace in its velvet case in the pocket of his overcoat and went out with the intention of asking Haasberg to take care of it for him, and only to hand it back to him when on the following evening the train *deluxe* was on the point of starting. He had been in sight of Haasberg's lodgings when, without the slightest warning, a dull blow on the back of his head coming he knew not whence, robbed him of consciousness.

This explanation, however, was voted almost unanimously to be very false, and it was, on the whole, as well that the Saunders's had decided to remain abroad for a time. The ladies especially—and above all those who had put their money together for the necklace—were very bitter against him. At best, they averred, he had proved himself a despicable coward as well as a fool, and in any case, he had failed in his trust.

On the other hand, Sir Montague Bowden was having a very rough time of it; he had already had one or two very unpleasant word-tussles with some outspoken friends of his, and there was talk of a slander action that would certainly be a cause celebre when it came on. Thus, the arguments went on in endless succession until one day—well do I remember the excitement that spread throughout the town as soon as the incident became known—there was a terrible row in one of the big clubs in Piccadilly.

Sir Montague Bowden was insulted by one of his fellow members: he was called a thief, and asked what share he was getting out of the sale of the necklace. Of course, the man who spoke in this unwarrantable fashion was drunk at the time, but nevertheless it was a terrible position for Sir Montague, because as his opponent grew more and more abusive and he himself more and more indignant, he realised that he had practically no friends who would stand by him in the dispute. Some of the members tried to stop the row and others appeared indifferent, but no one sided with him, or returned abuse for abuse on his behalf.

It was in the very midst of this most unedifying scene—one perhaps unparalleled in the annals of London club life—that a club servant entered the room, and handed a telegram to Sir Montague Bowden.

Even the most sceptical there, and those whose brains were almost fuddled with the wrangling and the noise, declared afterwards that a mysterious Providence had ordained that the telegram should arrive at that precise moment. It had been sent to Sir Montague's private house in Lowndes Street; his secretary had opened it and sent it on to the club. As soon as Sir Montague had mastered its contents he communicated them to the member of the club, and it seems that there never had been such excitement displayed in any assembly of sober Englishmen as was shown in that club room on this momentous occasion.

The telegram had come all the way from the other end of Europe, and had been sent by the august lady in whose hands the priceless necklace, about which there was so much pother in England and France, had just been safely placed. It ran thus:

> Deeply touched by exquisite present just received through kind offices of Captain Saunders, from English ladies! Kind thoughts and beautiful necklace equally precious. Kindly convey my grateful thanks to all subscribers.

Having read out the telegram Sir Montague Bowden demanded an apology from those who had impugned his honour, and I understand that he got an unqualified one. After that, male tongues were let loose; the wildest conjectures flew about as to the probable solution of what appeared a more curious mystery than ever. By evening the papers had got hold of the incident, and all those who were interested in the affair shook their heads and looked portentously wise. But the hero of the hour was certainly Captain Saunders. From having been voted either a knave or a fool or both, he was declared all at once to be possessed of all the qualities which had made England great: prudence, astuteness and tenacity. However, as a matter of fact, nobody knew what had actually happened; the august lady had the necklace and Captain Saunders was returning to England without a stain on his character, but as to how these two eminently satisfactory results had come about, not even the wiseacres could say.

Captain and Mrs. Saunders arrived in England a few days later; everyone was agog with curiosity, and the poor things had hardly stepped out of the train before they were besieged by newspaper men and pressed with questions. The next morning the *Express Post* and the *Daily Thunderer* came out with exclusive interviews with Captain Saunders who had made no secret of the extraordinary adventure which had once more placed him in possession of the necklace. It seems that he and his wife on coming out of the Madeleine Church on Easter Sunday were hustled at the top of the steps by a man whose face they did not see, and who pushed past them very hastily and roughly. Arthur Saunders at once thought of his pockets and looked to see if his note-case had not disappeared.

To his boundless astonishment his hand came in contact with a long, hard parcel in the outside pocket of his overcoat, and this parcel proved to be the velvet case containing the missing necklace. Both he and his wife were flabbergasted at this discovery, and, scarcely believing in this amazing piece of good luck, they managed with the help of Mr. Haasberg, despite its being Easter Sunday, to obtain an interview with one of the great jewellers in the Rue de la Paix, who, well knowing the history of the missing necklace, was able to assure them that they had indeed been lucky enough to regain possession of their treasure. That same evening they left by the train *deluxe*, having been fortunate enough to secure seats; needless to say that the necklace was safely stowed away inside Captain Saunders's breast pocket.

All was indeed well that ended so well. But the history of the disappearance and re-appearance of the pearl necklace has remained a baffling mystery to this day. Neither the Saunders's nor Mr. Haasberg ever departed one iota from the circumstantial story which they had originally told and no one ever heard another word about the man with the walrus moustache and the gold-rimmed spectacles: the French police are still after him in connection with the assault on *le Capitaine* Saunders, but no trace of him was ever found.

To some people this was a conclusive proof of guilt, but then, having stolen the necklace, why should he have restored it? Though the pearls were very beautiful and there were a great number of them beautifully matched, there was nothing abnormal about them either in size or colour; there never could be any difficulty for an expert thief to dispose of them to Continental dealers. The same argument would of course apply to Mr. Haasberg whom some wiseacres still persisted in accusing. If he stole the necklace, why should he have restored it? Nothing could be easier than for a business man who travelled a great deal on the Continent to sell a parcel of pearls.

And there always remained the unanswered question: Why did Saunders take the pearls out of the strong room, and where was he taking them to when he was assaulted and robbed? Did the man with the walrus moustache really call at the Majestic that night? And if he was innocent, why did he disappear. Why? Why? Why?

3

The case had very much interested me at the time, but the mystery was a nine days' wonder as far as I was concerned, and soon far more important matters than the temporary disappearance of a few rows of pearls occupied public attention.

It was really only last year when I had renewed my acquaintance with the Man in the Corner that I bethought myself once more of the mystery of the pearl necklace, and I felt the desire to hear what the spook-like creature's theory was upon the subject.

"The pearl necklace?" he said with a cackle. "Ah, yes, it caused a good bit of stir in its day. But people talked such a lot of irresponsible nonsense that thinking minds had not a chance of arriving at a sensible conclusion."

"No," I rejoined amiably. "But you did."

"Yes, you are right there," he replied, "I knew well enough where the puzzle lay but it was not my business to put the police on the right track. And if I had I should have been the cause of making two innocent and clever people suffer more severely than the guilty party."

"Will you condescend to explain?" I asked, with an indulgent smile.

"Why should I not?" he retorted, and once again his thin fingers started to work on the inevitable piece of string. "It all lies in a nutshell, and is easily understandable if we realise that 'old Pasquier,' the man with the walrus moustache, was not the friend of the Saunders's, but their enemy."

I frowned. "Their enemy?"

"An old pal shall we say?" he retorted, "who knew something in the past history of one or the other of them that they did not wish their newest friends to know: really a blackmailer who, under the guise of comradeship, sat not infrequently at their fireside, watching an opportunity for extorting a heavy price for his silence and his good-will. Thus, he could worm himself into their confidence; he knew their private life; he heard about the necklace, and decided that here was the long sought for opportunity at last. Think it all over and you will see how well the pieces of that jigsaw puzzle fit together and make a perfect picture. Pasquier calls on the Saunders's a day or two before their departure and springs his infamous proposal upon them then. For the time being Arthur succeeds in giving him the slip; his journey is not yet. . . the necklace is not yet in his possession. . . but he knows the true quality of the blackmailer now and he is on the alert.

" He begins by going to Sir Montague Bowden and begging him to entrust the mission to somebody else. Judging by the butler's evidence, he even makes a clean breast of his troubles to Sir Montague who, however, makes light of them and advises consultation with Mr. Haasberg, who perhaps would undertake the journey. In any case it is too late to make fresh arrangements at this hour. Very reluctantly now, and hoping for the best, the Saunders's make a start. But the blackmailer, too, is on the alert, he has succeeded in spying upon them and in tracing them to the Majestic in Paris., The situation now has become terribly serious, for the blackmailer has thrown off the mask and demands the necklace under threats which apparently the Saunders's did not dare defy.

"But they are both clever and resourceful, and as soon as Haasberg's arrival rids them temporarily of their tormentor they put their heads together and invent a plot which was destined to free them for ever from the threats of Pasquier and at the same time would enable them to honour the trust which had been placed in them by the committee. In any case they had until the morrow to make up their minds. Remember the words which Mr. Haasberg overheard on the part of Pasquier: 'S'long old man. I'll wait till tomorrow.' Anyway, Pasquier must have gone off that evening confident that he had Captain Saunders entirely in his power and that the wretched man would on the morrow hand over the necklace without demur.

"Whether Arthur Saunders confided in Haasberg or no is doubtful. Personally, I think not. I believe that he and Mary did the whole thing between them. Arthur having parted from his brother-in-law went back to the hotel, took the necklace out of the strong room and then left it in Mary's charge. He threw the tin box away, there where it would surely be found again. Then he went as far as the Rue de Moncigny and crouched, seemingly unconscious, in the blind alley, having previously taken the precaution of saturating his handkerchief with chloroform.

"Thus, the two clever conspirators cut the ground from under the blackmailer's feet, for the latter now had the police after him for an assault, which he might find very difficult to disprove, even if he cleared himself of the charge of having stolen the necklace. Anyway, he would remain a discredited man, and his threats would in the future be defied, because if he dared come out in the open after that, public feeling would be so bitter against him for a crime which he had not committed that he would never be listened to if he tried to do Captain Saunders an injury. And it was with a view to keeping public indignation at boiling pitch against the supposed thief that the Saunders's kept up the comedy for so long. To my mind that was a very clever move. Then they came out with the story of the restoration of the necklace and became the heroes of the hour.

"Think it over," the funny creature went on as he finally stuffed his bit of string back into his pocket and rose from the table, "think it over and you will realise at once that everything happened just as I have related and that it is the only theory that fits in with the facts that are known; you'll also agree with me, I think, that Captain and Mrs. Saunders chose the one way of ridding themselves effectually of a dangerous blackmailer. The police were after him for a long time, as they still believed that he had something to do with the theft of the necklace and with the assault on M le Capitaine Saunders. But presently 1914 came along and what became of the man with the walrus moustache no one ever knew. What his nationality was was never stated at the time, but whatever it was, it would, I imagine, be a bar against his obtaining a visa on his passport for the purpose of visiting England and blackmailing Arthur Saunders.

"But it was a curious case."

The Mystery of the Russian Prince

1

There had been a great deal of talk about that time, in newspapers and amongst the public, of the difficulty an inexperienced criminal finds in disposing of the evidences of his crime—notably of course of the body of his victim. In no case perhaps was this difficulty so completely overcome—at any rate as far as was publicly known—as in that of the murder of the individual known as Prince Orsoff. I am thus qualifying his title because as a matter of fact the larger public never believed that he was a genuine prince—Russian or otherwise—and that even if he had not come by such a violent and tragic death the Smithsons would never have seen either their £10,000 again, or poor Louisa's aristocratic bridegroom.

I had been thinking a great deal about this mysterious affair, indeed it had been discussed at most of the literary and journalistic clubs as a possible subject for a romance or drama, and it was with deliberate intent that I walked over to Fleet Street that afternoon in order to catch the Man in the Corner in his accustomed tea-shop and get him to give me his views on the subject of the mystery that to this very day surrounds the murder of the Russian Prince.

"Let me just put the whole case before you," the funny creature began as soon as I had led him to talk upon the subject, "as far as it was known to the general public. It all occurred in Folkestone, you remember, where the wedding of Louisa Smithson, the daughter of a late retired grocer, to a Russian prince whom she had met abroad, was the talk of the town.

"It was on a lovely day in May, and the wedding ceremony was to take place at Holy Trinity Church. The Smithsons—mother and daughter—especially since they had come into a fortune, were very well known in Folkestone, and there was a large crowd of relatives and friends inside the church and another out in the street to watch the arrival of guests and to see the bride. There were camera men and newspaper men, and hundreds of idlers and visitors, and the police had much ado to keep the crowd in order.

"Mrs. Smithson had already arrived looking gorgeous in what I understand is known as amethyst *crepe-de-chine*, and there was a marvellous array of Bond Street gowns and gorgeous headgears, all of which kept the lookers-on fully occupied during the traditional quarter of an hour's grace usually accorded to the bride. But presently those fifteen minutes became twenty, the clergy had long since arrived, the guests had all assembled, the bridesmaids were waiting in the porch: but there was no bridegroom. Neither he nor his best man had arrived; and now it was half an hour after the time appointed for the ceremony, and, oh, horror!—the bride's car was in sight.

"The bride in church waiting for the bridegroom!—such an outrage had not been witnessed in Folkestone within the memory of the oldest inhabitant. One of the guests went at once to break the news to the elderly relative who had arranged to give the bride away, and who was with her in the car, whilst another, a Mr. Sutherland Ford, jumped into the first available taxi, having volunteered to go to the station in order to ascertain whether there had been any breakdown on the line, as the bridegroom was coming down by train from London with his best man.

"The bride, hastily apprised of the extraordinary *contretemps*, remained in the car, with the blinds pulled down, well concealed from the prying eyes of the crowd, whilst the fashionable guests, relatives, and friends had perforce to possess their souls in patience.

"And presently the news fell like a bombshell in the midst of this lively throng. A taxi drove up and from it alighted first Mr. Sutherland Ford, who had volunteered to go to the station for information, and then John and Henry Carter, the two latter beautifully got up, in frock coats, striped trousers, top hats, and flowers in their buttonholes, looking obviously like belated wedding guests. But still no bridegroom, and no best man. The three gentlemen, paying no heed to the shower of questions that assailed them, as soon as they had jumped out of the taxi ran straight into the church, leaving everyone's curiosity unsatisfied and public excitement at fever pitch. 'It was John and Henry Carter' the ladies whispered agitatedly; 'fancy their being asked to the wedding!'

"And those who were in the know whispered to those who were less favoured that young Henry had at one time been engaged to Louisa Smithson, before she met her Russian prince, and that when she threw him over, he was in such dire despair that his friends thought he would commit suicide.

"A moment or two later Mrs. Smithson was seen hurriedly coming out of church, her face pale and drawn, and her beautiful hat all awry. She made straight for the bride's car, stepped into it, and the car immediately drove off, whilst the wedding guests trooped out of the church and the terrible news spread like wildfire through the crowd and was presently all over the town. It seems that when the midday train, London to Folkestone, stopped at Swanley Junction, two passengers who were about to enter a first-class compartment in one of the corridor carriages were horrified to find it in a terrible state of disorder. They hastily called the guard, and on examination the carriage looked indeed as if it had been the scene of a violent struggle: the door on the off side was unlatched, two of the window straps were wrenched off, the antimacassars were torn off the cushions, one of the luggage racks was broken and the net hung down in strips, and over some of the cushions were marks unmistakably made by a bloodstained hand.

"The guard immediately locked the compartment and sent for the local police. No one was allowed in or out of the station until every passenger on the train had satisfied the police as to his or her identity. Thus, the train was held up for over two hours whilst preliminary investigations were going on. There appeared no doubt that a terrible murder had been committed, and telephonic communication all along the line presently established the fact that it must have been done somewhere in the neighbourhood of Sydenham Hill, because a group of men who were at work on the up side of the line at Penge when the down train came out of the tunnel noticed that the door of one of the first-class carriages was open.

"It swung to again just before the train steamed through the station. A preliminary search was at once made in and about the tunnel; it revealed on the platform of Sydenham Hill station a first-class single ticket of that day's issue, London to Folkestone, crushed and stained with blood, and on the permanent way, close to the entrance of the tunnel on the Penge side, a soft black hat, and a broken pair of *pince-nez*. But as to the identity of the victim there was for the moment no clue.

"After a couple of wearisome and anxious hours the passengers were allowed to proceed on their journey. Among these passengers, it appears, were John and Henry Carter, who were on their way to the Smithson wedding. Until they arrived in Folkestone, they had no more idea than the police who the victim of the mysterious train murder was: but in the station they caught sight of Mr. Sutherland Ford, whom they knew slightly. Mr. Ford was making agitated enquiries as to any possible accident on the line. The Carters put him *au fait* of what had occurred, and as there was no sign of the Russian prince amongst the passengers who had just arrived, all three men came to the horrifying conclusion that it was indeed the bridegroom elect who had been murdered. They communicated at once with the police, and there were more investigations and telephonic messages up and down the line before the Carters and Mr. Ford were at last allowed to proceed to the church and break the awful news to those most directly concerned.

"And in this tragic fashion did Louisa Smithson's wedding day draw to its end; nor, as far as the public was concerned, was the mystery of that terrible murder ever satisfactorily cleared up. The local police worked very hard and very systematically, but though presently they also had the help of one of the ablest detectives from Scotland Yard, nothing was seen or found that gave the slightest clue either as to the means which the murderer or murderers adopted for removing the body of their victim, or in what manner they made good their escape.'

The body of the Russian prince was never found, and, as far as the public knows, the murderer is still at large; and although, as time went on, many strange facts came to light, they only helped to plunge that extraordinary crime into darker mystery.

2

"The facts in themselves were curious enough, you will admit," the Man in the Corner went on after a while; "many of these were never known to the public, whilst others found their way into the columns of the halfpenny Press, who battened on the 'Mystery of the Russian prince' for weeks on end, and, as far as the unfortunate Smithsons were concerned, there was not a reader of the *Express Post* and kindred newspapers who did not know the whole of their family history.

"It seems that Louisa Smithson is the daughter of a grocer in Folkestone who had retired from business just before the War, and with his wife and his only child led a meagre and obscure existence in a tiny house in Warren Avenue somewhere near the tram road. They were always supposed to be very poor, but suddenly old Smithson died and it turned out that he had been a miser, for he left the handsome little fortune of £15,000 to be equally divided between his daughter and his widow.

"At once Mrs. Smithson and Louisa found themselves the centre of an admiring throng of friends and relatives, all eager to help them spend their money for their especial benefit; but Mrs. Smithson was shrewd enough not to allow herself to be exploited by those who in the past had never condescended to more than a bowing acquaintance with her. She turned her back on most of those sycophants, but at the same time she was, determined to do the best for herself and Louisa, and to this end she admitted into her councils her sister, Margaret Penny, who was saleswoman at a fashionable shop in London, and who immediately advised a journey up to town so that the question of clothes might at once be satisfactorily settled.

"In addition to valuable advice on that score, this Miss Penny seems to have succeeded in completely turning her sister's head. Certain it is that Mrs. Smithson left Folkestone a quiet, sensible, motherly woman, and that she returned, six weeks later, an arrogant, ill-mannered parvenue, who seemed to think that the possession of a few thousand pounds entitled her to ride roughshod over the feelings and sentiments of those who had less money than herself.

"She began by taking a suite of rooms at the Splendid Hotel for herself, her daughter, and her maid, then she sold her house in Warren Avenue, bought a car, and, though she and Louisa were of course in deep mourning, they were to be seen everywhere in wonderful Bond Street dresses and marvellous feathered hats. Finally, they announced their intention of spending the coming winter on the Riviera, probably Monte Carlo.

"All this extravagant behaviour made some people smile, others shrugged their shoulders and predicted disaster: but there was one who suffered acutely through this change in the fortune of the Smithsons. This was Henry Carter, a young clerk employed in an insurance office in London. He and his brother were Folkestone men, sons of a local tailor in a very small way of business, who had been one of old Smithson's rare friends. The elder Carter boy had long since cut his stick and was said to be earning a living in London by freelance journalism. The younger one, Henry, remained to help his father with the tailoring. He was a constant visitor in the little house in Warren Avenue, and presently became engaged to Louisa.

"There could be no question of an immediate marriage, of course, as Henry had neither money nor prospects; however, presently old

Carter died, the tailoring business was sold for a couple of hundred pounds, and Henry went up to London to join his brother and to seek his fortune. Presently he obtained a post in an insurance office, but his engagement to Louisa subsisted: the young people were known to be deeply in love with one another and Henry spent most weekends and all his holidays in Folkestone in order to be near his girl.

"Then came the change in the fortune of the Smithsons and an immediate coolness in Louisa's manner toward young Henry. It was all very well in the past to be engaged to the son of a jobbing tailor, while one was poor oneself, and one had neither wit nor good looks, but now. . .!

"In fact, already when they were in London Mrs. Smithson had intimated to Henry Carter that his visits were none too welcome, and when he appealed to Louisa, she put him off with a few curt words. The young man was in despair, and, indeed, his brother actually feared at one time that he would commit suicide.

"It was soon after Christmas of that same year that the curtain was rung up on the first act of the mysterious tragedy which was destined to throw a blight for ever after upon the life of Louisa Smithson. It began with the departure of herself and her mother for the Continent, where they intended to remain until the end of March. For the first few weeks their friends had no news of them, but presently Miss Margaret Penny, who had kept up a desultory correspondence with a pal of hers in Folkestone, started to give glowing accounts of the Smithsons' doings in Monte Carlo.

"They were staying at the Hotel de Paris, paying two hundred *francs* a day for their rooms alone, they were lunching and dining out every day of the week they had been introduced to one or two of the august personages who usually graced the Riviera with their presence at this time of the year, and they had met a number of interesting people. According to Miss Penny's account, Louisa Smithson was being greatly admired, and in fact several titled gentlemen of various nationalities had professed themselves deeply enamoured of her.

"All this Miss Penny recounted in her letters to her friends, with a wealth of detail and a marvellous profusion of adjectives, and finally in one of her letters there was mention of a certain Russian *grandee*—Prince Orsoff by name—who was paying Louisa marked attention. He also was staying at the 'Paris,' appeared very wealthy, and was obviously of very high rank for he never mixed with the crowd which was more than usually brilliant this year in Monte Carlo. This exclusiveness on his part was all the more flattering to the Smithsons, and, when he apprised them of his intention to spend the season in London, they had asked him to come and visit them in Folkestone, where Mrs. Smithson intended to take a house presently and there to entertain lavishly during the summer.

"After this preliminary announcement from Miss Penny, Louisa herself wrote a letter to Henry Carter. It was quite a pleasant chatty letter, telling him of their marvellous doings abroad, and of her own social successes. It did not do more, however, than vaguely hint at the Russian prince, his distinguished appearance and obvious wealth. Nevertheless, it plunged the unfortunate young man into the utmost depths of despair, and according to his brother John's subsequent account the latter had a terrible time with young Henry that winter. John himself was very busy with journalistic work which kept him away sometimes for days and weeks on end from the little home in London which the two brothers had set up for themselves with the money derived from the sale of the tailoring business. And Henry's state of mind did at times seriously alarm his brother, for he would either threaten to do away with himself, or vow that he would be even with that accursed foreigner.

"At the end of March, the Smithsons returned to England. During the interval Mrs. Smithson had made all arrangements for taking 'The Towers,' a magnificently furnished house facing the Leas at Folkestone, and here she and Louisa installed themselves preparatory to launching their invitations for the various tea-and tennis-parties, dinners and dances which they proposed to give during the summer.

"One might really quite truthfully say that the eyes of all Folkestone were fixed upon the two ladies. Their Paris dresses, their hats, their jewellery was the chief subject of conversation at tea-tables, and of course everyone was talking about the Russian prince, who—Mrs. Smithson had confided this to a bosom friend—was coming over to England for the express purpose of proposing to Louisa.

"There was quite a flutter of excitement on a memorable Friday afternoon when it was rumoured that Henry Carter had come down for a weekend, and had put up at a small hotel down by the harbour. Of course, he had come to see Louisa Smithson; everyone knew that, and no doubt he wished to make a final appeal to her love for him, which could not be entirely dead yet. Within twenty-four hours, however, it was common gossip that young Henry had presented himself at The Towers and been refused admittance. The ladies were out, the butler said, and he did not know when they would be home. This was on the Saturday. On the Sunday Henry walked about on the Leas all morning in the hope of seeing Louisa or her mother, and as he failed to do so he called again in the early part of the afternoon: he was told the ladies were resting. Later he came again and the ladies had gone out, and on the Monday, as presumably business called him back to town, he left by the early-morning train, without having seen his former *fiancée*. Indeed, people from that moment took it for granted that young Henry had formally been given his *congé*.

"Toward the middle of April Prince Orsoff arrived in London. Within two days he telephoned to Mrs. Smithson to ask her when he might come to pay his respects. A day was fixed and he came to 'The Towers' to lunch. He came again, and at his third visit he formally proposed to Miss Louisa Smithson and was accepted. The wedding was to take place almost immediately, and the very next day the exciting announcement had gone the round of the Smithsons' large circle of friends, not only in Folkestone but also in London.

"The effect of the news appears to have been staggering as far as the unfortunate Henry Carter was concerned. In the picturesque language of Mrs. Hicks, the middle-aged charlady who 'did' for the two brothers in their little home in Chelsea, ''e carried on something awful.' She even went so far as to say that she feared he might put 'is 'ead in the gas oven,' and that, as Mr. John was away at the time, she took the precaution every day when she left to turn the gas off at the meter.

"The following weekend Henry came down to Folkestone and again took up his quarters in the small hotel by the harbour. On the Saturday afternoon he called at 'The Towers' and refused to take 'No' for an answer when he asked to see Miss Smithson. Indeed he seems literally to have pushed his way into the drawing-room where the ladies were having tea. According to statements made subsequently by the butler, there ensued a terrible scene between Henry and his former *fiancée*, at the very height of which, as luck would have it, who should walk in but Prince Orsoff.

"That elegant gentleman, however, seems to have behaved on that trying occasion with perfect dignity and tact, making it his chief business to reassure the ladies and paying no heed to Henry's recriminations, which presently degenerated into vulgar abuse and ended in violent threats. At last, with the aid of the majestic butler, the young man was thrust out of the house, but even on the doorstep he turned and raised a menacing fist in the direction of Prince Orsoff and said loudly enough for more than one person to hear:

"'Wait! I'll be even with that —— foreigner yet.'

"It must indeed have been a terrifying scene for two sensitive and refined ladies like Mrs and Miss Smithson to witness. Later on, after the prince himself had taken his leave, the butler was rung for by Mrs. Smithson who told him that under no circumstances was Mr. Henry Carter ever to be admitted inside 'The Towers.'

"However, a Sunday or two afterwards, Mr. John Carter called and Mrs. Smithson saw him. He said that he had come down expressly from London in order to apologise for his brother's conduct. Henry, he said, was deeply contrite that he should thus have lost control over himself, his broken heart was his only excuse. After all, he had been and still was deeply in love with Louisa, and no man, worth his salt, could see the girl he loved turning her back on him without losing some of that equanimity which should of course be the characteristic of every gentleman.

"In fact Mr. John Carter spoke so well and so persuasively that Mrs. Smithson and Louisa, who were at bottom a quite worthy pair of women, agreed to let bygones be bygones, and said that, if Henry would only behave himself in the future, there was no reason why he should not remain their friend.

"This appeared a quite satisfactory state of things, and over in the little house in Chelsea Mrs. Hicks gladly noted that 'Mr. 'Enry seemed more like 'isself afterwards.' The very next weekend the two brothers went down to Folkestone together, and they called at 'The Towers' so that Henry might offer his apologies in person. The two gentlemen on that occasion were actually asked to stay to tea.

"Indeed, it seems as if Henry had entirely turned over a new leaf, and when presently the gracious invitation came for both brothers to come to the wedding they equally graciously accepted.

3

"The day fixed for the happy event was now approaching. The large circle of acquaintances, friends, and hangers-on which the Smithsons had gathered around them were all agog with excitement, wedding-presents were pouring in by every post. A kind of network of romance had been woven around the personalities of the future bride, her mother, and the Russian prince. The wealth of the Smithsons had been magnified a hundredfold, and Prince Orsoff was reputed to be a brother of the late *Czar*, who had made good his escape out of Russia bringing away with him most of the Crown jewels, which he would presently bestow upon his wife. And so on, *ad infinitum.*

"And upon the top of all that excitement and that gossip, and marvellous tales akin to the Arabian Nights, came the wedding day with its awful culminating tragedy.

"The Russian prince had been murdered and his body so cleverly disposed of that in spite of the most strenuous efforts on the part of the police not a trace of it could be found.

"That robbery had been the main motive of the crime was quickly enough established. The Smithsons—mother and daughter—had at once supplied the detective in charge of the case with proofs as to that. It seems that as soon as the unfortunate prince had become engaged to Louisa, he asked that the marriage should take place without delay. He explained that his dearest friend, Mr. Schumann, the great international financier, had offered him shares in one of the greatest post-war undertakings which had ever been floated in Europe, and which would bring in to the fortunate shareholders a net income of not less than £10,000 yearly for every £10,000 invested;.

"Mr. Schumann himself owned one half of all the shares and had, by a most wonderful act of disinterested generosity, allowed his bosom friend, Prince Orsoff, to have a few—a concession, by the way, which he had only granted to two other favoured personages, one being the Prince of Wales and the other the President of the French Republic. Of course, to receive £10,000 yearly for every £10,000 invested was too wonderful for words; the President of the French Republic had been so delighted with this chance of securing a fortune that he had put two million *francs* into the concern, and the Prince of Wales had put in £500,000.

"And it was so wonderfully secure, as otherwise the British Government would not have allowed the Prince of Wales to invest such a vast sum of money if the business was only speculative. Security and fortune beyond the dreams of thrift! It was positively dazzling. No wonder that this vision of untold riches made poor Mrs. Smithson's mouth water, the more so as she was quite shrewd enough to realise that at the rate she was going her share in the £15,000 left by the late worthy grocer would soon fade into nothingness. In the past few months, she and Louisa had spent considerably over £4,000 between them, and once her daughter was married to a *quasi*-royal personage, good old Mrs. Smithson did not see herself retiring into comparative obscurity on a few hundreds a year to be jeered at by all her friends.

"So she and Louisa talked the matter over together, and then they talked it over with Prince Orsoff on the occasion of his visit about ten days before the wedding. The prince at first was very doubtful if the great Mr. Schumann would be willing to make a further sacrifice in the cause of friendship. He was an international financier, accustomed to deal in millions; he would not look favourably—the prince feared—at a few thousands. Mrs. Smithson's entire fortune now only consisted of about £5,000; this she was unwilling to admit to the wealthy and aristocratic future son-in-law. So, the two ladies decided to pool their capital and then they begged that Prince Orsoff should ask the great Mr. Schumann whether he would condescend to receive £10,000 for investment in Mrs. Smithson's name in his great undertaking.

"Fortunately, the great financier did condescend to do this—he really was more of a philanthropist than a business man—but, of course, he could not be kept waiting, the money must reach him in Paris not later than May the 20th, which was the very day fixed for the wedding. It was all terribly difficult, and Mrs. Smithson was at first in despair as she feared she could not arrange to sell out her securities in time, and the difficulties were increased a hundredfold because, as Prince Orsoff explained to her, Mr. Schumann would even at the eleventh hour refuse to allow her to participate in the huge fortune if he found that she had talked about the affair over in England. The business had to be kept a profound secret for international reasons, in fact, if any detail relating to the business and to Mr. Schumann's participation in it were to become known, the whole of Europe would once more be plunged into war.

"To make a long story short, Mrs. Smithson and Louisa sold out all their securities, amounting between them to £10,000, Then they went up to London, drew the money out of their bank, changed it themselves into French money—so as to make it more convenient for Mr. Schumann—and handed the entire sum over to Prince Orsoff on the eve of the wedding. Of course, such fatuous imbecility would be unbelievable if it did not occur so frequently: vain, silly women, who have never moved outside their own restricted circle are always the ready prey of plausible rascals.

"Anyway, in this case the Smithsons returned to Folkestone that day, perfectly happy and with never a thought of anything but contentment for the present and prosperity in the future. The wedding was to be the next day; the bridegroom-elect was coming down by the midday train with his best man, whom he vaguely described as secretary to the Russian Embassy, and the bridal pair would start for Paris by the afternoon boat.

"All this the Smithsons related to the police inspector in charge of the case and subsequently to the Scotland Yard detective, with a wealth of details and a profusion of lamentations not unmixed with expletives directed against the unknown assassin, and thief. For indeed there was no doubt in the minds of Louise and her mother that the unfortunate prince, on whom the girl still lavished the wealth of her trustful love, had been murdered for the sake of the vast wealth which he had upon his person. It must have amounted to millions of *francs*, Mrs. Smithson declared, for he had the Prince of Wales' money upon him also, and probably that of the President of the French Republic, and at first, she and Louisa fastened their suspicions upon the anonymous best man, the so-called secretary of the Russian Embassy.

"Even when they were presently made to realise that there was no such thing as a Russian Embassy in London these days, and that minute inquiries both at home and abroad regarding the identity of a Prince Orsoff led to no result whatever, they repudiated with scorn the suggestion put forth by the police that their beloved Russian prince was nothing more or less than a clever crook who had led them by the nose, and that in all probability he had not been murdered in the train but had succeeded in jumping out of it and making good his escape across country.

"This the Smithson ladies would not admit for a moment, and with commendable logic they argued that if Prince Orsoff had been a crook and had intended to make away with their money he could have done that easily enough without getting into a train at Victoria and jumping out of it at Sydenham Hill.

"Pressed with questions, however, the ladies were forced to admit that they knew absolutely nothing about Prince Orsoff, they had never been introduced to any of his relations, nor had they met any of his friends. They did not even know where he had been staying in London. He was in the habit of telephoning to Louisa every morning, and any arrangements for his visits down to 'The Towers' or the ladies' trips up to town were made in that manner. As a matter of fact, Louisa and her future husband had not met more than a dozen times altogether, on some five or six occasions in Monte Carlo, and not more than six in England. It had been a case of love at first sight.

"The question of Mr. Schumann's vast undertaking was first discussed at 'The Towers.' After that the ladies wrote to their bank to sell out their securities, and subsequently went up to town for a couple of days to draw out their money, change it into French currency, and finally hand it over to Prince Orsoff. On that occasion he had met them at Victoria Station and taken them to a quiet hotel in Kensington, where he had engaged a suite of rooms for them. All financial matters were then settled in their private sitting-room.

"In answer to enquiries at that hotel, one or two of the employees distinctly remembered the foreign-looking gentleman who had called on Mrs and Miss Smithson, lunched with them in their sitting-room that day, and saw them into their cab when they went away the following afternoon. One or two of the station porters at Victoria also vaguely remembered a man who answered to the description given of Prince Orsoff by the Smithson ladies: tall, with a slight stoop, wearing *pince-nez,* and with a profusion of dark, curly hair, bushy eyebrows, long dark moustache, and old-fashioned imperial, which made him distinctly noticeable, he could not very well have passed unperceived.

"Unfortunately, on the actual day of the murder, not one man employed at Victoria Station could swear positively to having seen him, either alone or in the company of another foreigner; and the latter has remained a problematic personage to this day.

"But the Smithson ladies remained firm in their loyalty to their Russian prince. Had they dared they would openly have accused Henry Carter of the murder; as it was, they threw out weird hints and insinuations about Henry, who had more than once sworn that he would be even with his hated rival, and who had actually travelled down in the same train as the prince on that fateful wedding morning, together with his brother John, who no doubt helped him in his nefarious deed. I believe that the unfortunate ladies actually spent some of the money which now they could ill spare in employing a private detective to collect proofs of Henry Carter's guilt.

"But not a tittle of evidence could be brought against him. To begin with, the train in which the murder was supposed to have been committed was a nonstop to Swanley. Then how could the Carters have disposed of the body? The Smithsons suggested a third miscreant as a possible confederate; but the same objection against that theory subsisted in the shape of the disposal of the body. The murder—if murder there was—occurred in broad daylight in a part of the country that certainly was not lonely. It was not possible to suppose that a man would stand waiting on the line close to Sydenham Hill station until a body was flung out to him from the passing train, and then drag that body about until he found a suitable place in which to bury it: and all that without being seen by the workmen on the line or employees on the railway, or in fact any passer-by.

"Therefore, the hypothesis that Henry Carter or his brother murdered the Russian prince with or without the help of a confederate was as untenable as that the prince had travelled from Victoria to Sydenham Hill and there jumped out of the train, at risk of being discovered in the act, rather than disappear quietly in London, shave off his luxuriant hair, or assume any other convenient disguise, until he found an opportunity for slipping back to the Continent.

"But the Smithsons remained firm in their belief in the genuineness of their prince and in their conviction that he had been murdered—if not by the Carters, then by the mysterious secretary to the Russian Embassy or any other Russian or German emissary, for political reasons.

"And thus, the public was confronted with the two hypotheses, both of which led to a deadlock. No sensible person doubted that the so-called Russian prince was a crook and that he had a confederate to help him in his clever plot, but the mystery remained as to how the rascal or rascals disappeared so completely as to checkmate every investigation. The travelling by train that morning and setting the scene for a supposed murder was, of course, part of the plan, but it was the plan that was so baffling, because to an ordinary mind that disappearance could have been effected so much more easily and with far less risk without the train journey.

"Of course, there was not a single passenger on that train who was not the subject of the closest watchfulness on the part of the police, but there was not one—not excluding the Carters—who could by any possible chance have known that the prince carried a large sum of money upon his person. He was not likely to have confided the fact to a stranger, and the mystery of the vanished body was always there to refute the theory of an ordinary murderous attack for motives of robbery."

4

The Man in the Corner ceased talking and became once more absorbed in his favourite task of making knots in a bit of string.

"I see in the papers," I now put in thoughtfully, "that Miss Louisa Smithson has overcome her grief for the loss of her aristocratic lover by returning to the plebeian one."

"Yes," the funny creature replied drily, "she is marrying Henry Carter. Funny, isn't it? But women are queer fish! One moment she looked on the man as a murderer, now, by marrying him, she actually proclaims her belief in his innocence."

"It certainly was abundantly proved," I rejoined, "that Henry Carter could not possibly have murdered Prince Orsoff."

"It was also abundantly proved," he retorted, "that no one murdered the so-called prince."

"You think, of course, that he was an ordinary impostor?" I asked.

"An impostor, yes," he replied, "but not an ordinary one. In fact, I take off my hat to as clever a pair of scamps as I have ever come across."

"A pair?"

"Why, yes! It could not have been done alone."

"But the police . . ."

"The police," the spook-like creature broke in with a sharp cackle, "know more, in this case, than you give them credit for. They know well enough the solution of the puzzle which appears so baffling to the public, but they have not sufficient proof to effect an arrest. At one time they hoped that the scoundrels would presently make a false move and give themselves away, in which case they could be prosecuted for defrauding the Smithsons of £10,000, but this eventuality has become complicated through the masterstroke of genius which made Henry Carter marry Louisa Smithson."

"Henry Carter?" I exclaimed. "Then you do think the Carters had something to do with the case?"

"They had everything to do with the case. In fact, they planned the whole thing in a masterly manner."

"But the Russian prince at Monte Carlo?" I argued. "Who was he? If he was a confederate, where has he disappeared to?"

"He is still engaged in the free-lance journalism," the Man in the Corner replied drily, "and in his spare moments changes parcels of French currency back into English notes."

"You mean the brother!" I ejaculated with a gasp.

"Of course, I mean the brother," he retorted drily, "who else could have been so efficient a collaborator in the plot? John Carter was comparatively his own master. He lived with Henry in the small house in Chelsea, waited on by a charwoman who came by the day. It was generally given out that his reporting work took him frequently and for lengthened stays out of London. The brothers, remember, had inherited a few hundreds from their father, while the Smithsons had inherited a few thousands. We must suppose that the idea of relieving those ladies of those thousands occurred to them as soon as they realised that Louisa, egged on by her mother, would cold-shoulder her *fiancé*.

"John Carter, mind you, must be a very clever man, else he could not have carried out all the details of the plot with so much *sang-froid*. We have been told, if you remember, that he had, early in life, cut his stick and gone to seek fortune in London, therefore the Smithsons, who had never been out of Folkestone, did not know him intimately. His make-up as the prince must have been very good, and his histrionic powers not to be despised: his profession and life in London no doubt helped him in these matters. Then, remember also that he took very good care not to be a great deal in the Smithsons' company—even in Monte Carlo, he only let them see him less than half a dozen times, and as soon as he came to England he hurried on the wedding as much as he could.

"Another fine stroke was Henry's apparent despair at being cut out of Louisa's affections and his threats against his successful rival: it helped to draw suspicion on himself—suspicion which the scoundrels took good care could easily be disproved. Then take a pair of vain, credulous, unintelligent women, and a smart rascal who knows how to flatter them, and you will see how easily the whole plot could be worked. Finally, when John Carter had obtained possession of the money, he and Henry arranged the supposed tragedy in the train and the Russian prince's disappearance from the world as suddenly as he had entered it."

I thought the matter over for a moment or two. The solution of the mystery certainly appealed to my dramatic sense.

"But," I said at last, "one wonders why the Carters took the trouble to arrange a scene of a supposed murder in the train: they might quite well have been caught in the act, and in any case, it was an additional unnecessary risk. John Carter might quite well have been content to shed his role of Russian prince, without such an elaborate setting."

"Well," he admitted," in some ways you are right there, but it is always difficult to gauge accurately the mentality of a clever scoundrel. In this case I don't suppose that the Carters had quite made up their minds about what they would do when they left London, but that the plan was in their heads is proved by the hat, *pince-nez*, and railway ticket which they took with them when they started, and which, if you remember, were found on the line: but it was probably only because the train was comparatively empty, and they had both time and opportunity in the nonstop train, that they decided to carry their clever comedy through.

"Then think what an immense advantage in their future plans would be the Smithsons' belief in the death of their prince. Probably Louisa would never have dreamed of marrying if she thought her aristocratic lover was an impostor and still alive; she would never have let the matter rest; her mind would for ever have been busy with trying to trace him, and bring him back, repentant, to her feet. You know what women are when they are in love with that type of scoundrel, they cling to them with the tenacity of a leech. But once she believed the man to be dead, Louisa Smithson gradually got over her grief and Henry Carter wooed and won her on the rebound. She was poor now, and her friends had quickly enough deserted her; she was touched by the fidelity of her simple lover, and he thus consolidated his position and made the future secure.

"Anyway," the Man in the Corner concluded, "I believe that it was with a view to making a future marriage possible between Louisa and Henry that the two brothers organised the supposed murder. Probably if the train had been full and they had seen danger in the undertaking they would not have done it. But the *mise en scene* was easily enough set and it certainly was an additional safeguard. Now in another week or so Louisa Smithson will be Henry Carter's wife, and presently you will find that, John in London, and Henry and his wife, will be quite comfortably off. And after that, whatever suspicions Mrs. Smithson might have of the truth, her lips would have to remain sealed. She could not very well prosecute her only child's husband.

"And so, the matter will always remain a mystery to the public: but the police know more than they are able to admit because they have no proof.

"And now they never will have. But as to the murder in the train, well!—the murdered man never existed."

The Mysterious Tragedy in Bishop's Road

1

The Man in the Corner was in a philosophising mood that afternoon, and all the while that his thin claw-like fingers fidgeted with the inevitable piece of string he gave vent to various, disjointed, always sententious remarks.

Suddenly he said:

"We know, of course, that the world has gone dancing mad! But I doubt if the fashionable craze has ever been responsible before for so dark a tragedy as the death of old Sarah Levison. What do you think?"

"Well," I replied guardedly, for I knew that, whatever I might say, I should draw an avalanche of ironical remarks upon my innocent head, "I never have known what to think, and all the accounts of that brutal murder as they appeared in the cheaper Press only made obscurity all the more obscure."

"That was a wise and well-thought-out reply," the aggravating creature retorted with a dry chuckle, "and a non-committal one at that. Obscurity is indeed obscure for those who won't take the trouble to think."

"I suppose it is all quite clear to you?" I said, with what I meant to be withering sarcasm.

"As clear as the proverbial daylight," he replied undaunted.

"You know how old Mrs. Levison came by her death?"

"Of course, I do. I will tell you if you like."

"By all means. But I am not prepared to be convinced," I added cautiously.

"No," he admitted, "but you soon will be. However, before we reach that happy conclusion, I shall have to marshal the facts before you, because a good many of these must have escaped your attention.

Shall I proceed?"

"If you please."

"Well, then, do you remember all the personages in the drama?" he began.

"I think so."

"There were, of course, young Aaron Levison and his wife, Rebecca—the latter young, pretty, fond of pleasure, and above all of dancing, and he, a few years older, but still in the prime of life, more of an athlete than a business man, and yet tied to the shop in which he carried on the trade of pawnbroking for his mother. The latter, an old Jewess, shrewd and dictatorial, was the owner of the business: her son was not even her partner, only a well-paid clerk in her employ, and this fact we must suppose rankled in the mind of her smart daughter-in-law. At any rate, we know that there was no love lost between the two ladies; but the young couple and old Mrs. Levison and another unmarried son lived together in the substantial house over the shop in Bishop's Road."

"They had three servants and we are told that they lived well, old Mrs. Levison bearing the bulk of the cost of housekeeping. The younger son, Reuben, seems to have been something of a bad egg. He held at one time a clerkship in a bank, but was dismissed for insobriety and laziness; then after the war he was supposed to have bad health consequent on exposure in the trenches, and had not done a day's work since he was demobilised. But in spite, or perhaps because, of this, he was very markedly his mother's favourite; where the old woman would stint her hard-working, steady elder son, she would prove generous, even lavish, toward the loafer, Reuben; and young Mrs. Levison and he were as thick as thieves.

"What money Reuben extracted out of his mother he would spend on amusements, and his sister-in-law was always ready to accompany him. It was either the cinema or dancing—oh, dancing above all! Rebecca Levison was, it seems, a beautiful dancer, and night after night she and Reuben would go to one or other of the halls or hotels where dancing was going on, and often they would not return until the small hours of the morning.

"Aaron Levison was indulgent and easy-going enough where his young wife was concerned: he thought that she could come to no harm while Reuben was there to look after her. But old Mrs. Levison, with the mistrust of her race for everything that is frivolous and thriftless, thought otherwise. She was convinced in her own mind that

260

her beloved Reuben was being led astray from the path of virtue by his brother's wife, and she appears to have taken every opportunity to impress her thoughts and her fears upon the indulgent husband.

"It seems that one of the chief bones of contention between the old and the young Mrs. Levison was the question of jewellery. Old Mrs. Levison kept charge herself of all the articles of value that were pawned in the shop, and every evening after business hours Aaron would bring up all bits of jewellery that had been brought in during the day, and his mother would lock them up in a safe that stood in her room close by her bedside. The key of the safe she always carried about with her. For the most part these bits of jewellery consisted of cheap rings and brooches, but now and again some impoverished lady or gentleman would bring more valuable articles along for the purpose of raising a temporary loan upon them, and at the time of the tragedy there were some fine diamond ornaments reposing in the safe in old Mrs. Levison's room.

"Now young Mrs. Levison had more than once suggested that she might wear some of this fine jewellery when she went out to balls and parties. She saw no harm in it, and neither, for a matter of that, did Reuben. Why shouldn't Rebecca wear a few ornaments now and again if she wanted to?—they would always be punctually returned, of course, and they could not possibly come to any harm. But the very suggestion of such a thing was anathema to the old lady, and in her flat refusal ever to gratify such a senseless whim she had the whole-hearted support of her eldest son: such a swerving from traditional business integrity was not to be thought of in the Levison household.

On that memorable Saturday evening young Mrs. Levison was going with her brother-in-law to one of the big charity balls at the Kensington Town Hall, and her great desire was to wear for the occasion a set of diamond stars which had lately been pledged in the shop, and which were locked up in the old lady's safe. Of course, Mrs. Levison refused, and it seems that the two ladies very nearly came to blows about this, the quarrel being all the more violent as Reuben hotly sided with his sister-in-law against his mother.

2

"That then was the position in the Levison household on the day of the mysterious tragedy," the Man in the Corner went on presently: "an armed truce between the two ladies—the lovely Rebecca sore and defiant, pining to gratify a whim which was being denied her, and old

261

Mrs. Levison more bitter than usual against her, owing to Reuben's partisanship. Egged on by Rebecca, he was furious with his mother and vowed that he was sick of the family and meant to cut his stick in order to be free to lead his own life, and so on. It was all tall-talk, of course, as he was entirely dependent on his mother, but it went to show the ugliness of his temper and the domination which his brother's wife exercised over him. Aaron, on the other hand, took no part in the quarrel, but the servants remarked that he was unwontedly morose all day, and that his wife was very curt and disagreeable with him.

"Nothing, however, of any importance occurred during the day until dinner-time, which as usual was served in the parlour at the back of the shop at seven o'clock. It seems that as soon as the family sat down to their meal, there was another violent quarrel on some subject or other between the two ladies, Rebecca being hotly backed up by Reuben, and Aaron taking no part in the discussion; in the midst of the quarrel, and following certain highly offensive words spoken by Reuben, old Mrs. Levison got up abruptly from the table and went upstairs to her own room which was immediately overhead at the back of the house, next to the drawing-room, nor did she come downstairs again that evening.

"At half-past nine the three servants went up to bed according to the rule of the house. Old Mrs. Levison, who was a real autocrat in the management of the household, expected the girls, to be down at six every morning, but they were free to go to bed as soon as their work was done, and half-past nine was their usual time.

"Two of the girls slept at the top of the house, and the housemaid, Ida Griggs by name, who also acted as a sort of maid to old Mrs. Levison, occupied a small slip room on the half landing immediately above the old lady's bedroom. On the floor above this there was a large bedroom at the back and a bathroom and dressing-room in front, all occupied by Mr and Mrs. Aaron, and over that, the two maids' room, and one for Mr. Reuben, and a small spare room in which Mr. Aaron would sleep now and again when his wife was likely to be out late and he did not want to get his night's rest broken by her home-coming, or if he himself was going to be late home on a holiday night after one of those country excursions on his bicycle of which he was immensely fond and in which he indulged himself from time to time.

"On this fateful Saturday evening Aaron was kept late in the shop, but he finally went up to bed soon after ten, after he had seen to all the doors below being bolted and barred, with the exception of the front door which had to be left on the latch, Mrs. Aaron having the latch-key. Thus, the house was shut up and everyone in bed by half-past ten.

"In the meanwhile, the lovely Mrs. Rebecca and Reuben had dressed and gone to the ball.

"The next morning at a little before six, Ida Griggs, the house-maid, having got up and dressed, prepared to go downstairs: but when she went to open her bedroom door, she found it locked—locked on the outside. At first, she thought that the other girls were playing her a silly trick, and, presently hearing the patter of their feet on the stairs, she pounded against the door with her fists. It took the others some time to understand what was amiss, but at last they did try the lock on the outside, and found that the key had been turned and that Ida was indeed locked in.

"They let her out, and then consulted what had best be done, but for the moment it did not seem to strike any of the girls that this lock-ing of a door from the outside had a sinister significance. Anyway, they all went down into the kitchen and Ida prepared old Mrs. Levison's early cup of tea. This she had to take up every morning at half-past six; on this occasion she went up as usual, knocked at her mistress' door, and waited to be let in, as the old lady always slept behind locked doors. But no sound came from within, though Ida knocked repeat-edly and loudly called her mistress by name.

"Soon she started screaming and her screams brought the house-hold together: the two girls came up from the kitchen, Mr. Aaron came down from the top floor brandishing a poker, and presently Mrs. Aaron opened her door and peeped out clad in a filmy and ex-quisite nightgown, her eyes still heavy with sleep and her beautiful hair streaming down her back. But of old Mrs. Levison there was no sign. Mr. Aaron, genuinely alarmed, glued his ear to the keyhole, but not a sound could he hear. Behind that locked door absolute silence reigned.

"Fearing the worst, he set himself the task of breaking open the door, which after some effort, and the use of a jemmy, he succeeded in doing: and here the sight that met his eyes filled his soul with horror, for he saw his mother lying on the floor of her bedroom in a pool of blood. Evidently an awful crime had been committed. The unfortu-nate woman was fully dressed, as she had been on the evening before; the door of the safe was open with the key still in the lock, but no other piece of furniture appeared to be disturbed; the one window of the room was wide open and the one door had been locked on the inside; the other door, the one which gave on the front drawing-room, being permanently blocked by a heavy wardrobe; and below the open window the bunch of creepers against the wall was all broken and torn, showing plainly the way that the miscreant had escaped.

"After a few moments of awe-stricken silence Aaron Levison regained control of himself and at once telephoned—first for the police and then for the doctor, but he would not allow anything in the room to be touched, not even his mother's dead body.

"For this precaution he was highly commended by the police inspector who presently appeared upon the scene, accompanied by a constable and the divisional surgeon; the latter proceeded to examine the body. He stated that the unfortunate woman had been attacked from behind, the marks of fingers being clearly visible round her throat: in her struggle for freedom, she must have fallen backwards and in so doing struck her head against the corner of the marble washstand, which caused her death.

"In the meanwhile, the inspector had been examining the premises: he found that the back door which gave on the yard and the one that gave on the front area were barred and locked just as Mr. Aaron had left them before he went up to bed the previous night; on the other hand, the front door was still on the latch, young Mrs. Levison having apparently failed to bolt it when she came home from the ball. In the backyard the creeper against the wall below the window of Mrs. Levison's room was certainly torn, and the miscreant undoubtedly made his escape that way, but he could not have got up to the window save with the aid of a ladder, the creeper was too slender to have supported any man's weight, and the brick wall of the house offered no kind of foothold even to a cat.

"The yard itself was surrounded on every side by the backyards of contiguous houses, and against the dividing walls there were clumps of Virginia creeper and anaemic shrubs such as are usually found in London backyards. Now neither on those walls nor on the creepers and shrubs was there the slightest trace of a ladder being dragged across, or even of a man having climbed the walls or slung a rope over: there was not a twig of shrub broken or a leaf of creeper disturbed.

"With regard to the safe, it must either have been open at the time that the murderer attacked Mrs. Levison, or he had found the key and opened the safe after he had committed that awful crime. Certainly, the contents did not appear to have been greatly disturbed, no jewellery or other pledged goods of value were missing: Mr. Aaron could verify this by his books, but whether his mother had any money in the safe he was not in a position to say.

"There was no doubt that at first glance the crime did not seem to have been an ordinary one; whether robbery had been its motive, or its corollary, only subsequent investigation would reveal: for the moment the inspector contented himself with putting a few leading questions to the various members of the household, and subsequently questioning the neighbours. The public, of course, was not to know what the result of these preliminary investigations was, but the mid-day papers were in a position to assert that no one, with perhaps the exception of Ida Griggs, had seen or heard anything alarming during the night, and that the most minute inquiries in the neighbourhood failed to bring forth the slightest indication of how the miscreants effected an entrance into the house.

"The papers were also able to state that young Mrs. Levison returned from the ball in the small hours of the morning, but that Mr. Reuben Levison did not sleep in the house at all that night.

3

"Fortunately for me," my eccentric friend went on glibly, "I was up betimes that morning when the papers came out with an early account of the mysterious crime in Bishop's Road, I say fortunately, because, as you know, mysteries of that sort interest me beyond everything, and for me there is no theatre in the world to equal in excitement the preliminary investigations of a well-conceived and cleverly executed crime. I should indeed have been bitterly disappointed had circumstances prevented me from attending that particular inquest. From the first, one was conscious of an atmosphere of mystery that hung over the events of that night in the Bishop's Road household: here indeed was no ordinary crime; the motive for it was still obscure, and one instinctively felt that somewhere, in this vast city of London, there lurked a criminal of no mean intelligence who would probably remain unpunished.

"Even the evidence of the police was not as uninteresting as it usually is, because it established beyond a doubt that this was not a case of common burglary and housebreaking. Certainly, the open window and the torn creeper suggested that the miscreant had made his escape that way, but how he effected an entrance into Mrs. Levison's room remained an unsolved riddle. The absence of any trace of a man's passage on the surrounding walls of the backyard was very mysterious, and it was firmly established that the back door and the area door were secured, barred and bolted from the inside. A burglar might, of course, have entered the house by the front door, which was on the latch, using a skeleton key, but it still remained inconceivable how he gained access into Mrs. Levison's room.

"From the first the public had felt that there was a background of domestic drama behind the seemingly purposeless crime, for it did appear purposeless, seeing that so much portable jewellery had been left untouched in the safe. But it was when Ida Griggs, the housemaid, stood up in response to her name being called that one seemed to see the curtain going up on the first act of a terrible tragedy.

"Griggs was a colourless, youngish woman, with thin, sallow face, round blue eyes, and thin lips, and directly she began to speak one felt that underneath her placid, old-maidish manner there was an undercurrent of bitter spite, and even of passion.

For some reason which probably would come to light later on, she appeared to have conceived a hatred for Mrs. Aaron; on the other hand, she had obviously been doggedly attached to her late mistress, and in the evidence she dwelt at length on the quarrels between the two ladies, especially on the scene of violence that occurred at the dinner-table on Saturday and which culminated in old Mrs. Levison flouncing out of the room.

"'Mrs. Levison was that upset,' the girl went on, in answer to a question put to her by the coroner, 'that I thought she was going to be ill, and she says to me that women like Mrs. Aaron were worse than — as they would stick at nothing to get a new gown or a bit of jewellery. She also says to me. . .'

"But at this point the coroner checked her flow of eloquence as, of course what the dead woman had said could not be admitted as evidence. But nevertheless, the impression remained vividly upon the public that there had been a terrible quarrel between those two, and of course we all knew that young Mrs. Levison had been seen at the ball wearing those five diamond stars; we did not need the sworn testimony of several witnesses that were called and interrogated on that point. We knew that Rebecca Levison had worn the diamond stars at the ball, and that Police Inspector Blackshire found them on her dressing-table the morning after the murder.

"Nor did she deny having worn them. At the inquest she renewed the statement which she had already made to the police.

"'My brother-in-law, Reuben,' she said, 'was a great favourite with his mother, and when we were both of us ready dressed, he went into Mrs. Levison's room to say goodnight to her. He cajoled her into letting me wear the diamond stars that night. In fact, he always could make her do anything he really wanted, and they parted the best of friends.'

"'At what time did you go to the ball, Mrs. Levison?' the coroner asked.

"'My brother-in-law,' she replied, 'went out to call a taxi at half past nine, and he and I got into it the moment one drew up.'

"'And Mr. Reuben Levison had been in to say goodnight to his mother just before that?'

"'Yes, about ten minutes before.'

"'And he brought you the stars then,' the coroner insisted, 'and you put them on before he went out to call the taxi?'

"For the fraction of a second Rebecca Levison hesitated, but I do not think that anyone in the audience except myself noted that little fact. Then she said quite firmly:

"'Yes, Mr. Reuben Levison told me that he had persuaded his mother to let me wear the stars, he handed them to me and I put them on.'

"'And that was at half-past nine?'

"Again, Rebecca Levison hesitated, this time more markedly; her face was very pale and she passed her tongue once or twice across her lips before she gave answer.

"'At about half-past nine,' she said, quite steadily.

"'And about what time did you come home, Mrs. Levison?' the coroner asked her blandly.

"'It must have been close on one o'clock,' she replied. 'The dance was a Cinderella, but we walked part of the way home.'

"'What! In the rain?'

"'It had ceased raining when we came out of the Town Hall.'

"'Mr. Reuben Levison did not accompany you all the way?'

"'He walked with me across the park, then he put me into a taxicab and I drove home alone. I had my latch-key.'

"'But you failed to bolt the door after you when you returned. How was that?'

"'I forgot, I suppose.' the lovely Rebecca replied, with a defiant air. 'I often forget to bolt the door.'

"'And did you not see or hear anything strange when you came in?'

"'I heard nothing. I was rather sleepy and went straight up to my room. I was in bed within ten minutes of coming in.'

"She was speaking quite firmly now, in a clear though rather harsh voice: but that she was nervous, not to say frightened, was very obvious. She had a handkerchief in her hand, with which she fidgeted until it was nothing but a small, wet ball, and she had a habit of standing first on one foot then on the other, and of shifting the position of her hat. I do not think that there was a single member of the jury who did not think that she was lying, and she knew that they thought so, for now and again her fine dark eyes would scrutinise their faces and dart glances at them either of scorn or of anxiety. After a while she appeared very tired, and when pressed by the coroner over some trifling matters, she broke down and began to cry. After which she was allowed to stand down and Mr. Reuben Levison was called.

"I must say that I took an instinctive dislike to him as he stood before the jury with a jaunty air of complete self-possession. He had a keen, yet shifty eye, and sharp features, very like a rodent. To me it appeared at once that he was reciting a lesson rather than giving independent evidence. He stated that he had been present at dinner during the bitter quarrel between his mother and sister-in-law, and his mother was certainly very angry at the moment, but later on he went upstairs to bid her goodnight. She cried a little and said a few hard things, but in the end, she gave way to him as she always did: she opened the safe, got out the diamond stars and gave them to him, making him promise to return them the very first thing in the morning.

"'I told her,' Reuben went on glibly, 'that I would not be home until the Monday morning. I would see Rebecca into a taxi after the ball, but I had the intention of spending a couple of nights and the intervening Sunday with a pal who had a flat at Haverstock Hill. I thought then that my mother would lock the stars up again, however—she was always a woman of her word—once she had said a thing she would stick to it—and so, as I say, she gave me the stars and Mrs. Aaron wore them that night.'

"'And you handed the stars to Mrs. Aaron at half-past nine?' The coroner asked the question with the same earnest emphasis which he had displayed when he put it to young Mrs. Levison. I saw Reuben's shifty eye flash across at her, and I know that she answered that flash with a slight drop of her eyelids. Whereupon he replied as readily as she had done:

"'Yes, sir, it must have been about half-past nine.'

"And I assure you that every intelligent person in that room must have felt certain that Reuben was lying just as Rebecca had done before him. The inquest was developing on dramatic lines, and the chief actors in the play had come to a point of cerebral excitement that was plainly visible on their pale, set faces, and there were beads of moisture around their tightly-compressed lips which were not entirely attributable to the heat."

The Man in the Corner paused in his narrative. He drank half a glass of milk, smacked his lips, and for a few moments appeared intent on examining one of the complicated knots which he had made in his bit of string. Then after a while he resumed.

"The one member of the Levison family," he said, "for whom everyone felt sorry, was the eldest son, Aaron. Like most men of his race, he had been very fond of his mother, not because of any affection she may have shown him but just because she was his mother. He had worked hard for her all his life, and now through her death he found himself very much left out in the cold. It seems that by her will the old lady left all her savings, which, it seems, were considerable, and a certain share in the business, to Reuben, whilst to Aaron she only left the business nominally, with a great many charges on it in the way of pensions and charitable bequests and whatever was due to Reuben.

"But here I am digressing, as the matter of the will was not touched upon until later on, but there is no doubt that Aaron knew from the first that it would be Reuben who would primarily benefit by their mother's death. Nevertheless, he did not speak bitterly about his brother, and nothing that he said could be construed into possible suspicion of Reuben. He looked just a big lump of good nature, splendidly built, with the shoulders and gait of an athlete, but with an expression of settled melancholy in his face, and a dull, rather depressing voice. Seeing him there, gentle, almost apologetic, trying to explain away everything that might in any way cast a reflection upon his wife's conduct, one realised easily enough the man's position in the family—a kind of good-natured beast of burden, who would do all the work and never receive a 'thank you' in return.

"He was not able to throw much light on the horrible tragedy. He, too, had been at the dinner-table when the quarrel occurred, but directly after dinner he had been obliged to return to the shop, it being Saturday night and business very brisk. He had only one assistant to help him, who left at nine o'clock, after putting up the shutters; but he himself remained in the shop until ten o'clock to put things away and make up the books. He heard the taxi being called and his wife and brother going off to the ball; he was not quite sure as to when that was, but he dared say it was somewhere near half-past nine. As nothing of special value had been pledged that day in the course of business, he had no occasion to go and speak with his mother before going up to bed and, on the whole, he thought that, as she might still be rather sore and irritable, it would be best not to disturb her again, he did just knock at her door, and called out 'goodnight, mother.' But hearing no reply he thought she must already have been asleep.

"In answer to the coroner Aaron Levison further said that he had slept in the spare room at the top of the house for some time, as his wife was often very late coming home, and he did not like to have his night's rest broken. He had gone up to bed at ten o'clock and had neither seen nor heard anything in the house until six o'clock in the morning when the screams of the maid down below had roused him from sleep and made him jump out of bed in double-quick time.

"Although Aaron's evidence was more or less of a formal character, and he spoke very quietly without any show either of swagger or of spite, one could not help feeling that the elements of drama and of mystery connected with this remarkable case were rather accentuated than diminished by what he said. Thus, one was more or less prepared for those further developments which brought one's excitement and interest in the case to their highest point.

"Recalled, and pressed by the coroner to try and memorise every event, however trifling, that occurred on that Saturday evening, Ida Griggs, the maid, said that, soon after she had dropped to sleep, she woke with the feeling that she had heard some kind of noise, but what it was she could not define: it might have been a bang, or a thud, or a scream. At the time she thought nothing of it, whatever it was, because while she lay awake for a few minutes afterwards the house was absolutely still; but a moment or two later she certainly heard the window of Mrs. Levison's room being thrown open.

"'There did not seem to you anything strange in that?' the coroner asked her.

"'No, sir,' she replied, 'there was nothing funny in Mrs. Levison opening her window. I remember that it was raining rather heavily, for I heard the patter against the window panes, and Mrs. Levison may have wanted to look at the weather. I went to sleep directly after that and thought no more about it.'

"'And you don't know what it was that woke you in the first instance?'

"'No, sir, I don't,' the girl replied.

"'And you did not happen to glance at the clock at the moment?'

"'No, sir,' she said, 'I did not switch on the light.'

"But having disposed of that point, Ida Griggs had yet another to make, and one that proved more dramatic than anything that had gone before.

"'While I was clearing away the dinner things,' she said, 'Mr. Reuben and Mrs. Aaron were sitting talking in the parlour. At half-past eight Mrs. Aaron rang for me to take up her hot water as she was going to dress. I took up the water for her and also for Mrs. Levison, as I always did. I was going to help Mrs. Levison to undress, but she said she was not going to bed yet as she had some accounts to go through. She kept me talking for a bit, then while I was with her there was a knock at the door and I heard Mr. Reuben asking if he might come in and say goodnight. Mrs. Levison called out "goodnight, my boy," but she would not let Mr. Reuben come in, and I heard him go downstairs again.

"'A quarter of an hour or so afterwards Mrs. Levison dismissed me and I heard her locking her door after me. I went downstairs on my way to the kitchen: Mrs. Aaron was in the parlour then, fully dressed and with her cloak on; and Mr. Reuben was there, too, talking to her. The door was wide open and I saw them both and I heard Mrs. Aaron say quite spiteful like: "So she would not even see you, the old cat! She must have felt bad." And Mr. Reuben he laughed and said; "Oh—well, she will have to get over it." Then they saw me and stopped talking, and soon afterwards Mr. Reuben went out to call a taxi, and we girls went up to bed.'

"'It is all a wicked lie!' here broke in a loud, high-pitched voice, and Mrs. Aaron, trembling with excitement, jumped to her feet. 'A lie, I say. The woman is spiteful and wants to ruin me.'

"The coroner vainly demanded silence, and after a moment or two of confusion and of passionate resistance the lovely Rebecca was forcibly led out of the room. Her husband followed her, looking bigger and more meek and apologetic than ever before; and Ida Griggs was left to conclude her evidence in peace. She re-affirmed all that she had said and swore positively to the incident just as it had occurred in Mrs. Levison's room. Asked somewhat sharply by the coroner why she had said nothing about all this before, she replied that she did not wish to make mischief, but that truth was truth, and whoever murdered her poor mistress must swing for it, and that's all about it."

"Nor could any cross-examination upset her: she looked like a spiteful cat, but not like a woman who was lying.

"Reuben Levison had sat on, serene and jaunty, all the while that these damaging statements were being made against him. When he was recalled, he contented himself with flatly denying Ida Griggs' story, and reiterating his own.

"'The girl is lying,' he said airily, 'why she does so I don't know, but there was nothing in the world more unlikely than that my mother should at any time refuse to see me. Ask any impartial witnesses you like,' he went on dramatically, 'they will all tell you that my mother worshipped me: she was not likely to quarrel with me over a few bits of jewellery.'

"Of course, Mrs. Aaron, when she was recalled, corroborated Reuben's story. She could not make out why Ida should tell such lies about her.

"'But there,' she added, with tears in her beautiful dark eyes, 'the girl always hated me.'

"Yet one more witness was heard that afternoon whose evidence proved of great interest. This was the assistant in the shop, Samuel Kutz. He could not throw much light on the tragedy, because he had not been out of the shop from six o'clock, when he finished his tea, to nine, when he put up the shutters and went away. But he did say that, while he was having his tea in the back parlour, old Mrs. Levison was helping in the front shop, and Mr. Reuben was there, too, doing nothing in particular, as was his custom.

"When witness went back to the shop Mrs. Levison went through into the back parlour, and, as soon as she had gone, he noticed that she had left her bag on the bureau behind the counter. Mr. Reuben saw it too; he picked up the bag and said with a laugh: 'I'd best take it up at once, the old girl don't like leaving this about.' Kutz told him he thought Mrs. Levison was in the back parlour, but Mr. Reuben was sure she had since gone upstairs.

"'Anyway,' concluded witness, 'he took the bag and went upstairs with it.'

"This may have been a valuable piece of evidence or it may not," the Man in the Corner went on with a grin, "in view of the tragedy occurring so much later, it did not appear to at the time. But it brought in an altogether fresh element of conjecture, and while the police asked for an adjournment pending fresh inquiries, the public was left to ponder over the many puzzles and contradictions that the case presented. Whatever line of argument one followed, one quickly came to a dead stop. There was, first of all, the question whether Reuben Levison did cajole his mother into giving him the diamond stars, or whether he was peremptorily refused admittance to her room: but this was just a case of hard swearing between one party and the other, and here I must admit, that public opinion was inclined to take Reuben's version of the story. Mrs. Levison's passionate affection for her younger son was known to all her friends, and people thought that Ida Griggs had lied in order to incriminate Mrs. Aaron.

"But in this she entirely failed, and here was the first dead stop. You will remember that she said that, after she left Mrs. Levison, she went downstairs and saw Mrs. Aaron and Mr. Reuben fully dressed in the back parlour, and that afterwards she heard Mr. Reuben call a taxi: obviously, therefore, Mrs. Aaron had the diamonds in her possession then, since she was wearing them at the ball, and it is not conceivable that either of those two would have gone off in the taxi, leaving the other to force an entrance into Mrs. Levison's room, strangle her, and steal the diamonds.

"As Mrs. Aaron could not possibly have done all that in her evening dress, making her way afterwards from a first-floor window down into the yard by clinging to a creeper in the pouring rain, the hideous task must have devolved on Reuben, and even the police, wildly in search of a criminal, could not put the theory forward that a man would murder his mother in order that his sister-in-law might wear a few diamond stars at a ball.

"It was, in fact, the motive of the crime that seemed so utterly inadequate, and therefore public argument fell back on the theory that Reuben had stolen the diamond stars, just before dinner after he had found his mother's handbag in the shop, and that the subsequent murder was the result of ordinary burglary, the miscreant having during the night entered Mrs. Levison's room by the window while she was asleep. It was suggested that he had found the key of the safe by the bedside and was in the act of ransacking the place when Mrs. Levison woke, and the inevitable struggle ensued resulting in the old lady's death.

"The chief argument, however, against this theory was the fact that the unfortunate woman was still dressed when she was attacked, and no one who knew her for the careful, thrifty woman she was could conceive that she would go fast asleep leaving the safe door wide open. This, coupled with the fact that not the slightest trace could be found anywhere in the backyard of the house, or the adjoining yards and walls of the passage, of a miscreant armed with a ladder, constituted another dead stop on the road of public conjecture.

"Finally, when at the adjourned inquest Reuben Levison was able to bring forward more than one witness who could swear that he arrived at the ball at the Kensington Town Hall in the company of his sister-in-law somewhere about ten o'clock, and others who spoke to him from time to time during the evening, it seemed clear that he, at any rate, was innocent of the murder. Mr. Aaron had not gone up to bed until ten o'clock, and if Reuben had planned to return and murder his mother he could only have done so at a later hour, when he was seen by several people at the Kensington Town Hall.

"Subsequently the jury returned an open verdict and that abominable crime has remained unpunished until now. Though it appeared so simple and crude at first, it proved a terribly hard nut for the police to crack. We may say that they never did crack it. They are absolutely convinced that Reuben Levison and Mrs. Aaron planned to murder the old lady, but how they did it no one has been able to establish. As for proofs of their guilt, there are none and never will be, for, though they are perhaps a pair of rascals, they are not criminals. It is not they who murdered Mrs. Levison."

"You think it was Ida Griggs?" I put in quickly, as the Man in the Corner momentarily ceased talking.

"Ah!" he retorted with his funny, dry cackle, "you favour that theory, do you?"

"No, I do not," I replied. "But I don't see—"

"It is a foolish theory," he went on, "not only because there was absolutely no reason why Ida Griggs should kill her mistress—she did not rob her, nor had she anything to gain by old Mrs. Levison's death—but as she was neither a cat, nor a night moth, she could not possibly have ascended from a first-floor window to another window on the half landing above, and entered her own room that way, for we must not lose sight of the fact that her bedroom door was the next morning found locked on the outside, and the key left in the lock."

"Then," I argued, "it must have been a case of ordinary burglary."

"That has been proved impossible," he riposted—"proved to the hilt. No man could have climbed up the wall of the house without a ladder, and no man could have brought a ladder into the backyard without leaving some trace of his passage, however slight: against the

274

walls, around the yard, there were creepers and shrubs—it would be impossible to drag a heavy ladder over those walls without breaking some of them."

"But someone killed old Mrs. Levison," I went on, with some exasperation—"she did not strangle herself with her own fingers."

"No, she did not do that," he admitted with a dry laugh.

"And if the murderer escaped through the window, he could not vanish into thin air."

"No," he admitted again, "he could not do that."

"Well then?" I retorted.

"Well then, the murder must have been committed by one of the inmates of the house," he said; and now I knew that I was on the point of hearing the solution of the mystery of the five diamond stars, because his thin claw-like fingers were working with feverish rapidity upon his beloved bit of string.

"But neither Mrs. Aaron," I argued, "nor Reuben Levison—"

"Neither," he broke in decisively. "We all know that. It was not conceivable that a woman could commit such a murder, nor that Reuben would kill his mother in order to gratify his sister-in-law's whim. That, of course, was nonsense, and every proof, both of time and circumstance, both of motive and opportunity, was entirely in their favour. No. We must look for a deeper motive for the hideous crime, a stronger determination, and above all a more powerful physique and easier opportunity for carrying the plot through. Personally, I do not believe that there was a plot to murder; on the other hand, I do believe in the man who idolised his young wife and had witnessed a deadly quarrel between her and his mother, and I do believe in his going presently to the latter in order to try and soothe her anger against the woman he loved."

"You mean," I gasped, incredulous and scornful, "that it was Aaron Levison?"

"Of course, I mean that," he replied placidly; "and if you think over all the circumstances of the case, you will readily agree with me. We know that Aaron Levison loved and admired his wife; we know that he was very athletic, and altogether an outdoor man. Bear these two facts in mind and let your thoughts follow the man after the terrible quarrel at the dinner-table. For a while he is busy in the shop, probably brooding over his mother's anger and the unpleasant consequences it might have for the lovely Rebecca. But presently he goes upstairs determined to speak with his mother, to plead with her. Dreading that

Ida Griggs, with the habit of her kind, might sneak out of her room, and perhaps glue her ear to the keyhole, he turns the key in the lock of the girl's bedroom door. He knows that the interview with his mother will be unpleasant, that hard words will be spoken against Rebecca, and these he does not wish Ida Griggs to hear.

"Then he knocks at his mother's door, and asks admittance on the pretext that he has something of value to remit to her for keeping in her safe. She would have no reason to refuse. He goes in, talks to his mother; she does not mince her words. By now she knows that the diamond stars have been extracted from the safe, stolen by her beloved Reuben for the adornment of the hated daughter-in-law.

"Can't you see those two arguing over the woman whom the man loves and whom the older woman hates? Can't you see the latter using words which outrage the husband's pride and rouses his wrath till it gets beyond his control? Can't you see him in an access of unreasoning passion gripping his mother by the throat, to smother the insults hurled at his wife?—and can you see the old woman losing her balance, and hitting her head against the corner of the marble washstand and falling—falling—whilst the son gazes down, frantic and horror-struck at what he has done?

"Then the instinct of self-preservation is roused. Oh, the man was cleverer than he was given credit for! He remembers with satisfaction locking Ida Grigg's door from the outside; and now to give the horrible accident the appearance of ordinary burglary! He locks his mother's door on the inside, switches out the light, then throws open the window. For a youngish man who is active and athletic the drop from a first-floor window, with the aid of a creeper on the wall, presents but little difficulty, and when a man is faced with a deadly peril, minor dangers do not deter him.

"Fortunately, everything has occurred before he has bolted and barred the downstairs doors for the night. This, of course, greatly facilitates matters. He lets himself down through the window, jumps down into the yard, lets himself into the house through the back door, then closes up everything, and quietly goes upstairs to bed.

"There has not been much noise, even his mother's fall was practically soundless, and—poor thing!—she had not the time to scream; the only sound was the opening of the window; it certainly would not bring Ida Griggs out of her bed—girls of her class are more likely to smother their heads under their bedclothes if any alarming noise is heard. And so, the unfortunate man is able to sneak up to his room unseen and unheard. Whoever would dream of casting suspicion on him? He was never mixed up in any quarrel with his mother, and he had nothing much to gain by her death. At the inquest everyone was sorry for him; but I could not repress a feeling of admiration for the coolness and cleverness with which he obliterated every trace of his crime. I imagine him carefully wiping his boots before he went upstairs, and brushing and folding up his clothes before he went to bed. Cannot you?

"A clever criminal, what?" the whimsical creature concluded, as he put his piece of string in the pocket of his funny tweed coat. "Think of it—you will see that I am right. As you say, Mrs. Levison did not strangle herself, and a burglar from the outside could not have vanished into thin air."

The Mystery of the Dog's Tooth Cliff

The Man in the Corner was more than usually loquacious that day; he had a great deal to say on the subject of the strictures which a learned judge levelled against the police in a recent murder case.

"Well deserved," he concluded with his usual self-opinionated emphasis, "but not more so in this case than in many others, where blunder after blunder is committed and the time of the courts wasted without either judge or magistrate, let alone the police, knowing where the hitch lies."

"Of course, you always know," I remarked drily.

"Nearly always," he replied with ludicrous self-complacence. "Have I not proved to you over and over again that with a little reasonable common sense and a minimum of logic there is no such thing as an impenetrable mystery in criminology. Criminology is an exact science to which certain rules of reasoning invariably apply. The trouble is that so few are masters of logic and that fewer still know how to apply its rules. Now take the case of that poor girl, Janet Smith. We are likely to see some startling developments in it within the next two or three days. You'll see if we don't, and they will open the eyes of the police and public alike to what has been dear as daylight to me ever since the first day of the inquest."

I hastened to assure the whimsical creature that, though I was acquainted with the main circumstances of the tragedy, I was very vague as to detail, and that nothing would give me more pleasure than that he should enlighten my mind on the subject—which he immediately proceeded to do.

"You know Broxmouth, don't you?" he began after a while—"on the Wessex coast. It is a growing place, for the scenery is superb and the air acts on jaded spirits like sparkling wine. The only drawback—that is, from an artistic point of view—to the place, is that hideous barrack-like building on the West Cliff. It is a huge industrial school

278

recently erected and endowed by the trustees of the Woodforde bequest for the benefit of sons of temporary officers killed in the War, and is under the presidency of no less a personage than General Sir Arkwright Jones who has a whole alphabet after his name.

"The building is certainly an eyesore, and, before it came into being, Broxmouth was a real beauty spot. If you have ever been there, you will remember that fine walk along the edge of the cliffs, at the end of which there is a wonderful view as far as the towers of Barchester cathedral. It is called the 'Lovers' Walk,' and is patronised by all the young people in the neighbourhood. They find it romantic as well as exhilarating: the objective is usually Kurtmoor, where there are one or two fine hotels for plutocrats in search of rural surroundings, and where humble folk like you and I and the aforesaid lovers can get an excellent cup of tea at the Wheatsheaf in the main village street.

"But it is a daylight walk, for the path is narrow and in places the cliffs fall away, sheer and precipitous, to the water's edge, whilst loose bits of rock have an unpleasant way of giving way under one's feet. If you were to consult one of the Broxmouth gaffers on the advisability of taking a midnight walk to Kurtmoor, he would most certainly shake his head, and tell you to wait till the next day and take your walk in the morning. Accidents have happened there—more than one—though Broxmouth holds its tongue about that. Rash pedestrians have lost their footing and tumbled down the side of the cliff before now, almost always with fatal results.

"And so, at first when a couple of small boys, hunting for mussels at low tide in the early morning of May 5th last, saw the body of woman lying inanimate upon the rocks at the foot of the cliffs, and reported their discovery to the police, everyone began concluding that nothing but an accident had occurred, and went on to abuse the Town Council for not putting up along the more dangerous portions of the 'Lovers' Walk' some sort of barrier as a protection to unwary pedestrians.

"Later on, when the body was identified as that of Janet Smith, a well-known resident of Broxmouth, public indignation waxed high: the barrier along the edge of the Lovers' Walk became the burning question of the hour. But during the whole of that day the 'accident' theory was never disputed; it was only towards evening that whispers of 'suicide' began to circulate in and about Broxmouth, to be soon followed by the more ominous ones of 'murder.'

"And by the next morning Broxmouth had the thrill of its life when it became known throughout the town that Captain Franklin

Marston had been detained in connection with the finding of the body of Janet Smith, and that he would appear that day before the magistrate on a charge of murder.

"Properly to appreciate the significance of such an announcement, it would be necessary to be oneself a resident of Broxmouth where the Woodforde Institute, its affairs and its personnel are, as it were, the be-all and end-all of all the gossip in the neighbourhood. To begin with, the deceased was head matron of the Institute, and the man, now accused of the foul crime of having murdered her, was its secretary; moreover, the secretary and the pretty young matron were known to be very much in love with one another, and, as a matter of fact, Broxmouth had of late been looking forward to a very interesting wedding. The idea of Captain Marston—who by the way was very good-looking, very smart, and a splendid tennis player—being accused of murdering his sweetheart was in itself so preposterous, so impossible, that his numerous friends and many admirers were aghast and incredulous. 'There is some villainous plot here somewhere,' the ladies averred, and wanted to know what Major Gubbins's attitude was going to be under these tragic circumstances.

"Major Gubbins, if you remember, was headmaster of the school, and what's more he, too, had been very much in love with Janet Smith, but it appeared that his friendship with Captain Marston had prompted him to stand aside as soon as he realised which way the girl's affections lay. Major Gubbins was not so popular as the captain, he was inclined to be off-hand and disagreeable, so the ladies said, and moreover he did not play tennis, and, with the sublime inconsequence of your charming sex, they seemed to connect these defects with terrible accusation which was now weighing upon the major's successful rival.

"The executive of the Institute consisted, in addition to the three persons I have named, of its president, General Sir Arkwright Jones, who, it seems, took little if any interest in the concern. It seems as if, by giving it the prestige of his name, he had done all that he intended for the furtherance of the Institute's welfare. Then there were the governors, a number of amiable local gentlemen and ladies who played tennis all day and attended innumerable tea-parties and knew as much about administering a big concern as a terrier does of rabbit-rearing.

"In the midst of this official supineness, the murder of the young matron, followed immediately by the arrest of the secretary, had come as a bombshell, and now wise heads began to wag and ominous murmurs became current that for some time past there had been something very wrong in the management of the Woodforde Institute. Whilst, at the call of various august personages, money was pouring in from the benevolent public, the commissariat was being conducted on parsimonious lines that were a positive scandal: the boys were shockingly underfed and the staff of servants was constantly being changed because girls would not remain on what they called a starvation regime.

"Then again, no proper accounts had been kept since the inception of the Institute five years ago; entries were spasmodic, irregular and unreliable; books were never audited; no one apparently had the slightest idea of profit and loss or of balances; no one knew from week to week where the salaries and wages were coming from, or from quarter to quarter if there would be funds enough to meet rates and taxes; no one, in fact, appeared to know anything about the affairs of the Institute, least of all the secretary himself who had often remarked quite jocularly that he had never in all his life known anything about book-keeping and that his appointment by the governors rested upon his agreeable personality rather than upon his financial and administrative ability.

"As you see, the captain's position was, in consequence of this, a very serious one: it became still more so when presently two or three ominous facts came to light. To begin with, it seemed that he could give absolutely no account of himself during the greater part of the night of May 5th. He had left the Institute at about seven o'clock; he told the headmaster then that he was going for a walk which seemed strange as it was pouring with rain. On the other hand, the landlady at the room where he lodged told the police that when she herself went to bed at eleven o'clock the captain had not come in: she hadn't seen him since morning, when he went to work and at what time he eventually came home she couldn't say.

"But there was worse to come: firstly, a stick was found on the beach some thirty yards or less from the spot where the body itself was discovered; and secondly, the police produced a few strands of wool which were, it seems, clinging to the poor girl's hat-pin, and which presumably were torn out of a muffler during the brief struggle which must have occurred when she was first attacked and before she lost her footing and fell down the side of the cliff.

"Now the stick was identified as the property of Captain Marston, and he had been seen on the road with it in his hand in the early part of the evening. He was then walking alone on the 'Lover's Walk'; two Broxmouth visitors met him on their way back from Kurtmoor.

Knowing him by sight, they passed the time of day. These witnesses, however, were quite sure that Captain Marston was not then wearing a muffler, on the other hand they were equally sure that he carried the stick; they had noticed it as a very unusual one, of what is known as Javanese snake-wood with a round heavy knob and leather strap which the captain carried slung upon his arm.

"Of course, the matter interested me enormously; it is not often that a person of the social and intellectual calibre of Captain Marston stands accused of so foul a crime. It he was guilty, then indeed he was one of the vilest criminals that ever defaced God's earth, and in the annals of crime there were few crimes more hideous. The poor girl, it seems, had been in love with him right up to the end and, according to some well-informed gossips, the wedding day had actually been fixed.

"The unsuccessful rival, Major Gubbins, too, was an interesting personality, and it was difficult to suppose that he was entirely ignorant of the events which must of necessity have led up to the crime. Supposedly there had been a quarrel between the lovers; sundry rumours were current as to this and in a vague way those rumours connected this quarrel with the shaky financial situation of the Institute. But it was all mere surmise and very contradictory; no one could easily state what possible connection there could be between the affairs of the Institution and the murder of the chief matron.

"In the meanwhile, the accused had been brought up before the magistrate, and formal evidence of the finding of the body and of the arrest was given, as well as of the subsequent discovery of the stick which was identified by the two witnesses and of the strands of wool. The accused was remanded until the following Monday, bail being refused. The inquest was held a day or two later and I went down to Broxmouth for it. I remember how hot it was in that crowded courtroom: excited and perspiring humanity filled the stuffy atmosphere with heat. While the crowd jabbered and fidgeted, I had a good look at the chief personages who were about to enact a thrilling drama for my entertainment; you have seen portraits of them all in the illustrated papers, the British Army being well represented by a trio of as fine specimens of manhood as anyone would wish to see.

"The President, General Arkwright Jones, was there as a matter of course. He looked worried and annoyed that the even tenor of his pleasant existence should have been disturbed by this tiresome event; he is the regular type of British pre-war superior officer with ruddy face and white hair, something like a nice ripe tomato that has been packed in cotton wool. Then there was the headmaster, Major Gubbins, well-groomed, impassive, immaculate in dress and bearing; and finally, the accused himself, in charge of two warders, fine-looking man, obviously more of a soldier and an athlete than a clerk immersed in figures.

"Two other persons in the crowded room arrested my attention: two women. One of them dressed in deep black, thin-lipped, with pale round eyes and pursed-up mouth was Miss Amelia Smith, the sister with whom deceased had been living, and the other was Louisa Rumble who held the position of housekeeper at the Woodforde Institute. The latter was one of the first witnesses called, and her evidence was intensely interesting because it gave one the first clue as to the motive which underlay the hideous crime. The woman's testimony, you must know, bore entirely on the question of housekeeping and of the extraordinary scarcity of money in the richly-endowed Institute.

"'Often and often,' said the witness, a motherly old soul in a flamboyant bonnet, 'did I complain to Miss Smith when she give me my weekly allowance for the tradesmen's books: "'Tisn't enough, Miss Smith, I says to 'er, not to feed a family, I says, let alone thirty growin' boys and 'alf a dozen working girls." But Miss Smith she just shook 'er 'ead and says: "Committee's orders, Mrs. Rumble, I 'ave no power." "Why don't you speak to the captain?" I says to 'er, "'e 'as the 'andling of the money; it is a scandal," I says. "Those boys can't live on boiled bacon an' beans and not English nor Irish bacon, it ain't, neither," I says. "Pore lambs. The money I 'ave won't pay for beef or mutton for them, Miss Smith," I says, "and you know it." But Miss Smith, she only shook 'er 'ead and says she would speak to the captain about it.'

"Asked whether she knew if deceased had actually spoken to the secretary on the subject, Mrs. Rumble said most emphatically, 'Yes!'

"'What's more, sir,' she went on, 'I can tell you that the very day before she died, the pore lamb 'ad a reg'lar tiff with the captain about that there commissariat.'

"Mrs. Rumble had stumbled a little over the word, but strangely enough no one tittered; the importance of the old woman's testimony was impressed upon every mind and silenced every tongue. All eyes were turned in the direction of the accused. He had flushed to the roots of his hair, but otherwise stood quite still, with arms folded, and a dull expression of hopelessness upon his good-looking face.

"The coroner had asked the witness how she knew that Miss Smith had had words with the Captain Marston: 'Because I 'eard them two 'aving words, sir,' Mrs. Rumble replied. 'I'd been in the office to get my money and my orders from Miss Smith, and we 'ad the usual talk about American bacon and boiled beans with which I don't 'old, not for growing boys; then back I went to the kitchen, when I remembered I 'ad forgot to speak to Miss Smith about the scullery maid, who'd been saucy and given notice. So up I went again and I was just a goin' to open the office door when I 'eard Miss Smith say quite loud and distinck: "It is shameful," she says, "and I can't bear it," she says, "and if you won't speak to the general then I will. He is staying at the Queen's at Kurtmoor, I understand," she says, "and I am goin' this very night to speak with him," she says, "as I can't spend another night," she says, "with this on my mind." Then I give a genteel cough and...'

"The worthy lady had got thus far in her story when her volubility was suddenly checked by a violent expletive from the accused.

"'But this is damnable!' he cried, and no doubt would have said a lot more, but a touch on his shoulder from the warders behind him quickly recalled him to himself. He once more took up his outwardly calm attitude, and Mrs. Rumble concluded her evidence amidst silence more ominous than any riotous scene would have been.

"'I give a genteel cough,' she resumed, with unruffled dignity, 'and opened the door. Miss Smith, she was all flushed and I could see that she'd been crying; but the captain 'e just walked out of the room, and didn't say not another word.'

"By this time," the Man in the Corner went on drily, "we must suppose that the amateur detectives and the large body of unintelligent public felt that they were being cheated. Never had there been so simple a case. Here, with the testimony of Mrs. Rumble, was the whole thing clear as daylight—motive, quarrel, means, everything was there already. No chance of exercising those powers of deduction so laboriously acquired by a systematic study of detective fiction. Had it not been for the position of the accused and his popularity in Broxmouth society, all interest in the case would have departed in the wake of Mrs. Rumble, and at first when Amelia Smith, sister of the deceased, was called, her appearance only roused languid curiosity. Miss Amelia looked, what in fact, she was: a retired school marm, and wore the regular hall mark of impecunious and somewhat soured spinsterhood.

"'Janet often told me,' she said in the course of her evidence, 'that she was quite sure there was roguery going on in the affairs of the Institute, because she knew for a fact that subscriptions were constantly pouring in from the public, far in excess of what was being spent, for the welfare of the boys. I often used to urge her to go straight to the governors or even to the President himself about the whole matter, but she would always give the same disheartened reply. General Arkwright Jones, it seems, had made it a condition when he accepted the presidency that he was never to be worried about the administration of the place, and he refused to have anything to do with the handling of the subscriptions; as for the governors, my poor sister declared that they cared more for tennis parties than for the welfare of a lot of poor officers' children.'

"But a moment or two later we realised that Miss Amelia Smith was keeping her titbit of evidence until the end. It seems that she had not even spoken about it to the police, determined as she was, no doubt, to create a sensation for once in her monotonous and dreary life. So now she pursed up her lips tighter than before, and after a moment's dramatic silence, she said:

"'The day before her death, my poor sister was very depressed. In the late afternoon, when she came in for tea, I could see that she had been crying. I guessed, of course, what was troubling her, but I didn't say much. Captain Franklin Marston was in the habit of calling for Janet in the evening and they would go for a walk together; at eight o'clock on that sad evening I asked her whether Captain Marston was coming as usual, whereupon she became quite excited and said: "No, no, I don't wish to see him!" and after a while she added in a voice choked with tears: "Never again!"

"'About a quarter of an hour later,' Miss Amelia went on, 'Janet suddenly took up her hat and coat. I asked her where she was going and she said to me: "I don't know but I must put an end to all this. I must know one way or the other." I tried to question her further, but she was in an obstinate mood; when I remarked that it was raining hard, she said; "That's all right, the rain will do me good." And when I asked her whether she wasn't going to meet Captain Marston after all, she just gave me a look, but she made no reply. And so, my poor sister went out into the darkness and the rain, and I never again saw her alive.'

"She paused just long enough to give true dramatic value to her statement, and indeed there was nothing lukewarm now about the interest which she aroused; then she continued: 'As the clock was striking nine, I was surprised to receive a visit from the headmaster, Major Gubbins. He came with a message from Captain Marston to my sister; I told him that Janet had gone out. He appeared vexed, and told me that the captain would be terribly disappointed.'

"'What was this message?' the coroner asked, amidst breathless silence.

"'That Janet would please meet Captain Marston at the Dog's Tooth Cliff. He would wait for her there until nine o'clock.'

The Man in the Corner gave a short, sharp laugh, and with loving eyes contemplated his bit of string, in which he had just woven an elegant and complicated knot. Then he said:

"Now it was at the foot of the Dog's Tooth Cliff that the dead body of Janet Smith was found, and some thirty yards further on the stick which had last been seen in the hand of Captain Franklin Marston. Nervous women gave a gasp and scarcely dared to look at the accused for fear no doubt that they would see the hangman's rope around his neck, but I took a good look at him then. He had uttered a loud groan and buried his face in his hands, and I, with that unerring intuition of which I pride myself, knew that he was acting. Yes, deliberately acting a part—the part of shame and despair. You, no doubt, would ask me why he should have done this. Well, you shall understand presently. For the moment, and to all unthinking spectators, the attitude of despair on the part of the accused appeared fully justified.

"Later on, we heard the evidence of Major Gubbins himself. He said that about seven o' clock he met Captain Marston in the hall of the Institute.

"'He appeared flushed and agitated,' the witness went on, very reluctantly it seemed, but in answer to pressing questions put to him by the coroner, 'and told me he was going for a walk. When I remarked that it was raining hard, he retorted that the rain would do him good. He didn't say where he was going, but presently he put his hand on my shoulder and said in a tone of pleading and affection which I shall never forget: "Old man," he said, "I want you to do something for me. Tell Janet that I must see her again tonight; beg her not to deny me. I will meet her at our usual place on the Dog's Tooth Cliff. Tell her I will wait for her there until nine o'clock, whatever the weather. But she must come. Tell her she must."

"'Unfortunately,' the major continued, 'I was unable to deliver the message immediately as I had work to do in my office which kept me till close on nine o'clock. Then I hurried down to the Smiths' house and just missed Miss Janet who, it seems, had already gone out.'

"Asked why he had not spoken about this before, the major replied that he did not intend to give evidence at all unless he was absolutely forced to do so as a matter of duty. Captain Marston was his friend and he did not think that any man was called upon to give what might prove damnatory evidence against his friend.

"All of which sounded very nice and very loyal until we learned that William Peryer, batman at the Institute, testified to having overheard violent words between the headmaster and the secretary at the very same hour when the latter was supposed to have made so pathetic an appeal to his friend to deliver a message on his behalf. Peryer swore that the two men were quarrelling and quarrelling bitterly. The words he overheard were: 'You villain! You shall pay for this!' But he was so upset and so frightened that he could not state positively which of the two gentlemen had spoken them, but he was inclined to think that it was Major Gubbins.

"And so, the tangle grew, a tangled web that was dexterously being woven around the secretary of the Institute. The two Broxmouth visitors were recalled, and they once more swore positively to having met Captain Marston on the 'Lover's Walk' at about eight o'clock of that fateful evening. They spoke to him and they noticed the stick which he was carrying. They were on their way home from Kurtmoor, and they met the captain some two hundred yards or so before they came to the Dog's Tooth Cliff. Of this they were both quite positive.

"The lady remembered coming to the cliff a few minutes later: she was nervous in the dark and therefore the details of the incident impressed themselves upon her memory. Subsequently when they were nearing home, they met a lady who might or might not have been the deceased; they did not know her by sight and the person they met had her hat pulled down over her eyes and the collar of her coat up to her ears. It was raining hard then, and they themselves were hurrying along and paid no attention to passers-by.'

"We also heard that at about nine o'clock James Hoggs and his wife, who live in a cottage not very far from the Dog's Tooth Cliff, heard a terrifying scream. They were just going to bed and closing up for the night. Hoggs had the front door open at the moment and was looking at the weather. It was raining, but nevertheless he picked up his cap and ran out toward the cliff. A moment or two later he came up against a man whom he hailed; it was very dark, but he noticed that the man was engaged in wrapping a muffler round his neck. He asked him whether he had heard a scream, but the man said: 'No, I've not!' then hurried quickly out of sight. As Hoggs heard nothing more, or saw anything, he thought that perhaps after all he and his missis had been mistaken, so he turned back home and went to bed.

"I think," the Man in the Corner continued thoughtfully, "that I have now put before you all the most salient points in the chain of evidence collected by the police against the accused. There were not many faulty links in the chain you will admit. The motive for the hideous crime was clear enough: for there was the fraudulent secretary and the unfortunate girl who had suspected the defalcations and was threatening to go and denounce her lover, either to the President of the Institute or to the governors.

"And the method was equally clear: the meeting in the dark and the rain on the lonely cliff, the muffler quickly thrown round the victim's mouth to smother her screams, the blow with the stick, the push over the edge of the cliff. The stick stood up as an incontestable piece of evidence; the absence from home of the accused during the greater part of that night had been testified by his landlady, whilst his presence on the scene of the crime sometime during the evening was not disputed. As a matter of fact, the only point in the man's favour were the strands of wool found sticking to the girl's hat pin and Hoggs's story of the man whom he had seen in the dark, engaged in readjusting a muffler around his neck. Unfortunately, Hoggs, when more closely questioned on that subject, became incoherent and confused as men of his class are apt to do when pinned down to a definite statement.

"Anyway, the accused was committed for trial on the coroner's warrant, and of course reserved his defence. You probably, like the rest of the public, kept up a certain amount of interest in the Cliff murder, as it was popularly called, for a time, and then allowed your mind to dwell on other matters and forgot poor Captain Franklin Marston who was languishing in gaol under such a horrible accusation. Subsequently, your interest in him revived when he was brought up for trial the other day at the Barchester Assizes. In the meanwhile, he had secured the services of Messrs. Chamton and Inglewood, the noted solicitors, who had engaged Mr. Provost Boon, K.C., to defend their client.

"You know as well as I do what happened at the trial, and how Mr. Boon turned the witnesses for the Crown inside out and round about until they contradicted themselves and one another all along the line. The defence was conducted in a masterly fashion. To begin with the worthy housekeeper, Mrs. Rumble, after a stiff cross-examination which lasted nearly an hour, was forced to admit that she could not swear positively to the exact words which she overheard between the deceased and Captain Marston. All that she could swear to was that the captain and his sweetheart had apparently had a tiff. Then, as to Miss Amelia Smith's evidence: it also merely went to prove that the lovers had had a quarrel; there was nothing whatever to say that it was on the subject of finance, or that deceased had any intention either of speaking to the President about it, or of handing in her resignation to the governors.

"Next came the question of Major Gubbins's story of the message which he had been asked by his friend to deliver to the deceased. Now accused flatly denied that story, and denied it on oath. The whole thing, he declared, was a fabrication on the part of the major, who, far from being his friend, was his bitter enemy and unsuccessful rival. In support of his theory William Peryer's evidence was cited as conclusive. He had heard the two men quarrelling at the very moment when accused was alleged to have made a pathetic appeal to his friend. Peryer had heard one of them say to the other: 'You villain! You shall pay for this!' And, in very truth, the unfortunate captain was paying for it, in humiliation and racking anxiety.

"Then there came the great, the vital question of the stick, and of the strands of wool so obviously torn out of a muffler. With regard to the stick, the accused had stated that in the course of his walk he had caught his foot against a stone and stumbled, and that the stick had fallen out of his hand and over the edge of the cliff. Now this statement was certainly borne out by the fact that, as eminent counsel reminded the jury, the stick was found more than thirty yards away from the body. As for the muffler, it was a graver point still; strands of wool were found sticking to the girl's hat pin and James Hoggs, after hearing a scream at nine o'clock that evening, ran out toward the cliff and came across a man who was engaged in readjusting a muffler round his throat.

"That was incontestable. Of course, Mr. Boon argued, it was easy enough to upset a witness of the type of James Hoggs, but an English jury's duty was not to fasten guilt on the first man who happens to be handy, but to see justice meted out to innocent and guilty alike. The evidence of the muffler, argued the eminent counsel, was proof positive of the innocence of the accused. The witnesses who saw him in the Lover's Walk on that fateful night had declared most emphatically that he was not wearing a muffler. Then where was the man with the muffler? Where was the man who was within a few yards of the scene of the crime five minutes after James Hoggs had heard the scream— the man who had denied hearing the scream, although both Hoggs and his wife heard it over a quarter of a mile away?

"'Yes, gentlemen of the jury,' the eminent counsel concluded with a dramatic gesture, 'it is the man with the muffler who murdered the unfortunate girl. If he is innocent, why is he not here to give evidence? There are no side tracks that lead to the cliffs at this point, so the man with the muffler must have seen something or someone; he must know something that would be of invaluable assistance to the elucidation of this sad mystery. Then why does he not come forward? I say because he dare not. But let the police look for him, I say. The accused is innocent; he is the victim of tragic circumstances, but his whole life, his war record, his affection for the deceased, all proclaim him to be guiltless of such a dastardly crime, and above all there stands the incontestable proof of his innocence, the muffler, gentlemen of the jury—the muffler!

"He said a lot more than that, of course," the Man in the Corner went on, chuckling drily to himself, "and said it a lot better than ever I can repeat it, but I have given you the gist of what he said. You know the result of the trial. The accused was acquitted, the jury having deliberated less than a quarter of an hour. There was no getting away from that muffler, even though every other circumstance pointed to Marston as the murderer of Janet Smith. On the whole his acquittal was a popular one, although many who were present at the trial shook their heads and thought that if they had been on the jury Marston would not have got off so easily, but for the most part these sceptics were not Broxmouth people.

"In Broxmouth the captain was personally liked, and the proclamation of his innocence was hailed with enthusiasm; and, what's more, those same champions of the good-looking secretary—they were the women mostly—looked askance on the headmaster who, they averred, had woven a Machiavellian net for trapping and removing from his path for ever a hated and successful rival.

"The police have received a perfect deluge of anonymous communications suggesting that Major Gubbins was identical with the mysterious man with the muffler, but of course such a suggestion is perfectly absurd, since at the very hour when James Hoggs heard the scream and a very few minutes before he met the man with the muffler, Major Gubbins was paying his belated visit to Miss Amelia Smith and delivering the alleged message. Even those ladies who disliked the headmaster most cordially had to admit that he could not very well have been in two places at the same time. The Dog's Tooth Cliff is a good half-hour's walk from Miss Smith's house to the 'Lover's Walk' itself and is not accessible to cyclists or motors.

"And thus, to all intents and purposes the Cliff murder has remained a mystery, but it won't be one for long. Have I not told you that you may expect important developments within the next few days? And I am seldom wrong. Already in this evening's paper you will have read that the entire executive of the Woodforde Institute has placed its resignation in the hands of the governors, that several august personages have withdrawn their names from the list of patrons, and that though the President has been implored not to withdraw his name, he has proved adamant on the subject, and even refused to recommend successors to the headmaster, the secretary or the matron; in fact, he has seemingly washed his hands of the whole concern."

"But surely," I now broke in, seeing that the Man in the Corner threatened to put away his piece of string and to leave me without the usual epilogue to his interesting narrative, "surely General Sir Arkwright Jones cannot be blamed for the scandal which undoubtedly has dimmed the fortunes of the Woodfordfe Institute!"

"Cannot be blamed?" the Man in the Corner retorted sarcastically. "Cannot be blamed for entering into a conspiracy with his secretary and his headmaster to defraud the Institute, and then to silence for ever the one voice that might have been raised in accusation against him."

"Sir Arkwright Jones?" I exclaimed incredulously, for indeed the idea appeared to me preposterous then, as the general's name was almost a household word before the catastrophe. "Impossible!"

"Impossible!" he reiterated. "Why? He murdered Janet Smith; of that you will be as convinced within the next few days as I am at this hour. That the three men were in collusion I have not the shadow of doubt. Marston only made love to Janet Smith in order to secure her silence, but in this he failed and the girl boldly accused him of roguery as soon as she found him out. It would be inconceivable to suppose that being the bright, intelligent girl that she admittedly was, she could remain for ever in ignorance of the defalcations in the books; she must and did tax her lover of irregularities, she must have and indeed did threaten to put the whole thing before the governors.

"So much for the lover's quarrel overheard by Mrs. Rumble. I believe that the fate of the poor girl was decided on then and there by two of the scoundrels; it only remained to consult with their other accomplice as to the means for carrying their hideous project through. Janet had announced her determination to go to Kurtmoor that self-

291

same evening, the only question was which of those three miscreants would meet her in the darkness and solitude of the 'Lovers' Walk.'

"But in order at the outset to throw dust in the eyes of the public and the police and not appear to be in any way associated with one another, Marston and Gubbins made pretence of a violent quarrel which Peryer overheard; then Gubbins, in order to make sure that the poor girl would carry out her intention of going over to Kurtmoor that evening, went to her house with the supposed message from Marston, and incidentally secured thereby his own alibi. This made him safe. Marston in the meanwhile went to arrange matters with Arkwright Jones. His position was of course more difficult than that of Gubbins.

"If there was to be murder—and my belief is that the scoundrels had been resolved on murder for some time before—the first suspicion would inevitably fall on the secretary who had kept the books and who had had the handling of the money. The miscreants had some sort of vague plan in their heads: of this there can be no doubt; they were only procrastinating, hoping against hope that chance would continue to favour them. But now the hour had come, the danger was imminent; within the next four and twenty hours Janet Smith, being promised no redress on the part of the President, would place the whole matter before the governors. Unless she was effectually made to hold her tongue.

"We can easily suppose that Marston would be clever enough to arrange to meet Arkwright Jones, without arousing suspicion. We do know that soon after he finally quarrelled with Janet Smith, he walked over to Kurtmoor; the two witnesses who spoke with him stated that they met him whilst they themselves were walking to Broxmouth. It was then past eight o'clock. Arkwright Jones had either dined at his hotel or not; we do not know, for it never struck the police to enquire at once how the popular general had spent his time on that fateful evening. You know what those sort of unconventional seaside places are: people spend most of their time out of doors, and there would be nothing strange, let alone suspicious, in any visitor going out for an hour after dinner, even if it rained.

"Then surely you can in your mind see those two scoundrels putting their villainous heads together, and, as suspicion of any foul play would of necessity at once fall on Marston, Jones decided to take the hideous onus on himself. He went to the Dog's Tooth Cliff to meet Janet Smith himself and borrowed Marston's stick to aid him in his abominable deed. He was clever enough, however, to throw it over the edge of the cliff some distance away from the scene of his crime. We do not know, of course, whether the poor girl recognised him, or whether he just fell on her in the dark; she gave only one scream before she fell. They were clever scoundrels we must admit, but chance favoured them too, especially in one thing: she favoured them when she prompted Arkwright Jones to put a muffler round his throat.

"This one fact as you know saved Marston's neck from the gallows; but for the strands of wool in the girl's hat pin and Hoggs's brief view of a man manipulating a muffler nothing but Jones's own confession could have saved his accomplice. Whether he would have confessed remains a riddle which no one will ever solve. But as to the whole so-called mystery, I saw daylight through it the moment I realised that Marston's despair and humiliation during the inquest was a pretence. If he feigned despair, it was because he desired temporarily to be the victim of circumstantial evidence. From that point to the unravelling of the tangled skein was but a step for a mind bent on logic.

"But," I argued, for indeed I was bewildered and really incredulous, "what will be the end of it all? Surely three scoundrels like that will not go scot free. There will be an inquiry into the affairs of the Institute: the governors—"

"The governors have talked of an inquiry," the funny creature broke in with a chuckle, "but if you had any experience of these private charities, you would know that the thing their administrators wish to avoid is publicity. The President of the Woodforde Institute had sufficient influence on the committee, you may be sure, to stifle any suggestion of creating public scandal by any sort of inquiry."

"But the question of the finances of the Institute is anyhow public property now and—"

"And it will be allowed to sink into oblivion. The executive has resigned. Marston and Gubbins will leave the country, and everything will be conveniently hushed up."

"But Arkwright Jones—" I protested.

"You see the papers regularly," he rejoined drily, "watch them and you will see. .. "

I don't know when he went, but a moment or two later I found myself sitting alone at the table in the blameless tea shop. The matter interested me more than I cared to admit but, for once, I was not altogether prepared to accept the funny creature's deductions.

Twenty-four hours later, however, I had to own that he had been right, when the following piece of sensational news appeared in the *Evening Post*.

TRAGIC SEQUEL TO THE CLIFF MURDER.

An extraordinary sequel to the mysterious tragedy of the Dog's Tooth Cliff, near Broxmouth, occurred last night, when on the self-same spot where Miss Janet Smith met her death three months ago, General Sir Arkwright Jones lost his footing and fell a distance of two hundred feet on to the rocks below. It was a beautiful moonlight evening, and the tide being low, a number of visitors were down on the beach at the time, but those who immediately hurried to the general's assistance found life already extinct. The distinguished soldier, who will be deeply mourned, must have been killed on the spot.

Indeed, now general public opinion as well as every inhabitant of Broxmouth will bring pressure to bear upon the Borough Council to see that a suitable barrier is erected along the dangerous portions of the beautiful 'Lover's Walk.' The double tragedy of this year's season renders such an erection imperative.

I was probably the only reader of that paragraph who guessed that the once distinguished soldier had not come accidentally by his death. No doubt the police had followed up the clue of the man with the muffler and were actually on the track of the miscreant, when the latter, guessing that exposure was imminent, preferred to put an end to his own miserable life.

I have since heard from friends at Broxmouth that Marston has gone to the Malay States, and that Gubbins is doing something in Germany. Curious creature Marston must have been! Imagine after Jones had returned from his infamous errand and told him that the hideous deed was done, imagine Marston walking back to Broxmouth along the 'Lover's Walk' in the rain and the darkness, past the Dog's Tooth Cliff, at the foot of which the body of the murdered girl lay! I wonder what would be the views of the Man in the Corner on the psychology of a man with nerve enough for such an ordeal.

The Tytherton Case

"What do you make of this?" the Man in the Corner said to me that afternoon. "A curious case is it not?" And with his claw-like fingers he indicated the paragraph in the Evening Post which I had just been perusing with great interest.

"At best," I replied, "it is a very unpleasant business for the Carysforts."

"And at the worst?" he retorted with a chuckle.

"Well . . .!" I remarked drily.

"Do you think they are guilty?" he asked.

"I don't see who else . . ."

"Ah!" he broke in, with his usual lack of manners, "that is such a stale argument. One doesn't see who else, therefore one makes up one's mind that so and so must be guilty. I'll lay an even bet with anyone that out of a dozen cases of miscarriage of justice, I could point to ten that were directly due to that fallacious reasoning. We all admit that there is a motive underlying every crime, and my argument is that public and police alike are far too ready to presuppose a motive that is half the time of their own creation, and, having done that, they start working upon a flimsy foundation, waste a vast amount of time, and in the meanwhile give the real criminal every chance of escape. Now take as an example the Tytherton case, in which you are apparently interested.

"It was an unprecedented outrage which stirred the busy provincial town to its depths, the victim, Mr. Walter Stonebridge, being one of its most noted solicitors. He had his office in Tytherton High Street and lived in a small, detached house on the Great West Road. The house stood in the middle of a small garden, and had only one story above the ground floor; the front door opened straight on a long, narrow hall which ran along the full depth of the house. On the left side of this hall there were two doors, one leading to the drawing-room and the other to a small morning-room. At the end of the hall was the staircase, and beyond it, down a couple of steps, there was a tiny dining-room and the usual offices. The back door opened straight on the kitchen, and on the floor above there were four bedrooms and a bathroom. Mr. Walter Stonebridge was a bachelor and his domestic staff consisted of a married couple—Henning by name—who did all that was necessary for him in the house.

"It was on the last evening of February. The weather was fair and bright. The Hennings had gone upstairs to their room as usual at ten o'clock. Mr. Stonebridge was at the time, sitting in the morning-room. He was in the habit of sitting up late, reading and writing. On this occasion he told the Hennings to close the shutters and lock the back door as usual, but to leave the front door on the latch as he was expecting a visitor. The Hennings thought nothing of that, as one or two gentlemen-friends, or sometimes clients of Mr. Stonebridge, would now and then drop in late to see him.

"Anyway, they went contentedly to bed. A little while later—they could not exactly recollect at what hour because they had already settled down for the night—they heard the front door bell, and immediately afterwards Mr. Stonebridge's footsteps along the hall. Then suddenly they heard a crash followed by what sounded like a struggle, then a smothered cry, and finally silence. Henning was out of bed and on the landing in an instant and he had just switched on the light there when he heard Mr. Stonebridge's voice calling up to him from below:

"'That's all right, Henning. I caught my foot in this confounded rug. That's all.'

Henning looked over the banister, and seeing nothing he shouted down:

"'Shall I give you a 'and, sir?' But Mr. Stonebridge at once replied, quite cheerily: 'No, no! I'm all right. You go back to bed.'

"And Henning did as he was told, nor did he or his wife hear anything more during the night. But in the early morning when Mrs. Henning came downstairs she was horror-struck to find Mr. Stonebridge in the dining-room, lying across the table to which he was securely pinioned with a rope; a serviette taken out of the sideboard drawer had been tied tightly round his mouth and his eyes were blindfolded with his own pocket handkerchief. The woman's screams brought her husband upon the scene; together they set to work to rescue their master from his horrible plight. At first, they thought that he was dead, and Henning was for fetching the police immediately, but his wife declared that Mr. Stonebridge was just unconscious and she started to apply certain household restoratives and made Henning force some brandy through Mr. Stonebridge's lips. Presently the poor man opened his eyes and gave one or two other signs of returning consciousness, but he was still very queer and shaky. The Hennings then carried him upstairs, undressed him and put him to bed, and then Henning ran for the doctor.

"Well, it was days, or in fact weeks, before Mr. Stonebridge had sufficiently recovered to give a coherent statement of what happened to him on that fateful night, and—which was just as much to the point—what had happened the previous day. The doctor had pre-scribed complete rest in the interim. The patient had suffered from concussion and I know not what, and those events had got so mixed up in his brain that to try and disentangle them was such an effort that every time he attempted it it nearly sent him into a brain fever. But in the meanwhile, his friends had been busy—notably Mr. Stonebridge's head clerk, Mr. Medburn, who was giving the police no rest. There was, even without the evidence of the principal witness concerned, plenty of facts to go on to make out a case against the perpetrator of such a dastardly outrage.

"That robbery had been the main motive of the assault was easily enough established—a small fire and burglar proof safe which stood in a corner of the morning-room had been opened and ransacked. When examined it was found to contain only a few trinkets which had prob-ably a sentimental value, but were otherwise worthless. The key of the safe—one of a bunch—was still in the lock, which went to prove ei-ther that Mr. Stonebridge had the safe open when he was attacked, or what was more likely—considering the solicitor's well-known careful habits—that the assailant had ransacked his victim's pockets after he had knocked him down. A pocket-book, torn, and containing only a few unimportant papers lay on the ground; there had been a fire in the room at the time of the outrage and careful analysis of the ashes found in the hearth revealed the presence of a quantity of burnt paper.

"But robbery being established as the motive of the outrage did not greatly help matters, because while Mr. Stonebridge remained in such a helpless condition, it was impossible to ascertain what booty his assailant had carried away. Soon, however, the first ray of light was thrown upon what seemed until this hour an impenetrable mystery.

It appears that Mr. Medburn was looking after the business in High Street during his employer's absence, and one morning—it was on the Monday following the night of the outrage—he had a visit from a client who sent in his name as Felix Shap. The head clerk knew something about this client who had recently come over to England from somewhere abroad in order to make good his claim to certain royalties on what is known as the Shap Fuelettes—a kind of cheap fuel which was launched some time before the war by Sir Alfred Carysfort, Bart., of Tytherton Grange, and out of which that gentleman made an immense fortune, and, incidentally, got his title thereby.

"This man Shap—a Dutchman by birth—was, it appears the original inventor and patentee of these Fuelettes, and Mr. Carysfort, as he was then, had met him out in the Dutch East Indies and had bought the invention from him for a certain sum down, and then exploited it in England first and afterwards all over the world at immense profit. Sir Alfred Carysfort died about a year ago, leaving a fortune of over a million sterling, and was succeeded in the title and in the managing directorship of the business by his eldest son David, a married man with a large family. The business had long since been turned into a private limited liability company, the bulk of the shares being held by the managing director.

"The fact that the patent rights of the Shap Fuelettes had been sold by the inventor to the late Alfred Carysfort had, never been in dispute. It further appeared that Felix Shap had at one time been a very promising mining engineer, but that in consequence of incurable, intemperate habits he had gradually drifted down the social scale; he lost one good appointment after another until he was just an under-paid clerk in the office of an engineer in Batavia, whose representative in England was Mr. Alfred Carysfort. The latter was on a visit to the head office in Batavia some twelve years ago when he met Shap, who was then on his beam-ends. He had recently been sacked by his employers for intemperance and was on the fair way of becoming one of those hopeless human derelicts who usually end their days either on the gallows or in a convict prison.

"But at the back of Shap's fuddled mind there had lingered throughout his downward career the remembrance of a certain invention which he had once patented and which he had always declared would one day bring him an immense fortune; but though he had spent quite a good deal of money in keeping up his patent rights, he had never had the pluck and perseverance to exploit or even to perfect his invention. Alfred Carysfort, on the other hand, was brilliantly clever, he was ambitious, probably none too scrupulous, and at once he saw the immense possibilities, if properly worked, of Shap's rough invention, and he set to work to obtain the man's confidence, and, presumably, by exercising certain persuasion and pressure he got the wastrel to make over to him in exchange for a few hundred pounds the entire patent rights in the Fuelettes.

"The transaction was, as far as that goes, perfectly straightforward and above board; it was embodied in a contract drawn up by an English solicitor, who was the British Consul in Batavia at the time; nor was it—taking everything into consideration—an unfair one. Shap would never have done anything with his invention, and a clean, wholesome and entirely practical fuel would probably have been thus lost to the world; but there remains the fact that Alfred Carysfort died a dozen years later worth more than a million sterling, every penny of which he had made out of an invention for which he had originally paid less than five hundred.

"Mr. Medburn had been put in possession of these facts some weeks previously when Mr. Felix Shap had first presented himself at the private house of Mr. Stonebridge; he came armed with a letter of introduction from a relative of Mr. Stonebridge's whom he had met out in Java, and he was accompanied by a friend—an American named Julian Lloyd—who was piloting him about the place, and acting as his interpreter and secretary, as he himself had never been in England and spoke English very indifferently. His passport and papers of identification were perfectly in order; he appeared before Mr. Stonebridge as a man still on the right side of sixty who certainly bore traces on his prematurely wrinkled face and in his tired lustreless eyes of a life spent in dissipation rather than in work, but otherwise he bore himself well, was well dressed and apparently plentifully supplied with money.

"The story that he told Mr. Stonebridge through the intermediary of his friend, Julian Lloyd, was a very curious one. According to his version of various transactions which took place between himself and the late Sir Alfred Carysfort, the latter had, sometime after the signing of the original contract, made him a definite promise in writing that should the proceeds in the business of the Shap Fuelettes exceed £10,000 in any one year, he, Sir Alfred, would pay the original inventor out of his own pocket a sum equivalent to twenty *per cent* of all such profits over and above the £10,000, with a minimum of £200.

" Mr. Shap had brought over with him all the correspondence

relating to this promise, and, moreover, he adduced as proof positive that Sir Alfred had looked on that promise as binding, and had at first loyally abided by it, the fact that until 1916 he had paid to Mr. Felix Shap the sum of £200 every year. These sums had been paid half-yearly through Sir Alfred's bankers, and acknowledgments were duly sent by Shap direct to the bank, all of which could of course be easily verified. But in the year 1916 these payments suddenly ceased. Mr. Shap wrote repeatedly to Sir Alfred, but never received any reply. At first, he thought that there were certain difficulties in the way owing to the European War, so after a while he ceased writing. But presently there came the Armistice; Mr. Shap wrote again and again, but was again met by the same obstinate silence.

"In the meanwhile, he had come to the end of his resources; he had spent all that he had ever saved, but nevertheless he was determined that as soon as he could scrape up a sufficiency of money, he would go to England in order to establish his rights. Then in 1922 he heard of Sir Alfred Carysfort's death. It was now or never if he did not mean to acquiesce silently in the terrible wrong which was being put upon him.

"Fortunately, he had a good friend in Mr. Julian Lloyd, who had helped him with money and advice, and at last he had arrived in England. It was for Mr. Stonebridge to say whether the papers and correspondence which he had brought with him were sufficient to establish his claim in law. Mr. Medburn remembered Mr. Stonebridge telling him all about these matters and emphasising the fact that Felix Shap had undoubtedly a very strong case and that he could not understand a man in the position of Sir Alfred Carysfort thus wilfully repudiating his own signature.

"'There is not only the original letter,' Mr. Stonebridge had concluded, 'making a definite promise to pay certain sums out of his own pocket if the profits of the company exceeded £10,000 in any one year, but there are all the covering letters from Sir Alfred's bankers whenever they sent cheques on his behalf to Shap—usually twice a year for sums that varied between £100 and £150. I cannot understand it!' he had reiterated more than once, and Mr. Medburn, who also had a great deal of respect for the Carysforts, who were among the wealthiest people in the county, was equally at a loss to understand the position.

"However, Mr. Stonebridge, after he had seen the late Sir Alfred's bankers about the payments to Shap and consulted an expert on the subject of the all-important letter signed by the late Alfred Carysfort, sought an interview with Sir David. From the first there seemed to be an extraordinary amount of acrimony brought into the dispute by both sides; this was understandable enough on the part of Felix Shap, who felt he was being defrauded of his just dues by men who were literally coining money out of the product of his brain; but the greatest bitterness really appeared to come from the other side.

"At first Sir David Carysfort refused even to discuss the question; he was quite sure that if his father had made promises of payments to anyone, he was the last man in the world to repudiate such obligations. Sir David had not yet had time to go through all his father's papers, but he was quite convinced that correspondence, or documents, would presently be found, which would set at nought the original letter produced by Mr. Shap. But, of course, the payments to Shap up to and including the year 1916 could not be denied; there was the testimony of Sir Alfred's bankers that sums in accordance with Sir Alfred's instructions, varying between £100 and £150, were paid by cheque every half-year to the order of Felix Shap in Batavia. In 1916 these payments automatically ceased, Sir Alfred giving no further orders for these to be made. Mr. Stonebridge naturally desired to know what explanation Sir David would give about those payments.

"At first Sir David denied all knowledge as to the reason or object of the payments, but after a while he must have realised that public opinion was beginning to raise its voice on the subject, and that it was not exactly singing the praises of Sir David Carysfort, Bart. Although Mr. Stonebridge had, of course, been discretion itself, Mr. Shap had admittedly not the same incentive to silence, and what's more his friend, Mr. Lloyd, made it his business to get as much publicity for the whole affair as he could.

"Paragraphs in the local papers had begun to appear with unabated regularity, and though there were no actual comments on the case as a whole, no prejudging of respective merits, there were unmistakable hints that it would be in Sir David's interest to put dignity on one side and come out frankly into the open with explanations and suggestions. Soon the London papers got hold of the story, and you know what that means. The Radical Press simply battened on a story which placed a poor, down-at-heel inventor in the light of a victim to the insatiable greed and frank dishonesty of a high-born profiteer.

"Whether it was pressure from outside, or from his own family, that suddenly induced Sir David to 'come out into the open' is not generally known; certain it is that presently he condescended to give an explanation of the mysterious half-yearly payments made by his father to Felix Shap, and the explanation was so romantic and frankly so far-fetched that most people, especially men, refused to accept it—notably Mr. Stonebridge. It was not the business of a lawyer to listen to sentimental stories, least of all was it the business of the lawyer acting on the other side. The story told by Sir David, namely, was this:

"The late Sir Alfred, when quite a young man, had gone out as clerk to that same engineering firm in Batavia whom he represented later on; it was then that he first met Felix Shap, who had not yet begun to go downhill. An intimacy sprang up between Alfred Carysfort and Shap's sister, Berta, and the two were secretly married in Batavia. A year later Berta had a son whose birth she only survived by a few hours. The marriage had been an unhappy one from the first, and Carysfort was only too thankful when his firm called him back to England and he was able to shake off the dust of Batavia from his feet, as he hoped for ever.

"He never spoke of his marriage, nor did he ever recognise or have anything to do with his son. By some pecuniary arrangement entered into with Felix Shap the latter undertook to provide for and look after the boy, to give him his own name, and never to trouble his brother-in-law about him again. A deed-poll was, Sir David believed, duly executed, and the boy assumed the name of Alfred Shap.

"Some years later there occurred the transaction over the Shap Fuelettes. Alfred Carysfort had come to Batavia on business: he had met Felix Shap again who by this time had become a hopeless wastrel. The contract for the sale of the patent rights in the Fuelettes was duly executed, but whether, after seeing his son once more, the call of the blood became more insistent in the heart of Alfred Carysfort or whether he merely yielded to blackmail, Sir David could not say; certain it is that after a while when the profits of the Shap Fuelettes Company became substantial Sir Alfred took to sending over a couple of hundred pounds every year to Shap for the benefit of young Alfred. Then the war broke out; young Alfred joined the Australian Expeditionary Force and was killed in Gallipoli in August, 1915. As soon as Sir Alfred had definite news of the boy's death, he naturally stopped all further payments to Shap.

"The story as you see sounded plausible enough, and if it proved to be untrue, it would reflect great credit on Sir David's gift of imagination. Felix Shap, as was only to be expected, denied it from beginning to end; the whole thing, he declared, was an impudent falsehood, based on a semblance of truth. It was quite true that he had adopted and for years had cared for his sister's son, who was subsequently killed in Gallipoli; it was also true that Alfred Carysfort had years ago paid some attention to his sister Berta, but there never was any question of marriage between them, young Carysfort deeming himself far too grand and well-born to marry the daughter of an obscure East Indian trader. Berta had subsequently married a man of mixed blood who deserted her and went off somewhere—Argentina or Honduras—Shap did not know where; at any rate he was never heard of again.

"In proof of his version of the romantic story, Felix Shap actually had a copy of his sister's marriage certificate, as well as one or two letters written at different times to his sister Berta by her rascally husband. He had, indeed, plenty of proofs for his assertions; but when Mr. Stonebridge asked for confirmation of Sir David's story, the latter appeared either unprepared or unwilling to produce any, whereupon Mr. Stonebridge, on behalf of his client, entered an action for the recovery of certain royalties due to him on the sales of the Shap Fuelettes, the amount to be presently agreed on after examination of the audited accounts.

"Thus, matters stood when on that Wednesday night in February last Mr. Stonebridge was found gagged and unconscious, the victim of a murderous and inexplicable assault. And on the Saturday following Mr. Felix Shap, accompanied by his friend, Mr. Lloyd, called on Mr. Medburn at the office in High Street. They had read in the papers certain details which had filled Shap with apprehension; they had read that the safe in the morning-room in Mr. Stonebridge's house had been obviously ransacked, and that the analysis of the ashes in the grate had revealed the presence of a large quantity of burnt paper.

"'My friend Mr. Shap would like you to put his mind at rest Mr.—er—Medburn,' Mr. Lloyd said in an anxious, agitated tone of voice, 'that the papers relating to this case, which I entrusted to Mr. Stonebridge, are safely locked up in a safe at this office.'

"Unfortunately, the head clerk was not able to satisfy Mr. Shap on that point. Mr. Stonebridge had never brought the papers to the office, nor had Mr. Medburn ever seen them. His impression was—he regretted to say—that Mr. Stonebridge had, for the time being, kept all papers relating to this particular case at his private house, just as he had always seen Mr. Shap there rather than at the office. Of course, Medburn hastened to assure his visitor, Mr. Stonebridge may have kept the documents in some other secure place; Mr. Medburn couldn't say, not having access to all his employer's papers, and in any case, he would make a comprehensive search for the missing documents, and if nothing was found he would at once inform the police.

"An evening or two later the papers came out with flaring headlines: 'Amazing developments in the Tytherton outrage. Missing documents. Sensational turn in the Shap Fuelettes case.' And so on. The head clerk had made an exhaustive search amongst his employer's papers, but not a trace could he find of any documents relative to Mr. Snap's case. One and all had disappeared: the original letter from Alfred Carysfort promising to pay an extra twenty *per cent* on the profits of the Shap Fuelette Company under certain conditions, the letters from the scoundrel who had been Berta's husband together with the copy of Berta's marriage certificate—everything was gone, every proof of the truth of the story which Felix Shap had come all this way to tell.

2

"The next exciting incident," the Man in the Corner continued glibly, "in this remarkably mysterious case, was the news that Mr. Allan Carysfort, eldest son of Sir David Carysfort, Bart., had been detained in connection with the assault upon Mr. Stonebridge and the disappearance of certain papers, the property of Mr. Felix Shap of Batavia.

"Young Allan Carysfort, who was a subaltern in a cavalry regiment, had come home from India recently, and, as a matter of fact, he had arrived at the Grange, the family seat just outside Tytherton, the very evening of the outrage. Acting upon, certain information received the police had detained him. He was to be brought before the magistrates on the following day and in the meanwhile it was generally understood that some highly sensational evidence had been collected by the police.

"It has been asserted that Sir David Carysfort and his family were the last to realise how very strong public opinion had been against them ever since Shap's story and the loss of the documents had become generally known. Though there had been no hint of it in the Press, the public loudly declared that the Carysforts must have had something to do with the outrage, seek him whom the crime benefits being a most excellent adage. But imagine the sensation when Allan Carysfort, the eldest son of Sir David Carysfort, Bart., was arrested! Need I say that the following day when the young man was, brought before the magistrates the court was crowded. David was a magistrate, too, but of course he did not sit that day. To see his eldest son arraigned before his brother Beaks must have been a bitter pill for his pride to swallow.

"We had the usual formal evidence of arrest, the medical evidence, and so on, after which we quickly plunged into exciting business. Mr Stonebridge we were soon told had made a statement. He was not yet strong enough to appear in person but he had made a statement, so at last the public was to be initiated into the mysteries that surrounded the inexplicable assault.

"'After my servants had gone to bed,' Mr. Stonebridge had stated, 'I sat awhile reading in the morning-room. I was expecting the visit of Mr. Shap, as we had talked over the possibility of a quiet chat at my house that evening on the subject of his affairs. He and Mr. Lloyd, who were both of them very fond of the cinema, were in the habit of dropping in after the show, on their way home. At about a quarter to eleven—I am sure it was not later—there was a ring at the front door bell, and I went to open the door.

"'No sooner had I done this than a shawl or muffler of some sort was thrown over my face, and I was made to lose my balance by the thrust of a foot between my two shins. I came down backwards with a crash. The whole thing occurred in fewer seconds that it takes to describe; the next moment I had the sensation of cold steel against my temple, I heard an ominous click, and a husky voice whispered in my ear, "Your servant is coming out of his room. Speak to him, tell him you are all right, or I shoot." What could I do? I was utterly helpless and a revolver was held to my temple.

"'The muffler was then lifted from my mouth, I could feel the man bending over me, I could feel his hot breath on my forehead, and a few seconds later I heard Henning come out of his room upstairs and switch on the light on the top landing. "If he comes downstairs," the voice whispered close to my ear, "I shoot." Then it was,' Mr. Stonebridge went on to say, 'that I shouted up to Henning that I had only tripped over a rug, and that I was quite all right. I don't think I ever looked death so very near in the face before. The next moment I heard Henning switch off the light upstairs and go back to his room. After that I remember nothing more. I only have a vague recollection of a sudden terrible pain in my head; everything else is a blank until I found myself in bed, and with vague stirrings of memory bringing a return of that same appalling headache.'

"The great point about Mr. Stonebridge's evidence was that he was utterly unable to identify his assailant. He was not even sure whether he had been attacked by two men or one, since he had been blind-folded at the outset, and all that he heard was a husky voice that spoke in a whisper. He was ready to admit that he may have left the safe un-locked when he went to answer the front door bell, and he certainly had the papers relating to Mr. Shap's case on his desk as he had been going through them earlier in the evening. Those papers, therefore, had undoubtedly been burned in the grate, and it was obvious that the theft and destruction of those papers was the motive of the assault.

"After that we went from excitement to excitement. We did not get it all the same day of course; Allan Carysfort appeared, as far as I can remember, three or four times before the local magistrates; in between times he was out on bail, this having been fixed at £1,000 in two recognisances of £500 each, with an additional £500 on his own. It seems that when he was arrested, he had made a statement, to which he had since unreservedly subscribed.

"He said that he had arrived in London from Southampton on Monday the 26th, and after seeing to some business in town, he took the 8.10 pm train on the 28th to Tytherton, where he arrived at 9.50, having dined on board. His father met him at the station with the car, but it was such a beautiful moonlit night Sir David and himself de-cided that they would walk to the Grange and then sent the car home with a message to Lady Carysfort that they would be home at about eleven o'clock.

"Carysfort had been asked whether it was not strange that after be-ing absent from home so long, he should have elected to put off seeing his mother till a much later hour.

"'Not at all,' he replied. 'Sir David wished to put me *au fait* of cer-tain family matters before I actually saw Lady Carysfort. These mat-ters,' he added emphatically in reply to questions put to him by the magistrate, 'had nothing whatever to do with financial business, least of all were they in any relation to Mr. Shap and his affairs. Sir David and I,' he went on calmly, 'walked about for a while and then Sir David remembered that he wished to see a friend at the County Club. He went in there, but I preferred to take another turn out of doors, as I had not had a taste of English country air for nearly two years.'

"Asked how long he had walked about Tytherton waiting for Sir David, Carysfort thought about half an hour, and when questioned as to the direction he had taken, he said he really couldn't remember. The police of course had adduced certain witnesses whose testimony would justify the course they had taken in arresting a gentleman in the position of Mr. Alan Carysfort. There was, first of all, Felix Shap himself and his friend Julian Lloyd. They deposed that at about half-past ten, or perhaps a little earlier, they were on their way to see Mr. Stonebridge, as the latter had expressed a wish to see them both and have another quiet talk over a cigar and a glass of wine; Shap and Lloyd had been to the P.P.P cinema in High Street, and they left just before the end to go to Mr. Stonebridge's house.

"They were within fifty yards of it when they saw a man turn out of the nearest side street and go up to Mr. Stonebridge's house. The man went through the garden gate and up to the front door. Shap and Lloyd saw him in the act of ringing the bell. It was then somewhere between 10.30 and 10.45. Mr. Stonebridge was so very much in the habit of seeing friends, and even those clients with whom he was intimate, late in the evenings, that Mr. Shap and Mr. Lloyd didn't think anything of the incident; but, at the same time, they made up their minds to postpone their own visit to Mr. Stonebridge until they could be quite sure of seeing him alone. So, they turned then and there and went straight back to the Black Swan where they lodged.

"I may add that with commendable reserve both these witnesses refused to identify Allan Carysfort with Mr. Stonebridge's visitor on that memorable Wednesday evening. The man they saw had an overcoat and wore a Glengarry cap. More they could not say, as they had not seen his face clearly. On the other hand, the hall-porter at the County Club, another witness for the Treasury, had no cause for such reserve. He said that on the evening of February 28th Sir David Carysfort came to the Club a little before half-past ten. Mr. Allan was with him then, but he didn't come in.

"The hall-porter heard him say to Sir David: 'Very well then! I'll pick you up here in about half an hour!' And Sir David rejoined: 'Yes; don't be late!' Mr. Allan did return to the Club at about eleven o'clock and the two gentlemen then went off together. The hall-porter remembered the incident on that date quite distinctly, because he recollected being much surprised at seeing Mr. Allan Carysfort, who he thought was still abroad.

"After that there was another remand, Allan Carysfort's solicitor having asked and obtained an adjournment for a week. But by this time, as you may imagine, not only the county, but London society too were absolutely horror-struck. To think that a man in the position of the Carysforts should have stooped to such an act, not only of violence, but of improbity, was indeed staggering. Nor did public opinion swerve from this attitude one hair's breadth, even though at the next hearing all the proofs which the police had adduced against the accused were absolutely confuted. Fortunately for Carysfort, his solicitors had been successful in finding two witnesses, Miriam Page and Arthur Ormeley, who had seen Mr. Allan Carysfort, whom they knew by sight, strolling by the river at a quarter to eleven. They—like the hall-porter at the County Club—remembered the circumstance very clearly because they did not know that Mr. Allan was home from abroad, and were astonished to see him there.

"The point of the evidence of three witnesses was that the river where they had seen Allan Carysfort strolling at a quarter to eleven is at the diametrically opposite end of the town to that where lies the Great West Road. Now the hall-porter had seen Allan Carysfort outside the County Club at half-past ten and again at eleven. If Carysfort was strolling by the river at a quarter to eleven, and there was no reason to impugn the credibility of the witnesses, he could not possibly have been the man whom Mr. Snap and Mr. Lloyd saw ringing the bell of Mr. Stonebridge's house at about that same hour.

"Allan Carysfort was discharged by the magistrates as you know. There was no definite proof against him. But public opinion is ever an uncertain quantity, and it is still dead against the Carysforts. In the public mind two facts have remained indelibly fixed: firstly, that the Carysforts had everything to gain by the destruction of Felix Shap's papers, and, secondly, that there was nobody else who could possibly have benefited by it. Since then, also, Mr. Stonebridge has made a declaration that nothing was stolen out of his safe and pocket-book except the papers and letters belonging to Felix Shap. So, what would you? Although Allan Carysfort was discharged by the magistrates, really because there was no tangible evidence against him, he did not leave the court without a stain on his character. The stain was there, and there it is to this day.

"It will take the Carysforts years to live the scandal down; though some friends have remained loyal, there are always the enemies, the envious, the uncharitable, and they insist that the two witnesses—the only two, mind you, whose evidence did clear Allan Carysfort of suspicion—had been bought and should not be believed, while others simply declare that Sir David and his son employed some ruffian to do the dirty work for them."

He gave a dry cackle and contemplated me through his huge horn-rimmed spectacles.

"And you are of that opinion, too, I imagine," he said.

"Well, it seems the only likely explanation," I replied guardedly.

"Surely you don't suppose," he retorted, "that a business man like David Carysfort would place himself so entirely in the hands of a ruffian that he would for ever after be the victim of blackmail! Why, it would have been cheaper to buy off Felix Shap!"

"But," I rejoined, "I don't see who else had any interest in doing away with those documents."

"I'll tell you," he rejoined dryly. "Felix Shap himself."

"What do you mean?" I queried, with as much lofty scorn as I could command.

"I mean," he replied, "that all Felix Shap's documents were forgeries."

"Forgeries?" I exclaimed.

"Yes, spurious! False affidavits! Forgeries the lot of 'em. My belief is that Stonebridge began to suspect this himself, and I think he has had a narrow escape of being murdered outright by those two rascals. As it is they have destroyed every proof of their villainy, and old Stonebridge, I imagine, is content to let things remain as they are rather than admit publicly that he was completely taken in by two very plausible rogues."

"But," I urged, "what about the handwriting expert?"

The funny creature laughed aloud.

"Yes!" he said, "what about the expert? If there had been two, they would have disagreed. And mind you at a distance of twelve years a signature would be difficult of absolute identification. Everyone's handwriting undergoes certain modifications in the course of years. Experts," he reiterated, "Bah!"

"But," I went on impatiently, "I don't see the object of the whole scheme."

"The object was blackmail," the whimsical creature retorted, "and it succeeded admirably. Already we read that Messrs. Shap and Lloyd are staying at expensive hotels in London, that they have granted interviews to pressmen and written articles for halfpenny newspapers. We shall hear of them as cinema stars presently. They have had the most gorgeous, the most paying publicity, and presently Sir David Carysfort will have had enough of them and will put a few more hundreds in their pockets just to be rid of them. That was the object of the whole scheme, my dear young lady! And see how well it was carried out. Of course, the addle-headed Dutchman never thought of it. I imagine that the whole scheme originated in the fertile brain of Mr. Julian Lloyd, and it was thoroughly well thought out from the manufacture of the documents and letters down to the assault on the silly old country attorney.

"And, mind you, the rascals originally went to a silly country attorney; they would have been afraid to go to a London lawyer lest he be too sharp for them. The only mistake they made were the letters purported to be written to Berta Shap by the husband who is supposed to have disappeared, and the copy of Berta's marriage certificate. It is those letters that gave me the clue to the whole thing; old Stonebridge was too dull to have seen through those letters. If they were genuine why should Felix Shap have brought them over to England? They had nothing whatever to do with any contract about the Shap Fuelettes.

"If they were genuine, how could he guess that he would have to disprove a story of a secret marriage and of young Alfred being the son of Sir Alfred Carysfort? By wanting to prove too much, he, to my mind, gave himself away, and one can but marvel that neither lawyers nor police saw through the roguery. Of course, the moment one understands that one set of papers was spurious, it is easily concluded that all the others were forgeries. And the late Sir Alfred Carysfort, anxious only to obliterate every vestige of that early marriage of his, unwittingly played into the hands of those two scoundrels by destroying all the correspondence that he had ever had with Shap.

"Think it all over, you will see that I am right. Look at this paragraph again in the *Evening Post*, does it not bear out what I say?"

The paragraph in the evening paper to which the Man in the Corner was pointing read as follows:

"Among the passengers on the Dutch liner *Stadt Rotterdam* is Mr. Felix Shap, the hero of a recent celebrated case. He is returning to Batavia, having, through a misadventure which has remained an impenetrable mystery to this day, been deprived of all the proofs that would have established his claim to a substantial share of the profits in the Shap Fuelettes Company. Fortunately, Mr. Shap had enlisted many sympathies in England that his friends had no difficulty in collecting a considerable sum of money which was presented to him on his departure in the form of a purse and as a compensation for the ill-luck which has attended him since he set foot in this country.

"Mr. Shap will now be able to take abroad with him the assurance that British public opinion is always on the side of the victims of an adverse and unmerited fate."

"Yes!" the funny creature concluded with a cackle, "until the victims are found out to be rogues. Mr. Felix Shap and his friend, Mr. Julian Lloyd, will be found out some day."

The next moment he had gone with that rapidity which was so characteristic of him, and I might have thought that he was just a spook who had come to visit me whilst I dozed over my cup of tea, only that on the table by the side of an empty glass was a piece of string adorned with a series of complicated knots.

The Mystery of Brudenell Court

1

"Did you ever make up your mind about that Brudenell Court affair," the Man in the Corner said to me that day.

"No," I replied. "As far as I am concerned the death of Colonel Forburg has remained a complete mystery."

"You don't think," he insisted "that Morley Thrall was guilty?"

"Well," I said, "I don't know what to think."

"Then don't do it," he rejoined with a chuckle, "if you don't know what to think, then it's best not to think at all. At any rate wait until I have told you exactly what did happen—not as it was reported in the newspapers, but in the sequence in which the various incidents occurred.

"On Christmas Eve, last year, while the family were at dinner, there was a sudden commotion and cries of 'Stop thief!' issuing from the back premises of Brudenell Court, the country seat of a certain Colonel Forburg. The butler ran in excitedly to say that Julia Mason, one of the maids, was drawing down the blinds in one of the first-floor rooms when she saw a man fiddling with the shutters of the French window in the smoking-room downstairs. She at once gave the alarm, whereupon the man bolted across the garden in the direction of the five-acre field. The colonel and his stepson, as well as two male guests who were dining with them, immediately jumped up and hurried out to help in the chase. It was a very dark night, people were running to and fro, and for a few moments there was a great deal of noise and confusion, through which two pistol shots in close succession were distinctly heard.

"The ladies—amongst whom was Miss Monica Glenluce, the colonel's stepdaughter—had remained in the dining-room, and the dinner was kept waiting, pending the return of the gentlemen. They straggled in one by one, all except the colonel. The ladies eagerly asked for news; the gentlemen could not say much—the night was very dark and they had just waited about outside until some of the indoor men who had given chase came back with the news that the thief had been caught. This news was confirmed by young Glenluce, Miss Monica's brother, who was the last to return. He had actually witnessed the capture.

"The thief had bolted straight across the five-acre meadow, but doubled back before he reached the stables, turned sharply to the right through the kitchen garden and then jumped over the boundary wall of the ground into the lane beyond, where he fell straight into the arms of the local constable who happened to be passing by. Young Glenluce had great fun out of the chase; he had guessed the man's purpose and instead of running after him across the meadow, he had gone round it, and had reached the boundary wall only a few seconds after the thief had scaled it. The was some talk about the gun shots that had been heard and everyone supposed that Colonel Forburg, who was a violent tempered man, had snatched up a revolver before giving chase to the burglar and had taken a pot-shot at him; it was fortunate that he had missed him.

"The incident would then have been closed and the interrupted dinner proceeded with, but for the fact that the host had not yet returned. Nothing was thought of this at first, for it was generally supposed that the colonel had been kept talking by one of his men, or perhaps by the constable who had effected the capture; it was only when close on half an hour had gone by that Miss Monica became impatient. She got the butler to telephone both to the stables and to the lodge, but the colonel had not been seen at either place, either during or after the incident with the burglar; communication with the police station brought the same result; nothing had been seen or heard of the colonel.

"Genuinely alarmed now, Monica gave orders for the grounds to be searched; it was just possible that the colonel had fallen whilst running, and was lying somewhere, helpless in the dark, perhaps un-conscious... Everyone began recalling those pistol shots and a sense of tragedy spread over the entire house. Monica blamed herself for not having thought of all this before.

"A search party went out at once; for a while stable-lanterns and electric torches gleamed through the darkness and past the shrubber-ies. Then suddenly there were calls for help, the wandering lights cen-tred in one spot, somewhere in the middle of the five-acre meadow near the big elm tree. Obviously there had been an accident. Monica ran to the front door, followed by all the guests. Through the darkness a group of men were seen slowly wending their way toward the house: one man was running ahead, it was the chauffeur. Young Glenluce, half-guessing that something sinister had occurred, went forward to meet him.

"What had happened was indeed as tragic as it was mysterious; the search party had found the colonel lying full-length in the meadow. His clothes were saturated with blood, he had been shot in the breast and was apparently dead. Close by a revolver had been picked up. It was impossible to keep the terrible news from Miss Monica. Her brother broke the news to her. She bore up with marvellous calm, and it was she who at once gave the necessary orders to have her stepfather's body taken upstairs and to fetch both the doctor and the police.

"In the meanwhile, the guests had gone back into the house. They stood about in groups, awestruck and whispering. They did not care to finish their dinner, or to go up to their rooms, as in all probability they would be required when the police came to make enquiries. Monica and Gerald Glenluce had gone to sit in the smoking-room.

"It was the most horrible Christmas Eve anyone in that house had ever experienced."

2

"Murder committed from any other motive than that of robbery." the Man in the Corner went on after a moment's pause, "always excites the interest of the public. There is nearly always an element of mystery about it, and it invariably suggests possibilities of romance. In this case, of course, there was no question of robbery. After Colonel Forburg fell, shot, as it transpired at close range and full in the breast, his clothes were left untouched; there was loose silver in his trouser pocket, a few treasury notes in his letter-case, and he was wearing a gold watch and chain and a fine pearl stud.

"The motive of the crime was therefore enmity or revenge, and, here the police were at once confronted with a great difficulty. Not, mind you, the difficulty of finding a man who hated the colonel sufficiently to kill him, but that of choosing among his many enemies one who was most likely to have committed such a terrible crime. He was the best hated man in the county.

"Known as 'Remount Forburg' he was generally supposed have made his fortune in some shady transactions connected with the Remount Department of the War Office during Boer War, more than twenty years ago. His first wife was said to have died of a broken heart, and he had no children of his own; some ten years ago he had married a widow with two young children. She had a considerable fortune of her own, and when she died, she left it in trust for her children, but she directed that her husband should be the sole guardian of Monica and Gerald until they came of age; moreover, she left him the interest on the whole of the capital amount for as long as they were in his house and unmarried. After his death the money would revert unconditionally to them.

"Of course, it was a foolish, one might say a criminal will, and one obviously made under the influence of her husband. One can only suppose that the poor woman had died without knowing anything of 'Remount Forburg's' character. Since her death his violent temper and insufferable arrogance had alienated from the children every friend they ever had. Only some chance acquaintances ever came anywhere near Brudenell Court now. Naturally everyone said that the colonel's behaviour was part of a scheme for keeping suitors away from his stepdaughter Monica, who was a very beautiful girl; as for Gerald Glenluce, Monica's younger brother, he had been sadly disfigured when he was a schoolboy through a fall against a sharp object that had broken his nose and somewhat mysteriously deprived him of the sight of one eye. Those who suffered most from Colonel Forburg's violent tempers declare that the boy's face had been smashed in by a blow from a stick, and that the stick had been wielded by his stepfather.

"Be that as it may, Gerald Glenluce had remained, in consequence of his disfigurement, a shy, retiring, silent boy, who neither played games nor rode to hounds and had no idea how to handle a gun; but he was essentially the colonel's favourite. Where Forburg was harsh and dictatorial with everyone else he would always unbend to Gerald, and was almost gentle and affectionate toward him. Perhaps an occasional twinge of remorse had something to do with that soft side of his disagreeable character. Certainly, that softness did not extend to Monica.

"He made the girl's life almost unbearable with his violence which amounted almost to brutality. The girl hated him openly and said so. Her one desire was to get away from Brudenell Court by any possible means. But owing to her mother's foolish will she had no money of her own, and the few friends she had were not sufficiently rich, or sufficiently disinterested, to give her a home away from her stepfather, nor would the colonel, for the matter of that, have given his consent to her living away from him. As for marriage, it was a difficult question. Young men fought shy of any family connection with 'Remount Forburg.' The latter's nickname was bad enough, but there were rumours of secrets more unavowable still in the past history of the colonel. Certain it is that though Monica excited admiration wherever she went, und though one or two of her admirers did go to the length of openly courting her, the courtship never matured into an actual engagement.

"Something or other always occurred to cool off the ardour of the wooers. Suddenly they would either go on a big game shooting expedition, or on a tour round the world, or merely find that country air did not suit them. There would perhaps be a scene of fond farewell, but Monica would always understand that the farewell was a definite one, and, as she was an intelligent as well as a fascinating girl, she put two and two together, and observed that these farewell scenes were invariably preceded by a long interview behind closed doors between her stepfather and her admirer of the moment.

"Small wonder then that she hated the colonel. She hated him as much as she loved her brother. A great affection had, especially of late, developed between these two; it was a love born of an affinity of trouble and sense of injustice. On Gerald's part there was also an element of protection toward the beautiful sister; the fact that he was so avowedly the spoilt son of his irascible stepfather enabled him many a time to stand between Monica and the colonel's unbridled temper.

"Latterly, however, some brightness and romance had been introduced into the drab existence of Monica Glenluce by the discreet courtship of her latest admirer, Mr. Morley Thrall. Mr. Thrall was a wealthy man, not too young and of independent position, who presumably did not care whether county society would cut him or no in consequence of his marriage with the stepdaughter of 'Remount Forburg.'

"Subsequent events showed that he had observed the greatest discretion while he was courting Monica. No one knew that there was an understanding between him and the girl, least of all the colonel. Mr. Morley Thrall came, not too frequently, to Brudenell Court; while there he appeared to devote most of his attention to his host and to Gerald, and to take little if any notice of Monica. She had probably given him a hint of rocks ahead, and he had succeeded in avoiding the momentous interview with the colonel which Monica had learned to look on with dread.

"Mr. Morley Thrall had been asked to stay at Brudenell Court for Christmas, the other guests being a Major Rawstone, with his wife and daughter, Rachel. They were all at dinner on that memorable Christmas Eve when the tragedy occurred, and all the men hurried out of the dining-room in the wake of their host when first the burglary alarm was given."

3

"Thus, did matters stand at Brudenell Court when directly after the holidays, Jim Peyton, a groom recently in the employ of Colonel Forburg, was brought before the magistrates charged with the murder of his former master. There was a pretty stiff case against him too. It seems that he had lately been dismissed by Colonel Forburg for drunkenness, and that before dismissing him the colonel had given him a thrashing which apparently was well deserved, because while he was drunk, he very nearly set fire to stables, and an awful disaster was only averted by the timely arrival of the colonel himself upon the scene.

"Be that as it may, the man went away swearing vengeance. Subsequently he took out a summons for assault against Colonel Forburg and only got damages of one shilling. This had occurred a week before Christmas. There were several witnesses there who could swear to the threatening language used by Peyton on more than one occasion since then, and of course he had been caught in the very act of trying to break into the house through the French window of the smoking-room.

"On the other hand, the revolver with which 'Remount Forburg' had been shot, and which was found close to the body with two empty chambers, was identified as the colonel's own property, one which he always kept, loaded, in a drawer of his desk in the smoking-room. And—this is the interesting point—the shutters of the smoking-room were found by the police inspector, who examined them subsequently, to be bolted on the inside, just as they had been left earlier in the evening by the footman whose business it was to see to the fastening of windows and shutters on the ground floor.

"This fact—the shutters being bolted on the inside—was confirmed by Miss Monica Glenluce who had been the first to go into the smoking-room after the tragic event. Her brother joined her subsequently. Both of these witnesses said that the room looked absolutely undisturbed, the shutters were bolted, the drawer of the desk was closed: they had remained in the room until after the visit of the police inspector.

"After the positive evidence of these two witnesses, the police prosecution had of necessity to fall back on the far-fetched theory that Colonel Forburg himself, before he hurried out in order to join in the chase against the burglar, had run into the smoking-room and picked up his revolver, and that, having overtaken Peyton, he had threatened him; that Peyton had then jumped on him, wrenched the weapon out of his hand and shot him. It was a far-fetched theory certainly, and one which the defence quickly upset. Gerald Glenluce for one was distinctly under the impression that the colonel ran from the dining-room straight out into the garden, and the young footman who was watching the fun from the front door, and saw the colonel run out, was equally sure that he had not a revolver in his hand.

"Peyton got six months hard for attempted house-breaking, there really was no evidence against him to justify the more serious charge; but when the charge of murder was withdrawn, it left the mystery of 'Remount Forburg's' tragic end seemingly more impenetrable than before. Nevertheless, the coroner and jury laboured conscientiously at the inquest. No stone was to be left unturned to bring the murderer of 'Remount Forburg' to justice, and, in this laudable effort the coroner had the able and unqualified assistance of Miss Glenluce.

"However bitter her feelings may have been in the past towards her stepfather while he lived, she seemed determined that his murderer should not go unpunished. Nay more, there appeared to be in all her actions during this terrible time a strange note of vindictiveness and animosity, as if the unknown man who had rid her of an arrogant and brutal tyrant had really done her a lasting injury.

"It was entirely through her energy and exertions that certain witnesses were induced to come forward and give what turned out to be highly sensational evidence. The police who were convinced that James Peyton was guilty had turned all their investigations in the direction of proving their theories; Miss Monica, on the other hand, had seemingly made up her mind that the murderer was to be sought for inside the house; it even appeared as if she had certain suspicions which she only desired to confirm. To this end she had questioned and cross-questioned everyone who was in the house on that fatal night, well knowing how reluctant some people are to be mixed up in any way with police proceedings. But at last, she had forced two persons to speak, and it was on the first day of the inquest that at last a glimmer of light was thrown upon the mysterious tragedy.

"After the medical evidence which went to establish beyond a doubt that Colonel Forburg died from a gunshot wound inflicted at close range, both balls having penetrated the heart, Miss Glenluce was called. Replying to the coroner who had put certain questions to her with regard to the colonel's state of mind just before the tragedy, she said that he appeared to have a premonition that something untoward was about to happen. When the butler ran into the dining-room saying that a burglar had been seen trying to break into the house, the colonel had jumped up from the table at once.

"'I did the same,' Miss Monica went on, 'as I was genuinely alarmed; but my stepfather in his peremptory way ordered me to sit still. "I believe," he said to me with a funny laugh, "that it's a put-up job. It's some friend of Thrall's giving him a hand" I could not, of course, understand what he meant by that, and I looked at Mr. Thrall for an explanation. I must add that Mr. Thrall had been extraordinarily moody all through dinner; he looked flushed and I noticed particularly that he never spoke either to my stepfather, to my brother, or to me. However, at the moment I failed to catch his eye, and the very next second he was out of the room, on the heels of Colonel Forburg.'

"This was remarkable evidence to say the least of it, but nevertheless it was confirmed by two witnesses who heard the colonel make that strange remark: one was Rachel Rawstone, the young friend who was dining at Brudenell Court that Christmas Eve, and the other was Gerald Glenluce.

"Of course, by this time the public was getting very excited: they were like so many hounds heading for a scent, and the jury was beginning to show signs of that obstinate prejudice which culminated presently in a ridiculous verdict. But there was more to come. Thanks again to Miss Monica's insistence the footman at Brudenell Court, a lad named Cambalt, had been induced to come forward with a story which he had evidently intended to keep hidden within his bosom, if possible. He gave his evidence with obvious reluctance and in a scarcely audible voice. It was generally noticed, however, that Miss Monica urged him frequently to speak up.

"Cambalt deposed that just before dinner on Christmas Eve he had gone in to tidy the smoking-room before the gentlemen came down from dressing. As he opened the door, he saw Mr. Morley Thrall standing in the middle of the room facing Colonel Forburg who was seated at his desk. Young Mr. Glenluce was standing near the mantelpiece with one foot on the fender staring into the fire. Mr. Thrall, according to witness, was livid with rage.

"''E took a step forward like,' Cambalt went on, amidst breathless silence on the part of the public and jury alike. 'and 'e raised 'is fist. But the colonel 'e just laughed, then 'e opened the drawer of the desk and took out a revolver and showed it to Mr. Thrall and says: "'Ere y'are, there's a revolver 'andy, anyway." Then Mr. Thrall, 'e swore like anything and says: "You blackguard! You d—d scoundrel! You ought to be shot like the cur you are." I thought 'e would strike the colonel, but young Mr. Glenluce 'e just stepped quickly in between the two gentlemen and 'e says 'Look 'ere. Thrall, I won't put up with this! You jess get out!" Then one of the gentlemen seed me and Mr. Thrall 'e walked out of the room.'

"'And what happened after he had gone?' the coroner asked.

"'Oh!' the witness replied, 'the colonel 'e threw the revolver back into the drawer and laughed sarcastic like. Then 'e 'eld out 'is 'and to Mr. Gerald and says: "Thanks my boy. You did 'elp me to get rid of that ruffian." After that,' Cambalt concluded, 'I got on with my work, and the gentlemen took no notice of me.'

"This witness was very much pressed with questions as to what happened later on when the burglary alarm was given and the gentlemen all hurried out of the house. Cambalt was in the hall at the time and he made straight for the front door to see some of the fun. He said that the colonel was out first and the other three gentlemen, Mr. Gerald, Mr. Rawstone and Mr. Morley Thrall went out after him; Mr. Thrall was the last to go outside; he ran across the garden in the direction of the five-acre field. Major Rawstone remained somewhere near the house, but it was a very dark night, and he, Cambalt, soon lost sight of the gentlemen. Presently, however, Mr. Thrall came back toward the house.

"It was a few minutes after the shots had been fired and witness heard Mr. Thrall say to Major Rawstone: 'I suppose it's that fool Forburg potting away at the burglar; he'll get himself into trouble if he doesn't look out.' Soon after that Mr. Gerald came running back with the news that the burglar had fallen into the arms of a passing constable and Cambalt then returned to his duties in the dining-room.

"As you see," the Man in the Corner went on glibly, "the witness's evidence was certainly sensational. The jury, which was composed of farm labourers, with the local butcher at foreman, had by now fully made up its silly mind that Mr. Morley Thrall had taken the opportunity of sneaking into the smoking-room, snatching up the revolver and shooting 'Remount Forburg,' whom he hated, because the colonel was opposing his marriage with Miss Monica.

"It was all as clear as daylight to those dunderheads, and from that moment they simply would not listen to any more evidence. They had made up their minds; they were ready with their verdict and it was: Manslaughter against Morley Thrall. Not murder you see! The dolts who had all of them suffered from 'Remount Forburg's' arrogance and violent temper would not admit that killing such vermin was a capital crime.

"What I am telling you would be unbelievable if it were not a positive fact. It is no use quoting British justice and dilating on the absolute fairness of trial by jury. A coroner's inquest fortunately is not a trial. The verdict of a coroner's jury, such as the one which sat on the Brudenell Court affair, though it may have very unpleasant consequences for an innocent person, cannot have fatal results. In this case it cast a stigma on a gentleman of high position and repute, and the following day Mr. Morley Thrall, himself J.P., was brought up before his brother magistrates on an ignominious charge.

4

"It is not often," the Man in the Corner resumed after a while, "that so serious a charge is preferred against a gentleman of Mr. Morley Thrall's social position, and I am afraid that the best of us are snobbish enough to be more interested in a gentleman criminal than in an ordinary Bill Sykes.

"I happened to be present at that magisterial inquiry when Mr. Morley Thrall, J.P., was brought in between two warders, looking quite calm and self-possessed. Everyone of us there noticed that when he first came in, and in fact throughout that trying inquiry, his eyes sought to meet those of Miss Glenluce who sat at the solicitor's table; but whenever she chanced to look his way, she quickly averted her gaze again, and turned her head away with a contemptuous shrug. Gerald Glenluce, on the other hand, made pathetic efforts at bowing sympathy with the accused, but he was of such unprepossessing appearance and was so shy and awkward that it was small wonder Morley Thrall took little if any notice of him.

"Very soon we got going. I must tell you first of all that the whole point of the evidence rested upon a question of time. If the accused took the revolver out of the desk in the smoking-room, when did he do it? The footman, Cambalt, reiterated the statement which he had made at the inquest. He was, of course, pressed to say definitely whether after the quarrel between Mr. Morley Thrall and the colonel which he had witnessed, and before everyone went in to dinner, Mr. Thrall might have gone back to the smoking-room and extracted the revolver from the drawer of the desk; but Cambalt said positively that he did not think this was possible. He himself, after he had tidied the smoking-room, had been in and out of the hall preparing to serve dinner. The door of the smoking-room gave on the hall, between the dining room and the passage leading to the kitchens. If anyone had gone in or out of the smoking-room at that time Cambalt must have seen them.

"At this point Miss Glenluce was seen to lean forward and to say something in a whisper to the Clerk of the Justices, who in his turn whispered to the chairman on the Bench, and a moment or two later that gentleman asked the witness:

"'Are you absolutely prepared to swear that no one went in or out of the smoking-room while you were making ready to serve dinner?'

"Then, as the young man seemed to hesitate, the magistrate added more emphatically:

"'Think now! You were busy with your usual avocations; there would have been nothing extraordinary in one of the gentlemen going in or out of the smoking-room at that hour. Do you really believe and are you prepared to swear that such a very ordinary incident would have impressed itself indelibly upon your mind?'

"Thus, pressed and admonished, Cambalt retrenched himself behind a vague,

'No sir! I shouldn't like to swear one way or the other.'

"Whereat Miss Monica threw a defiant look at the accused who, however, did not as much as wink an eyelid in response.

"Presently when that lady herself was called no one could fail to notice that she, like the coroner's jury the previous day, had absolutely made up her mind that Morley Thrall was guilty, otherwise her attitude of open hostility toward him would have been quite inexplicable. She dwelt at length on the fact that Mr Thrall had paid her marked attention for months, and that he had asked her to marry him.

She had given him her consent, and between them they had decided to keep their engagement a secret, until after she, Monica, had attained her twenty-first birthday, when she would be free to marry whom she chose.

"'Unfortunately,' the witness went on, suddenly assuming a dry, pursed-up manner, 'Colonel Forburg got wind of this. He was always very much set against my marrying at all, and between tea and dinner on Christmas Eve he and I had some very sharp words together on the subject, at the end of which my stepfather said very determinedly: "Christmas or no Christmas, the fellow shall leave my house by the first available train tomorrow, and tonight I am going to give him a piece of my mind.'

"Just for a moment after Miss Glenluce had finished speaking, the accused seemed to depart from his attitude of dignity and reserve, and an indignant 'Oh!' quickly repressed, escaped his lips. The public by this time was dead against him. They are just like sheep, as you know, and the verdict of the coroner's jury had prejudiced them from the start, and the police, aided by Miss Glenluce, had certainly built up a formidable case against the unfortunate man. Everyone felt that the motive for the crime was fully established already. 'Remount Forburg' had had a violent quarrel with Morley Thrall, then had turned him out of the house, and the latter, furious at being separated from the girl he loved, had killed the man who stood in his way.

"I should be talking until tomorrow morning were I to give you in detail all the evidence that was adduced in support of the prosecution. The accused listened to it all with perfect calm. He stood with arms folded, his eyes fixed on nothing. The 'Oh!' of indignation did not again cross his lips, nor did he look once at Miss Monica Glenluce. I can assure you that at one moment that day things were looking very black against him.

"Fortunately for him, however, he had a very clever lawyer to defend him in the person of his distinguished cousin, Sir Evelyn Thrall. The latter, by amazingly clever cross-examination of the servants and guests at Brudenell Court, had succeeded in establishing the fact that at no time, from the moment that the burglary alarm was given until after the two revolver shots had been heard, was the accused completely out of sight of someone or other of the witnesses. He was the last to leave the dining-room. Mrs. Rawstone and her daughter testified to that. He had stayed behind one moment after the other three gentlemen had gone out in order to say a few words to Monica Glenluce. Miss Rawstone was standing inside the dining-room door and she was quite positive that Mr. Thrall went straight out into the garden.

"On the other hand, Major Rawstone saw him in the forecourt coming away from the five-acre meadow only a very few moments after the shots were fired, and gave it absolutely as his opinion that it would have been impossible for the accused to have fired those shots.

This is where the question of time came in.

"'When a man who bears a spotless reputation,' Major Rawstone argued, 'finds that he has killed a fellow creature, he would necessarily pause a moment, horror-struck with what he has done; whether the deed was premeditated or involuntary he would at least try and ascertain if life was really extinct. It is inconceivable that any man, save an habitual and therefore callous criminal, would just throw down his weapon and with absolute calm, hands in pocket and without a tremor in his voice make a casual remark to a friend. Now I saw Mr. Morley Thrall perhaps two minutes after the shots were fired; in that time, he could not have walked from the centre of the field to the forecourt where I was standing and he had not been running as his voice was absolutely clear and he came walking towards me with his hands in pockets.'

"As was only to be expected Sir Evelyn Thrall made the most of Major Rawstone's evidence, and I may say that it was chiefly on the strength of it that the charge of murder against the accused was withdrawn, even though the Clerk to the Magistrates, perpetually egged on by Miss Glenluce, did his best to upset Major Rawstone. When the lady found that this could not be done, she tried to switch back to the idea that accused had abstracted the revolver out of the morning-room before dinner and immediately after his quarrel with Colonel Forburg.

"The footman Cambalt's evidence on this point had been somewhat discounted by his refusing to state positively that no one could have gone into the smoking-room at that time without his seeing them. But against this theory there was always the argument—of which Sir Evelyn Thrall made the most as you know—that before dinner the accused could not have known that there would be an alarm of burglary which would give him the opportunity of waylaying the colonel in the open field.

"With equal skill, too, Sir Evelyn brought forward evidence to bear out the statement made by the accused on the matter of his quarrel with Colonel Forburg.

"'Just before dinner,' Mr. Thrall stated, 'Colonel Forburg told me he had something to say to me in private. I followed him into the smoking-room and there he gave me certain information with regard to his past life and also with regard to Miss Glenluce's parentage which made it absolutely impossible for me, in spite of the deep regard which I have for that lady, to offer her marriage. Miss Glenluce is the innocent victim of tragic circumstances in the past, and Forburg is just an unmitigated blackguard, and I told him so, but I had my family to consider and very reluctantly I came to the conclusion that I could not introduce any relation of Colonel Forburg into its circle. Colonel Forburg did not stand in the way of my marrying his stepdaughter, it is I who most reluctantly withdrew.'

"Whilst the accused was cross-examined upon this statement, and he gave his answers in firm, dignified tones, Miss Monica never took her eyes off him, and surely if looks could kill, Mr. Morley Thrall would not at that moment have escaped with his life, so full of deadly hatred and contempt was her gaze. The accused had signed a much fuller statement than the one which he had made in open court: it contained a detailed account of his interview with Colonel Forburg, and of the circumstances which finally induced him to give up all thoughts of asking Miss Glenluce to be his wife. These facts were not made public at the time for the sake of Miss Monica and of the unfortunate Gerald, but it seems that the transactions which had earned for the colonel the sobriquet of 'Remount Forburg' were so disreputable and so dishonest that not only was he cashiered from the army, but he served a term of imprisonment for treason, fraud and embezzlement.

"He had no right to be styled colonel any longer, and quite recently had been threatened with prosecution if he persisted in making further use of his army rank. But that was not all the trouble. It seems that in his career of improbity he had been associated with a man named Nosdel, a man of Dutch extraction whom he had known in South Africa. This man was subsequently hanged for a particularly brutal murder, and it was his widow who was 'Remount Forburg's' second wife and the mother of Monica and of Gerald, who had been given the fancy name of Glenluce.

"Obviously a man in Mr Morley Thrall's position could not marry into such a family, and it appears that whenever there was a question of a suitor for Monica, 'Remount Forburg' would tell the aspirant the whole story of his own shady past and, above all, that of Monica's father. Sir Evelyn Thrall had been clever enough to discover one or two gentlemen who had had the same experience as his cousin Morley; they, too, just before their courtship came to a head had had a momentous interview with 'Remount Forburg,' who found this means of choking off any further desire for matrimony on the part of a man who had family connections to consider.

"But it was very obvious that Mr. Morley Thrall had no motive for killing 'Remount Forburg'; he would have left Brudenell Court that very evening, he said, only that young Glenluce had begged him, for Monica's sake, not to make a scene; anyway, he was leaving the house next day and had no intention of ever darkening its doors again.

"Poor Monica Glenluce or Nosdel, ignorant of the hideous cloud that hung over her entire life, ignorant too of what passed between her stepfather and Mr. Morley Thrall, nothing but hatred and contempt for the man whose love, she believed, had proved as unstable as that of any of her other admirers. For charity's sake one must suppose that she really thought him guilty at first, and hoped that when the clouds had rolled by, he would return to her, more ardent than before. Presumably he found means to make her understand that all was irrevocably at an end between them as far as he was concerned, whereupon her regard for him turned bitterness and desire for revenge.

"And, indeed, but for the cleverness of a distinguished lawyer, poor Morley Thrall might have found himself the victim of a judicial error brought about by the deliberate enmity of a woman. Had he been committed for trial, she would have had more time at her disposal to manufacture evidence against him, which I am convinced she had a mind to do.

"As it is," I now put in tentatively, for the Man in the Corner had been silent for some little while, "the withdrawal of the charge of murder against Morley Thrall did not help to clear up the mystery of 'Remount Forburg's' tragic death."

"Not as far as the public is concerned," he retorted drily.

"You have a theory?" I asked.

"Not a theory," he replied. "I know who killed 'Remount Forburg.'"

"How do you know?" I riposted.

"By logic and inference," he said. "As it was proved that Morley Thrall did not kill him, and that Miss Monica could not have done it, as the ladies did not join in the chase after the burglar, I looked about me for the only other person in whose interest it was to put that blackguard out of the way."

"You mean—?"

"I mean the boy Gerald, of course. Openly and before the other witness Cambalt, he stood up for his stepfather against Thrall who was not measuring his words, but just think how the knowledge which he had gained about his own parentage and that of his sister must have rankled in his mind. He must have come to the conclusion that while this man—his stepfather—lived, there would be no chance for him to make friends, no chance for the sister whom he loved ever to have a home, a life of her own. Whether that interview on Christmas Eve was the first inkling which he had of the real past history of his own and Forburg's family, it is impossible to say. Probably he had suspicions of it before, when, one by one, Monica's suitors fell away after certain private interviews with the colonel. Morley Thrall must have been a last hope, and that, too, was dashed to the ground by the same infamous means.

"I am not prepared to say that the boy got hold of the revolver that night with the deliberate intention of killing his stepfather at the earliest opportunity: he may have run into the smoking-room to snatch up the weapon, only with a view to using it against the burglar; certain it is that he overtook 'Remount Forburg' in the five-acre field and that he shot him then and there. Remember that the night was very dark, and that there was a great deal of running about and of confusion. The boy was young enough and nimble enough after he had thrown down the revolver to run across the field and then to go back to the house by a roundabout way.

" It is easy enough in a case like that to cover one's tracks, and, of course, no one suspected anything at the time. Even the sound of firing created but little astonishment; it was so very much on the cards that the colonel would use a revolver without the slightest hesitation against a man who had been trying to break into his house. It was just the sort of revenge that a man of Gerald's temperament—disfigured, shy, silent and self-absorbed—would seek against one whom he considered the fount of all his wrongs."

"But," I objected, "how could young Glenluce run into the smoking-room, pick up the revolver out of a drawer, and run back through the hall with servants and guests standing about. Someone would be sure to see him."

"No one saw him," the funny creature retorted, "for he did it at the moment of the greatest confusion. The butler had run in with the news of the burglary, the colonel jumped up and ran out through the hall, the guests had not yet made up their minds what to do. In moments like this there are always just a few seconds of pandemonium, quite sufficient for a boy like Gerald to make a dash for the smoking-room."

"But after that—"

"After that he took the revolver out of the drawer and ran out

327

through the French window."

"But the shutters were found to be bolted on the inside," I argued, "when they were subsequently examined by police inspector."

"So they were," he admitted. "Miss Monica had already been in there with young Gerald. They had seen to the shutters."

"Then you think that Monica knew?" I asked.

"Of course, she did."

"Then her desire to prove Morley Thrall guilty—?"

"Was partly hatred of him and partly the desire to shield her brother," the funny creature concluded as he collected his traps, his bit of string and his huge umbrella. "Think it over; you will see that I am right. I am sorry for those two, aren't you? But they are selling Brudenell Court, I understand, and their mother's fortune has become theirs absolutely. They will go abroad together, make a home for themselves, and one day, perhaps, everything will be forgotten, and a new era of happiness will arise for the innocent, now that the guilty has been so signally punished. But it was an interesting case. Don't you agree with me?"

The Mystery of the White Carnation

"I suppose that it is a form of snobbishness," the Man in the Corner began abruptly.

I gave such a jump that I nearly upset the contents of a cup of boiling tea which I was conveying to my mouth. As it was, I scalded my tongue and nearly choked.

"What is?" I queried with a frown, for I was really vexed with the creature. I had no idea he was there at all. But he only smiled and concluded his speech, quite unperturbed.

". . .that creates additional interest in a crime when it concerns people of wealth or rank."

"Snobbishness," I rejoined, "of course it's snobbishness! And when the little suburban madam has finished reading about Lady Stick-inthemud's reception at Claridge's, she likes to turn to Lord Tomnoodle's prospective sojourn in gaol."

"You were thinking of the disappearance of the Australian millionaire?" he asked blandly.

"I don't know that I was," I retorted.

"But of course, you were. How could any journalist worthy of the name fail to be interested in that intricate case?"

"I suppose you have your theory—as usual?

"It is not a theory," the creature replied, with that fatuous smile of his which always irritated me; "it is a certainty."

Then, as he became silent, absorbed in the contemplation of a wonderfully complicated knot in his beloved bit of string, I said with gracious condescension:

"You may talk about it, if you like."

He did like, fortunately for me, because, frankly, I could not see daylight in that maze of intrigue, adventure and possibly crime, which was described by the Press as "The Mystery of the White Carnation."

"The events were interesting from the outset," he began after a while, whilst I settled down to listen, "and so were the various actors in the society drama. Chief amongst these was, of course, Captain Shillington, an Australian ex-officer, commonly reputed to be a millionaire, who, with his mother and sister, rented Mexfield House in Somerset Street, Mayfair, the summer before last. It appears that Lord Mexfield's younger son, the Honourable Henry Buckley, who was an incorrigible rake and whom his father had sent on a tour round the world in order to keep him temporarily out of mischief, not to say out of gaol, had met a married brother of Captain Shillington's out in the Antipodes; they had been very kind to him, and so on, with the result that when came the following London season the family turned up in England and, after spending a couple of days at the Savoy, they moved into the Mexfields' house in Somerset Street.

"Lord and Lady Mexfield were abroad that year and Henry Buckley and his sister Angela were living with an aunt who had a small house somewhere in Mayfair.

"Although the Shillingtons were reputed to be very wealthy, they appeared to be very quiet, simple folk, and it certainly seemed rather strange that they should have gone to the expense of a house in town, when obviously they had no social ambitions and did not mean to entertain. As a matter of fact, as far as Mrs. Shillington and her daughter were concerned, nobody could have lived a quieter, more retiring life than they did. Mrs. Shillington was an invalid and hardly ever went outside her front door, and the girl Marion seemed to be suffering from a perpetual cold in the head.

"They seemed to be in a chronic state of servant trouble. Mrs. Shillington was dreadfully irritable and one set of servants after another were engaged only to leave without notice after a few days. The only faithful servant who remained was a snuffy old man who came to them about a month after they moved into Mexfield House. He and a charwoman did all the work of cooking and valeting and so on. Presumably the old man could not have got a situation elsewhere as his appearance was very unprepossessing, and therefore he was willing to put up with what the servants' registry offices would term 'a very uncomfortable situation.'

"Captain Shillington, the hero of the tragic adventure, on the other hand, went about quite a good deal. He was certainly voted to be rather straitlaced, not to say priggish, but he was very good looking and a fine dancer. Henry Buckley introduced him to some of his smart friends and Lady Angela constituted him her dancing partner. This partnership soon developed into warmer friendship, and presently it was given out that Lady Angela Buckley, only daughter of the Earl and Countess of Mexfield, was engaged to Captain Denver Shillington, the Australian millionaire. Lady Angela confided to her friends that her *fiancé* was the owner of immense estates in Western Australia, on a portion of which rich deposits of gold had lately been discovered. He certainly had plenty of money to spend, and on one occasion he actually paid Henry Buckley's gambling debts to the tune of two or three hundred pounds.

"On the whole, society pronounced the match a suitable one. Lady Angela Buckley was no longer in her first youth, whilst her brother, to whom she was really devoted, would be all the better for a somewhat puritanical, strait-laced and above all wealthy brother-in-law.

2

"That, then, was the position," the old Man in the Corner continued, after a while, "and the date of Lady Angela Buckley's marriage to Captain Denver Shillington had been actually fixed when the public was startled one afternoon towards the end of the summer by the sensational news in all the evening papers: 'Mysterious disappearance of a millionaire.' This highly coloured description applied, as it turned out, to Captain Shillington, the *fiancé* of Lady Angela Buckley. It seems that during the course of that same morning a young lady, apparently in deep distress and suffering from a streaming cold in the head, had called at Scotland Yard.

"She gave her name and address as Marion Shillington of Mexfield House, Somerset Street, Mayfair, and stated that she and her mother were in the greatest possible anxiety owing to the disappearance of her brother, Captain Denver Shillington. They had last seen him on the previous Friday evening at about nine o'clock when he left home in order to pick up his *fiancée*, Lady Angela Buckley, whom he was escorting that night to a reception in Grosvenor Square. He was wearing full evening dress and a soft hat. Miss Shillington couldn't say whether he had any money in his pockets. She thought that probably he was carrying a gold cigarette case which Lady Angela had given him, but, as a matter of fact, he never wore any jewellery.

"No one in the house had heard him come in again that night, and his bed had not been slept in. Questioned by the police, Miss Shillington explained that neither she nor her mother felt any alarm at first because there had been some talk of Captain Shillington going away with his *fiancée* to stay with friends over the weekend somewhere near Newmarket. It was only this morning, Wednesday, that Mrs. Shillington first began to worry when there was still no sign or letter from him.

"'My brother is a very good son,' Miss Shillington continued, explaining to the police, "and always very considerate to mother. It was so unlike him to leave us without news all this while and not to let us know when to expect him home. So, I rang up Lady Angela Buckley, who is his *fiancée*, to see if I could get news through her, as I could see mother was beginning to get anxious.

"'Mr. Henry Buckley, Lady Angela's brother, answered the 'phone. I asked after his sister and he told me that she was staying on in the country a day or two longer. He himself had come back to town the previous night. I then asked him, quite casually, if he knew whether Denver—that's my brother—would be returning with Angela. And his answer to me was, "Denver? Why, I haven't seen him since Friday, and I can tell you he is in for a row with Angela. She was furious with him that he never wrote once to her while she was away." I was so upset that I hung up the receiver and just sat there wondering what to do next. But Mr. Buckley rang up a moment or two later and asked quite cheerily if there was anything wrong. "Good old Square-toes!" he said, meaning my brother, whom he always used to chaff by calling him 'Square-toes,' "don't tell me he has gone off on the spree without letting you know. I say, that's too bad of him, though. But I shouldn't be anxious, if I were you. Boys, you know, Miss Shillington, will be boys, and I like old Square-toes all the better for it."'

"Miss Shillington," the old Man in the Corner went on, "was, as usual, suffering from a streaming cold, and between spluttering and crying she had reduced two or three handkerchiefs to wet balls. At best she is no beauty, and with a red nose and streaming eyes she presented a most pitiable spectacle.

"'I made Mr. Buckley assure me once more,' she said, 'that he had seen nothing of Denver since Friday. That night he and Lady Angela and Denver were at a reception in Grosvenor Square. They all left about the same time. Angela and Denver went presumably straight home; at any rate, he, Mr. Buckley, saw nothing more of them after they got into their car. He himself went to spend an hour or two at his club and came home about two am. The next morning, after breakfast, he drove his sister out to Tatchford, near Newmarket, where they spent the weekend with some friends. And that was all Mr. Buckley could say to me.' Miss Shillington concluded, vigorously blowing her nose: 'He came home last night from Tatchford, and was expecting Lady Angela in a couple of days. Denver had not been at Tatchford at all, and he had not once written to Angela all the while she was away.'

"Of course, the police inspector to whom Miss Shillington related all these facts had a great many questions to put to her. For one thing he wanted to know whether she had been in communication with Lady Angela Buckley since this morning.

"'No,' the girl replied, 'I have not, and so far, I haven't said anything to mother. As soon as I felt strong enough, I put on my things and came along here.'

"Then the inspector wanted to know if she knew of any friends or acquaintances of her brother with whom he might have gone off for a weekend jaunt without saying anything about it, either at home or to his *fiancée*. He put the questions as delicately as he could, but the sister flared up with indignation. It seems that the captain's conduct had always been irreproachable. He was a model son, a model brother, and deeply in love with Angela. Miss Shillington also refused to believe that he could have been enticed to a place of ill-fame and robbed by one of the usual confidence-tricksters.

"'My brother is exceptionally shrewd,' she declared, 'and a splendid business man. Though he is not yet thirty he has built up an enormous fortune out in Australia, and administers his estates himself to the admiration of everyone who knows him. He is not the sort of man who could be fooled in that way.'

"But beyond all this, and beyond giving a detailed description of her brother's appearance, the poor girl had very little to say, and the detective who was put in charge of the case could only assure her that enquiries would at once be instituted in every possible direction, and that the police would keep her informed of everything that was being done. Obviously, the person most likely to be able to throw some light upon the mystery was Lady Angela Buckley, but as you know, the advent of this charming lady upon the scene only helped to complicate matters.

"It appears that Henry Buckley, delighted at what he jocosely called, "Old Square-toes" falling from grace," had rung up his sister in order to tell her the startling news over the telephone. Lady Angela being a very modern young woman, her brother thought that she might storm for a bit, but in end see the humorous side of the situation. But not at all! Lady Angela took the affair entirely *au tragique*.

Over telephone she only exclaimed 'Great Lord!' but at o'clock after noon she arrived at the flat, having taken the first train up to town and not even waiting for her maid to pack her things. Mr. Henry Buckley was just going out to lunch. Without condescending to explain anything, his sister dragged him off then and there to Scotland Yard. "Something happened to Denver," was all that she would say. "Something dreadful, I am sure."

In vain did her brother protest that she would only be making a fool of herself by rushing to the police like this, that old Square-toes had only gone on the spree, and that anyway he ought to consult with the Shillingtons before doing anything silly; Lady Angela would not listen to reason. "You don't know! You don't know!" she kept on re-iterating with ever-increasing agitation. 'He has been murdered, I tell you. Murdered!"

"By the time that the pair arrived at Scotland Yard Lady Angela was in a state bordering on hysterics, and her brother appeared both sulky and perplexed. They saw the same Inspector who had interviewed Miss Shillington, and certainly his amazement was no whit less than that of Mr. Henry Buckley's when Lady Angela, having mentioned the disappearance of Captain Denver Shillington, said abruptly. 'Yes, he has disappeared, and incidentally, he had my pearls in his pocket.' The Inspector made no immediate comment; men of his calling are used to those kinds of surprises, but Henry Buckley gave a gasp of horror.

"'Your pearls?' he exclaimed. 'What pearls? Not—?'

"'Yes,' Lady Angela rejoined coolly. 'The Glenarm pearls. All of them!'

"'But—' Henry Buckley stammered, wide-eyed and white to the lips.

"His sister threw him what appeared to be a warning glance, then she turned once more to the police inspector.

"'My brother is upset,' she said calmly, 'because he knows that the pearls are of immense value. The late Lord Glenarm left them to me in his will. He made a huge fortune by a successful speculation in sugar. He had no daughters of his own and late in life he married my mother's sister. He was my godfather, and when he first bought the pearls and gave them to his wife as a wedding present, he said that after her death and his they should belong to me. They were valued for probate at twenty-five thousand pounds.'

"Henry Buckley was still speechless, and it was in answer to several questions put to her by the inspector that Lady Angela gave the full history, as far as she knew it, of the disappearance of her pearls.

"'I was going to spend the weekend with some friends at Tatchford, near Newmarket,' she said. 'My brother at first had decided not to come with me. On the Friday evening I went with Captain Shillington to a ball at the Duchess of Flint's in Grosvenor Square. I wore my pearls; on the way home in the car Captain Shillington appeared very anxious as to what I should do about the pearls whilst I was away. He wanted me to take them to the bank first thing in the morning before I left. But I knew I couldn't do this because my train was at nine-fifty from Liverpool Street. Captain Shillington had once or twice before shown anxiety about the pearls and urged me to keep them at the bank when I was not wearing them, but he had never been so insistent as that night.'

"Lady Angela appeared to hesitate for a moment or two. She glanced at her brother with a curious expression, both of anxiety and contempt. It seemed as if she were trying to make up her mind to say something that was very difficult to put in so many words. The inspector sat silent and impassive, waiting for her to continue her story, and at last she did make up her mind to speak.

"'I had a safe in the flat,' she went on glibly, 'where I keep my jewellery, but Captain Shillington did not seem satisfied. He argued and argued, and at last he persuaded me to let him have the pearls while I was away and he would deposit them at his own bank until my return.'

"Presumably at this point the lady caught an expression on the face of the inspector which displeased her, for she added with becoming dignity, 'I am engaged to be married to Captain Denver Shillington.'

"'My God!' Henry Buckley exclaimed at this point, and with a groan he buried his face in his hands.

"Mind you," the Man in the Corner proceeded, after moment's pause, "the public had no information as to the exact words, and so on, that passed between Lady Angela, her brother Henry, and the officials of Scotland Yard. All that I am telling you, and what I am still about to tell you, came out bit by bit in the papers. Sensation lovers were immensely interested in the case from the outset, because although both public and police are familiar enough with the tragi-comedy of the good-looking young blackguard who gets confiding females to entrust him with their little bits of jewellery, this was the first time that the confidence trick had been played by a well-known man about town—reputed wealthy since he had gone to the length of paying a friend's gambling debts—on a society lady who was not in her first youth and must presumably have had some knowledge of the world she lived in.

"Lady Angela had concluded her statements by saying that during the drive home in the car she took off her pearls and handed them to her *fiancé* who slipped them into his pocket just as they were, although when presently the car drew up at her door, she suggested running up to her room to get the case for them. The captain, however, declared this to be unnecessary. What he said was, 'I will sleep with them under my pillow tonight, and tomorrow morning first thing I will take them round to the bank for you.' After this he said goodnight. Lady Angela let herself into the house with her latch-key, and Captain Shillington then dismissed the car, saying that he would enjoy a bit of a walk as the rooms at Grosvenor Square had been so desperately hot.

"And it was at this point," the Man in the Corner now said with deliberate emphasis as he worked away at an exceptionally intricate knot in his beloved bit of string, "it was at this point that certain facts leaked out which lent to the whole case a sinister aspect.

"It appears that on the Saturday morning at break of day one of the boats belonging to the Thames District Police found a grey Homburg hat floating under one of the old steamship landing stages and stuck to one of the wooden piles close by a man's silk scarf. There was no name inside the hat or any other clue as to the owner's identity, but both the scarf, which had once been white or light grey, and the hat were terribly soiled and torn, and both were stained with blood. The police had tried on the quiet to trace the owner of the hat and scarf but without success. After Lady Angela had told her story of the missing pearls, the things were shown to Miss Shillington, who at once identified the hat as belonging to her brother; the scarf, however, she knew nothing about.

"But this was not by any means all. It appears that for some reason which was never quite clear, Captain Shillington, after he said goodnight to Lady Angela, altered his mind about the proposed walk. It may have started to rain, or he may not, after all, have liked the idea of walking about the streets at night with twenty-five thousand pounds' worth of pearls in his pocket. Be that as it may, he hailed a passing taxi and drove to Mexfield House. The driver came forward voluntarily in answer to an advertisement put in the papers by the police. He stated that he remembered the circumstance quite well because of what followed. He remembered taking up a fare outside Stanhope Gate and being ordered to drive to Mexfield House in Somerset Street. When he slowed down close to Mexfield House, he noticed a man with his hands in his pockets lounging under the doorway of one of the houses close by.

"As far as he could see the man was in evening dress and wore a light overcoat. He had on a silk hat tilted right to his eyes so that only the lower part of his face was visible, and he had a white or pale grey scarf tied loosely round his face. The chauffeur also noticed that he had a large white flower, probably a carnation, in his buttonhole. After the taxi-man had put down his fare he drove off, and as he did so he saw the man in the light overcoat step out from under the doorway where he had been lounging, and turn in the direction of Maxfield House. What happened after that he didn't know, as he drove away without taking further notice, but the police were already in touch with another man who had been watching that night in Somerset Street, where a portion of the road was up for repair.

"This man whose name, I think, was William Rugger, remembered quite distinctly seeing a 'swell' in a light overcoat and wearing a light-coloured scarf round his neck, loafing around Mexfield House. He remembered the taxi drawing up and a gentleman getting out of it, whereupon the one in the light overcoat and the scarf went up to him and said, 'Hallo, Denver!' at which the other gent, the one who had come in the taxi, appeared very surprised, for Rugger heard him say; 'Good Lord, Henry, what are you doing here?'

"Rugger didn't hear any more because the gentleman in the light overcoat then took the other one by the arm and together the pair of them walked away down the street. When they had gone Rugger noticed a large white carnation lying on the pavement; he picked it up and subsequently took it home to his missus.

"You may imagine what a stir and excitement this story—which pretty soon leaked out in all its details—caused amongst the public. It seems that, although neither the taxi driver nor the man Rugger had seen the face of the man who had stepped out from under a neighbouring doorway and accosted Captain Shillington, they were both of them quite positive that he was in evening dress, and that he wore a silk hat, a light overcoat, and had a pale grey or white scarf wound round his neck. And besides that, there was the white carnation. But, of course, the crux of the whole evidence was Rugger's assertion that he heard one gentleman—the one who got out of the cab—say to the other in tones of great surprise, 'Good Lord, Henry, what are you doing here?'

"Questioned again and again he never wavered in this statement. He heard the name Henry quite distinctly and it stuck in his mind because his eldest boy was Henry. He was also asked whether the gentleman who had stepped out of the taxi—obviously Captain Shillington since the other had called to him 'Hello, Denver!'—walked away reluctantly or willingly when he was thus summarily taken hold of by the arm. Rugger was under the impression that he walked away reluctantly; he freed his arm once, but the other got hold of him again, and, though Rugger did not catch the actual words, he certainly thought that the two gentlemen were quarrelling.

"And thus, public opinion which at first had been dead against the Australian captain now went equally dead against Henry Buckley. Ugly stories were current of his extravagance, his gambling debts, his addiction to drink. People who knew him remembered one or two ugly pages in his life's history: altercations with the police, raids on gambling clubs of which he was a prominent member; there was even a fraudulent bankruptcy which had been the original cause of his being sent out to Australia by his harassed parents until the worst of the clouds had rolled by.

"The only thing that told in his favour, as far as the public was concerned, was the bitter vindictiveness displayed against him by Miss Shillington. That the girl had cause for bitterness was not to be denied. For a time, at any rate, public opinion had branded her brother as a common trickster and a thief, and she and her mother had no doubt suffered terribly under the stigma; in consequence of this, Mrs. Shillington's health, always in a precarious state, had completely broken down and the old lady had taken to her bed, not suffering from any particular disease, but just from debility of mind and body, obstinately refusing to see a doctor, declaring that nothing would cure her except the return of her son.

"And on the top of all that came the growing conviction that the son never would return and that he had been foully murdered for the sake of Lady Angela's pearls, which he so foolishly was carrying in his pocket that night. No wonder then, that his sister Marion felt bitter against the people who were the original cause of all these disasters; no wonder that she threw herself heart and soul into the search for evidence against the man whom she sincerely believed to be guilty of a most hideous crime.

"It was mainly due to her that the police came on the track of

William Rugger, the night-watchman, and through the latter that the driver of the taxi-cab was advertised for, because Rugger remembered seeing the gentleman alight from a taxi outside Mexfield House. But Miss Shillington's valuable assistance in the matter of investigation went even further than that. She at last prevailed upon the old man-servant at Mexfield House to come forward like a man and to speak the truth. He was a poor creature, not really old, probably not more than fifty, but timid and almost abject. He had at first declined to make any statement whatever, declaring that he had nothing to say.

"To every question put to him by the police he gave the one answer, 'I saw nothing, sir, I 'eard nothing. I went to bed as usual on the Friday night. The captain 'e never expected me to sit up for 'im when 'e out to parties, and I never 'ear 'im come in, as I sleep at top of the 'ouse. No, sir, I didn't 'ear nothing that night. The last I seed of the captain was at nine o'clock when 'e got into the car and said goodnight to me.' When he was shown the bloodstained hat, he burst out crying and said, 'Yes, sir! Yes, sir! That is the captain's 'at. My Lord! What 'as come of 'im?' He also failed to identify the scarf as being his master's property.

"Then one day Miss Shillington, still suffering from a cold in the head, but otherwise very business-like and brisk, arrived at Scotland Yard with the man—James Rose was his name—in tow. By what means she had persuaded him to speak the truth at last no one ever knew, but in a tremulous voice and shaken with nervousness, he did tell what he swore to be the truth. 'I must 'ave dropped to sleep in the dining-room,' he said. 'I was very tired that evening, and I remember after I 'ad cleared supper away I just felt as 'ow I couldn't stand on my legs any longer, and I sat down in an armchair and must 'ave dozed off.

"'What woke me was the front door bell which rings in the 'all as well as in the basement. I looked at the clock, it was past midnight. Captain forgot 'is key, that's what I thought. Lucky I 'adn't gone to bed, or I should never 'ave 'eard 'im. Funny 'is forgetting 'is key, I thought. Never done such a thing before, I thought, and went to open the door for 'im. But it wasn't the captain,' Rose went on, his voice getting more and more husky as no doubt he realised the deadly im-portance of what he was about to say. 'No, it wasn't the captain,' he reiterated, and shook his head in a doleful manner.

"'Who was it?' the inspector demanded.

"'The young gentleman who sometimes came to the 'ouse,' Rose repeated under his breath. "Mr. 'Enery Buckley it was, sir. Yes, Mr.

'Enery, that's 'oo it was.'

"'What did he say?' Rose was asked.

"''E asked if the captain was in, and I said no, not as I knew, but I would go and see. So up I went to the captain's room and saw 'e wasn't there. Not yet. And I told Mr. 'Enery so when I came down again.'

"'Then what happened?'

"'Mr. 'Enery 'e told me that 'e wouldn't wait and that I was to tell the captain 'e 'ad called, and that 'e would call again in 'arf an hour. I said that I was going to bed and I wouldn't probably see the captain. 'E might be ever so late. Then Mr 'Enery 'e just said, "Very good," and "Never mind," and "Goodnight, Rose," 'e said, and then I let 'im out.'

"'Well, and what happened after that?'

"'I don't know, sir,' the old man concluded. 'I went to bed and I never seed the captain again, nor yet Mr. 'Enery—not from that day to this, sir. No, not again sir.' And Rose once more shook his head in the same doleful manner. Of course, the police were very down on him for keeping back this valuable piece of information, and they were even inclined to look with suspicion upon the man. They wanted to know something about his antecedents, and why he seemed so frightened of facing the police authorities. Fortunately for him, however. Miss Shillington could give them all the information they wanted. She said that James Rose had been for years in the service of a Mrs. O'Shea who was a great friend of Mrs. Shillington's.

"When Mrs. O'Shea died she left him a hundred pounds. But the poor thing had never been very strong and he was nothing to look at, he couldn't get another place, and the hundred pounds vanished bit by bit. About a month ago Mrs. Shillington, who was requiring a manservant, advertised for one in the *Daily Mail*. Rose answered the advertisement and though the poor thing in the meanwhile had gone terribly downhill physically, Mrs Shillington, who remembered how honest and respectable he had always been when he was in Mrs. O'Shea's service, engaged him out of compassion for the sake of old times. Miss Shillington gave him a excellent character and the police were satisfied.

"I think," the old Man in the Corner said, amorously contemplating a marvellously intricate knot which he had had just made in his bit of string, "I think that the police were mainly satisfied because at last they felt that 'they had made out a case.' From that moment the detectives and inspectors in charge became absolutely convinced that Henry Buckley had enticed Captain Denver Shillington to some place of ill fame close to the river and there, in collusion probably with other disreputable characters, had robbed and murdered him. To say the least, the case looked black enough against Buckley.

"His fast living, his mountain of debt, the absence in him of moral rectitude as proved by his fraudulent bankruptcy, told against him; and now it was definitely proved that he had sought out and actually been in the company of Captain Shillington the night that the latter disappeared. A light grey overcoat similar to the one described by Rugger and the chauffeur as worn by the gentleman who was loafing round Somerset Street was found to be a part of his wardrobe; no one could swear, however, as to the scarf, but it turned out that he never went out in the evening without wearing a large white carnation in his buttonhole.

"The fact that he had not stated from the beginning that he had called at Mexfield House that night, and subsequently met the missing man and walked away with him, naturally told terribly against him. Obviously, the man lost his head. Questioned by the police, he tried at first to deny the whole thing: he declared that the man with the white carnation and the light-coloured scarf was some other man whose name happened to be Henry, and he tried to upset Rose's evidence by declaring that the man lied and that he had never called at Mexfield House that night. But, unfortunately for him, he had taken a taxi from his club to the house, the taxi-driver was found, and the noose was further tightened round the Honourable Henry Buckley's neck.

"In vain did he assert after that that Denver Shillington had told him to call at Mexfield House at a quarter-past midnight on that fatal Friday. He was no longer believed. He admitted that he was in financial difficulties, and that he had spoken about these to Captain Shillington earlier in the evening. He admitted, tardily enough, that he went to Mexfield House hoping that Denver would give him some money in order to wipe out his most pressing debts. When he found that the captain had not yet come home, he left a message with the manservant and thought he would go on to the club for a little while and return later to see Shillington. Unfortunately, he drank rather heavily whilst he was at the club and never thought any more about his money worries or about the captain. In fact, he remembered nothing very clearly beyond the fact that he went home in the small hours and went straight to bed.

"He then went on to say that he woke up the next morning with a splitting headache. It was pouring with rain and London was looking particularly beastly, as he picturesquely termed it. He recollected that his sister Angela had planned to go down with old Square-toes to some friends near Newmarket for the weekend. He, too, had been asked but had declined the invitation, but now he began to wish he hadn't; while he was out of town money-lenders couldn't dun him, and a breath of country air would certainly do him good.

"And he was just cogitating over these matters at eight a.m. on that Saturday morning when his sister Angela came into his room. 'She told me,' he went on, 'that old Square-toes was unable to accompany her to these friends in Cambridgeshire, that she didn't want to go alone, and would I hire a car and drive her down. She offered to pay for the car, and, as the scheme happened to suit me, I agreed. We drove down to Tatchford, and on the Tuesday I had an unpleasant reminder from one of my creditors and thought that I must get back to see what old Square-toes would do for me.

"I got home that same evening, and the next morning early Miss Shillington rang me up and told me over the 'phone that they had heard nothing of Captain Shillington since the previous Friday and that they were getting anxious. And that's all I know." he concluded. 'I swear that I never set eyes on Shillington after he drove off from the Duchess of Flint's with my sister in his car. I did call at Mexfield House, but it was at Shillington's suggestion, but when the man told me that the captain was not yet home, I did not loaf about the street, I went straight back to the club and then home.'

"Of course, all this was very clear and very categorical but there were one or two doubtful points in Buckley's statements, which the police—dead out now to prove him guilty of murder—made the most of. Firstly, there was his former denial on oath that he had not called at Mexfield House that night. It was only when he was confronted with the testimony of the taxi-cab driver that he made the admission. The employees at his club, which, by the way, was in Hanover Square, had seen him come in at about half-past eleven. He went out again twenty minutes later and the hall-porter saw him hail a taxi-cab. He was once more in the club at half past twelve, and it is a significant fact that two of the young members chaffed him subsequently because he had not got the usual white carnation in his buttonhole.

"Then again it was more than strange that on the Friday he was so worried about his debts that he went in the middle of the night to his friend's house in order to try and borrow money from him, and yet when according to his own statements he never even saw his friend, off he went the very next morning to the country, stayed away four days, and on his return did not make any attempt seemingly to see the captain or to ask him for money. Thirdly, it was equally inconceivable that Captain Shillington should have appointed to see Buckley at that hour of the night, however pressed the latter might have been for money. Why should he? The next morning would have done just as well, whether he meant to help him or whether he did not, and, according to the testimony of the night-watchman, William Rugger, when he was accosted by Buckley, he exclaimed in tones of great surprise, 'Good Lord, Henry, what are you doing here?' These are not words which a man would say to a friend whom he had appointed to meet at this very hour.

"However, this portion of the taxi-driver's and Rugger's testimony Buckley still strenuously denied. He could deny the other. He had called at Mexfield House and reluctantly admitted that it had been nothing but 'blue funk' that had prompted him at first to hold his tongue about that and then to deny the fact altogether.

"But, above all, there was yet another fact which to the police was more conclusive, more damning than any other, and that was that on the Wednesday morning the Honourable Henry Buckley had called at Messrs. Foster and Turnbull, the well-known pawnbrokers of Oxford Street, and had pledged a pair of diamond ear-rings and a couple of valuable bracelets there for which he received three hundred and fifty pounds.

"Here again, if Buckley had volunteered this statement, all might have been well, but it was the pawnbrokers who gave information to the police. It turned out that the ear-rings and the two bracelets were the property of his sister, Lady Angela. Buckley declared that she had given them to him and she, very nobly, did her best to corroborate this statement of his, but it had become impossible to believe a word he said. Lady Angela's valiant efforts on his behalf were thought to be unconvincing, and, as a matter of fact, the public has never known from that day to this whether Henry Buckley stole his sister's jewellery or whether she gave them to him voluntarily."

3

"Mind you, there can be no question but that the police acted very injudiciously when they actually preferred a charge of murder against Henry Buckley. There were two such damning flaws in the chain of evidence that had been collected against him that the man ought never to have been arrested. Even the magistrate was of that opinion. As you know, if there is the slightest doubt about such a serious charge, the magistrates will always commit a man for trial and let a jury of twelve men pronounce on the final issue rather than decide such grave matters on their own. But in this case, there were really no proofs. There were deductions; the accused was a young blackguard, a moral coward and a liar. There was the bloodstained scarf, the hat and the white carnation, there was the testimony of the taxi-driver and the night-watchman that Henry Buckley had been in the company of Captain Shillington that night, but there was no proof that he had murdered his friend and stolen the pearls.

"To begin with, if there had been a murder, where was it committed, and what became of Captain Shillington's body? Of course, the police still hope to find traces of it, but, as you know, they have not yet succeeded. Various theories are put forward that Henry Buckley was member of a gang of ruffians with headquarters in some obscure corner of London close to the river, and that he enticed the captain there and murdered him with the help of his criminal associates with whom he probably shared the proceeds of the crime. But over a year has gone by since Shillington disappeared and the police are no nearer finding the body of the missing man.

"The magistrate dismissed the case against Henry Buckley. There was not sufficient evidence to commit him for trial. What told most in his favour in the end was the question of time. He was able to prove that he was at his club in Hanover Square at half-past midnight on the fateful night. Now according to James Rose's testimony, it was after midnight when he, Buckley, called at Mexfield House. Even supposing that Shillington had arrived in the taxi five minutes later, it was inconceivable that a man could entice another to an out-of-the-way part of London, murder him—even if he left others to dispose of the body—and walk back unconcernedly to Hanover Square, all in less than half an hour.

"Nor were the pearls or any large sum of money ever traced to Henry Buckley. He was just as deeply in debt after the disappearance of Captain Shillington as he had been before. Now he has gone on another tour round the world, and the Shillingtons—mother and daughter—have given up all hopes of ever seeing the gallant captain, who was such a model son, again. A little while ago the illustrated papers published photos of the two ladies on board a P. & O steamer bound for Australia, but the public had forgotten all about Lady Angela's pearls and the mysterious white carnation. No one was interested in the old lady with the white hair and stooping figure who was carried on board in a chair, and who obstinately refused to be interviewed by newspaper men eager for copy. The case is relegated, as far as the public is concerned, to the category of undiscovered crimes."

"But," I argued, as the Man in the Corner became silent, absorbed in the untying of an intricate knot which had made a little while ago, "surely the police have found out who the man was who accosted Captain Shillington in Somerset Street that night, the man with the light-coloured scarf which was subsequently found in the river by the side of the missing man's hat, the man who called the captain 'Denver,' and whom the latter called 'Henry' and was so surprised to see. If it was not Henry Buckley, who was it?"

"Ah!" the exasperating creature retorted with a fatuous smile, "who was it? That's just the point—a point just as dark as that a man like Captain Shillington could be enticed at that hour of the night to an out-of-the-way part of London, and at a moment when he had his *fiancée's* jewellery worth twenty-five thousand pounds in his pocket. Don't you think that that point is absolutely inconceivable?"

"Well," I said, "it does seem—"

"Of course, it does," he broke in eagerly. "I ask you: is it likely? At one moment we are told that Captain Shillington was a pattern of all the virtues and that his business acumen and abilities had earned for him not only a fortune but the admiration of all those who knew him; and the very next we are asked to suppose that he would meekly allow a young blackguard whom he knew to be dishonest and unscrupulous to drag him 'reluctantly' to some obscure haunt of a gang of criminals. Surely that should have jumped to the eyes of my sane person who had studied the case."

"I don't suppose," I retorted, "that Captain Shillington allowed Buckley to drag him very far. Most people believed at the time that he was attacked directly he rounded the corner of Somerset Street. There are one or two entrances to mews just about there—"

"Yes," the funny creature rejoined excitedly, "but not one nearer than fifty yards from Mexfield House. And do you think that the immaculate Australian would have walked ten yards at night with young Buckley and with those pearls in his pocket? Why should he? He was outside his own door. Wouldn't he have taken Henry into the house with him if he wished to speak to him? No! No! The whole theory is inconceivable. . . ."

"But Captain Shillington disappeared," I argued, "and so did the pearls, and his hat was found floating in the river, torn and blood-stained. You cannot deny that."

"I certainly cannot deny," he replied, "that a bloodstained hat will float on the water if it is thrown—say from a convenient bridge."

"But the scarf?" I retorted.

"A scarf will obey the same laws of Nature as a hat."

"But surely you are not going to tell me—?"

"What?"

"That the whole thing was a confidence trick, after all?"

"I am certain that it was. A clever one, I'll admit, and even I was puzzled at the time. I couldn't think who 'Henry' could possibly be. It wasn't young Buckley, that was obvious. The alibi was conclusive as to that; the miscreants who had planned to throw dust in the eyes of the police by trying to fasten a hideous crime on that unfortunate young Buckley set their stage rather too elaborately when they devised the trick about the scarf. By identifying the murderer with the wearer of the scarf, they saved Buckley from the gallows; without it, there might have remained some doubt in the minds of some of the jury.

"But, of course, it raised a tremendous puzzle. Who was the 'Henry' of Somerset Street? And was it not a curious coincidence that he should be wearing an overcoat similar to the one habitually worn by Henry Buckley and a white carnation which many friends would at once associate with that unfortunate young man? From the examination of the puzzle to its solution was but a step. I came at once to the conclusion that here was no coincidence but a deliberate attempt to impersonate Henry Buckley, the man most likely in the eyes of the public to waylay, and even murder a man whom he knew to be in possession of valuable jewellery. Such a deliberate attempt, therefore, argued that Captain Shillington himself must have been in it.

'Good Lord, Henry, what in the world are you doing here?' was obviously intended for any passer-by to hear in the same way that the white carnation was intended for any chance passer-by to pick up. Having established the *mise en scène* the two scoundrels walked off, having previously provided themselves with a bloodstained hat which presently Miss Shillington would identify as the property of her brother.

"Miss Shillington?" I broke in eagerly, "then you think that the whole Australian family was in the conspiracy? And what about the man Rose?"

346

"The whole family," he rejoined, "only consisted of two. Man and wife most likely."

"But the man Rose?" I insisted.

"An excellent part, alternately played with remarkable skill by the captain and his female accomplice."

"Do reconstruct the whole thing for me," I pleaded. "I own that I am bewildered."

And from my bag I extracted a brand-new piece of string which I handed to him with an engaging smile. Nothing could have pleased the fatuous creature more. With long, claw-like fingers twiddling the string, he began leisurely:

"Nothing could be more simple. Captain Shillington takes leave of his *fiancée*, having the pearls in his pocket. It is then about half-past eleven. Henry Buckley has gone to his club, Shillington having appointed to see him at Mexfield House soon after midnight. There is, therefore, plenty of time. Shillington hurries home, changes his personality into that of James Rose, as he often has done before, and subsequently interviews Henry Buckley on the doorstep. You can see that, can't you?"

"Easily," I replied.

"Then as soon as he has got rid of Buckley, our friend the captain quits the personality of a snuffy, middle-aged manservant, and becomes himself once more. He goes back to the neighbourhood of Mayfair, hails a taxi and drives to Mexfield House. But in the meanwhile, the female confederate—we'll call her Miss Shillington for convenience sake—in male attire and evening-dress, wearing a light overcoat, a light-coloured scarf and a white carnation in her buttonhole, lounges under a doorway in Somerset Street, waiting to play her part. Now do you see how simple it all is?"

"Perfectly," I admitted. "As you said before, they had provided themselves with a blood-stained hat which presently they threw into the river, together with the scarf; and what happened after that?"

"They walked home quietly and went to bed."

"What? Both of them? . . . But the mother?"

"I don't believe in the mother," he retorted blandly. "Do you?"

"I thought—"

"She takes to her bed—she never sees a doctor—she and her daughter never see anyone—they have no friends—no servants save the man Rose; put two and two together, my dear," the funny old man concluded as he slipped the piece of string in his pocket. "Captain

Shillington was the only one in that house who ever went outside the doors. The mother never did—no one ever saw her—the daughter had a perpetual cold in the head—the man Rose had no one to speak for him, no one to relate his past history, except Miss Shillington. Where is he now? What has become of him? There's nobody to enquire after him, so the police don't trouble. The two Shillingtons—supposed to be mother and daughter—went back to Australia last year, but not the man Rose. Then, where is he? But I say that the two passengers on board that P & O boat were not mother and daughter, but male and female confederates in as fine a bit of rascality as I've ever seen. And the man Rose never existed. He was just a disguise assumed from time to time by Captain Shillington.

"It is not difficult, you know, to assume a personality of that sort. The police inspectors who questioned him had never seen Captain Shillington, and dirt and shabby clothes are very perfect disguises. Now the pair of them are knocking about the world somewhere, they will dispose of the pearls to Continental dealers not over scrupulous where a good bargain can be struck. If you will just think of Captain Shillington impersonating James Rose and a decrepit old woman alternately and of Miss Shillington impersonating Henry Buckley on that one occasion you will see how conclusive are my deductions. I have a snapshot here of the two Australian 'ladies' taken on board the boat. This muffled-up bundle of bonnet and shawl is supposed to be Mrs. Shillington; it might as well be M. Poincare or the *Kaiser*, don't you think?

"And here is a snapshot of James Rose giving evidence in the magistrate's court. Unfortunately, I have no photo of Captain Shillington or I could have shown you just how to trace the personality of the handsome young man about town under that of the snuffy, dirty, ill-kempt, unwashed and badly clothed, stooping figure of an out-at-elbows servant."

He threw a bundle of newspaper cuttings down on the table. I gazed at them still puzzled, but nevertheless convinced that he was right. When I looked up again, I only saw a corner of his shabby checked ulster disappearing through the swing-doors.

The Mystery of the Montmartre Hat

"It was during a foggy, rainy night in November a couple of years ago," the Man in the Corner said to me that day, "that the inhabitants of Wicklow Lane, Southwark, were startled by a terrible row proceeding from one of the houses down the street. There was a lot of shouting and banging, then a couple of pistol shots, after that nothing more. It was then just after midnight. The dwellers in Wicklow Lane are all of them poor, they are all of them worried with the cares of large families, small accommodation, and irregular work, all of which we must take it make for indifference to other people's worries, and, above all, to other people's quarrels.

"Rows were not an unknown occurrence in Wicklow Lane, not always perhaps at dead of night and not necessarily accompanied by pistol shots, but nevertheless sufficiently frequent not to arouse more than passing interest. Half a dozen tousled heads—no more—were thrust out of the windows to ascertain what this particular row was about; but as everything was quiet again, as no police was in sight to whom one might give directions, and the mixture of rain and fog was particularly unpleasant, the tousled heads after a few minutes disappeared again, and once more peace reigned in Wicklow Lane.

"Of course, the next morning the event of the night was mentioned and mildly discussed, both by the men whilst going to their work and by the ladies whilst scrubbing their door steps. Everyone agreed that the pistol shots were fired soon after midnight, but no one seemed to be very clear in which particular house the row had occurred. Two or three of the people who lived in No 11 and No. 15 respectively would have it that it occurred 'next door,' but as the house next door to them both could only be the one between them, namely No. 13, and as No. 13 had been empty for months, this testimony was at first strongly discounted.

"Presently, however, a helmeted and blue-coated representative of the law came striding leisurely down the lane. Within a minute or two he was surrounded by a number of excited ladies, all eager to give him their own version of the affair. You can see him, can't you?" the Man in the Corner went on with a grin, "stalking up the street, his thumbs thrust into his belt, his face wearing that marvellous look of impassivity peculiar to the force, and followed by this retinue of gesticulating ladies, dressed in what they happened to have picked up in neighbouring 'ole clo' shops, and by a sprinkling of callow youths and unkempt, unshaven men.

"You can see him solemnly plying the knocker on the dilapidated front door of No. 13, while for the space of a minute or two the gesticulating ladies, the youths and the men were silent and motionless. But not a sound came in response to the Bobby's vigorous knocking. The house was silent as the grave; just above the front door a weather-worn board, swaying and creaking in the wind, mutely gave it out that the lease of these desirable premises was to be sold and that the key could be had on application to Messrs. J. Whiskin and Sons, of Newnham Road, S.E. The ladies, with cheeks blanched under the grime, looked aghast at one another; the youths tittered nervously, the men swore. No one appeared altogether displeased. Here was a real excitement at last to vary the monotony of life, something that would keep gossip alive at the 'White Lion' for many a day to come.

"The majestic representative of the law then blew his whistle. This broke the spell of silence and voluble tongues started wagging again. Soon the second representative of the law appeared, as ponderous, as impassive as his mate. He was quickly put in possession of all the known and unknown facts connected with the mysterious occurrence. Leaving his mate in charge, he stalked off to get assistance.

"Well, you remember no doubt what happened after that. A police inspector called straightway on Messrs. Whiskin and Sons and elicited from them the information that effectively No. 13 Wicklow Lane was for sale, had been for some time, and that on the previous morning— it was, of course, Thursday—a well-dressed gentleman had called to make enquiries about the house. Young Mr. Whiskin gave him the key and asked him to be sure and return it before 1 pm as the office closed early on Thursdays. Well, the gentleman hadn't come back yet with the key, but Mr. Whiskin was not troubling much about that, there being nothing in the house—nor for a matter of that in the street— likely to tempt a thief.

"Young Mr. Whiskin thought that he would be able to identify the gentleman if he saw him again. He had rather a red face and a thick nose which suggested that he was accustomed to good living, rough ginger-coloured hair, and a straggly ginger beard and walrus moustache, all of which gave him rather a peculiar appearance. He wore a neat brown lounge suit, a light overcoat, and grey Homburg hat, and he was carrying a large parcel under his arm. Mr. Whiskin added that he had never seen the man before or since.

"As soon as these facts became known there was more voluntary information forthcoming. It appears that one or two of the residents in Wicklow Lane remembered seeing a man in light overcoat and soft grey hat, and carrying a parcel under his arm, enter No. 13 with a latch-key. No one had taken 'pertikler notice,' however, chiefly because the occurrence was not an unusual one. Often people would go in to look at the empty house and come out again after inspection.

"Unfortunately, too, because of this there was distinct confusion of evidence, some witnesses declaring that the man carried a large parcel and that he went away again, but not until the evening; others would have it that he had a very small parcel and that he wore a bowler hat; others that the man with the bowler hat was another person altogether and did not call till the evening, whilst this again was contradicted by another witness who said that the man who called in the evening had very conspicuous ginger-coloured hair and beard, but that he certainly wore a bowler hat. And through this mass of conflicting evidence there was always the fact that the fog was very thick that night and that no one therefore was able to swear very positively to anything.

"This, then, being all the information that could be gathered for the moment from the outside, the police next decided to force an entry into the empty house. Its unlucky number justified, as you know, its sinister reputation, because the first sight that greeted the inspector when he entered the front room on the ground floor was the body of a man lying in a pool of blood. At first glance he looked like a foreigner—youngish, and with jet-black hair and moustache. By side of him there was a damp towel, also stained with blood. Closer examination revealed the fact that he was not dead, but he seemed in a dead faint, and the inspector sent one of the men off at once to telephone for the divisional surgeon.

"The wounded man was dressed in a dark suit. He had on a gold watch of foreign make, twenty pounds in notes and some loose silver in his pockets, and a letter addressed to 'Allen Lloyd, Esq.' at an hotel at Boulogne. The letter was a private one relating unimportant family events; it was signed by a Christian name only, and bore a London postmark but no address. The police inspector took charge of the letters and the money, and as the divisional surgeon had now arrived and was busy with the wounded man, he proceeded to examine the premises.

"The houses in Wicklow Lane all have small yards at the back. These yards end in a brick wall, the other side of which there is a railway cutting. It was obvious that No. 13 had been untenanted for some time. The dust of ages lay over window and door frames, over broken mantelpieces and dilapidated stoves. There was not a stick of anything anywhere; even the rubbish in the basement—such as is found in every empty house, residue left over by the last tenant—had been picked over until there was nothing left but dust and a few empty bottles.

"The front room in which the wounded man lay revealed very little. Two bullets were found lodged in one of the walls; one, quite close to the ceiling, suggesting that it had been fired in the air, and the other at a height of seven feet from the ground. The dust on the floor had certainly been disturbed, but by how many pairs of feet it was impossible say. On the other hand, the back room on the same floor had quite a grim tale to tell. It gave on the small backyard with the wall as a background, beyond which was the railway cutting. The window in this room was open.

"In one corner there was an ordinary sink which showed that water had been running from the tap quite recently; there was a small piece of soap in the sink which had also recently been used. On the mantelpiece a small oak-framed mirror was propped up against the wall and beside it on the shelf there was the remnant of a burnt-out candle and a box of matches, half empty. And thrown down on the floor, in a corner of the room, were a black Inverness cape and soft black hat with a very wide brim, such as are usually affected by French students.

"It was, of course, difficult to reconstruct the assault just at present, the wounded man being still in a state of stupor and unable to give any account of himself, but the revolver was found lying at the bottom of the yard close to the end wall.

"In the meanwhile, the divisional surgeon had concluded his examination. He pronounced the wound to have been caused by one of the bullets that had lodged in the wall of the front room. It had been fired at very close range, as the flesh was singed all round the wound. The bullet had gone right through the left deltoid, front to back and slightly upwards, just grazed the top of the shoulder and then lodged in the wall. The surgeon was inclined to think that the wound was self-inflicted, but this theory was thought to be untenable, because if a man was such an obviously poor shot, he would surely have chosen some other way of putting an end to himself, unless, indeed, he was a lunatic, which might account for any incongruity in the known facts, even to the noise—the shouting and the banging—that all the neighbours agreed had preceded the revolver shots.

"But there certainly was one fact which discounted the attempted suicide theory and that was the undoubted presence of another man upon the scene—the man with the ginger hair and the thick nose who had called for the key at Messrs. Whiskin and Sons, and whom several witnesses had actually seen entering the empty house—the man with the parcel. Now no one saw him come out again by the front door. He must have been in the house when the foreigner with the jet-black hair came and joined him, and he must have slipped out later on in the dark, under cover of the fog and rain, either by the front door when nobody happened to be passing by, or over the wall and then by the railway cutting.

"Now what had brought these two men together in an empty house, in one of the worst slums in London? One man was wounded; where was the other? Had the revolver been dropped by one of them in his flight or flung out of the window by a lunatic? Was it attempted suicide by a madman or murder consequent on a quarrel, or blackmail? None of these questions was ever answered, nor was the man with the ginger-coloured hair ever found. There was absolutely no clue by which he might be traced; the earth just swallowed him up as if he had been a spook.

"Nor was the identity of the wounded man ever satisfactorily established. Who he was, where he came from, who were his associates and what were his antecedents, he never revealed. He was detained in hospital for a time as he certainly was suffering from loss of memory. But presently they had to let him go. He had money and he was otherwise perfectly sane, but to every question put to him he only answered 'I don't know! I can't remember!' He spoke English without the slightest trace of foreign accent; all that was foreign about him was his jet-black hair and beard. Nor was the history of the revolver ever traced to its source. Where was it bought? To whom was it sold, and by whom? Nobody ever knew."

"But where did the man go after he left the hospital?" I now asked, seeing that the funny creature looked like curling himself up in his corner and going to sleep. "Surely he was kept under observation when they let him out!"

"Of course, he was," he replied glibly, "and for some time after that."

"Then where did he go," I reiterated impatiently, "when he was discharged from hospital?"

"He asked the way to the nearest public library and went straight there; he looked down the columns of the Morning Post, scribbled a few addresses on a scrap of paper, then took a taxi and drove to one of the private hotels in Mexborough Gate, where he engaged a room, paying a fortnight's board and lodging in advance. Here he lived for some considerable time. He was always plentifully supplied with money, he bought himself clothes and linen, but where he got the money from was never discovered.

"For a time, he was watched both by the police and by amateur detectives eager for copy, but nothing was ever discovered that would clear up the mystery. From time to time letters came for him at the hotel in Mexborough Gate. They were addressed to Allen Lloyd, Esq., which may or may not have been a taken-up name. Presumably these letters contained remittances in cash. They were never traced to their source. Anyway, he always paid his weekly bills at the hotel, but he never spoke to anyone in the place, nor, as far as could be ascertained, did he ever meet anyone or enter any house except the one he lodged in.

"Then one fine day he left the hotel, never to return. He went out one afternoon and nothing has been seen or heard of him from that day to this. The mysterious Mr. Allen Lloyd has disappeared in the whirlpool of London, leaving no trace of his identity. He had paid his bill at the hotel that very day. He left no debts and just a very few personal belongings behind. To all intents and purposes the matter was relegated in the public mind to the category of unsolved and unsolvable mysteries."

2

The Man in the Corner had paused. From the capacious pocket of his tweed ulster, he now extracted a thick piece of string; his claw-like fingers set to work. The problem which the police and public had never been able to solve had, I had no doubt, presented few difficulties to his agile brain.

"Tell me," I suggested.

He went on working away for a little while at an intricate knot, then he said: "If you want to know more, you will have to listen to what will seem to you an irrelevant story."

I professed my willingness to listen to anything he might choose to tell me.

"Very well, then," he said. "Let me take your mind back to that same winter two years ago. Do you remember the extraordinary theft of a valuable collection of gems, the property of Sir James Narford?"

"I do."

"Do you know who Sir James Narford was?"

"I would prefer you to tell me," I replied.

"Sir James Narford," the funny creature went on glibly, "was a young gentleman who had been employed during the war in one of the Government departments; he was the only son of his father who was an impoverished Irish baronet. Soon after the Armistice Sir James went to South America to visit some relations. He must have made a very favourable impression on one of these—an eccentric old cousin who died a very few months later and left to his English relative a marvellous collection of pearls and other gems. Some of these were of priceless value, and as is the way with anything that is out of the common, all sorts of stories grew around the romantic legacy.

"The great worth and marvellous beauty of the jewels were told and retold, with many embellishment no doubt, in the English papers. It was asserted that the Brazilian Government had valued them for probate at a million pounds sterling; that there were diamonds—some still uncut—that would make the Koh-i-noor or the Orloff look like small bits of glass, and so on. I daresay you can remember some of the legends that gathered around Sir James Narford's gems. By the time the lucky owner of the fabulous treasure, who had gone out again to Brazil in order to fetch away his jewels, had returned to England, he was the object of universal interest, and he and his gems were photographed and paragraphed all over the place.

"But as I told you, the recipient of this princely legacy had always been a poor man. We may take it that the payment of legacy duty on forty thousand pounds' worth of gems had impoverished him still further. Busybodies, of course tried to persuade him to sell the gems; he had numberless letters from diamond and pearl merchants, asking for permission to see them with a view to purchase, but, naturally enough, he didn't want to do anything in a hurry; he deposited his treasure at the bank and then thought things over. He didn't want to sell for he was inordinately proud of his new possession and of the notoriety which it had conferred upon him. It was even rumoured that he had received more than one hint from fair lips that if he proposed marriage, the owner of such beautiful jewels would be certain of acceptance.

"I don't know who first suggested the idea to Sir James Narford that he should exhibit the gems for the benefit of disabled soldiers and sailors. It was a splendid idea; 2s. 6d. was to be charged for admission, and, after deducting expenses of rent and attendants, the profits were to go to that very laudable able charity. Suitable premises were secured in Sackville Street. These consisted of a shop with a large plate-glass front and a small room at the back; the entrance was through a front door and passage which were common to the rest of the house, and there were two doors in the passage, one of which gave into the shop and the other into the back room. Sir James spent a little money in getting up the place in modern style and he had some cases made for the display of the gems. The door which gave from the passage into the shop was condemned and a heavy piece of furniture placed against it. The back room was only to be used as an office and ante-room with communicating doors leading into the shop.

"In the daytime the gems were displayed in glass cases ranged right and left of the shop; at night they were locked up in a safe which stood in the middle of the shop, facing the plate-glass window and with a blazing electric light kept on all night, just above the safe. This is a very usual device with jewellers in a smaller way of business. The policeman on night duty can see at once if there is anything wrong.

"Everything being ready. Sir James Narford asked a distinguished lady friend of his to declare the show open, and for the first fortnight—this, I must tell you, was in October—there was a steady stream of visitors, ladies for the most part, who came to gaze on the much-advertised gems. You might wonder what pleasure there could be in looking at things one could never hope to possess, especially at loose gems, however precious, which to my mind only become beautiful when they are mounted and set in artistic designs. However, I do not profess to understand feminine mentality; all I know is that Sir James Narford declared himself on more than one occasion satisfied with the result of his little venture.

"True that after the first fortnight the attendance at the show fell off considerably, and a few people did wonder why Sir James should continue to keep it open for so long. Those who had been most curious to see the gems of fabulous value had flocked in the first few days, after that there was only a very thin sprinkling of people up from the country, or foreigners who paid their 2s. 6d. admission for the sight. But be that as it may, the jewels were certainly getting an additional amount of advertisement, and when presently the owner would put them up for sale, as no doubt he intended to do, they would fetch a higher figure in consequence. In the meantime, Sir James went on living very quietly in a small service flat in George Street, waited on by a faithful servant, a man named Ruggles whom he had known for years.

"Every day he would stroll round to Sackville Street to look at his treasure and to talk to one or two friends. At six o'clock the exhibition would be closed and Sir James would himself deposit all the gems into the safe, lock up the premises, and take the key back with him to his flat. He went out very little in society and only occasionally to his club. His one extravagance appeared to be a mania for travelling in all sorts of out-of-the-way places; he had been seemingly in every corner of Europe—in Czecho-Slovakia and Yugo-Slavia, in Montenegro, Bosnia and Bessarabia. Before this whenever he went off on his travels, he would take his man with him and shut up the flat, but on the occasion which presently arose he left Ruggles in charge of the exhibition in Sackville Street.

"This was early in November, about a fortnight after the opening of the exhibition; and when Sir James had gone it was Ruggles who, every night at six o'clock, put the gems away in the safe and locked up the premises. He then made a point of going for a brisk walk and returned to the flat at about half-past seven, had his supper, read his paper, and then went to bed at about ten o'clock with the keys of the safe and of the Sackville Street premises underneath his pillow.

"One of the staff in the flats at George Street always got his supper ready for him—some cold meat, bread and cheese and half a pint of beer, which the lift-boy invariably fetched for him from the Crown and Sceptre round the corner. He prepared his own breakfast in the morning and his other meals he took in Sackville Street. They were sent in from one of the cheaper restaurants in Piccadilly.

"Every morning the charwoman who cleaned the steps outside the block of flats in George Street would see Ruggles come out of the house and walk away in the direction of Sackville Street. Even on Sundays he would stroll round as far as the shop to see that everything was all right.

"It was on a snowy morning in January that the charwoman failed to see Ruggles at his accustomed time. As the quiet neighbourhood did not as a rule lend itself much to gossip, the present opportunity was not to be missed. The charwoman, on meeting with the lift-boy, imparted to him the priceless news that Mr. Ruggles must either be ill or had gone and overslept himself. Whereupon the lift-boy was ready with the startling information that he had just observed that one of the glass panels in the front door of Sir James Narford's flat was broken. 'The glass wasn't broken in the evening, ten-thirty,' he went on to say, 'when I took a party down who'd been visitin' Miss Jenkins.'

"It seems that Miss Jenkins was maid to a lady who had a flat on the same floor as Sir James Narford. But there was the length of a passage with staircase and lift between the two flats, and neither the lady nor the maid, when spoken to by the lift-boy about the broken glass panel, had heard anything during the night. Now all this seemed very strange, more especially as the morning hours wore on and there was still no sign of Mr. Ruggles. The lift-boy was kept busy for the next hour taking the staff of the service flats up and down in his lift, as everyone wished to have a look at the broken panel and wanted to add their quota of opinion as to what had gone on last night in Sir James Narford's flat.

"At ten o'clock the housekeeper, more responsible or more enterprising than the rest of the staff, resolved to knock at the flat door. No answer came. She then tried to peep through the broken glass panel and to apply her ear to it. For a time all was silence. The charwoman, the lift-boy, the scullery-maid and the head housemaid stood by on the landing, holding their breath. Suddenly they all gave a simultaneous gasp! A groan—distinctly a groan—was heard issuing from inside the flat! The group of watchers looked at one another in dismay. 'What's to be done?' they murmured.

"The lift-boy had the key of the flat, but as the front door was bolted on the inside, the key in itself was no use. The housekeeper, with the air of a general in command about to order a deathly charge, said resolutely, 'I shall force my way in!' And it was the lift-boy who gasped, awe-stricken, 'You kin put your 'and through the broken panel, mum, and pull the bolt.'

"Somehow this bright idea which had occurred to the lift-boy made everyone there feel still more uncomfortable. The housekeeper, who had been so bold a while ago, stammered something about fetching the police, and when at the precise moment the lift-bell rang, the head housemaid declared herself ready to faint. But it was only Sir

James Narford who had rung for the lift from below. He had arrived by the night mail from Paris, and had only his small suit-case with him. The lift-boy had the satisfaction of being the first to impart the exciting news to him. "'E took it badly, 'e did!' was that young gentleman's comment on Sir James's reception of the news.

"Without taking the slightest notice of the group of excited women on the landing, Sir James went straight to his front door, thrust his hand through the broken panel, drew back the inside bolt and stepped into his flat. The next moment the agitated crowd on the landing heard him cry out, 'My God, Ruggles, what has happened?' A feeble voice which was scarcely recognisable as that of Ruggles, was then heard talking in short, jerky sentences, and a few moments later Sir James's voice could be distinctly heard speaking on the telephone.

"'He is telephoning for the police,' the housekeeper solemnly announced to the staff.

"Well," the Man in the Corner continued after a while, "let me shorten my tale by telling you briefly the story which Ruggles told the police. It did not amount to a great deal, but such as it was it revealed a degree of cunning and of daring in the ways of burglary that have seldom been equalled. Ruggles, it seems, had as usual put away the gems in the safe and locked up the premises in Sackville Street and then walked home to the flat, very glad, he declared, that his responsibility would cease before another day went by, as he expected Sir James home from abroad the following morning. He had his supper as usual, but when he settled down to read his paper, he felt so sleepy that he just went and bolted the front door, placed the keys underneath his pillow and went straight to bed.

"He remembered nothing more until he felt himself roughly shaken and heard his master's voice calling to him. It took him some time to collect himself; he felt dazed and his head ached terribly. When Sir James told him that it was past ten o'clock, he could not conceive how he could have overslept himself in this way. Through force of habit, he put his hand under his pillow to grope for the keys. They had gone! Then Sir James telephoned to the police. That was all that Ruggles could say. His condition was pitiable; alternately bemoaning his fate and cursing himself for a fool, he knelt at his master's feet and with hands clasped begged for forgiveness.

"'I'd have done anything in the world for Sir James,' he kept reiterating to the police officer, 'and 'ere I've been the ruin of 'im, just through over-sleepin.'

359

"The police inspector got quite impatient with him, and at one time, I think, he thought that the man was acting a part. But Sir James Narford himself indignantly repudiated any suggestion of the sort. 'I would trust Ruggles,' he said emphatically, 'as I would myself. I have known him for thirty years and he was in my father's service before that. I trust him with my keys, with money, with everything. He would have plenty of opportunity to rob me comfortably if he had a mind. What would a man of his class do with valuable gems?'

"All the same I fancy that the police did not altogether lose sight of the possibility that Ruggles might know something about the affair, but in spite of very clever questioning and cross-questioning, his story never varied even in the minutest detail. All that he added to his original statement that was of any value was the description of a foreign visitor at Sackville Street whom, in his own words, he 'didn't like the looks of.'

"This was a youngish man, with very sallow complexion, jet-black hair and moustache, and wearing a peculiar-looking caped overcoat and black soft hat with a very wide brim, who had remained over half an hour in the shop, apparently deeply interested in the gems. At one time he asked Ruggles whether he might have the glass cases opened so that he could examine the stones and pearls more closely. This request Ruggles very naturally refused. The young man then put a lot of questions to him: 'Where did the gems come from? What was their value? Were they insured? Where were they kept at night? Was the safe burglar-proof or only fire-proof?' and so on.

"It seems that two ladies who were visiting the exhibition at the same time noticed this same young man with the sallow complexion and the jet-black hair. They heard him questioning Ruggles and remarked upon his foreign accent, which was neither Italian nor Spanish; they thought he might be Portuguese. His clothes were certainly very outlandish. The ladies had noticed the caped coat, a kind of black Inverness, and the hat *à la* Montmartre. The presence of this foreigner in the shop in Sackville Street became still more significant later on, when another fact came to light—a fact in connection with the half-pint of beer which the lift-boy from the flats in George Street had fetched as usual on the evening preceding the robbery, from the Crown and Sceptre public-house. A few drops of the beer had remained in the mug beside the remnants of Ruggles' supper. On examination the beer was found to contain chloral.

"The lift-boy at first was probably too scared to throw any light on this circumstance. He had, he declared, fetched the beer as usual from the Crown and Sceptre, taken it up to No. 4, Sir James Narford's flat, and put it upon the table in the sitting-room where Mr. Ruggles' supper was already laid for him. After repeated questions from the police inspector, however, he recollected that on his way from the public-house to the flats, a gentleman accosted him and asked him the way to Regent Street. The boy, holding the mug of beer in one hand, pointed out the way with the other, and probably turned his head in the same direction as he did so. He couldn't say for certain. The gentleman seemed stupid and didn't understand the directions all at once; the boy had to repeat them again and again, and altogether was in conversation with the gentleman quite a while.

"It was dark at the time, but he did see that the gentleman wore a funny sort of coat and a funny hat, and, as the boy picturesquely put it, ''e spoke queer-like, as if 'e wor a Frenchman.' To a lift-boy presumably every foreigner is Frenchman if he be not a German, and though the lad's description of the coat and hat only amounted to his calling them 'funny,' there seemed little doubt but that the man who visited the shop in Sackville Street and the one who accosted the lift-boy in George Street were one and the same. There was also little doubt but that he poured the drug into the mug of beer while the boy's head was turned away. And finally, all doubts were set at rest when the 'funny coat and hat' were discovered tied up in a bundle in the area of an empty house, two doors higher up the street.

"Unfortunately, although these few facts were definitely established, all traces of the man himself vanished after that. How he got into the block of flats could not be ascertained. He might have slipped in after the lift-boy, while the latter went upstairs with the beer, and concealed himself somewhere in the basement. It was impossible to say. The street door was kept open as usual until eleven o'clock, and until that hour the boy was in attendance at the lift; he had been up and down several times, taking up residents or their visitors, and while he ran to fetch the beer one of the maids saw to the lift if the bell rang.

"At eleven o'clock every evening the street door was closed, but not bolted; it was provided with a Yale lock and every resident had one key in case they came in late; the lift was not worked after that hour, but there was a light kept on every landing. These lights the housemaid switched off the first thing every morning when she did the stairs, and, as a matter of fact, she remembered that on that memorable morning the light on the top floor landing—which is the landing outside Sir James Narford's flat—was already switched off when she went to do it.

"And those are all the facts," the Man in the Corner went on slowly, while he paused in his work of fashioning intricate knots in his beloved bit of string, "all the facts that were ever known in connection with the theft of Sir James Narford's gems. Of course, as you may well suppose, not only the official but also the public mind at once flew to the mysterious personage originally found wounded in an empty house in Wicklow Lane.

"There could be no shadow of doubt that this man and the one who visited the shop in Sackville Street, who accosted the lift-boy, drugged Ruggles' beer and robbed him of his keys, were one and the same. There was the black caped coat, the Montmartre hat, the jet-black hair and the foreign look. True, the wounded man of Wicklow Lane spoke English without any foreign accent, but the latter could easily be assumed. Indeed, it all seemed plain sailing, and as soon as the word went round about the robbery in Sackville Street and the description was given of the foreign-looking individual with the jet-black hair, the police thought they had a perfectly clear case.

"A clear case, yes!" the funny creature went on, with a grin, "but not an easy one, because when the police called at the hotel in Mexborough Square, they learned that the mysterious Mr. Allen Lloyd had been gone three days. He paid his bill, he had walked out of the house one dark afternoon and not been seen or heard of since. He went off carrying a paper parcel which no doubt contained the few belongings he had bought of late.

"Of course, he was the thief and a marvellously cunning one. Just think what it meant. It meant, first of all, the presence of mind and daring to accost the lift-boy and engage him in conversation whilst pouring a drug into a mug of beer; then it meant sneaking into the block of flats in George Street, breaking the glass panel of a door, entering the flat, stealing the keys, sneaking out of the building again, going round to Sackville Street, watching until the police on duty had passed by, entering the house, opening the safe, collecting the gems—all in full view of the street, mind you, or in absolute darkness—then relocking the safe and again watching for the opportunity to sneak out of the house until the man on duty was out of sight. Clever? I should think it would have been clever, if it had ever been done!"

"How do you mean, if it had ever been done?" I ejaculated with some impatience. "Whoever the thief was—and suppose that you have your theory—he must have done those things."

"Oh, no, he did not!" the funny creature asserted emphatically, "he merely put all the gems away in his own pocket after the exhibition was closed for the night, instead of locking them up in the safe."

"Then you think it was Ruggles?" I exclaimed.

"In conjunction with his master."

"Sir James Narford? But why?"

"For the sake of the insurance money."

"But man alive!" I ejaculated, "that was the tragedy of the whole thing. I remember reading about it at the time. I suppose that it was either out of meanness or because he had so little ready money, but Sir James Narford had only insured his treasure for £20,000, whereas the jewels—"

"Were not worth a penny more than that," the Man in the Corner broke in with his bland smile. "The public may have been bamboozled with tales of fabulous value—nowadays people talk as glibly of millions as the past generation did of thousands—but insurance companies don't usually listen to fairy tales."

"But even so," I argued, "the jewels must have been worth more than the insurance after all the advertisement they got. Why shouldn't Sir James have sold them, rather than take the risk of stealing them?"

"But, my dear young lady," he retorted, "can't you see that the jewels can still be sold and that they will be—abroad—presently—one by one? Twenty thousand pounds insurance money is good, but you double the amount and it is better."

"But what about the wounded man in Wicklow Lane?" I asked.

"A red herring across the trail," he replied, with a smile, "only with this difference, that it was dragged across before the hounds were on the scent. And that is where the immense cleverness of the man comes in. To create a personality on whom to draw suspicion of a crime and then make that personality disappear before the crime is committed, is as clever a bit of rascality as I have ever seen. It needed absolute coolness and a knowledge of facial make-up, in both of which we must take it Sir James Narford was a past-master. Think then how easy everything else would be for him.

"Just let me reconstruct the whole thing for you from beginning to end, that is, from the moment when Sir James Narford first conceived the idea of doubling the value of his gems, and took his man Ruggles as partner in that fine piece of rascality. He couldn't have done it without a partner, of course, and probably this was not the first villainy those two scoundrels carried through together. Well then, Narford, having given instructions to Ruggles and arranged certain matters of detail with him, begins his campaign by ostensibly starting on a journey. He crossed over to France probably and then back to England. It is easy enough for a man to disappear in crowded trains or railway stations if there is no one on his track; easy enough for him to stay in one hotel after another in any big town if he chooses hotels whose proprietors have reason to dread the police and will not volunteer information if any of their visitors are 'wanted.'

"A month only of such wanderings and Sir James Narford, habitually a very dapper man with sleek, sandy hair cropped very close, a tiny tooth-brush moustache and shaven cheeks and chin, can easily be transformed into one with shaggy hair and beard and walrus moustache. Add to this a nose built out with grease-paint and highly-coloured, and cheeks stained a dull red, and you have the man who called for the key of that empty house at Messrs. Whiskin and Sons, with a parcel under his arm which contained the black cape and Montmartre hat purchased abroad at some time previously, during the course of his wanderings. That's simple, is it not?" the funny creature continued, while his thin, claw-like fingers worked away feverishly at his piece of string.

"Now, all that our rascal wants is to change his clothes and his face; so, late that evening, by preconcerted plan, Ruggles meets him at the empty house under cover of the fog. Here he and his precious master change clothes with one another. Narford then completes his toilet by applying to his shaggy hair and beard one of those modern dyes that are so much advertised for the use of ladies desiring to possess raven locks. And so, we have the explanation of all the conflicting evidence of the witnesses who saw a man with a parcel and yet were so much at variance both as to the time when they saw him, as to his appearance, and even as to the size of the parcel.

"Having thus created the personality of a foreign-looking individual in black clothes, you will easily see how important it was for the general scheme that the comedy of the row and the pistol shots in the empty house should be enacted. Attention had to be drawn to the created personage, attention coupled with mystery, and at this stage of the scheme there was not the slightest danger of the wounded man in Wicklow Lane being in any way connected with Sir James Narford of George Street, Mayfair. Time was no object.

"The mysterious Allen Lloyd of Wicklow Lane might be detained days, weeks, even months, but he would have to be let out some time or other. He was perfectly harmless apparently, and otherwise sane; he could not be kept for ever at the country's expense. He was eventually discharged, went to an hotel and lived there quietly a while longer until he thought that the time was ripe for complete disappearance.

"In the meanwhile, we must suppose that he was in touch with Ruggles. Ruggles made a point of taking a brisk walk every evening. Well, winter evenings are dark and London is a very crowded place. Ruggles would bring what money was required. What more easy than to meet in a crowd?

"Then at last the two rascals thought that the time was ripe. The mysterious Mr. Allen Lloyd disappeared from the hotel in Mexborough Gate; he went to Sackville Street where he shaved off his shaggy moustache and beard and cut his hair once more so close that nothing of the dyed ends could be seen. He changed into his own clothes which Ruggles kept there ready for him. Then he slipped round to Victoria Station and crossed over to France, only in order to return to England openly this time as Sir James Narford, and just in time to find Ruggles just aroused from a drugged sleep and the whole flat seething with excitement. But it was he who in black cape and Montmartre hat visited the shop in Sackville Street, it was Ruggles who the following night spoke to the lift boy, even while Narford was procuring for himself a perfect alibi by crossing over quite openly from France.

"Ruggles' task was, of course, much easier. All he had to do was to put the gems in his pocket and these Narford took over from him in the morning at the flat before he telephoned for the police. To put on the black cape and hat and to accost the lift-boy was easy enough on a dark, snowy night in January. And now all the excitement has died down. The whole thing was so cleverly planned that the real rascal was never suspected. Ruggles may have been but nothing could really be brought up against him. The gems haven't been found and to all appearances he has not benefited by the robbery. He is just the faithful, trusted servant of his master.

"Sir James Narford has got his money from the Insurance Company and since then has left for abroad. By the way," the Man in the Corner concluded, as he gathered up his precious bit of string and slipped it in the pocket of his ulster, "I heard recently that he has bought some property in Argentina and has settled down there permanently with his friend Ruggles. I think he was wise to do that, and if you care to publish my version of that mysterious affair, you are at liberty to do so. I don't think that our friend would sue you for defamation of character, and, anyway, I'll undertake to pay damages if the case comes into court."

The Miser of Maida Vale

"One of the most puzzling cases I ever remember watching," the Man in the Corner said to me that day, "was the one known to the public as that of 'The Miser of Maida Vale.' It presented certain altogether novel features, and for once I was willing to admit that, though the police had a very hard nut to crack in the elucidation of the mystery, and in the end failed to find a solution, they were at one time very near putting their finger on the key of the puzzle. If they had only possessed some of that instinct for true facts with which Nature did so kindly endow me, there is no doubt that they would have brought that clever criminal to book."

I wish it were in my power to convey something of that air of ludicrous complacency with which he said this. I could almost hear him purring to himself, like a lean, shabby old cat. He had his inevitable bit of string in his hand and had been in rapturous contemplation of a series of knots which he had been fashioning until the moment when I sat down beside him and he began to speak. But as soon as he embarked upon his beloved topic, he turned his rapturous contemplation on himself. He just sat there and admired himself, and now and again blinked at me, with such an air of self-satisfaction that I longed to say something terribly rude first and then to flounce out of the place, leaving him to admire himself at his leisure.

But, of course, this could not be. To use the funny creature's own verbiage, Nature had endowed me with the journalistic instinct. I had to listen to him; I had to pick his brains and to get copy out of him. The irresistible desire to learn something new, something that would thrill my editor as well as my public compelled me to swallow my impatience, to smile at him—somewhat wryly perhaps—and then to beg him to proceed.

I was all attention.

"Well," he said, still wearing an irritating air of condescension, "do you remember the case of the old miser of Maida Vale?"

"Only vaguely," I was willing to admit.

"It presented some very interesting features," he went on blandly, "and, assuming that you really only remember them vaguely, I will put them before you as clearly as possible, in order that you may follow my argument more easily later on.

"The victim of the mysterious tragedy was, as no doubt you remember, an eccentric old invalid named Thornton Ashley, the well-known naval constructor, who had made a considerable fortune during the war and then retired, chiefly, it was said, owing to ill-health. He had two sons, one of whom, Charles, was a misshapen, undersized creature, singularly unprepossessing both in appearance and in manner, whilst the other, Philip, was a tall, good-looking fellow, very agreeable and popular wherever he went.

"Both these young men were bachelors, a fact which, it appears, had been for some time a bone of contention between them and their father. Old Ashley was passionately fond of children and the only desire of his declining years was to see the grandchildren who would ultimately enjoy the fortune which he had accumulated. Whilst he was ready to admit that Charles, with his many afflictions, did not stand much chance with the fair sex, there was no reason at all why Philip should not, marry, and there had been more than one heated quarrel between father and son on that one subject.

"So much so, indeed, that presently Philip cut his stick and went to live in rooms in Jermyn Street. He had a few hundreds a year of his own, left to him by a godmother. He had been to Rugby and to Cambridge and had been a temporary officer in the war; pending his obtaining some kind of job he settled down to live the life of a smart young bachelor in town, whilst his brother Charles was left to look after the old man, who became more and more eccentric as his health gradually broke up.

"He sold his fine house in Hyde Park Gardens, his motor and the bulk of his furniture, and moved into a cheap flat in Maida Vale, where he promptly took to his bed, which he never left again. His eccentricities became more and more pronounced and his temper more and more irascible. He took a violent dislike to strangers, refused to see anybody except his sons and two old friends, Mr. Oldwall, the well-known solicitor, and Dr. Fanshawe-Bigg, who visited him from time to time, and whose orders he obstinately refused to obey. Worst of all, as far as the unfortunate Charles was concerned, he became desperately mean, denying himself (and, incidentally, his son) every luxury, subsisting on the barest necessities, and keeping no servant to wait on him except a daily 'char.'

"Soon his miserliness degenerated into a regular mania.

"'Charles and I are saving money for the grandchildren you are going to give me one day,' he would say with a chuckle whenever Philip tried to reason with him on the subject of this self-denying ordinance. 'When you have an establishment of your own, you can invite us to come and live with you. There will be plenty then for housekeeping, I promise you!'

"At which the handsome Philip would laugh and shrug his shoulders and go back to his comfortable rooms in Jermyn Street. But no one knew what Charles thought about it all. To an outsider his case must always have appeared singularly pathetic. He had no money of his own and his delicate health had made it impossible for him to take up any profession: he could not cut his stick like his brother Philip had done, but truth to tell, he did not appear to wish to do so. Perhaps it was real fondness for his father that made him seem contented with his lot. Certain it is that as time went on, he became a regular slave to the old man, waiting on him hand and foot, more hard-worked than the daily 'char,' who put on her bonnet and walked out of the flat every day at six o'clock when her work was done, and who had all her Sundays to herself.

"All the relaxation that Charles ever had were alternate weekends, when his brother Philip would come over and spend Saturday to Monday in the flat, taking charge of the invalid. On those occasions Charles would get on an old bicycle, and with just a few shillings in his pocket which he had saved during the past fortnight out of the meagre housekeeping allowance which he handled, he would go off for the day somewhere into the country, nobody ever knew where. Then on Monday morning he would return to the flat in Maida Vale, ready to take up his slave's yoke, to all appearance with a light heart.

"'Charles Ashley is wise,' the gossiping acquaintances would say, 'he sticks to the old miser. Thornton Ashley can't live for ever, and Oldwall says that he is worth close a quarter of a million.'

"Philip, on the other hand, could have had no illusions with regard to his father's testamentary intentions. The bone of contention—Philip's celibacy—was still there, making bad blood between father and son; more than once the old miser had said to him with a sardonic grin: 'Let me see you married soon, my boy, and with a growing family around you, or I tell you that my money shall go to that fool Charles, or to the founding of an orphan asylum or the establishment of a matrimonial agency.'"

"Mr. Oldwall the solicitor, a very old friend of the Ashleys, and who had seen the two boys grow up, threw out as broad a hint to Philip on that same subject as professional honour allowed.

"'Your father,' he said to him one day, 'has got that mania for saving money, but otherwise he is perfectly sane you know. He'll never forgive you if you don't gratify his wish to see you married. Hang it all, man, there are plenty of nice girls about. And what on earth would poor old Charles do with a quarter of a million, I'd like to know.'

"But for a long time, Philip remained obstinate and his friends knew well enough the cause of this obstinacy; it had its root in a pre-war romance. Philip Ashley had been in love—some say that he had actually been engaged to her—with a beautiful girl, Muriel Balleine, the daughter of the eminent surgeon, Sir Arnold Balleine. The two young people were thought to be devoted to one another. But the lovely Muriel had, as it turned out, another admirer in Sir Wilfred Peet-Jackson, the wealthy ship-owner, who worshipped her.

"Philip Ashley and Wilfred Peet-Jackson were great friends; they had been at school and 'Varsity together. In 1915 they both obtained a commission in the Coldstreams and in 1916 Peet-Jackson was very severely wounded. He was sent home to be nursed by the beautiful Muriel in her father's hospital in Grosvenor Square. His case had already been pronounced hopeless, and Sir Arnold himself, as well as other equally eminent surgeons, gave it as their opinion that the unfortunate young man could not live more than a few months—if that.

"We must then take it that pity and romance played their part in the events that ensued. Certain it is that London society was one day thrilled to read in its *Times* that Miss Muriel Balleine had been married the previous morning to Sir Wilfred Peet-Jackson, the wealthy ship-owner and owner of lovely Deverill Castle in Northamptonshire. Her friends at once put it about that Muriel had only yielded to a dying man's wish, and that there was nothing mercenary or calculating in this unexpected marriage; she probably would be a widow within a very short time and free to return to her original love and to marry Philip Ashley.

"But in this case, like in so many others in life, the unexpected occurred. Sir Wilfred Peet-Jackson did not die—not just then. He lived six years after the doctors had said that he must die in six months. He remained an invalid and he and his beautiful wife spent their winters in the Canaries and their summers in Switzerland, but Muriel did not become a widow until 1922, and Philip Ashley all that time never looked at another girl; he was even willing to allow a fortune to slip away from him, because he always hoped that the woman whom he had never ceased to worship would be his wife one day.

"Probably old Ashley knew all that; probably he hated the idea that this one woman should spoil his son's life for always; probably he thought that threat of disinheritance would bring Philip back out of the realms of romance to the realities of life. All this we shall never know. The old man spoke to no one about that, not even to Mr. Oldwall, possibly not even to Charles. By the time that Sir Wilfred Peet-Jackson had died and Philip had announced his engagement to the beautiful widow, Thornton Ashley was practically a dying man. However, he did have the satisfaction before he died of hearing the good news. Philip told him of his engagement one Saturday in May when he came for his usual fortnightly weekend visit.

"Strangely enough although the old man must have been delighted at this tardy realisation of his life's desire, he did not after that make any difference in his mode of life. He remained just as irascible, just as difficult and every bit as mean as he had always been; he never asked to see his future daughter-in-law, whom he had known in the past, though she did come once or twice to see him; nor did he encourage Philip to come and see him any more frequently than he had done before. The only indication he ever gave that he was pleased with the engagement was an obvious impatience to see the wedding-day fixed as soon as possible, and one day he worked himself up into a state of violent passion because Philip told him that Lady Peet-Jackson was bound to let a full year lapse before she married again, out of respect for Wilfred's memory."

2

"Of course, a good deal of gossip was concentrated on all these events. Although Thornton Ashley had, for the past three years, cut himself adrift from all social intercourse, past friends and acquaintances had not altogether forgotten him, whilst Philip Ashley and Lady Peet-Jackson had always been well-known figures in a certain set in London. It was not likely, therefore, that their affairs would not be discussed and commented on at tea-parties and in the clubs. Philip Ashley was exalted to the position of a hero. By his marriage he would at last grasp the fortune which he had so obstinately and romantically evaded: true love was obtaining its just reward, and so on. Lady Peet-Jackson, on the other hand, was not quite so leniently dealt with by the gossips. It was now generally averred that she had originally thrown Philip Ashley over only because Peet-Jackson was a very rich man and had a handle to his name, and that she was only returning to her former love now, because Thornton Ashley had already one foot in the grave and was reputed to be worth a quarter of a million.

"I have a photograph here," the Man in the Corner went on, and threw a bundle of newspaper cuttings down before me, "of Lady Peet-Jackson. As no doubt you will admit, she is very beautiful, but the face is hard; looking at it one feels instinctively that she is not a woman who would stand by a man in case of trouble or disgrace. But it is difficult to judge from these smudgy reproductions, and there is no doubt that Philip Ashley was madly in love with her. That she had enemies, especially amongst those of her own sex, was only natural in view of the fact that she was exceptionally beautiful, had made one brilliant marriage and was on the point of making another.

"But the two romantic lovers were not the sole food of the gossip-mongers. There was the position of Charles Ashley to be discussed and talked over. What was going to become of him? How would he take this change in his fortune? If rumour, chiefly based on Mr. Oldwall's indiscretions, was correct, he would be losing that reputed quarter of a million if Philip's marriage came off. But in this case gossip had to rest satisfied with conjectures. No one ever saw Charles, and Philip, when questioned about him, had apparently very little to say.

"'Charles is a queer fish,' he would reply. 'I don't profess to know what goes on inside him. He seems delighted at the prospect of my marriage, but he doesn't say much. He is very shy and very sensitive about his deformity, and he won't see anyone now, not even Muriel.'

"And thus, the stage was set," the funny creature continued with a fatuous grin," for the mysterious tragedy which has puzzled the public and the police as much as the friends of the chief actors in the drama. It was set for the scene of Philip Ashley's marriage to Muriel Lady Peet-Jackson, which was to take place very quietly at St. Saviour's, Warwick Road, early in the following year.

"On August 27th old Thornton Ashley died, that is to say he was found dead in his bed by his son Charles, who had returned that morning from his fortnightly weekend holiday. The cause of death was not in question at first; though Dr. Fanshawe-Bigg was out of town at the moment, his locum tenens knew all about the case, and had seen the invalid on the Thursday preceding his death. In accordance with the amazing laws of this country, he gave the necessary certificate without taking a last look at the dead man, and Thornton Ashley would no doubt have been buried then and there without either fuss or ceremony, but for the amazing events which thereupon followed one another in quick succession.

"The funeral had been fixed for Thursday the 30th, but within twenty-four hours of the old miser's death it had already transpired that he had indeed left a considerable fortune which included one or two substantial life insurances, and that the provisions of his will were very much as Philip Ashley and his friends had surmised. After sundry legacies to various charitable institutions concerned with the care of children, Thornton Ashley had left the residue of his personality to whichever of his sons was first married within a year from the time of the testator's death, the other son receiving an annuity of three hundred pounds.

"This clearly was aimed at Philip as poor misshapen Charles had always been thought to be out of the running. Moreover, a further clause in the will directed that in the event of both the testator's sons beings still unmarried within that given time, then the whole of the residue was to go to Charles, with an annuity of one hundred pounds to Philip and a sum of ten thousand pounds for the endowment of an orphan asylum at the discretion of the Charity Organisation Society.

"There were a few conjectures as to whether Charles Ashley, who, by his brother's impending marriage, would be left with a paltry three hundred pounds a year, would contest his father's will on the grounds of *non-compos mentis*, but, you know, it is always very difficult in this country to upset a will, and the provisions of this particular one were so entirely in accord with the wishes expressed by the deceased on every possible occasion, that the plea that he was of unsound mind when he made it would never have been upheld, quite apart from the fact that Mr. Oldwall, who drew up the will and signed it as one of the witnesses, would have repudiated any suggestion that his client was anything but absolutely sane at the time.

"Everything then appeared quite smooth and above board when suddenly, like a bolt from the blue, came the demand from the Insurance Company in which the late Mr. Thornton Ashley had a life policy for forty thousand pounds for a postmortem examination, the company not being satisfied that the deceased had died a natural death.

Naturally, Dr. Percy Jutt, who had signed the death certificate, was furious, but he was overruled by the demands of the Insurance Company, backed by no less a person than Charles Ashley. Indeed, it soon transpired that it was in consequence of certain statements made by Mr. Triscott, a local solicitor, on behalf of Charles Ashley to the general manager of the company, that the latter took action in the matter.

"Philip Ashley, through his solicitor, Mr. Oldwall, and backed by Dr. Jutt, might perhaps have opposed the proceedings, but quite apart from the fact that opposition from that quarter would have been impolitic, it probably also would have been unsuccessful. Anyway, the sensation-mongers had quite a titbit to offer to the public that afternoon: the evening papers came out before midday with flaring headlines: 'The Mystery Miser of Maida Vale.' Also 'Sensational Developments' and 'Sinister Rumours.'

"By four o'clock in the afternoon some of the papers had it that a postmortem examination of the body of the late Mr. Thornton Ashley had been conducted by Dr. Dawson, the divisional surgeon, and that it had revealed the fact that the old miser had not died a natural death, traces of violence having been discovered on the body. It was understood that the police were already in possession of certain facts and that the coroner of the district would hold an inquest on Thursday the 30th, the very day on which the funeral was to have taken place.

3

"Now I have attended many an inquest in my day," the Man in the Corner continued after a brief pause, during which his claw-like fingers worked away with feverish energy at his bit of string, "but seldom have I been present at a more interesting one. There were so many surprises, such an unexpected turn of events, that one was kept on tenterhooks the whole time as to what would happen next.

"Even to those who were in the know, the witnesses in themselves were a surprise. Of course, everyone knew Mr. Oldwall, the solicitor and life-long friend of old Thornton Ashley, and the divisional surgeon, whose evidence would be interesting; then there was poor Charles Ashley and handsome brother, Philip, now the owner of a magnified fortune, whose romantic history had more than once been paragraphed in the Press. But what in the world had Mr. Triscott, a local lawyer whom nobody knew, and Mrs. Trapp, a slatternly old 'char,' to do with the case? And there was also Dr. Percy Jutt who had not come out of the case with flying professional colours, and who must have cursed the day when he undertook the position of locum tenens for Dr. Fanshawe-Bigg.

"The proceedings began with the sensational evidence of Dr. Dawson, the divisional surgeon, who had conducted the post-mortem. He stated that the deceased had been in an advanced state of *uraemia*, but this had not actually been the cause of death. Death was due to heart-failure caused by fright and shock following on violent aggression and an attempt at strangulation. There were marks round the throat, and evidences of a severe blow having been dealt to the face and cranium, causing concussion. In the patient weak state of health, shock and fright had affected the heart's action with fatal results.

"All the while that the divisional surgeon gave evidence, going into technical details which the layman could not understand. Dr. Percy Jutt had obvious difficulty to control himself. He had a fidgety, nervous way with him and was constantly biting his nails. When he, in his turn, entered the witness-box, he was as white as a sheet and tried to hide his nervousness behind a dictatorial, blustering manner. In answer to the coroner, he explained that he had been acting as locum tenens for Dr. Fanshawe-Bigg who was away on holiday. He had visited the deceased once or twice during the past fortnight, and had last seen him on the Thursday preceding his death. Dr. Fanshawe-Bigg had left him a few notes on the case.

"'I found,' he went on to explain, 'the deceased in an advanced stage of *uraemia*, and there was very little that I could do, more especially as I was made to understand that my visits were not particularly wanted. On the Thursday deceased was in a very drowsy state, this being one of the best-known symptoms of the disease, and I didn't think that he could live much longer. I told Mr. Charles Ashley so; at the same time, I did not think that the end would come quite so soon.

"'However, I was not particularly surprised when on the Monday morning I received a visit from Mr. Charles Ashley who told me that his father was dead. I found him very difficult to understand,' Dr. Jutt continued in reply to a question from the coroner, 'emotion had, I thought, addled his speech a little. He may have tried to tell me something in connection with his father's death, but I was so rushed with work that morning, and, as I say, I was fully prepared for the event, that all I could do was to promise to come round sometime during the day, and, in the meanwhile, in order to facilitate arrangements for the funeral, I gave the necessary certificate. I was entirely within my rights,' he concluded, with somewhat aggressive emphasis, and, as far as I can recollect, Mr. Charles Ashley said nothing that in any way led me to think that there was anything wrong.'

"Mr. Oldwall, the solicitor, was the next witness called, and his testimony was unimportant to the main issue. He had drafted the late Mr. Thornton Ashley's will in 1919, and had last seen him alive before starting on a short holiday sometime in June. Deceased had just heard then of his son's engagement and witness thought him looking wonderfully better and brighter than he had been for a long time.

"'Mr. Ashley,' the coroner asked, 'didn't say anything to you then about any alteration to his will?'

"'Most emphatically, no!' the witness replied.

"'Or at any time?'

"'At no time,' Mr. Oldwall asserted.

"These questions put by the coroner in quick succession had, figuratively speaking, made everyone sit up. Up to now the general public had not been greatly interested; one had made up one's mind that the old miser had kept certain sums of money, after the fashion of his kind, underneath his mattress; that some evildoer had got wind of this and entered the flat when no one was about, giving poor Thornton Ashley a fright that had cost him his life.

"But with this reference to some possible alteration in the will the case at once appeared more interesting. Suddenly one felt on the alert, excitement was in the air, and when the next witness, a middle-aged, dapper little man, wearing spectacles, a grey suit and white spats, stood up to answer questions put to him by the coroner, a suppressed gasp of anticipatory delight went round the circle of spectators.

"The witness gave his name as James Triscott, solicitor of Warwick Avenue. He said that he had known the deceased slightly, having seen him on business in connection with the lease of 73, Malvine Mansions, the landlord being a client of his. On the previous Friday, that is, the 24th, witness received a note written in a crabbed hand and signed 'A. Thornton Ashley,' asking him to call at Malvine Mansion any time during the day. This Mr. Triscott did that same afternoon. The door was opened by Mr. Charles Ashley whom he had also met once or twice before, who showed him into the room where the deceased lay in bed, obviously very ill but perfectly conscious and reasonable.

"'After some preliminary talk,' the witness went on, 'the deceased explained to me that he was troubled in his mind about a will which he had made some four years previously, and which had struck him of late as being both harsh and unjust. He desired to make a new will, revoking the previous one. I naturally told him that I was entirely at his service, and he then dictated his wishes to me. I made notes and promised to have the will ready for his signature by Monday. The thought of this delay annoyed him considerably, and he pressed me hard to have everything ready for him by the next day. Unfortunately, I couldn't do that. I was obliged to go off into the country that evening on business for another client, and couldn't possibly be back before midday Saturday, when my clerk and typist would both be gone. All I could do was to promise faithfully to call again on Monday at eleven o'clock with the will quite ready for signature. I said I would bring my clerk with me, who could then sign as a witness.

"'I quite saw the urgency of the business,' Mr. Triscott, went on in his brisk, rather consequential way, 'as the poor old gentleman certainly looked very ill. Before I left, he asked me to let him at least have a copy of my notes before I went away this evening. This I was able to promise him. I got my clerk to copy the notes and to take them round to the flat later on in the day.'

"I can assure you," the Man in the Corner said, "that while that dapper little man was talking, you might have heard the proverbial pin drop amongst the public. You see, this was the first that anyone had ever heard of any alteration in old Ashley's will, and Mr. Triscott's evidence opened up a vista of exciting situations that was positively dazzling. When he ceased speaking, you might almost have heard the sensation-mongers licking their chops like a lot of cats after a first bite at a succulent meal; glances were exchanged, but not a word spoken, and presently a sigh of eagerness went round when the coroner put the question which everyone had been anticipating:

"'Have you got the notes, Mr. Triscott, which you took from the late Mr. Thornton Ashley's dictation?'

"At which suggestion Mr. Oldwall jumped up, objecting that such evidence was inadmissible. There was some legal argument between him and the coroner, during which Mr. Triscott, still standing in the witness-box, beamed at his colleague and at the public generally through his spectacles. In the end the jury decided the point by insisting on having the notes read out to them.

"Briefly, by the provisions of the new will, which was destined never to be signed, the miser left his entire fortune with the exception of the same trifling legacies and of an annuity of a thousand pounds a year to Philip, to his son Charles absolutely, in grateful recognition for years of unflagging devotion to an eccentric and crabbed invalid.

Mr. Triscott explained that on the Monday morning he had the document quite ready by eleven o'clock and that he walked round with it to Malvine Mansions, accompanied by his clerk. Great was his distress when he was met at the door by Charles Ashley, who told him that old Mr. Thornton Ashley was dead.

"That was the substance of Mr. Triscott's evidence, and I can assure you that even I was surprised at the turn which events had taken. You know what the sensation-mongers are; within an hour of the completion of Mr. Triscott's evidence it was all over London that Mr. Philip Ashley had murdered his father in order to prevent his signing a will that would deprive him—Philip—of a fortune. That is the way of the world," the funny creature added with a cynical smile. "Philip's popularity went down like a sail when the wind suddenly drops, and in a moment public sympathy was all on the side of Charles who had been done out of a fortune by a grasping and unscrupulous brother.

"But there was more to come.

"The next witness called was Mrs. Triscott, the wife of the dapper little solicitor, and her presence here in connection with the death of old Thornton Ashley seemed as surprising at first as that of her husband had been. She looked a hard, rather common, but capable woman, and after she had replied to the coroner's preliminary questions, she plunged into her story in a quiet, self-assured manner. She began explaining that she was a trained nurse, but had given up her profession since her marriage. Now and again, however, either in an emergency or to oblige a friend, she had taken care of a patient.

"'On Friday evening last,' she continued, 'Mr. Triscott, who was just going off into the country, on business, said to me that he had a client in the neighbourhood who was very ill, and about whom, for certain reasons, he felt rather anxious. He went on to say that he was chiefly sorry for the son, a delicate man, who was sadly deformed. Would I, like a good Samaritan, go and look after the sick man during the week end? It seems that the doctor had ordered absolute rest, and Mr. Triscott feared that there might be some trouble with another son because, as a matter of fact, the old man had decided to alter his will.

"'I knew nothing about Mr. Thornton Ashley's family affairs,' the witness said, in reply to a question put to her the coroner, and calmly ignoring the sensation which her statement was causing, 'beyond what I have just told that Mr. Triscott said to me, but I agreed to go to Malvine Mansions and see if I could be of any use. I arrived at the flat on Friday evening and saw at once what the invalid was suffering from. I had nursed cases of *uraemia* before, and I could see that the poor old man had not many more days to live. Still, I did not think that the end was imminent. Mr. Charles Ashley, who had welcomed me most effusively, looked to need careful nursing almost as much as his father did. He told me that he had not slept for three nights, so I just packed him off to bed and spent the night in an armchair in the patient's room.

"'The next morning Mr. Philip Ashley arrived and I was told of the arrangement whereby Mr. Charles got a weekend holiday once a fortnight. welcomed the idea for his sake, and as he seemed very anxious about his father, and remembering what my husband had told me, I promised that I would stay on in the flat until his return on the Monday. Thus, only was I able to persuade him to go off on his much needed holiday. Directly he had gone, however, I thought it my duty to explain to Mr. Philip Ashley that really his father was very ill. He was only conscious intermittently and that in such cases the only thing that could be done was to keep the patient absolutely quiet. It was the only way, I added, to prolong life and to ensure a painless and peaceful death.

"'Mr. Philip Ashley,' the witness continued, 'appeared more annoyed than distressed when I told him this, and asked me by whose authority I was here, keeping him out of his father's room, and so on. He also asked me several peremptory questions as to who had visited his father lately, and when I told him that I was the wife of a well-known solicitor in the neighbourhood, he looked for a moment as if he would give way to a violent fit of rage. However, I suppose he thought better of it, and presently I took him into the patient's room, who was asleep just then, begging him on no account to disturb the sufferer.

"'After he had seen his father, Mr. Ashley appeared more ready to admit that I was acting for the best. However, he asked me—rather rudely, I thought, considering that the patient was nothing to me and I was not getting paid for my services—how long I proposed staying in the flat. I told him that I would wait here until his brother's return, which I was afraid would not be before ten o'clock on Monday morning. Whereupon he picked up his hat, gave me a curt good-day, and walked out of the flat.

"'To my astonishment,' the witness now said, amidst literally breathless silence on the part of the spectators, 'it had only just gone eight on the Monday morning when Mr. Philip Ashley turned up once more. I must say that I was rather pleased to see him. I was expecting Mr. Triscott home and had a lot to do in my own house. The patient, who had rallied wonderfully the last two days, had just gone off into a comfortable sleep, and as I knew that Mr. Charles would be back soon, I felt quite justified in going off duty and leaving Mr. Philip in charge, with strict injunctions that he was on no account to disturb the patient. If he woke, he might be given a little barley-water first and then some beef-tea, all of which I had prepared and put ready. My intention was, directly I got home, to telephone to Dr. Jutt and ask him to look in at Malvine Mansions sometime during the morning. Unfortunately, when I got home, I had such a lot to do, that frankly, I forgot to telephone to the doctor, and before the morning was over, Mr. Triscott had come home with the news that old Mr. Thornton Ashley was dead.

"This," the Man in the Corner continued, "was the gist of Mrs. Triscott's evidence at that memorable inquest. Of course, there were some dramatic incidents during the course of her examination; glances exchanged between Philip Ashley and Mr. Oldwall, and between him and the dapper little Mr. Triscott. The latter, I must tell you, still beamed at everybody; he looked inordinately proud of his capable business-like wife, and very pleased with the prominence which he had attained through this mysterious and intricate case.

4

"The luncheon interval gave us all a respite from tension that had kept our nerves strung up all morning. I don't think that Philip Ashley, for one, ate much lunch that day. I noticed, by the way, that he and Mr. Oldwall went off together, whilst Mr and Mrs. Triscott took kindly charge of poor Charles. I caught sight of the three of them subsequently in a blameless tea-shop. Charles was indeed a pathetic picture to look upon; he looked the sort of man who lives on his nerves, with no flesh on his poor misshapen bones, and a hungry craving expression in his eyes, as in those of an underfed dog.

"We had his evidence directly after luncheon. But, a matter of fact, he had not much to say. He had last seen his father alive on the Saturday morning when he went off on his fortnightly weekend holiday. He had cycled to Dorking and spent his time there at the 'Running Footman,' as he had often done before. He was well known in the place. On Monday morning he made an early start and got to Malvine Mansions soon after ten and let himself into the flat with his latch-key. He expected to find his brother or Mrs. Triscott there, but there was no one. He then went into his father's room, and, at first, thought that the old man was only asleep. The blinds were down and the room very dark.

"He drew up the blind and went back to his father's bedside. Then only did he realise that the old man was dead. Though he was very ignorant in such matters, he thought that there was something strange about the dead man, and he tried to explain this to Dr. Jutt. But the latter seemed too busy to attend to him, so when Mr. Triscott came to call later on, he told him of this strange feeling that troubled him. Mr. Triscott then thought that as Dr. Jutt seemed so indifferent about the matter, it might be best to see the police.

"'But this,' Charles Ashley explained, 'I refused to do, and then Mr. Triscott asked me if I knew whether my dear father had any life insurances, and, if so, in what company. I was able to satisfy him on that point, as I had heard him speak to Mr. Oldwall about a life policy he had in the Empire of India Life Insurance Company. Mr. Triscott then told me to leave the matter to him, which I was only too glad to do.'

"Witness was asked if he knew anything of his father's intentions with regard to altering his will, and to this he gave an emphatic 'No!' He explained that he had taken a note from his father to Mr. Triscott on the Friday and that he had seen Mr. Triscott when the latter called at the flat that afternoon, but when the coroner asked him whether he knew what passed between his father and the lawyer on that occasion, he again gave an emphatic 'No!'

"He had accepted gratefully Mr. Triscott's suggestion that Mrs. Triscott should come over for the weekend to take charge of the invalid, but he declared that this arrangement was in no way a reflection upon his brother. On the whole then, Charles Ashley made a favourable impression upon the public and jury for his clear and straightforward evidence. The only time when he hesitated—and did so very obviously—was when the coroner asked him whether he knew of any recent disagreement between his father and his brother Philip, a disagreement which might have led to Mr. Thornton Ashley's decision to alter his will.

"Charles Ashley did hesitate at this point and, though he was hard-pressed by the coroner, he only gave ambiguous replies, and when he had completed his evidence, he left one under the impression that he might have said something if he would, and that but for his many afflictions the coroner would probably have pressed him much harder.

"This impression was confirmed by the evidence of the next witness, a Mrs. Trapp, who had been the daily char at Malvine Mansions. She began by explaining to the coroner that she had done the work at the flat for the past two years. At first, she used to come every morning for a couple of hours, with the exception of Sundays, but for the last two months or so she came on the Sundays, but stayed away on the Monday; on Wednesdays she stayed the whole day, until about six, as Mr. Charles always did a lot of shopping those afternoons.

"Asked whether she remembered what happened at the flat on the Wednesday preceding Mr. Thornton Ashley's death she said that she did remember quite well. Mr. Philip Ashley called; he did do that sometimes on a Wednesday when his brother was out. He stayed about an hour and, in Mrs. Trapp's picturesque language, he and his father 'carried on awful!'

"'I couldn't 'ear what they said,' Mrs. Trapp explained with eager volubility, 'but I could 'ear the ole gentleman screaming. I 'ad 'eard 'im storm like that at Mr. Philip once before—about a month ago. But Lor' bless you, Mr. Philip 'e didn't seem to care, and on Wednesday when I let 'im out of the flat 'e just looked quite cheerful like. But the ole gentleman 'e was angry. I 'ad to give 'im a nip o' brandy, 'e was sort o' shaken after Mr. Philip went.'

"You see then, don't you?" the Man in the Corner said with a grim chuckle, "how gradually a network of sinister evidence was being woven around Philip Ashley. He himself was conscious of it, and he was conscious also of the wave of hostility that was rising up against him. He looked now, not only grave, but decidedly anxious, and he held his arms tightly crossed over his chest, as if in the act of making a physical effort to keep his nerves under control.

"He gave me the impression of a man who would hate any kind of publicity, and the curious, eager looks that were cast upon him, especially by the women, must have been positive torture to a sensitive man. However, he looked a handsome and manly figure as he stood up to answer the questions put to him by the coroner. He said that he had arrived at the flat on the Saturday at about midday, explaining to the jury that he always came once a fortnight to be with his father, whilst his brother Charles enjoyed a couple of days in the country. On this occasion, however, he was told that his father was too ill to see him.

"Charles, however, went off on his bicycle as usual, but contrary to precedent a lady had apparently been left in charge of the invalid. Witness understood that this was Mrs. Triscott, the wife of a neighbour, who had kindly volunteered to stay over the weekend. She was an experienced nurse and would know what to do in case the patient required anything. For the moment he was asleep and must not be disturbed.

"'I naturally felt very vexed,' the witness continued, 'at being kept out of my father's room, and I may have spoken rather sharply at the moment, but I flatly deny that I was rude to Mrs. Triscott, or that I was in a violent rage. I did get a glimpse of my father as he lay in bed, and I must say that I did not think that he looked any worse than he had been all along. However, I was not going to argue the point. I preferred to wait until the Monday morning when my brother would be home, and I could tackle him on the subject.

"At this point the coroner desired to know why, in that case, when the witness was told that his brother would not be at the flat before ten o'clock, he turned up there as early as half-past eight.

"'Because,' the witness replied, 'I was naturally rather anxious to know how things were, and because I hoped to get a day on the river with a friend, and to make an early start if possible. However, when I got to the flat, Mrs. Triscott wanted to get away, and so I agreed to stay there and wait until ten o'clock, when, so Mrs. Triscott assured me, my brother would certainly be home. As a matter of fact, he always used to get home at that hour with clockwork regularity on the Monday mornings after his holiday.

"'My father was asleep and Mrs. Triscott left me instructions what to do in case he required anything. At half-past nine he woke. I heard him stirring and I went into his room and gave him some barley-water and sat with him for a little while. He seemed quite cheerful and good-tempered and, honestly, I did not think that he was any worse than he had been for weeks. Just before ten o'clock he dropped off to sleep again. I knew that my brother would be in within the next half-hour and, as this would not be the first time that my father was left alone in the flat, I did not think that I should be doing anything wrong by leaving him. I went back to my chambers and was busy making arrangements for the day when I had a telephone message from my brother that our father was dead.'

"Questioned by the coroner as to the disagreement which he had had with his father on the previous Wednesday, Mrs Philip Ashley indignantly repudiated the idea that there was any quarrel.

"'My father,' he said, 'had a very violent temper and a very harsh, penetrating voice. He certainly did get periodically angry with me whenever I explained to him that my marriage to Lady Peet-Jackson could not, in all decency, take place for at least another six months. He would storm and shriek for a little while,' the witness went on, 'but we invariably parted the best of friends.'

The Man in the Corner paused for a little while, leaving me both interested and puzzled. I was trying to piece together what I remembered of the case with what he had just told me, and I was longing to hear his explanation of the events which followed that memorable inquest. After a little while the funny creature resumed:

"I told you," he said, "that a wave of hostility had risen in the public mind against Philip Ashley. It came from a sense of sympathy for the other son, who, deformed and afflicted, had been done out of a fortune. True, that it would not have been of much use to him, and that in the original will ample provision had been made for his modest wants, but it now seemed as if, at the eleventh hour, the old miser had thought to make reparation toward the son who had given up his whole life to him, whilst the other had led one of leisure, independence and gaiety.

"What had caused old Thornton Ashley thus to change his mind was never conclusively proved; there were some rumours already current that Philip Ashley was in debt and had appealed to his father for money, a fatal thing to do with a miser. But this also was never actually proved. The only persons who could have enlightened the jury on the subject were Philip Ashley himself and his brother Charles, but each of them, for reasons of his own, chose to remain silent.

"And now you will no doubt recall the fact which finally determined the jury to bring in their sensational verdict, in consequence of which Philip Ashley was arrested on the coroner's warrant on a charge of attempted murder. It seemed horrible, ununderstandable, unbelievable, but nevertheless a jury of twelve men did arrive at that momentous decision after deliberation lasting less than half an hour.

"What I believe weighed with them in the end was the fact that the assistant who came with the divisional surgeon to conduct the post-mortem found underneath the bed of the deceased a walking-stick with a rather heavy knob, and the crumpled and torn copy of the notes for the new will which Mr. Triscott had prepared. Philip Ashley when confronted with the stick admitted that it was his. He had missed it on the Saturday when he was leaving the flat, as he was under the impression that he had brought one with him; however, he did not want to spend any more time looking for it, as he was obviously so very much in the way.

"Now both the charwoman and Mrs. Triscott swore that the patient's room had been cleaned and tidied on the Sunday, and that there was no sign of a walking-stick in the room then."

"And so," the Man in the Corner went on, with a cynical shrug of his lean shoulders, "Philip Ashley went through the terrible ordeal of being hauled up before the magistrate on the charge of having attempted to murder his father, an old man with one foot in the grave. He pleaded 'Not Guilty' and reserved his defence. The whole of the evidence was gone through all over again, of course, but nothing new had transpired. The case was universally thought to look very black against the accused, and no one was surprised when he was eventually committed for trial.

"Public feeling remained distinctly hostile to him. It was a crime so horrible and so unique you would have thought that no one would have believed that a well-known, well-educated man could possibly have been guilty of it. Probably, if the event had occurred before the war, public opinion would have repudiated the possibility, but so many horrible crimes have occurred in every country these past few years that one was just inclined to shrug one's shoulders and to murmur, 'Perhaps, one never knows!'

"One thing remained beyond a doubt: old Mr. Thornton Ashley died of shock or fright following a violent and dastardly assault, finger-marks were discovered round his throat, and there were evidences on his face and head that he had been repeatedly struck with what might easily have been the walking-stick which was found under his bed. Add to this the weight of evidence of the new will about to be signed, and of the quarrel between father and son on the previous Wednesday, and you have as good a motive for the murder as any prosecuting counsel might wish for. Philip Ashley would not, of course, hang for murder, but it was even betting that he would get twenty years.

"Anyway, I don't think that, as things were, anyone blamed Lady Peet-Jackson for her decision. A week before Philip Ashley's trial came on, she announced her engagement to Lord Francis Firmour, son of the Marquis of Ettridge, whom she subsequently married.

"But Philip Ashley was acquitted—you remember that? He was acquitted because Sir Arthur Inglewood was his counsel, and Sir Arthur is the finest criminal lawyer we possess; and, because the evidence against him was entirely circumstantial, it was demolished by his counsel with masterly skill. Whatever might be said on the subject of motive, there was nothing whatever to prove that the accused knew anything of his father's intentions with regard to a new will; and there was only a charwoman's word to say that Philip had quarrelled with his father on that memorable Wednesday.

"On the other hand, there was Mr. Oldwall and Dr. Fanshawe-Bigg, old friends of the deceased, both swearing positively that Thornton Ashley had a peculiarly shrill and loud voice, that he would often get into passions about nothing at all, when he would scream and storm, and yet mean nothing by it. The only evidence of any tangible value was the walking-stick, but even that was not enough to blast a man's life with such a monstrous suspicion.

"Philip Ashley was acquitted, but there are not many people who followed that case closely who believed him altogether innocent at the time. What Lady Peet-Jackson thought about it no one knows. It was for her sake that the unfortunate man threw up the chances of a fortune, and when it came within his grasp it still seemed destined to evade him in the end. In losing the woman for whom he had been prepared to make so many sacrifices, poor Philip lost the fortune a second time, because, as he was not married within the prescribed time-limit, it was Charles who inherited under the terms of the original will. But I think you will agree with me that any sensitive man is well out of a union with a hard and mercenary woman.

"And now there has been another revolution in the wheel of Fate. Charles Ashley died the other day in a nursing-home of heart-failure following an operation. He died intestate and his brother is his sole heir. Funny, isn't it, that Philip Ashley should get his father's fortune in the end? But Fate does have a way sometimes of dealing out compensations after she has knocked a man about beyond his deserts. Philip Ashley is a rich man now, and there is a rumour, I am told, current in the society papers, that Lady Francis Firmour has filed a petition for divorce, and that the proceedings will be undefended. But can you imagine any man marrying such a woman after all that she made him suffer?'

Then, as the funny creature paused and appeared entirely engrossed in the fashioning of complicated knots in his beloved bit of string, I felt that it was my turn to keep the ball rolling.

"Then you, for one," I said, "are quite convinced that Philip Ashley did not know that his father intended to make a new will, and did not try to murder him?"

"Aren't you?" he retorted.

"Well," I rejoined, somewhat lamely, "someone did assault the old miser, didn't they? If it was not Philip Ashley then it must have been just an ordinary burglar who thought that the old man had some money hidden away under his mattress."

"Can't you theorise more intelligently than that?" the tiresome creature asked, in his very rude and cynical manner. I would gladly have slapped his face, only—I did want to know.

"Your own theory," I retorted, choosing to ignore his impertinence, "seek him first whom the crime benefits."

"Well, and whom did that particular crime benefit the most?"

"Philip Ashley, of course," I replied. "But you said yourself—"

"Philip Ashley did not benefit by the crime," the old scarecrow broke in, with a dry cackle. "No, no, but for the fact that a merciful Providence removed Charles Ashley so very unexpectedly out of this wicked world, Philip would still be living on a few hundreds a year, most of which he would owe to the munificence of his brother."

"That," I argued, "was only because that Peet-Jackson woman threw him over, otherwise—"

"And why did she throw him over? Because old Thornton Ashley died under mysterious circumstances and Philip Ashley was under a cloud because of it. Anyone could have foreseen that that particular woman would throw him over the very moment that suspicion fell upon him."

"But Charles—" I began.

"Exactly," he broke in, excitedly, "it was Charles who benefited by the crime. It was he who inherited the fortune."

"But, by the new will he would have inherited anyhow. Then why in the world—"

"You surely don't believe in that new will, do you? The way in which I marshalled the facts before you ought to have paved the way for more intelligent reasoning."

"But Mr. Triscott—" I argued.

"Ah, yes," he said, "Mr. Triscott—exactly. The whole thing could only be done in partnership, I admit. But does not everything point to a partnership in what, to my mind is one of the ugliest crimes in our records? You ought be able to follow the workings of Charles Ashley's mind, a mind as tortuous as the body that held it. Let me put the facts more briefly before you.

"While Philip obstinately remained a bachelor, all was well. Charles stuck to the old miser, carefully watching over his interests lest they became jeopardised. But presently Lady Peet-Jackson became a widow and Philip gaily announced his engagement. From that hour Charles, of course, must have seen the fortune on which he had already counted slipping away irretrievably from his grasp. Can you not see in your mind's eye that queer, misshapen creature setting his crooked brain to devise a way out of the difficulty? Can you not see the plan taking shape gradually, forming itself slowly into a resolve—a resolve to stop his brother's marriage at all costs?

"But how? Philip, passionately in love with Muriel Peet-Jackson, having won her after years of waiting, was not likely to give her up. No, but she might give him up. She had done it once for the sake of ambition, she might do it again if... if... Well, Charles Ashley, obscure, poor, misshapen, was not likely to find a rival who would supplant his handsome brother in any woman's affections. Certainly not! But there remained the other possibility, the possibility that Philip, poor—or, better still, disgraced—might cease to be a prize in the matrimonial market. Disgraced! But how? By publicity? By crime? Yes, by crime! Now, can you see the plan taking shape?

"Can you see Charles cudgelling his wits as to what crime could most easily be fastened on a man of Philip's personality and social position? Probably a chance word dropped by his father put the finishing touch to his scheme, a chance word on the subject of a will. And there was the whole plan ready. The unsigned will, the assault on the dying man, and there were always plenty of quarrels between the peppery old miser and his somewhat impatient son. As for Triscott, the dapper little local lawyer, I suppose it took some time for Charles Ashley's crooked schemes to appear as feasible and profitable to him. Of course, without him nothing could have been done, and the whole of my theory rests upon the fact that the two men were partners in the crime.

"Where they first met, and how they became friends, I don't profess to know. If I had had anything to do with the official investigation of that crime I should first of all have examined the servant in the Triscott household, and found out whether or no Mr. Charles Ashley had ever been a visitor there. In any case, I should have found out something about Triscott's friends and Triscott's haunts. I am sure that it would then have come to light that Charles Ashley and Mr. Triscott had constant intercourse together.

"I cannot bring myself to believe in that unsigned will. There was nothing whatever that led up to it, except the supposed quarrel on the Wednesday. But, if that old miser did want to alter his will, why should he have sent for a man whom he hardly knew and whom, mind you, he would have to pay for his services, rather than for his friend, Old-wall, who would have done the work for nothing? The man was a miser, remember. His meanness, we are told, amounted to a mania; a miser never pays for something he can get for nothing.

"There was also another little point that struck me during the in-quest as significant. If Triscott was an entire stranger to Charles Ashley, why should he have taken such a personal interest in him and in the old man to the extent of sending his wife to spend two whole days and nights in charge of an invalid who was nothing to him? Why should Mrs. Triscott have undertaken such a thankless task in the house of a miser where she would get no comforts and hardly anything to eat? Why, I say, should the Triscotts have done all that if they had not some vital self-interest at stake?

"And I contend that that vital self-interest demand that one of them should be there, in the flat, on the watch to see that no third per-son was present whilst Philip spent his time by his father's bedside—a witness, such as Lady Peet-Jackson, perhaps, or some friend—whose testimony might demolish the whole edifice of lies which had been so carefully built up. And, did you notice another point? The charwoman, by a new arrangement, was never at the flat on a Monday morning, and that arrangement had only obtained for the past two months. Now why? Charwomen stay away, I believe, on Sundays always, but I ask you, have you ever heard of a charwoman having a holiday on a Monday?"

I was bound to admit that it was unusual, whereupon the old scare-crow went on with excitement that grew as rapidly as did the feverish energy of his fingers manipulating his bit of string.

"And now propel your mind back to that same Monday morn-ing, when, the coast being clear, Charles Ashley, back at the flat and alone with the old man, was able at last to put the finishing touch to his work of infamy. One pressure of the fingers, one blow with the walking-stick, and the curtain was rung down finally on the hideous drama which he had skilfully invented. Think of it all carefully and intelligently," the Man in the Corner concluded, as he stuffed his be-loved of string into the capacious pocket of his checked ulster, "and you will admit that there is not a single flaw in my argument—"

"The walking-stick," I broke in, quickly.

"Exactly," he retorted, "the walking-stick. Charles was quick enough to grasp the significance of that, and on Saturday, while his brother's back was turned, he carefully hid the walking-stick, knowing that it would be a useful piece of evidence presently. Do you, for a moment suppose," he added, drily, "that any man would have been such a fool as to throw his walking-stick and the crumpled notes of the will underneath his victim's bed? They could not have been left there, remember, they could not have rolled under the bed, as the walking-stick had a crook handle, they must deliberately have been thrown there.

"No, no!" he said, in conclusion, "there is no flaw. It is all as clear as daylight to any receptive intelligence, and though human justice did err at first, and it looked, at one time, as if the innocent alone would suffer and the guilty enjoy the fruits of this crime, a higher Justice interposed in the end. Charles has gone, and Philip is in possession of the fortune which his father desired him to have. I only hope that his eyes are opened at last to the true value of the beautiful Muriel's love, and that it will be some other worthier woman who will share his fortune and help him forget all that he endured in the past."

"And what about the Triscotts?" I asked

"Ah!" he said, with a sigh, "they are the wicked who prosper, and higher Justice has apparently forgotten them, as it often does forget the evil-doer, for a time. We must take it that they were well paid for their share in the crime, and, if the unfortunate Charles had lived, he probably would have been blackmailed by them and bled white. As it is, they have gone scot-free. I made a few enquiries in the neighbourhood lately and I discovered that Mr. Triscott is selling his practice and retiring from business. Presently we'll hear that he has bought himself a cottage in the country. Then, perhaps, your last doubt will vanish and you will be ready to admit that I have found the true solution of the mystery that surrounded the death of the miser of Maida Vale."

The next moment he was gone and I just caught sight of the corner of his checked ulster disappearing through the swing-doors.

The Fulton Gardens Mystery

"Are you prepared to admit," the Man in the Corner said abruptly as soon as he had finished his glass of milk, "that sympathy, understanding, largeness of heart—what?—are invariably the outcome of a big brain? It is the fool who is censorious and cruel. Your clever man is nearly always sympathetic. He understands, he appreciates, he studies motives and understands them. During the war it was the fools who tracked down innocent men and women under pretence that they were spies; it was the fools who did not understand that a German might be just as fine a patriot as a Briton or a Frenchman if he served his own country. The hard, cruel man is almost always a fool; the back-biting old maid invariably so.

"I am tempted to say this," he went on, "because I have been thinking over that curious case which newspaper reporters have called the Fulton Gardens Mystery. You remember it, don't you?"

"Yes," I said, "I do. As a matter of fact, I knew poor old Mr. Jessup slightly and I was terribly shocked when I heard about that awful tragedy. And to think that that horrid young Leighton—"

"Ha!" my eccentric friend broke in, with a chuckle, "then you have held on to that theory, have you?"

"There was no other possible!" I retorted.

"But he was discharged."

I shrugged my shoulders under pretence of being unconvinced. As a matter of fact, all I wanted was to make the funny creature talk. "A flimsy alibi," I said coldly.

"And a want of sympathy," he rejoined.

"What has sympathy got to do with a brutal assault on a defenceless old man? You can't deny that Leighton had something, at any rate, to do with it?"

"I did not mean sympathy for the guilty," he argued, "but for the women who were the principal witnesses in the case."

"I don't see—" I protested.

"No, but I do. I understood, and in a great measure I sympathised."

At which expression of noble sentiment I burst out laughing. I couldn't help it. In view of his preamble just now his fatuous statement was funny beyond words.

"You being the clever man who understands, *etcetera*," I said, as seriously as I could, "and I the censorious and cruel old maid who is invariably a fool."

"You put it crudely," he rejoined complacently, "and had you not given ample proof of your intelligence before now I might have thought it worthwhile to refute the second half of your argument. As for the first. . ."

"Hadn't you better tell me about the Fulton Garde Mystery?" I broke in impatiently.

"Certainly," he replied, in no way abashed. "I have meant to talk to you about it all along, only that you would digress."

"Pax!" I retorted, and with a conciliatory smile I handed him a beautiful bit of string. He pounced on it with thin hands that looked like the talons of a bird, and he gloated on that bit of string for all the world as on a prey.

"I daresay," he began, "that to most people the mystery appeared baffling enough. But to me. . . Well, there was the victim of what you very properly call the cowardly assault, your friend—or acquaintance—Mr. Seton Jessup, a man on the wrong side of sixty, but very active and vigorous for his years. He carried on the business of pearl merchant in Fulton Gardens, but he did not live there, as you know. He was a married man, had sons and daughters and a nice house in Fitzjohn's Avenue. He also owned the house in Fulton Gardens, a four-storied building of the pattern prevalent in that neighbourhood.

"The ground floor, together with the one above that, and the basement were used by Mr. Jessup himself for his business: on the ground-floor he had his office and showroom, above that were a couple of reception rooms where he usually had his lunch and saw a few privileged customers, and in the basement, there was a kitchen with scullery and pantry, a small servants' hall and a strong room for valuables.

"The top storey of all was let to a surgical-instrument maker who did not sleep on the premises, and the second floor—that is the one just below the surgical-instrument maker and immediately above the reception rooms—was occupied by Mrs. Tufnell, who was cook-housekeeper to Mr. Jessup, and her niece, Ann Weber, who acted as the house-parlourmaid. Mrs. Tufnell's son, Mark, who was a junior clerk in the office, did not sleep in the house. He was considered to be rather delicate and lived with a family somewhere near the Alexandra Palace.

"All these people, as you know, played important parts in the drama that was enacted on the 16th of November at No. 13, Fulton Gardens—an unlucky number, by the way, but one which Mr. Jessup did not change to the usual 12a when he bought the house because he despised all superstition. He was a hard-headed, prosperous business man; he worked hard himself and expected hard work from his employees. Both his sons worked in the office, one as senior clerk and the other as showman, and in addition to young Mark Tufnell there was another junior clerk—a rather unsatisfactory youth named Arthur Leighton, who was some sort of a relation of Mrs. Jessup's.

"But for this connection he never would have been kept on in the business, as he was unpunctual, idle and unreliable. The housekeeper, as well as some of the neighbours, had been scandalised lately by what was picturesquely termed the 'goings on of that young Leighton with Ann, the housemaid at No. 13.'

"Ann Weber was a very pretty girl, and like many pretty girls, she was fond of finery and of admiration. As soon as she entered Mr. Jessup's service she started a flirtation with Mark Tufnell, then she dropped him for a while in favour of the youngest Mr. Jessup; then she went back to Mark and seemed really in love with him that time until, finally, she transferred her favours to Arthur Leighton, chiefly because he was by far the most generous of her admirers. He was always giving her presents of jewellery which Mark Tufnell could not afford, and young Jessup apparently did not care to give her. But she did not, by any means, confine her flirtations to one man: indeed, it appears that she had a marvellous facility for keeping several men hanging about her dainty apron-strings.

"She was not on the best of terms with her aunt, chiefly because the latter noted with some asperity that her son was far from cured of his infatuation for the pretty housemaid. The more she flirted with Leighton and the others the greater did his love for her appear, and all that Mrs. Tufnell could hope for was that Mr. Leighton would many Ann one day soon, when he would take her right away and Mark would then probably make up his mind to forget her. Young Leighton was doing very well in business apparently, for he always had plenty of money to spend, whilst poor Mark had only a small salary, and, moreover, had nothing of the smart, dashing about him which had made the other man so attractive to Ann.

2

"And now," the Man in the Corner continued after a while, "we come to that 16th of November when the mysterious drama occurred at No. 13, Fulton Gardens. As a general rule, it seems, Mr. Jessup was in his office most evenings until seven o'clock. His clerks and showmen finished at six, but he would, almost invariably, stay on an hour longer to go through his accounts or look over his stock. On this particular evening, just before seven o'clock, he rang for the housekeeper, Mrs. Tufnell, and told her that he would be staying until quite late, and would she send him in a cup of tea and a plate of sandwiches in about an hour's time.

"Mrs. Tufnell owned to being rather disappointed when she had this order because her son Mark had arranged to take her and Ann to the cinema that evening, and now, of course, they could not leave until after Mr. Jessup had gone, in case he wanted anything, and he might be staying on until all hours. However, Mark stayed to supper, and after supper Mrs. Tufnell got the tea and sandwiches ready and took the tray up to Mr. Jessup herself. Mr. Jessup was then sitting at his desk with two or three big books in front of him, and Mrs. Tufnell noticed that the safe in which the cash was kept that came in after banking hours was wide open.

"Mrs. Tufnell put down the tray and was about to leave the room again when Mr. Jessup spoke to her.

"'I expect Mr. Leighton back presently. Show him in here when he comes. But I don't want to see anybody else, not any of you. Understand?'

"It seems that he said this in such a harsh and peremptory manner that Mrs. Tufnell was not only upset but quite frightened. Mr. Jessup had always been very kind and considerate to his servants, and the housekeeper declared that she had never been spoken to like that before. But we all know what those sort of people are: they have no understanding, and unless you are perpetually smiling at them you turn huffy at the slightest word of impatience. Undoubtedly Mr. Jessup was both tired and worried and no great stress was laid by the police subsequently on the fact that he had spoken harshly on this occasion. Even to you at this moment I daresay that this seems a trifling circumstance, but I mention it because to my mind it had a great deal of significance, and I think that the police were very wrong to dismiss it quite so lightly.

"Well, to resume. Mr. Jessup was in his office with his books and with the safe, where he kept all the cash that came in after banking hours, open. Mrs. Tufnell saw and spoke to him at eight o'clock and he was then expecting Arthur Leighton to come to him at nine.

"No one saw him alive after that.

"The next morning Mrs. Tufnell was downstairs as usual at a quarter to seven. After she had lighted the kitchen fire, done her front steps and swept the hall, she went to do the ground-floor rooms. She told the police afterwards that from the moment she got up she felt that there was something wrong in the house. Somehow or other she was frightened; she didn't know of what, but she was frightened. As soon as she had opened the office door, she gave a terrified scream. Mr. Jessup was sitting at his desk just as Mrs. Tufnell had seen him the night before, with his big books in front of him and the safe door open.

"But his head had fallen forward on the desk and his arms were spread out over his books. Mrs. Tufnell never doubted for a second but that he was dead, even before she saw the stick lying on the floor and that horrible, horrible, dull red stain which spread from the back of the old man's head, right down to his neck and stained his collar and the top of his coat. Even before she saw all that she knew that Mr. Jessup was dead.

"Terrified, she clung to the open door; she could do nothing but stare and stare, for the room, the furniture, the motionless figure by the desk had started whirling round and round before her eyes, so that she felt that at any moment she might fall down in a dead faint. It seemed ages before she heard Ann's voice calling to her, asking what was the matter. Ann was lazy and never came downstairs before eight o'clock. She had apparently only just tumbled out of bed when she heard Mrs. Tufnell's scream. Now she came running downstairs, with her bare feet thrust into her slippers and a dressing-gown wrapped round her.

"'What is it, auntie?' she kept on asking as she ran, 'What has happened?'

"And when she reached the office door, she only gave one look into the room and exclaimed, 'Oh, my God! He's killed him!'

"Somehow Ann's exclamation of horror brought Mrs. Tufnell to her senses. With a great effort she pulled herself together, just in time, too, to grip Ann by the arm, or the girl would have measured her length on the tiled floor behind her. As it was, Mrs. Tufnell gave her a vigorous shake:

"'What do you mean, Ann Weber?' she demanded in a hoarse whisper. 'What do you mean? Who has killed him?'

"But Ann couldn't or wouldn't utter another word. She was as white as a sheet and, staggering backwards, she had fallen up against the banisters at the foot of the stairs and was clinging to them, wide-eyed, with twitching mouth and shaking knees.

"'Pull yourself together, Ann Weber,' Mrs. Tufnell said peremptorily, 'and run and fetch the police at once.'

"But Ann looked as if she couldn't move. She kept reiterating in a dry, meaningless manner, 'The police! The police!' until Mrs. Tufnell, who by now had gathered her wits together, gave her a vigorous push and then went upstairs to put on her bonnet. A few minutes later she had gone for the police.

3

"I don't know," the Man in the Corner went on glibly, "whether you remember all the circumstances which made that case such a puzzling one. Indeed, it well deserved the popular name that the evening papers bestowed on it—'The Fulton Gardens Mystery'—for it was, indeed, a mystery, and to most people it has so remained to this day."

"Not to you," I put in, with a smile, just to humour him, as I could see he was waiting to be buttered-up before he would proceed with his narrative.

"No, not to me," he admitted, with his fatuous smile. "If the members of the police force who had the case in hand had been psychologists, they would not have been puzzled, either. But they were satisfied with their own investigations and with all that was revealed at the inquest, and they looked no further, with the result that when the edifice of their deductions collapsed, they had nowhere to turn. Time had gone on, evidences had become blurred, witnesses were less sure of themselves and less reliable, and a certain blackguard, on whom I for one could lay my fingers at this moment, is going through the world scot-free.

"But let me begin by telling you the facts as they were revealed at the inquest. You can then form your own conclusions, and I daresay that these will be quite as erroneous as those arrived at by the public and the police.

"The drama began to unfold itself when Mr. Ernest Jessup, the younger son of the deceased gentleman, was called. He began by explaining that he was junior clerk in his father's office, and that he, along with all the other employees, had remarked on the 16th that the guv'nor did not seem at all like himself. He was irritable with everybody, and just before luncheon he called Arthur Leighton into his office and apparently some very hot words passed between the two. Witness happened to be in the hall at the moment, getting his hat and coat, and the housemaid was standing by. They both heard very loud voices coming from the office. The guv'nor was storming away at the top of his voice.

"'That's poor Leighton getting it in the neck,' witness remarked to Ann Weber.

"But the girl only giggled and shrugged her shoulders. Then she said: 'Do you think so?'

"'Yes,' witness replied; 'aren't you sorry to see your devoted admirer in such hot water?'

"Again, the girl giggled and then ran away upstairs. Mr. Leighton was not at the office the whole of that afternoon, but witness understood, either from his father or from his brother—he couldn't remember which—that Leighton was to come in late that night to interview the guv'nor.

"Witness was next questioned as to the events that occurred at Mr. Jessup's home in Fitzjohn's Avenue, while the terrible tragedy was enacted in Fulton Gardens. It seems that Mr. Jessup had an old mother who lived in St. Albans, and that he went sometimes to see her after business hours and stayed the night. As a general rule when he intended going, he would telephone home in the course of the afternoon. On the 16th he rang up at about five o'clock and said that he was staying late at the office—later than usual—and they were not to wait dinner for him.

"Mrs. Jessup took this message herself and had recognised her husband's voice. Then, later on in the evening—it might have been half-past eight or nine—there was another telephone message from the office. Witness went to the telephone that time. A voice, which at first he did not think that he recognised, said: 'Mr. Jessup has gone to St. Albans. He caught the 7.50 and won't be home tonight.'

"In giving evidence witness at first insisted on the fact that he did not recognise the voice on the telephone. It was a man's voice, and sounded like that of a person who was rather the worse for drink. He asked who was speaking and the reply came quite clearly that time: 'Why, it's Leighton, you ass! Don't you know me?' Witness then asked:

'Where are you speaking from?' and the reply was: 'From the office, of course. I've had my wigging and am getting consoled by our Annie-bird.' Annie-bird was the name the pretty housemaid went by among the young clerks at the office.

"Witness then hung up the receiver and gave his mother the message. Neither Mrs. Jessup nor anyone else in the house thought anything more about it, as there was nothing whatever unusual about the occurrence. Witness only made some remarks about Arthur Leighton having been drinking again, and there the matter unfortunately remained until the following morning, when witness and his brother arrived at the office and were met with the awful news.

"Both Mrs. Jessup and Mr. Aubrey, the eldest son, corroborated the statements made by the previous witness with regard to the telephone messages on the evening of the 16th. Mr. Aubrey Jessup also stated that he knew that his father was worried about some irregularities in Arthur Leighton's accounts; and that he meant to have it out with the young clerk in the course of the evening. Witness had begged his father to let the matter rest until the next day, as Leighton, he thought, had got the afternoon off to see a sick sister, but the deceased had rejected the suggestion with obvious irritation.

"'Stuff and nonsense!' he said. 'I don't believe in that sick sister a bit. I'll see that young blackguard tonight.'

"The next witness was Mrs. Tufnell, who was cook-housekeeper at Fulton Gardens. She was a middle-aged, capable-looking woman, with a pair of curiously dark eyes. I say 'curiously' because Mrs. Tufnell's eyes had that velvety quality which is usually only met with in Southern countries. I have seldom seen them in England, except, perhaps, in Cornwall. Apart from her eyes, there was nothing either remarkable or beautiful about Mrs. Tufnell. She may have been good looking once, but that was a long time ago. When she stood up to give evidence, her face appeared rather bloodless, weather-beaten, and distinctly hard. She spoke quite nicely and without any of that hideous Cockney accent one might have expected from a cook in a City office.

"She deposed that on the 16th, just before the luncheon hour, she was crossing the hall at 13, Fulton Gardens. The door into the office was ajar and she heard Mr. Jessup's voice raised, evidently in great wrath. Mrs. Tufnell also heard Mr. Leighton's voice, both gentlemen, as she picturesquely put it, going at one another hammer and tongs. Obviously, though she wouldn't admit it, Mrs. Tufnell stopped to listen, but she does not seem to have understood much of what was said. However, a moment or two later, Mr. Jessup went to the door in order to shut it, and while he did so, Mrs. Tufnell heard him say quite distinctly:

"'Well, if you must go now, you must, though I don't believe a word about your sister being ill. But you may go; only, understand that I expect you back here this evening not later than nine. I shall have gone through the accounts by then, and...'

"At this point the door was shut and witness heard nothing more. But she reiterated the statements which she had already made to the police, and which I have just retold you, about Mr. Jessup staying late at the office and her taking him in some sandwiches, when he told her that he was expecting Mr. Leighton at about nine o'clock and did not wish to be disturbed by anybody else. Witness was asked to repeat what the deceased had actually said to her with reference to this matter, and she laid great stress on Mr. Jessup's harsh and dictatorial manner, so different, she said, to his usual gentlemanly ways.

"'"I don't want to see anybody else—not any of you," that's what he said,' Mrs. Tufnell replied, with an air of dignity, and then added: 'As if Ann Weber or I had ever thought of disturbing him when he was at work!'

"Witness went on to relate that, after she had taken in the tray of tea and sandwiches, she went upstairs and found Ann Weber sitting in her room by herself. Mark, the girl explained, had gone off, very disappointed that they couldn't all go together to the cinema. Mrs. Tufnell argued the point for a moment or two, as she didn't see why Ann should have refused to go if she wanted to see the show. But the girl seemed to have turned sulky. Anyway, it was too late, she said, as Mark had gone off by himself: he had booked the places and didn't want to waste them, so he was going to get another friend to go with him.

"Mrs. Tufnell then settled down to do some sewing and Ann turned over the pages of a magazine. Mrs. Tufnell thought that she appeared restless and agitated. Her cheeks were flushed and at the slightest sound she gave a startled jump. Presently she said that she had some silver to clean in the pantry, and went downstairs to do it. Some little time after that there was a ring at the front door bell, and Mrs. Tufnell heard Ann going through the hall to open the door. A quarter of an hour went by, and then another.

"Mrs. Tufnell began to wonder what Ann was up to. She put down her sewing and started to go downstairs. The first thing that struck her was that all the lights on the stairs and landing were out; the house appeared very silent and dark; only a glimmer came from one of the lights downstairs in the hall at the foot of the stairs.

"Mrs. Tufnell went down cautiously. Strangely enough, it did not occur to her to turn on the lights on her way. After she had passed the first-floor landing she heard the sound of muffled voices coming from the hall below. Thinking that she recognised Ann's voice, she called to her: 'Is that you, Ann?' And Ann immediately replied: 'Coming, aunt.' 'Who are you talking to?' Mrs. Tufnell asked, and as Ann did not answer this time, she went on: 'Is it Mr. Leighton?' And Ann said: 'Yes. He is just going.'

"Mrs. Tufnell stood there, waiting. She was half-way down the stairs between the first floor and the hall, and she couldn't see Ann or Mr. Leighton, but a moment or two later she heard Ann's voice saying quite distinctly: 'Well, goodnight, Mr. Leighton, see you tomorrow as usual.' After which the front door was opened, then banged to again, and presently Ann came tripping back across the hall.

"'You go to bed now, Ann,' Mrs. Tufnell said to her. 'I'll see Mr. Jessup off when he goes. He won't be long, now, I daresay.'

"'Oh, but,' Ann said, 'Mr. Jessup has been gone some time.'

"'Gone some time?' Mrs. Tufnell exclaimed. 'He can't have been gone some time. Why, he was expecting Mr. Leighton, and Mr. Leighton has only just gone.'

"Ann shrugged her shoulders: 'I can only tell you what I know, Mrs. Tufnell,' she said, acidly. 'You can come down and see for yourself. The office is shut up and all the lights out.'

"'But didn't Mr. Leighton see Mr. Jessup?'

"'No, he didn't. Mr. Jessup told Mr. Leighton to wait and then he went away without seeing him.'

"'That's funny,' Mrs. Tufnell remarked, dryly. 'What was Mr. Leighton doing in the house, then, all this time? I heard the front door bell half an hour ago and more.'

"'That's no business of yours. Aunt Sarah,' the girl retorted pertly. 'And it wasn't half an hour, so there!'

"Mrs. Tufnell did not argue the point any further. Mechanically she went downstairs and ascertained in point of fact that the door of the office and the showroom on the ground floor were both locked as usual, and that the key of the office was outside in the lock. This was entirely in accordance with custom. Mrs. Tufnell, through force of habit, did just turn the key and open the door of the office. She just peeped in to see that the lights were really all out. Satisfied that everything was dark she then closed and relocked the door. Ann, in the meanwhile, stood half-way up the stairs, watching. Then the two women went upstairs together. They had only just got back in their room when the front door bell rang once more.

"'Now, whoever can that be?' Mrs. Tufnell exclaimed.

"'Don't trouble, aunt,' Ann said with alacrity. 'I'll run down and see.'

"Which she did. Again, it was some time before she came back, and when she did get back to her room she seemed rather breathless and agitated.

"'Someone for Mr. Jessup,' she said in answer to Mrs. Tufnell's rather acid remark that she had been gone a long time. 'He kept me talking ever such a while. I don't think he believed me when I said Mr. Jessup had gone.'

"'Who was it?' witness asked.

"'I don't know,' the girl replied. 'I never saw him before.'

"'Didn't you ask his name?'

"'I did. But he said it didn't matter—he would call again tomorrow.'

"After that the two women sat for a little while longer, Mrs. Tufnell sewing, and Ann still rather restlessly turning over the pages of a magazine. At ten o'clock they went to bed. And that was the end of the day as far as the household of Mr. Jessup was concerned.

"You may well imagine that all the amateur detectives who were present at the inquest had made up their minds by now that Arthur Leighton had murdered Mr. Seton Jessup, and robbed the till both before and after the crime. It was a simple deduction easily arrived at and presenting the usual features. A flirty minx, an enamoured young man, extravagance, greed, opportunity and supreme temptation. Amongst the public there were many who did not even think it worthwhile to hear further witnesses. To their minds the hangman's rope was already round young Leighton's neck. Of course, I admit that at this point it seemed a very clear case. It was only after this that complications arose and soon the investigations bristled with difficulties.

4

"After a good deal of tedious and irrelevant evidence had been gone through, the inquest was adjourned and the public left the court on the tiptoe of expectation as to what the morrow would bring. Nor was anyone disappointed, for on the morrow the mystery deepened even though there was plenty of sensational evidence for newspaper reporters to feed on.

"The police, it seems, had brought forward a very valuable witness in the person of the point policeman, who was on duty from eight o'clock onwards on the evening of the 16th at the corner of Clerkenwell Road and Fulton Gardens. Number 13 is only a few yards up the street. The man had stated, it seems, that soon after half-past eight he had seen a man come along Fulton Gardens from the direction of Holborn, go up to the front door of Number 13 and ring the bell. He was admitted after a minute or two and he stayed in the house about half an hour.

"It was a dark night and there was a slight drizzle; the witness could not swear to the man's identity. He was slight and of middle height and walked like a young man. When he arrived, he wore a bowler hat and no overcoat, but when he came out again he had an overcoat on and a soft grey hat and he carried the bowler in his hand. Witness noticed as he walked away up Fulton Gardens towards Finsbury this time, he took off the soft hat, slipped it into the pocket of his overcoat and put on the bowler.

"About ten minutes later, not more, another visitor called at No. 13. He also was slight and tallish, and he wore an overcoat and a bowler hat. He turned into Fulton Gardens from Clerkenwell Road, but on the opposite corner to the one where witness was standing. He rang the bell and was admitted and stayed about twenty minutes. He walked away in the direction of Holborn. Witness would not undertake to identify either of these two visitors: he had not been close enough to them to see their faces, and there was a good deal of fog that night as well as the drizzle. There was nothing suspicious looking about either of the men. They had walked quite openly up to the front door, rung the bell and been admitted. The only thing that had struck the constable as queer was the way the first visitor had changed hats when he walked away.

"Witness swore positively that no one else had gone in or out of No. 13 that night except those two visitors. How important this evidence was you will understand presently.

After this young Tufnell was called. He was a shy-looking fellow, with a nervous manner altogether out of keeping with his dark expressive eyes—eyes which he had obviously inherited from his mother and which gave him a foreign as well as a romantic appearance. He was said to be musical and to be a talented amateur actor. Everyone agreed, it seems, that he had always been a very good son to his mother until his love for Ann Weber had absorbed all his thoughts and most of his screw. He explained that he was junior clerk to Mr Jessup, and as far as he knew had always given satisfaction.

"On the 16th he had also noticed that the guv'nor was not quite himself. He appeared unusually curt and irritable with everybody. Witness had not been in the house all the evening. When his mother told him that neither she nor Ann could go to the cinema with him he went off by himself, and after the show he went straight back to his digs near the Alexandra Palace. He only heard of the tragedy when he arrived at the office as usual on the morning of the 17th.

"His evidence would have seemed uninteresting and unimportant but for the fact that while he gave it he glanced now and again in the direction where Ann Weber sat beside her aunt. It seemed as if he were all the time mutely asking for her approval of what he was saying, and presently when the coroner asked him whether he knew the cause of his employer's irritability, he very obviously looked at Ann before he finally said: 'No, sir, I don't!'

"After that Ann Weber was called. Of course, it had been clear all along that she was by far the most important witness in this mysterious case, and when she rose from her place looking very trim and neat in her navy-blue coat and skirt, with a jaunty little hat pulled over her left eye, and wearing long amber ear-rings that gave her pretty face a piquant expression, everyone settled down comfortably to enjoy the sensation of the afternoon.

"Ann, who was thoroughly self-possessed, answered the coroner's preliminary questions quite glibly, and when she was asked to relate what occurred at No. 13, Fulton Gardens on the night of the 16th, she plunged into her story without any hesitation or trace of nervousness.

"'At about half-past eight,' she said, 'or it may have been later—I won't swear as to the time—there was a ring at the front door bell. I was down in the pantry and as I came upstairs, I heard the office door being opened. When I got into the passage, I saw Mr. Jessup standing in the doorway of the office. He had his spectacles on his nose and a pen in his hand. He looked as if he had just got up from his desk.'

"'If that's young Leighton,' he said to me, 'tell him I'll see him tomorrow. I can't be bothered now.' Then he went back into the office and shut the door.

"'I opened the door to Mr. Leighton,' witness continued, 'and he came in looking very cold and wet. I told him that Mr. Jessup didn't want to see him tonight. He seemed very pleased at this but he wouldn't go away, and when I told him I was busy, he said that I couldn't be so unkind as to turn a fellow out into the rain without giving him a drink. Now I could see that already Mr. Leighton had had a bit too much, and I told him so quite plainly. But there! he wouldn't take "No" for an answer, and as it really was jolly cold and damp, I told him to go and sit down in the servants' hall while I got him a hot toddy. I went down into the kitchen and put the kettle on and cut a couple of sandwiches. I don't know where Mr. Leighton was during that time or what he was doing. I was in the kitchen some time because I couldn't get the kettle to boil as the fire had gone down and we have no gas downstairs.

"'When I took the tray into the servants' hall Mr. Leighton was there, and again I told him that I didn't think he ought to have any more whisky, but he only laughed and was rather impudent, so I just put the tray down, and then I thought that I would run upstairs and see if Mr. Jessup wanted anything. I was rather surprised when I got to the hall to see that all the lights up the stairs had been turned off. There's a switch down in the hall that turns off the lot. The whole house looked very dark. There was but a very little light that came from the lamp at the other end of the hall, near the front door.

"'I was just thinking that I would turn on the lights again when I saw what I could have sworn was Mr. Jessup coming out of his office. He had already got his hat and coat on, and when he came out of the office, he shut the door and turned the key in the lock, just as Mr. Jessup always did. It never struck me for a moment that it could be anybody but him. Though it was dark, I recognised his hat and his overcoat, and his own way of turning the key. I spoke to him,' witness continued in answer to a question put to her by the coroner, 'but he didn't reply; he just went straight through the hall and out by the front door. Then after a bit Mr. Leighton came up, and I told him Mr. Jessup had gone. He was quite pleased and stopped talking in the hall for a moment, and then aunt called to me and Mr. Leighton went away.'

"Witness was then questioned as to the other visitor who called later that same evening, but she stated that she had no idea who it was. 'He came about nine,' she explained, 'and I went down to open the door. He kept me talking ever such a time, asking all sorts of silly questions; I didn't know how to get rid of him, and he wouldn't leave his name. He said he would call again and that it didn't matter.'

"Ann Weber here gave the impression that the unknown visitor had stopped for a flirtation with her on the doorstep and her smirking and pert glances rather irritated the coroner. He pulled her up sharply by putting a few straight questions to her. He wanted to pin her down to a definite statement as to the time when (1) she opened the door to Mr. Leighton; (2) she saw what she thought was Mr. Jessup go out of the house, and (3) the second visitor arrived. Though doubtful as to the exact time, Ann was quite sure that the three events occurred in the order in which she had originally related them and in this she was, of course, corroborating the evidence of the point policeman.

"But there was the mysterious contradiction. Ann Weber swore that Mr. Leighton followed her up from the servants' hall just after she had seen the mysterious individual go out by the front door. On the other hand, she couldn't swear what happened while she was busy in the kitchen getting the hot toddy for Mr. Leighton. She had been trying to make the fire burn up, and had rattled coals and fire-irons. She certainly had not heard anyone using the telephone, which was in the office, and she did not know where Mr. Leighton was during that time.

"Nor would she say what was in her mind when first she saw her employer lying dead over the desk and exclaimed: 'My God! He has killed him!' And when the coroner pressed her with questions, she burst into tears. Except for this her evidence had, on the whole, been given with extraordinary self-possession. It was a terrible ordeal for a girl to have to stand up before a jury and, roughly speaking, to swear away the character of a man with whom she had been on intimate terms. . . . The character, did I say? I might just as well have said the life, because whatever doubts had lurked in the public mind about Arthur Leighton's guilt, or at least complicity in the crime, those doubts were dispelled by the girl's evidence.

"For I need not tell you, I suppose, that every man present that second day at the inquest had already made up his mind that Ann Weber was lying to save her sweetheart. No one believed in the mysterious impersonator of Mr. Jessup. It was Arthur Leighton, they argued, who had murdered his employer and robbed the till, and Ann Weber knew it and had invented the story in order to drag a red herring across the trail.

"I must say that the man himself did not make a good impression when he was called in his turn. As he stepped forward with a swaggering air, and a bold glance at coroner and jury, the interest which he aroused was not a kindly one. He was rather a vulgar-looking creature, with a horsey get-up, high collar, stock-tie, fancy waistcoat and so on. His hair was of a ginger colour, his eyes light and his face tanned. Everyone noticed that he winked at Ann Weber when he caught her eye, and also that the girl immediately averted her glance and almost imperceptibly shrugged her shoulders. Thereupon Leighton frowned and very obviously swore under his breath.

"Questioned as to his doings on the 16th, he admitted that 'the guv'nor had been waxy with him, because,' as he put it with an indifferent swagger, 'there were a few pounds missing in the till.' He also admitted that he had not been looking forward to the evening's interview, but that he had not dared refuse to come. In order to kill time and to put heart into himself, he had gone with a couple of friends to the Café Royal in Regent Street and they all had whiskies and sodas till it was time for him to go to Fulton Gardens. His friends were to wait for him until he returned, when they intended to have supper together. Witness then went to Fulton Gardens and saw Ann Weber, who told him that the guv'nor didn't wish to see him. This, according to his own picturesque language, was a little bit of all right. He stayed for a few minutes talking to Ann, and she gave him a hot toddy. He certainly didn't think he had stayed as long as half an hour, but then, when a fellow was taking to a pretty girl... eh?... what? ...

"The coroner curtly interrupted his fatuous explanations by asking him at what time he had left his friends, and at what time he had met them again subsequently. Witness was not very sure; he thought he left the Café Royal about half-past eight, but it might have been earlier or later. He took a bus to the bottom of Fulton Gardens. It was beastly cold and wet, and he was very grateful to Ann for giving him a hot drink. He denied that he had been drinking too much or that he had demanded the hot drink. It was Ann Weber who had offered to get it for him. Jolly pretty girl, Annie-bird, and not shy.

"Witness concluded his evidence by swearing positively that he had waited in the servants' hall all the while that Ann Weber got him the toddy; he had followed her down and not gone upstairs or seen anything of Mr. Jessup all the time he was in the house. When he left Fulton Gardens, he tried to get a bus back to Regent Street, but many of them were full and it was rather late before he got back to the Café Royal.

"It was very obvious that as the coroner continued to put question after question to him, Arthur Leighton became vaguely conscious of the feeling of hostility towards him which had arisen in the public mind. He lost something of his swagger, and his face under the tan took on a greyish hue. From time to time he glanced at Ann Weber, but she obstinately looked another way.

"Undoubtedly he felt that he was caught in a network of damnatory evidence which he was unable to combat. The day ended, however, with another adjournment; the police wanted a little more time before taking drastic action. The public so often blame them for being in too great a hurry to fasten an accusation on the flimsiest grounds that one is pleased to record such a noteworthy instance when they really did not leave a single stone unturned before they arrested Arthur Leighton on the charge of murder. They did everything they could to find some proof of the existence and identity of the individual whom Ann Weber professed to have seen while Leighton was still in the house. But all their efforts in that direction came to naught, whilst Leighton himself denied having had an accomplice just as strenuously as he did his own guilt.

"He was brought up before the magistrate, charged with the terrible crime. No one, the police argued, had so strong a motive for the crime or such an opportunity. Alternatively, no one else could have admitted the mysterious impersonator of Mr. Jessup into the house, the accomplice who did the deed, whilst Leighton engaged Ann Weber's attention, always supposing that he did exist, which was never proved, and which the evidence of the police constable refuted. People who dabbled in spiritualism and that sort of thing were pleased to think that the mysterious personage whom the housemaid saw was the ghost of poor old Jessup, who was then lying murdered in his office, stricken by Leighton's hand. But even the most physically-minded individual was unable to give a satisfactory explanation for the ghost having changed hats while he walked away from that fateful No. 13.

"Altogether the question of hats played an important role in the drama of Leighton's arrest and final discharge. The magistrate did not commit him for trial because the case for the prosecution collapsed suddenly like a pack of cards. It was the question of hats that saved Leighton's neck from the hangman's rope. You remember, perhaps, that in his evidence he had stated that before starting to interview his irate employer he had been with some friends at the Café Royal in Regent Street, and that subsequently he met these friends there for supper. Well, although it appeared impossible to establish definitely the time when Leighton left the Café Royal to go to Fulton Gardens, there were two or three witnesses prepared to swear that he was back again at a quarter to ten.

"Now this was very important. It seems that his friends who were waiting at the Café Royal were getting impatient, and at twenty minutes to ten by the clock one of them—a fellow named Richard Hurrill—said he would go outside and see if he could see anything of Leighton. He strolled on as far as Piccadilly Circus where the 'buses stop that come from the City, and a minute or two later he saw Leighton step out of one. He seemed a little fuzzy in the head, and Hurrill chaffed him a bit. Then he took him by the arm and led him back in triumph to the Café Royal.

"Now mark what followed," the funny creature went on, whilst all at once his fingers started working away as if for dear life on his bit of string. "A hat—a soft grey hat—with an overcoat wrapped round it, were found in the area of a derelict house in Blackhorse Road, Walthamstow, close to the waterworks, and identified as the late Mr. Seton Jessup's overcoat and hat. I don't suppose that you have the least idea where Blackhorse Road, Walthamstow is, but let me tell you that it is at the back of beyond in the north-east of London.

"If you remember, the point policeman had stated that the first visitor had called at No. 13, Fulton Gardens, at half-past eight and stayed half an hour. He then walked away in the direction of Finsbury. That visitor, the police argued, was Arthur Leighton who had murdered Mr. Jessup and sent the telephone message to Fitzjohn's Avenue; then, hearing Ann Weber moving about downstairs and frightened at being caught by her, he had put on the deceased's hat and coat slipped out of the house. Ann, however, had recognised him. She had involuntarily given him away when the housekeeper asked her whom she was talking to, so she invented the story of having seen what she thought was Mr. Jessup in order to save her sweetheart.

"It was a logical theory enough, but here came the evidence of the hat. The man who walked away from Fulton Gardens at nine o'clock, whom the point policeman saw changing his hat in the street at that hour, could not possibly have gone all the way to Walthamstow, either by bus or even part of the way in a taxi, and back again to Piccadilly Circus all in the space of forty-five minutes. And Leighton, mind you, stepped out of a bus when his friend met him, and I can tell you that the police worked their hardest to find a taxi-man who may have picked up a fare that night in the neighbourhood of Clerkenwell and driven out to Walthamstow and then back to Holborn. That search proved entirely fruitless.

On the other hand, Leighton had paid his bus fare from Holborn, and the conductor vaguely recollected that he had got in at the corner of Clerkenwell Road. Well, that being proved, the man couldn't have done in the time all that the prosecution declared that he did.

"After he was discharged, the Press started violently abusing the police for not having directed their attention to the second visitor who called at Fulton Gardens ten minutes or so after the first one had left. But this person appeared as elusive and intangible as the mysterious wearer of Mr. Jessup's hat and coat. The point policeman saw him in the distance and Ann Weber admitted him into the house and chatted with him for over twenty minutes. She didn't know him, but she declared that she could easily recognise him if she saw him again. For some time after that the poor girl was constantly called upon by the police to see, and if possible, identify, the mysterious visitor. Half the shady characters in London passed, I believe, before her eyes during the next three months. But this search proved as fruitless as the other. The murder of Mr. Seton Jessup has remained as complete and as baffling a mystery as any in the annals of crime.

"Many there are—you amongst the number—who firmly believe that Arthur Leighton had, at any rate, something to do with it. I know that the family of the deceased were convinced that he did. Mr. Aubrey Jessup, the eldest son of the deceased, who was one of the executors under his father's will, and who had gone through the accounts of the business, had noted certain irregularities in Leighton's books; he also declared that various sums which had come in on the 16th after banking hours were missing from the safe. Moreover, young Leighton himself had admitted that 'the guv'nor was waxy with him because a few pounds were missing from the till.'

"All these facts, no doubt, had influenced the police when they applied for a warrant for his arrest, but there was no getting away from the evidence of that hat and coat found ten miles and more away from the scene of the crime, and of the bus conductor who could swear that out of forty-five minutes which the accused had to account for, he had spent twenty in a bus."

"It is all very mysterious," I put in, because my eccentric friend had been silent for quite a long time, while his attention was entirely taken up by the fashioning of a whole series of intricate knots. "I am afraid that I was one of those who blamed the police for not directing their investigations sooner in the direction of the second visitor. He seems to me much, more mysterious than the first. We know who the first one was—"

"Do we?" he retorted with a chuckle. "Or rather, do you?"

"Well, of course, it was Arthur Leighton," I rejoined impatiently. "Mrs. Tufnell saw him—"

"She didn't," he broke in, quickly. "The house was pitch dark; she heard voices and she asked whether she was speaking to Mr. Leighton."

"And Ann said yes!" I riposted.

"She said yes," he admitted with an irritating smile.

"And Leighton himself in his evidence—"

"Leighton in his evidence." the funny creature broke in excitedly, "admitted that he had called at the house, he admitted that he remembered vaguely that Ann Weber told him that Mr. Jessup had decided not to see him, and that to celebrate the occasion he got the girl to make him a whisky toddy. But, apart from these facts, he only had the haziest notions as to the time when he came and when he left or how long he stayed. Nor were his precious friends at the Café Royal any clearer on that point. They had all of them been drinking and only had the haziest notion of time until twenty minutes to ten, when they got hungry and wanted their supper."

"But what does that prove?" I argued with an impatient frown.

"It proves that my contention is correct; that the first visitor was not Leighton, that it was someone for whom Ann Weber cared more than she did for Leighton, as she lied for his sake when she told her aunt that she was speaking to Leighton in the hall. The whole thing occurred just as the police supposed. The first visitor called and while Ann Weber was down in the kitchen getting him something to eat and drink, he entered the office, probably not with any evil intention, and saw his employer sitting at his desk with the safe containing a quantity of loose cash, invitingly open. Let us be charitable and assume that he yielded to sudden temptation. Mr. Jessup's coat, hat and stick were lying there on a chair. The stick was one of those heavily weighted ones which men like to carry nowadays. He seizes the stick and strikes the old man on the head with it, then he collects the money from the safe and thrusts it into his pockets.

"At that moment Ann Weber comes up the stairs. I say that this man was her lover; she had returned to him, as she did once before. Imagine her horror first and then her desire—her mad desire—to save him from the consequences of his crime. It is her woman's wit which first suggests the idea of telephoning to Fitzjohn's Avenue: she who thinks of plunging the house in darkness. And now to get the criminal out of the house. It can be done in a moment, but just then Mrs. Tufnell opens her door on the second floor and begins to grope her way downstairs. It is impossible to think quickly enough how to meet this situation. Instinct is the only guide, and instinct suggests impersonating the deceased, to avoid the danger of Mrs. Tufnell peeping in at the office door.

"The criminal hastily dons his victim's hat and coat, and he is almost through the hall when Mrs. Tufnell calls to Ann:

'Is it Mr. Leighton?' and Ann on the impulse of the moment replies: 'Yes, it is! He is just going.' And so, the criminal escapes unseen. But there is still the danger of Mrs. Tufnell peeping in at the office door, so Ann invents the story of having seen Mr. Jessup walk out of the house some time before. So, for the moment danger is averted; the housekeeper does peep in at the door, but only in order to satisfy herself that the lights are out, and the women then go upstairs together.

"Ten minutes later there is another ring at the bell. This time it is Arthur Leighton and Ann Weber has sufficient presence of mind not to let him see that there is anything wrong in the house. She asks him in, she tells him Mr. Jessup cannot see him, she gets him a drink and sends him off again. I don't suppose for a moment that at this stage she has any intention of using him as a shield for her present sweetheart, but undoubtedly the thought had by now crept into her mind to utilise Leighton's admitted presence in the house for the purpose of confusing the issues. Nor do I think that she had any idea that night that Mr. Jessup was dead. She probably thought that he had only been stunned by a blow from the stick: hence her exclamation when she realised the truth, 'My God, he has killed him!' Then only did she concentrate all her energies and all her wits to saving her sweetheart—even at the cost of another man.

"Women are like that sometimes," the Man in the Corner went on with a chuckle, "the instinct of the primitive woman is first of all to save her man, never mind at whose expense. The cave-man's instinct is to protect his woman with his fists—but she, conscious of physical weakness, sets her wits to work, and if her man is in serious danger, she will lie and she will cheat—aye, and perjure herself if need be. And those flirtatious minxes of which Annie-bird is a striking example are only cave-women with a veneer of civilisation over them.

"She did save her man by dragging a red herring across his trail, and she left Fate to deal with Leighton. Once embarked on a system of lies she had to stick to it or her man was doomed. Fortunately, she could rely on the other woman. A mother's wits are even sharper than those of a sweetheart."

"A mother?" I ejaculated. "Then you think that it was——?"

"Mark Tufnell, of course," he broke in, dryly. "Didn't you guess? As he could not go with his beloved to the cinema, he thought he would spend a happy evening with her. What made him originally go into the office we shall never know. Some trifle, no doubt, some message for his employer; it is those sort of trifles that so often govern the destinies of men. Personally, I think that he was very much in the same boat as young Leighton: some trifling irregularities in his account. The deceased speaking so harshly to Mrs. Tufnell that night first directed my attention to young Tufnell. He didn't want to see any of them that night: he was irritated with Mark quite as much as with Leighton, but out of consideration for the housekeeper whom he valued he said little about her son.

"Perhaps he had ordered the young man to come to his office; as I said just now, this little point I cannot vouch for. But if I have not succeeded in convincing you that the first visitor at No. 13, Fulton Gardens was Mark Tufnell, and that it was he who went out in Mr. Jessup's hat and overcoat, changed hats in the street and wandered out as far as Walthamstow in order to be rid of the *pieces de conviction* then you are less intelligent than I have taken you to be. Mark Tufnell, remember, lives in the north of London; he was supposed to have gone to the cinema that night, therefore the people with whom he lodged thought nothing of his coming home late."

"That poor mother!" I ejaculated, "I wonder if she suspects the truth."

"She knows it," the funny creature said, "you may be sure of that. There was a bond of understanding between those two women, and they never once contradicted each other in their evidence. A worthless young blackguard has been saved from the gallows; my sympathy is not with him, but with the women who put up such a brave fight for his sake."

"Do you know what happened to them all subsequently?" I asked.

"Not exactly. But I do know that Mr. Seton Jessup in his will left his housekeeper an annuity of £50. I also know that young Tufnell has gone out to Australia, and that if you ever dine with a friend at the Alcyon Club you will notice an exceptionally pretty waitress who will make eyes at all the men. Her name is Ann Weber!"

A Moorland Tragedy

The Man in the Corner had finished his glass of milk and ceased to munch his bun; from the capacious pocket of his huge tweed coat, he extracted a piece of string, and for a while he sat contemplating it, with his head on one side, so like one of those bald-headed storks at the zoo.

"I always had a great predilection for that mystery," he said, *a propos* of nothing at all. "It still fascinates me."

"What mystery?" I asked; but as usual he took no notice of my question.

"It was more romantic than the common crimes of today; in fact, I don't know if you will agree with me, but to me it has quite an eighteenth-century atmosphere about it."

"If you were to tell me to what particular crime you refer," I said coldly, "I might tell you whether I agree with you or not."

He looked at me as if he thought me an idiot, then he rejoined dryly:

"You don't mean to say that you have never thought of the Moorland Tragedy!"

"Yes," I said, "often!"

"And don't you think that the story is as romantic as any you have read in fiction recently?"

"Yes, I do think that the story is romantic but only because of its *mise en scène*. The same thing might have occurred in a London slum, and then it would have been merely sordid. Of course, it is all very mysterious, and I for one have often wondered what has become of that Italian—I forget his name."

"Antonio Vissio. A queer creature, wasn't he? And we can well imagine with what suspicion he was regarded by the yokels in the neighbouring villages. Yorkshire yokels! Just think of them in connection with an exotic creature like Vissio. He had a curious history,

413

too. His people owned a little farm somewhere in the mountains near Santa Catarina in Liguria, and during the war an English Intelligence officer—Captain Arnott—lodged with them for a time. They were, it seems, extraordinarily kind to him. The family consisted of a widow, two daughters, and the son Antonio. As he was the only son of a widow, he was, of course, exempt from military service and helped his mother to look after the farm.

"His passion, however—and one, by the way, which is very common to Italian peasants—was shooting. There is very little game in that part of Italy, and it means long tramps before you can get as much as a rabbit or a partridge; but there was nothing that Antonio loved more than those tramps with a gun and a dog, and when Captain Arnott had leisure the two of them would go off together at daybreak and never return till late at night.

"Sometime in 1917 Captain Arnott was transferred to another front. He got his majority the following year, and after the war he retired with the rank of lieut. colonel. He hadn't seen the Vissio family for some time, but he always retained the happiest recollections of their kindness to him and of Antonio's pleasant companionship. It was not to be wondered at, therefore, that when in 1919 that terrible explosion occurred at the fort of Santa Catarina, which was only distant a quarter of a mile from the Vissio's farm, Colonel Arnott should at once think of his friends, and, as he happened to be at Genoa on business at the time, he motored over to Santa Catarina to see if he could ascertain anything of their fate.

"He found the village a complete devastation, the isolated farms for miles around nothing but masses of wreckage. I don't know how many people—men, women and children—had been killed, there were over two hundred injured, and those who had escaped were herding together amongst the ruins of their homes. It was only by dint of perseverance and the exercise of an iron will that Colonel Arnott succeeded at last in finding Antonio Vissio.

"There was nothing left of the farm but dust and ashes. The mother and one of the girls had been killed by the falling in of the roof, and the younger daughter was being taken care of by some sisters in a neighbouring convent which had escaped total destruction. Antonio was left in the world all alone, homeless, moneyless; Italy is not like England where at times of disaster money comes pouring at once out of the pockets of the much abused capitalists to help the unfortunate. There was no money poured out to help poor Antonio and his kindred.

"Colonel Arnott was deeply moved at sight of the man's loneliness. He worked hard to try and get him a job in England right away from the scenes of the disaster that must perpetually have awakened bitter memories. Finally, he succeeded. A friend of his, Lord Crookhaven, who owned considerable property in the North Riding, agreed to take Vissio as assistant to one of his gamekeepers, a fellow named William Topcoat. Of course, this was an ideal life for Antonio. He could indulge his passion for shooting to his heart's content, and, incidentally, he would learn something of the science of preserving, and of the game laws as they exist in all the sporting countries.

"I don't suppose that Antonio ever realised quite how unpopular he was from the first in his new surroundings. The Yorkshire yokels looked upon him as a *dago*, and the fact that he had not fought in the war did not help matters. During the first six months he did not speak a word of English, and even after he had begun to pick up a sentence or two, he always remained unsociable. To begin with, he didn't drink: he hated beer and said so. He didn't understand cricket and was bored with football. He didn't bet and he was frightened of horses. All that he cared for was his gun, and he went about his work not only conscientiously but intelligently, took great interest in the rearing of young birds and was particularly successful with them.

"After he had been in England a year, he fell madly in love with Winnie Gooden. And that is how the tragedy began."

2

"An Italian peasant's idea of love is altogether different to that of an English yokel. The latter will begin by keeping company with his sweetheart: he will walk out with her in the twilight, and sit beside her on the stile, chewing the end of a straw and timidly holding her hand. Kisses are exchanged and sighs, and usually no end of jokes and chaff. On the whole the English yokel is a cheerful lover. Not so the Italian. With him love is the serious drama of life; he is always prepared for it to turn to tragedy. His love is overwhelming, tempestuous. With one arm he fondles his sweetheart, but the other hand is behind his back, grasping a knife.

"So, it was with Antonio Vissio. Winnie Gooden was the daughter of one of the gardeners at Markthwaite Hall, Lord Crookhaven's residence. She was remarkably pretty, and I suppose that she was attracted by the silent, rather sullen Italian, who, by the way, was extraordinarily good looking. Dark eyes, a soft creamy skin, quantities of wavy hair;

everyone admitted that the two of them made a splendid pair when they walked out together on Sunday afternoons. Thanks to the kindness of Colonel Arnott, Vissio had succeeded in selling the bit of land on which his farm had stood, so he had a good bit of money, too, and though James Gooden, the father, was said to be averse to the idea of his daughter marrying a foreigner, it was thought that Winnie would talk her father over easily enough if she really meant to have Antonio; but people didn't think that she was seriously in love with him.

"During the spring of 1922, Mr. Gerald Moville came home from Argentina where he was said to be engaged cattle-rearing. He was the youngest son of Sir Timor Moville whose property adjoined that of Lord Crookhaven. His arrival caused quite a flutter in feminine hearts for miles around, for smart young men are scarce in those parts, and Gerald Moville was both good looking and smart, a splendid dancer, a fine tennis and bridge player, and, in fact was possessed of the very qualities which young ladies of all classes admire, and which were so sadly lacking in the other young men of the neighbourhood.

"The fact that he had always been very wild, and that it was only through joining the Air Force at the beginning of the war that he escaped prosecution for some shady transaction in connection with a bridge club in London, did not seriously stand against him, at any rate with the ladies; the men, perhaps, cold-shouldered him at first, and he was not made an honorary member of the County Club at Richmond, but he was welcome at all their tea and garden parties, the dances and the tennis matches throughout the North Riding, and in social matters it is, after all, the ladies who rule the roost.

"The Movilles, moreover, were big people in the neighbourhood, whom nobody would have cared to offend. The eldest son was colonel commanding a smart regiment—I forget which; one daughter had married an eminent K.C., and the other was the wife of a bishop; so for the sake of the family, if for no other reason, Gerald Moville was accepted socially and his *peccadilloes*, of which it seems there was more than the one in connection with the bridge club, were conveniently forgotten; besides which it was declared that he was now a reformed character. He had joined the Air Force quite early in the war, been a prisoner of the Germans until 1919 when he went out to Argentina where he had made good, and where, it was said, he was making a huge fortune.

"This rumour also helped, no doubt, to make Gerald Moville popular, even though he himself had laughingly sworn on more than one occasion that he was not a marrying man: he was in love with too many girls ever to settle down with one. He certainly was a terrible flirt and gave all the pretty girls of the neighbourhood a very good time; he had hired a smart little two-seater at Richmond, and motor excursions, lunches at the Wheatsheaf at Reeth, jade ear-rings or wrist-watches—the girls, who were ready to flirt with him and to amuse him could get anything they wanted out of him.

"But it was soon pretty evident that though Gerald Moville flirted with many, it was Winnie Gooden whom he admired the most. From the first he ran after that girl in a way that scandalised the village gossips. She, of course, was flattered by his attentions, but did not show the slightest inclination to throw Antonio over. She was sensible enough to know that Gerald Moville would never marry her, and she made it very clear that though he amused her, her heart would remain true to her Italian lover. But here was the trouble. Antonio was not the man to run in double harness. His fiery Southern blood rose in revolt against any thought of rivalry. He had won Winnie's love and meant to hold it against all comers, and more than once in public and in private he threatened to do for any man who came between him and Winnie.

"You would have thought that those who were in the know would have foreseen the tragedy from the moment that Winnie Gooden started to flirt with Gerald Moville; nevertheless, when it did occur there was universal surprise quite as much as horror, and there seemed to be no one clever enough to understand the psychological problem that was the true key of that so-called mystery."

3

"Lord Crookhaven's property, you must know," the Man in the Corner resumed, after a moment's pause, "extends right over Markthwaite Moor, which is a lonely stretch of country, intersected by gullies, down which, during the heavy rains in spring and autumn, the water rushes in torrents. There are one or two disused stone quarries on the moor, and, except for the shooting season when Lord Crookhaven has an occasional party of sportsmen to stay with him at the Hall, who are out after the birds all day, this stretch of country is singularly desolate.

"Topcoat's cottage, where Vissio lodged, is on the edge of the moor on the Markthwaite side; about a couple of miles away to the north the moor is intersected by the secondary road which runs from Kirkby Stephen and joins up with the main road at Richmond, and three or four miles again to the north of the road is the boundary wall that divides Lord Crookhaven's property from that of his neighbour Sir Timothy Moville.

"It was in September 1922 that the tragedy occurred which made Markthwaite Moor so notorious at the time. Topcoat was walking across the moor in the company of the Italian, both carrying their guns, when about half a mile away, on the further side of the quarry known as the Poacher's Leap, the gamekeeper spied a man who appeared to be crouching behind some scrub. Without much reflection he pointed his crouching figure out to Vissio and said: "'There's a fellow who is up to no good. After the birds again, the damned thief. Run along, my lad, and see if you can't put a shot or two into his legs.'

"Topcoat swore subsequently, that when he said this, he had not recognised who the crouching figure was. But he was a very hard man where poachers were concerned; he had been much worried with them lately, and a day or two ago had been reprimanded by Lord Crookhaven for want of vigilance. This, no doubt, had irritated his temper, and made him rather 'jumpy.'

"Vissio, with his gun on his shoulder, went off in the direction of the Poacher's Leap. Topcoat watched him until a bit of sharply rising ground hid him from sight. A moment or two later the crouching figure stood up and Topcoat recognised Mr. Gerald Moville. He had always had exceptionally fine sight, and Mr. Moville had certain tricks of gait and movement which were unmistakable even at that distance. Topcoat immediately shouted to Vissio to come back, but apparently the Italian did not hear him, and the last thing that the gamekeeper saw on that eventful morning was Mr. Moville suddenly turn and walk towards the high bit of ground behind which Vissio had just disappeared.

"And that was the last," my eccentric neighbour concluded with a chuckle all his own, "that has been seen up to this hour of those two men, Mr. Gerald Moville and Antonio Vissio. Topcoat waited for a while on the moor, and called to the Italian several times, but as he heard nothing in response and as it had started to rain heavily, he finally went home.

"Vissio did not turn up at the cottage the whole of that day, and he did not come home that night. The following morning, which was a Thursday, Topcoat walked across to the Goodens' cottage to make enquiries, but no one had seen the Italian and Winnie knew nothing about him. The gamekeeper waited until the Saturday before he informed the police; that, of course, was a serious delay which ought never to have occurred, but you have to know that class of north country yokel intimately to appreciate this man's conduct throughout the affair. They all have a perfect horror of anything to do with the police. The type of delinquency most frequent in these parts is, of course, poaching, and the gamekeepers on the big estates look on themselves as the only efficient police for those cases. Half the time they don't turn the delinquent over to the magistrates at all, and administer a kind of rough justice as they think best. They hate police interference.

"In this case we must also bear Topcoat's subsequent statement in mind, which was that at first no suspicion of foul play had entered his head. He had not heard the report of a gun, and all he feared was that the Italian had tried to pick a quarrel with Mr. Moville and been soundly punished for his impertinence, and that probably he did not dare show his face until the trouble had blown over. Topcoat, however, spent a couple of days scouring the moor for the missing man, in case he had met with an accident and was lying somewhere unable to move.

"On the second day he found Vissio's gun lying in a gully close to the Poacher's Leap; it had not been discharged, and the next day—that is, on the Saturday—he, very reluctantly went to the police. Even then he made no mention of Mr. Gerald Moville; he only said that his assistant, an Italian named Antonio Vissio, who lodged with him,—had not been home for three days, and that he had last seen him on Markthwaite Moor on the previous Wednesday carrying a gun and walking in the direction of the Poacher's Leap.

"Poachers, of course, were at once suspected; Topcoat referred vaguely to Vissio having gone after a man whose movements had appeared suspicious. He was severely blamed for having delayed so long before informing the police; even if the Italian had not been the victim of foul play he might, it was argued, have met with a serious accident, and been lying for days, perhaps, with a broken leg out in the cold and wet, and might even have perished of exposure and neglect. But this latter theory Topcoat would not admit. He had scoured the moor, he declared, from end to end; if Vissio had been lying anywhere, he swore that he would have found him.

"Another three or four days were now spent by the police in scouring the moor, and it was only after a last fruitless search that Topcoat mentioned the fact that he had seen Mr. Gerald Moville the very morning and close to the spot where Vissio disappeared: that, as a matter of fact, he was the man after whom the Italian had gone, and that the two have met somewhere near the north end of the Poacher's Leap.

"Of course, to the general public—to you, for instance—Topcoat's attitude of reticence all this while must seem positively criminal; but it is useless to measure the conduct of people of that class in remote north-country districts by the ordinary rules of common sense. For a man in Topcoat's position to connect 'one of the gentry' with the disappearance of a gamekeeper's assistant—and a foreigner at that— would seem as preposterous as to imagine that the King of England would go poaching on his neighbour's estate. It simply couldn't be, and when the D.C.C., to whom Topcoat first made this statement, rebuked him with unusual severity, the gamekeeper turned sulky and declared that he didn't see he had done anything wrong.

"More than a week you see had elapsed since that Wednesday morning when Vissio had last been seen alive; for the past four days the police had worked very hard, but entirely in the dark. Now at last they felt that they had a glimmer of light to guide them in their search. The public, who had taken some interest at first in the Moorland Mystery, was beginning to tire of reading about this fruitless search for a missing *dago*. But now, suddenly, the mystery had taken a sensational turn. Topcoat's statement had found its way into the local papers and Mr. Gerald Moville's name was whispered in connection with the case. And hardly had the lovers of sensation recovered from this first shock of surprise, when they received another that was even more staggering.

"Mr. Gerald Moville, it seems, had left home on the very day that Vissio disappeared, and his people were without news of him. Just think what this sensational bit of news meant! It evoked at once in the mind of the imaginative, a drama of love and jealousy, a real romance such as is only dreamt of in the cinema, with an Italian *dago* as the jealous lover, and a handsome young Englishman as the victim of that jealousy. The police, holding on to this clue, turned their attention to the investigation of Mr. Gerald Moville's movements on the morning of that eventful Wednesday: they had to go very tactfully to work so as not to cause alarm to Sir Timothy and Lady Moville.

"It seems that Mr. Gerald had, on the Monday previously, announced his sudden intention to return immediately to Argentina. According to statements made by one or two of the servants, he did this at breakfast one morning after he had received a couple of official-looking letters that bore the Buenos Ayres' postmark. Lady Moville had been very distressed at this, and she and Sir Timothy tried to dissuade Mr. Gerald from going quite so soon; but he was quite determined to go, saying that there was some trouble at the farm which he must see to at once or it would mean a severe loss, not only to himself but to his partner. He finally announced that he would have to go up to London on the Wednesday at latest to see about getting a berth, if possible, in a boat that left Southampton for Buenos Ayres the following Saturday. Preparations for his departure were made accordingly.

"On the Tuesday the chauffeur took his luggage to Richmond and saw to its being sent off to London in advance. It was addressed to the Carlton Hotel. On the Wednesday Mr. Gerald had breakfast at half-past six as he wished to make an early start; he was going to drive the little two-seater back to the place in Richmond whence he had hired it, and then take the train that would take him to Dalton in time to catch the express up to London. He had said goodbye to his parents the evening before, and, having tipped all the servants lavishly, he made a start soon after seven.

"Two labourers going to their work saw the little car speeding along the road that intersects the moor; according their statement there were two people in the car, a man and a woman. They thought that the man who was driving might have been Mr. Moville, but the woman had on a thick veil and they had not particularly noticed who she was. On other hand one witness had seen the car standing unattended on the roadside within a hundred yards of a group of cottages one of which was occupied by Gooden. Whereupon Winnie was taken to task by the police.

"Amidst a flood of tears, she finally confessed that she had seen Mr. Moville on the Wednesday morning. He had called for her in his car very early; her father had only just gone to work, so it could not have much later than seven o'clock; he told her that he had some business to attend to in Richmond, would she like to come for a run and have lunch there with him. To this she willingly assented. On the way Mr. Moville told her that as a matter of fact he was going away for good, and that he could not possibly live without her. He begged her to come away with him; he would take her to London first and buy everything she wanted in the way of clothes, and then they would go on to Paris and travel all over the world and be the happiest couple on this earth.

"It seems that the girl at first was carried away by his eloquence; she was immensely flattered and thrilled by this romantic adventure, until something he said, or didn't say, some expression or some gesture— Winnie couldn't say what it was—but something seemed to drag her back. Probably it was just sound Yorkshire common sense. Anyway, she took fright, turned a deaf ear to Gerald Moville's blandishments, and insisted on being taken back to her father's cottage at once.

"Still to the accompaniment of a flood of tears Winnie went on to say that Mr. Gerald 'carried on terribly' when she finally refused to go away with him and he reproached her bitterly for having played with him, all the while that she was in love with that 'dirty *dago.*' But Winnie was firm and, in the end, the disappointed lover had to turn the car back and take the girl home again.

"It was then close upon nine o'clock. Mr. Gerald drove her to within half a mile of her father's cottage; here she got out and walked the rest of the way home. She had not seen Mr. Moville since. On the other hand, one of the neighbours told her that soon after she went off in the car that morning, Antonio Vissio had called at the cottage, and seemed in a terrible way when he was told that she had gone out with Mr. Moville.

"As you see the mystery was deepening. Instead of the one missing man, there were now two who had disappeared, and the question was what had become of Mr. Gerald Moville and his car. Enquiries at the garage where it belonged brought no light upon the subject. The car had not been returned, and nothing had been seen in Richmond of Mr. Moville or the car. Enquiries were then telegraphed all over the place and twenty-four hours later the car was traced to a small place called Falconblane, which is about twelve miles from Paisley, where it was left at a garage late on the Wednesday night by a man who had never since been to claim it.

"The people at the garage could only give a vague description, of this man. It was about eleven o'clock, a very dark night and just upon closing time. The man wore a big motor-coat and a cap with flaps over the ears; he had on a pair of goggles, and the lower part of his face looked coated with grime. It would be next to impossible to swear to his identity, but the assistant who took charge of the car said that the man spoke broken English. The police searched the car and found a handbag containing a number of effects such as a man would take with him if he was going on a long train journey: brush and comb, a novel, a couple of handkerchiefs and so on. Some of these effects bore the initials G. M.

"Pursuing their investigations further the police discovered that a man wearing a big motor-coat, goggles and a cap with flap-ears had taken a first-class ticket for Glasgow at Beith, which is a small place on a local branch line, in the early morning of Thursday, and had travelled to Glasgow by the 7.5 am. Glasgow being a very busy terminus no one appears to have noticed him there, but one of the porters found a motor-coat, a cap and a pair of goggles in one of the first-class carriages on the local from Beith, and a certain Mr. Etty, who was a gentleman's outfitter in the Station Road, stated that he had a customer in his shop early on Thursday morning who purchased a tweed cap and an overcoat off the peg. He had come in without either hat or coat, his face and hands were black with grime, and his hair looked covered with coal dust.

"He explained that he was an engineer who had been engaged all night on some salvage work down the line, where there had been a breakdown, and that he had somehow lost his coat and his cap. He paid for the goods with a £5 note which he took from a case out of his pocket, and the case appeared to be bulging over with notes. Mr. Etty thought that he might possibly be able to identify the man if he saw him again; one thing he did note about him, and that was that spoke broken English.

"But from that moment, in spite of strenuous efforts the part of the police, all traces of the man with the dirty face who spoke broken English vanished completely. And what's more all trace of Mr. Gerald Moville had also vanished. He did not go up to London, and all this while his luggage was at the Carlton Hotel waiting to be claimed. Nor was it ever claimed by him, because about a month after that tragic Wednesday in September the body of Mr. Gerald Moville was found in a 'gruff' or gully about three quarters of a mile from the Poacher's Leap. When I say that the body was found, I am wrong, for it was only a part of the body and that, of course, was completely decomposed.

"The head was missing and it was never found, in spite of the most strenuous efforts on the part of professional and amateur detectives, and lavish expenditure of money, thought and trouble on the part of Sir Timothy Moville. It lies buried, I imagine, somewhere on the moor. The clothes, though sodden, were, however, still recognisable, also the unfortunate man's wrist-watch, which had stopped at five minutes past eleven, his cuff-links, and his signet ring which had fallen from his fleshless finger and lay beside it in the 'gruff.'

"And about seventy yards higher up the gully a search-party found a knife of obviously foreign make, which still bore certain stains, which scientific analysis proved to be human blood. That knife was identified by Topcoat as the property of Vissio."

The Man in the Corner had been silent for a little while, as was his habit when he reached a certain stage of his narrative. At such moments it always seemed as if nothing in the world interested him, except the fashioning of innumerable and complicated knots in a bit of string. It was my business to set him talking again.

"Of course, there was an inquest after that," I said casually.

"Yes, there was," he replied dryly, "but it revealed nothing that the public did not already know. A few minor details—that was all. For instance, it came to light that when Mr. Moville left home on that fateful morning he was wearing the coat, cap and goggles which were subsequently found in the train at Glasgow station. It was easy to suppose that the murderer had stolen these from his victim, the cap and goggles being especially useful for purposes of disguise. The same supposition applies to money. Vissio, it was argued, had probably only a few shillings in his pocket when in a moment of mad jealousy, he killed Gerald Moville.

"That, of course, was the universally accepted theory, it was only desperate necessity that pushed him on to robbing the dead. Topcoat and others who knew Antonio well, declared that he was quite harmless except where Winnie Gooden was concerned, but it was more than likely that that morning he was tortured by one of his jealous fits. He had hated Gerald Moville from the first, and, according to the girl's own admissions, she must have given him definite cause for jealousy. That very morning, he had called at her cottage and found that she had gone out with his rival. Perhaps he knew that Moville was going away for good. Perhaps he guessed that he would try and induce Winnie to go with him. With such torturing fears in his heart, what wonder that when he met his rival on the lonely moor, he 'saw red,' and used his knife as Southerners, unfortunately, are only too apt to do?

"The coroner's jury returned a verdict of wilful murder against Antonio Vissio, and the police hold a warrant for his arrest. But more than two years have gone by since then, and Vissio has succeeded in eluding the police. For many weeks the public were deeply interested in the mystery the evening papers used to come out with the headlines; 'Where is Antonio Vissio?' and one great daily offered a reward of £500 for information that would lead to his apprehension. But, as you know, it has all been in vain. The public want to know how a man of unusual personality and speaking broken English could possibly lie *perdu* so long in this tight little island.

"And if he did leave the country, then how did he do it? He hadn't his passport with him, as that remained with his effects at Topcoat's Cottage. How then did he evade the passport officials at Glasgow or any other port of embarkation? It is done sometimes, we all know that, and in this case Vissio had four days' start before Topcoat gave information to police, but somehow the newspaper-reading public felt that if Vissio got out of the country, something would have betrayed him, someone would have seen him and furnished the first clue that would lead to discovery.

"And so, the disappearance of the Italian has been classed as one of the unsolved mysteries in the annals of crime. But to me the only point on which I am not absolutely clear (although even there I hold a theory), is why Gerald Moville should have gone wandering about the moor, after he had parted from Winnie Gooden, and when he hadn't very much time left to catch his train, if he didn't want to miss his connection at Dalton. That point did strike Inspector Dodsworth of the C.I.D who had been sent down from London to assist the local police in the investigation of the crime. I know Dodsworth very well, and he and I discussed that point once or twice. Of course, I was not going to give him the key to the whole mystery—a key, mind you, which I had discovered for myself—but I didn't object to talking over one or two of the minor details with the man, and I told him that in my opinion Moville undoubtedly went out on the moor in order to meet Vissio and have it out with him on the subject of Winnie.

"He wanted Winnie—badly—to come away with him, and I believe that he was just the sort of man who would think that he could bribe the Italian to stand aside for him, by offering him money. I believe those half-bred Spaniards and Portuguese out in Argentina are a most corrupt and venal lot, and Gerald Moville classed Vissio amongst that lot. I have no doubt whatever in my mind that Moville was walking across the moor to see if he couldn't find Vissio in Topcoat's cottage. It was obviously not for me to tell the police that the Poacher's, Leap is in a direct line between that cottage and the place where the two-seater was seen at a standstill on the roadside. But Dodsworth had to admit that I was right on that point."

"Then you think," I rejoined, "that Mr. Moville, after he parted from Winnie Gooden, set out to seek an interview with Antonio Vissio with a view to enter into an arrangement with him about the girl."

"Yes!" my eccentric friend assented with a nod.

"He wanted to bribe Vissio to stand aside for him?"

"Exactly."

"Then," I went on, "he met Vissio on the moor?"

"Yes!"

"Came out with his proposition?"

"Yes!"

"Which so enraged the Italian that he knocked the other man down and finally knifed him in accordance with the amiable custom of his country."

"No," the Man in the Corner retorted drily, "I didn't say that."

"But we know that the two men met and that—"

"And that one of them was killed," he broke in quickly. "But that man was not Gerald Moville."

"He was seen," I argued, "at Falconblane, at Beith and at Glasgow. The man with the dirty face, the motor-coat, and the goggles."

"Exactly," he broke in once more. "The man in the cap with the flap-ears, and wearing motor goggles; the man whose face and hair were in addition covered with grime. An excellent disguise, as it indeed proved to be."

"But the foreign accent. The man spoke broken English."

"There are few things," he said, with a sarcastic smile, "that are easier to assume than broken English, especially when only uneducated ears are there to hear."

"Then you think—?"

"I don't think," he replied curtly, "I know. I know that Gerald Moville met the Italian on the moor, that he quarrelled with him over Winnie Gooden, that he knocked him down, and that Vissio was killed in the fall. I can see the whole scene as plainly as if I had been there. Can't you see Moville realising that he had killed the man?— that inevitably suspicion would fall on him? Topcoat had seen him, witnesses had seen his car in the road, he was known to be the Italian's rival in Winnie's affections! Already he could feel the hangman's rope round his neck. But we must look on Gerald Moville as a man of resource, a man, above all, up to many tricks; for drawing a red herring across the trail of his own delinquencies.

"I will spare you the details of what I can see in my own mind as having happened after Moville had realised that Vissio was dead: the stripping of the body, the exchange of clothes down to the vest and shirt, the mutilation of the corpse with the victim's own knife, and the dragging of the body to a distant 'gruff' where it must inevitably remain hidden for days, until advanced decomposition had set in to

426

efface all identification marks.

"Fear no doubt lent ingenuity, and strength to the miscreant; and, as a matter of fact, Gerald Moville is one of the few criminals who committed no appreciable blunder when he set to work to obliterate all traces of his crime; he left the knife with its tell-tale stains on the spot, and that knife was identified as the property of the Italian, and the head which alone might have betrayed him, even if the body were not found for weeks, he took away with him to bury somewhere far away—goodness only knows where, but somewhere between York-shire and Scotland.

"I can see Gerald Moville after he had accomplished his grim task making his way back to his car—the loneliness of this stretch of coun-try would be entirely in his favour, more especially as it had begun to rain; I can see him driving along putting mile upon mile between himself and the scene of his crime. At one place he stopped—a lonely spot it must have been—where he disposed of his gruesome burden; then on and on, past the borders of Yorkshire, of Westmoreland and Cumberland and into Scotland, till he came close to the network of railway round about Paisley and Glasgow.

"Falconblane, a village tucked away on a lonely bit of country but boasting of a garage, must have seemed an ideal spot wherein to abandon the car altogether and take to the road, and this Moville did, trusting to the long night, and also to luck, to further efface his traces. Again, I can see him wandering restlessly through the dark hours of that night, not daring to enter a house and ask for a bed, determined at all costs to obliterate every vestige of his movements since the crime.

"Then in the morning he takes train for Glasgow, the busiest cen-tre wherein a man can disappear in a crowd; in the train he takes the precaution of divesting himself of the motor-coat, the goggles and the cap, but not of the grime that covers his face and hair. We know how he provided himself with a more suitable hat and coat; we know how all through his wanderings he kept up his broken English. At Glasgow all traces of him vanish; he has become a very ordinary-looking man, wearing quite ordinary clothes, and in Glasgow people are far too busy to take much notice of passers-by.

"We can easily conjecture how easy it was for Moville to leave the country altogether. He had plenty of money and it is never difficult for a man of resource to leave a British port for any destination he pleases, especially if he is of obviously British nationality. Money we all know will accomplish anything, and rogues will slip through a cordon of officials where the respectable citizens will be chivvied about and harassed with regulations. Moreover, we must always bear this in mind that the police were not on his track, nor on that of the Italian for that matter. Moville was free to come and go, and you may be sure that he was quite clever enough not to behave in any way that might create suspicion."

The Man in the Corner paused quite abruptly. A complicated knot was absorbing his whole attention. I felt thoughtful, meditative, and after a few minutes' silence I put my meditations into words.

"That is all very well," I said, "but, personally, I don't see that you have anything definite this time on which to base your theory. Both the men have disappeared; the police say that Vissio killed Moville; you assert the reverse and declare that Moville deliberately dressed up the body of the Italian in his own clothes, but you have nothing more to go on for your assertion than the police have for theirs."

"I was waiting for that," he rejoined with a dry chuckle. "But let me assure you that I have at least three psychological facts to go on for my assertion, whereas the police only go on two very superficial matters for theirs; they base their whole argument firstly on the clothes, watch, jewellery and so on found on a body that was otherwise unidentifiable, and secondly on a blood-stained knife known to have belonged to the Italian. Now I have demonstrated to you have I not, how easy it was for Moville to manufacture both these pieces of evidence. So, mark the force of my argument," the funny creature went on, gesticulating with his thin hands like a scarecrow blown by the wind. "First of all, why did Moville suddenly declare his intention of leaving England? In order to look after his partner's affairs? Not a bit of it. He left England because of some shady transaction out there in Argentina which was coming to light, and because of which he thought it best to disappear altogether for a time.

"My proof for this? you will ask. The simple proof that his parents accepted his disappearance for a whole week without making any enquiries about him either in Richmond, or London or the Shipping Company that controls the steamers to Buenos Ayres. Can you imagine that Sir Timothy Moville, having seen the last of his son on the Tuesday evening, would say and do nothing, when he was left eight days without news; he would have enquired in London; he knew to which hotel his son intended to go; someone would have enquired at Richmond whether the car had been left there. But no! There was not a single enquiry made for Gerald Moville by his parents, or his brothers and sisters, until after Topcoat had mentioned his name to the police and the latter had started their investigations.

"And why? Because his people knew where he was; that is to say they knew—or some of them knew—that Gerald had to lie low, at any rate for a time. Of course, his supposed death, under such tragic circumstances, must have been a terrible shock to them, but it is a remarkable fact you will admit that the offer of a substantial reward for the apprehension of the murderer did not come from Sir Timothy Moville; it came from one of the big dailies out for publicity.

"My whole argument rests on psychological grounds, and in criminal cases psychology is by far the surest guide. Now there was not a single detail in connection with the Moorland Tragedy that in any way suggested the hand of a man like Antonio Vissio. Can you see an Italian peasant, who, moreover, has lived all his life with a gun in his hand, solemnly laying that gun down before embarking on a quarrel with his rival? And yet the gun was found undischarged, lying in a gully. Vissio was much more likely to have shouldered it at sight of the man he hated and shot him dead, more especially as the Englishman would have an enormous advantage in a hand to hand fight, even if the other man had suddenly whisked out a knife.

"Vissio was not the type of man who would think of the consequences of his crime. Maddened by jealousy, he would kill his man at sight, but in his own country and also in France, there would be no disgrace attached to such a deed—no disgrace and very little punishment. The man who last year shot the English dancing girl on the Riviera because he thought that she was carrying on with another man, only got five years' imprisonment; Vissio would not realise that he would be amenable to English law, which does not look on homicide quite so leniently.

"Having killed his rival, the Italian would, in all probability, have swanked as far as the nearest village, had a good drink to steady his nerves, and then have boasted loudly of what he had done, certain that he would be leniently dealt with by a judge, and sympathised with by a jury, because of the torments of jealousy which he had endured until he could do so no longer. You can't imagine such a man sawing off his victim's head and wrapping it up in a newspaper taken out of the dead man's pocket.

"And this brings me to the final point in my argument, and one which ought to have struck the police from the first: the question of the car. How would Vissio know that he would find Moville's car conveniently stationed by the roadside? He would have to know that before he could dare walk across the moor, carrying his gruesome parcel. Now Vissio couldn't possibly know all that, and what's more, though he might not have been altogether ignorant of driving, he certainly was not expert enough to drive a car, all by himself for over a hundred miles, at top speed and for several hours in the dark.

"To my mind, if this fact had been driven home to the jury by a motoring expert, they never would have brought in a verdict against Vissio, and if you think the whole matter over you will be bound to admit that there is not a single flaw in my argument. From the point of view of possibility as well as of psychology, only one man could have committed that crime and that was Gerald Moville. I suppose his unfortunate parents will know the truth one day. Soon, probably, when the young miscreant is short of money and writes home for funds.

"Or else he may return to Argentina and under an assumed name start life anew. They are not over particular there as to a man's antecedents. They will, perhaps, think all the more of him, when they know that where a girl is concerned, he will stand no nonsense from a rival. Think it all over, you'll come to the conclusion that I'm right."

He gathered up his bit of string and took the spectacles from off his nose. For the first time I saw his pale, shrewd eyes looking down straight at me.

"I shan't see you again for some time," he said with a wry smile. "Won't you shake hands and wish me luck?"

"Indeed, I will," I replied, "but you are not going away, are you?"

He gave a curious, short, dry chuckle:

"I am going out of England for the benefit of my health," he said coolly.

I hadn't shaken hands with him, because the very next moment he had turned his back on me as if he thought better of it. The next morning, I read in the papers a curious account of some extensive robberies committed in the neighbourhood of Hatton Garden. The burglar had managed to escape, but the police were said to hold an important clue. A curious feature about those robberies was the way in which a knotted cord had been used to effect an entrance through a skylight. The newspaper reporters gave a very full description of this cord: it was photographed and reproduced in the illustrated papers. The knots in it were of a wonderful and intricate pattern.

They set me thinking—and wondering!

I have often been to that blameless tea-shop in Fleet Street since.

But the Man in the Corner is never there now, and the police have never been able to trace the large consignment of diamonds stolen from that shop in Hatton Garden and which has been valued at £80,000.

I wonder if I shall ever see my eccentric friend again.

Somehow, I think that I shall. And if I do, shall I see him sitting in his accustomed corner, with his spectacles on his nose, and his long, thin fingers working away at a bit of string—fashioning knots—many knots—complicated knots—like those in the cord by the aid of which an entrance was effected into that shop in Hatton Garden and diamonds worth £80,000 were stolen.

I wonder!!

LEONAUR

ALSO FROM LEONAUR
AVAILABLE IN SOFTCOVER OR HARDCOVER WITH DUST JACKET

MR MUKERJI'S GHOSTS *by S. Mukerji*—Supernatural tales from the British Raj period by India's Ghost story collector.

KIPLINGS GHOSTS *by Rudyard Kipling*—Twelve stories of Ghosts, Hauntings, Curses, Werewolves & Magic.

THE COLLECTED SUPERNATURAL AND WEIRD FICTION OF WASHINGTON IRVING: VOLUME 1 *by Washington Irving*—Including one novel 'A History of New York', and nine short stories of the Strange and Unusual.

THE COLLECTED SUPERNATURAL AND WEIRD FICTION OF WASHINGTON IRVING: VOLUME 2 *by Washington Irving*—Including three novelettes 'The Legend of the Sleepy Hollow', 'Dolph Heyliger', 'The Adventure of the Black Fisherman' and thirty-two short stories of the Strange and Unusual.

THE COLLECTED SUPERNATURAL AND WEIRD FICTION OF JOHN KENDRICK BANGS: VOLUME 1 *by John Kendrick Bangs*—Including one novel 'Toppleton's Client or A Spirit in Exile', and ten short stories of the Strange and Unusual.

THE COLLECTED SUPERNATURAL AND WEIRD FICTION OF JOHN KENDRICK BANGS: VOLUME 2 *by John Kendrick Bangs*—Including four novellas 'A House-Boat on the Styx', 'The Pursuit of the House-Boat', 'The Enchanted Typewriter' and 'Mr. Munchausen' of the Strange and Unusual.

THE COLLECTED SUPERNATURAL AND WEIRD FICTION OF JOHN KENDRICK BANGS: VOLUME 3 *by John Kendrick Bangs*—Including twor novellas 'Olympian Nights', 'Roger Camerden: A Strange Story', and ten short stories of the Strange and Unusual.

THE COLLECTED SUPERNATURAL AND WEIRD FICTION OF MARY SHELLEY: VOLUME 1 *by Mary Shelley*—Including one novel 'Frankenstein or the Modern Prometheus', and fourteen short stories of the Strange and Unusual.

THE COLLECTED SUPERNATURAL AND WEIRD FICTION OF MARY SHELLEY: VOLUME 2 *by Mary Shelley*—Including one novel 'The Last Man', and three short stories of the Strange and Unusual.

THE COLLECTED SUPERNATURAL AND WEIRD FICTION OF AMELIA B. EDWARDS *by Amelia B. Edwards*—Contains two novelettes 'Monsieur Maurice', and 'The Discovery of the Treasure Isles', one ballad 'A Legend of Boisguilbert' and seventeen short stories to cill the blood.

LEONAUR

ALSO FROM LEONAUR
AVAILABLE IN SOFTCOVER OR HARDCOVER WITH DUST JACKET

THE COMPLETE FOUR JUST MEN: VOLUME 2 *by Edgar Wallace*—*The Law of the Four Just Men & The Three Just Men*—disillusioned with a world where the wicked and the abusers of power perpetually go unpunished, the Just Men set about to rectify matters according to their own standards, and retribution is dispensed on swift and deadly wings.

THE COMPLETE RAFFLES: 1 *by E. W. Hornung*—*The Amateur Cracksman & The Black Mask*—By turns urbane gentleman about town and accomplished cricketer, life is just too ordinary for Raffles and that sets him on a series of adventures that have long been treasured as a real antidote to the 'white knights' who are the usual heroes of the crime fiction of this period.

THE COMPLETE RAFFLES: 2 *by E. W. Hornung*—*A Thief in the Night & Mr Justice Raffles*—By turns urbane gentleman about town and accomplished cricketer, life is just too ordinary for Raffles and that sets him on a series of adventures that have long been treasured as a real antidote to the 'white knights' who are the usual heroes of the crime fiction of this period.

THE COLLECTED SUPERNATURAL AND WEIRD FICTION OF WILKIE COLLINS: VOLUME 1 *by Wilkie Collins*—Contains one novel 'The Haunted Hotel', one novella 'Mad Monkton', three novelettes 'Mr Percy and the Prophet', 'The Biter Bit' and 'The Dead Alive' and eight short stories to chill the blood.

THE COLLECTED SUPERNATURAL AND WEIRD FICTION OF WILKIE COLLINS: VOLUME 2 *by Wilkie Collins*—Contains one novel 'The Two Destinies', three novellas 'The Frozen deep', 'Sister Rose' and 'The Yellow Mask' and two short stories to chill the blood.

THE COLLECTED SUPERNATURAL AND WEIRD FICTION OF WILKIE COLLINS: VOLUME 3 *by Wilkie Collins*—Contains one novel 'Dead Secret,' two novelettes 'Mrs Zant and the Ghost' and 'The Nun's Story of Gabriel's Marriage' and five short stories to chill the blood.

FUNNY BONES *selected by Dorothy Scarborough*—An Anthology of Humorous Ghost Stories.

MONTEZUMA'S CASTLE AND OTHER WEIRD TALES *by Charles B. Cory*—Cory has written a superb collection of eighteen ghostly and weird stories to chill and thrill the avid enthusiast of supernatural fiction.

SUPERNATURAL BUCHAN *by John Buchan*—Stories of Ancient Spirits, Uncanny Places & Strange Creatures.

www.ingramcontent.com/pod-product-compliance
Lightning Source LLC
Chambersburg PA
CBHW030348030726
47497CB00002B/238